THE BLOODY BUCKET

THE BLOODY BUCKET

Sgt. Thomas H. Schalata (left) bandages another soldier's hand

Tom Schalata

ARPress
ILLUMINATING IDEAS.
EMPOWERING VOICES

ARPress
45 Dan Road Suite 5
Canton MA 02021
Hotline: 1(888) 821-0229
Fax: 1(508) 545-7580

Ordering Information:
Quantity sales. Special discounts are available on quantity purchases by corporations, associations, and others. For details, contact the publisher at the address above.

Printed in the United States of America.

ISBN-13:   Softcover   979-8-89356-046-6
            eBook   979-8-89356-047-3

Library of Congress Control Number: 2024903168

Table of Contents

This book is dedicated to my late grandfather, Thomas H. Schalata, World War I Veteran, (referred to as Tommy in this book). "The Bloody Bucket" follows his life from peacetime service in Philadelphia, PA as a member of the Pennsylvania National Guard through his active duty In El Paso, TX, and ultimately in Europe during The Great War. It is also dedicated to my late father, Thomas E. Schalata, Sr., who would have been very proud of this project. In addition, all references to the Baldwin Locomotive Works, railroads in general, and the description and operation of locomotives are dedicated not only to my grandfather, who worked at Baldwin, and to my father for his great passion for trains, but to the late Greg Walleigh. Greg's boundless enthusiasm and knowledge on the subject were an inspiration to me. Special thanks to my friend, Fran Golembeski, who has shared with me an appreciation for railroad history. My research in this area was done as a tribute to all of these individuals. I am truly grateful to all my friends and family for their gracious love and support. Special recognition is given to my wife, Donna, who has been an essential advisor and confidant for all my projects. Inspiration to complete this project was provided by Andrew Kawczak, who reprinted his grandfather's memoirs (1914-1920), "Dying Echoes." Stanisław Kawczak was a Polish soldier in the Austrian Army in World War I. In remembrance of George A. Amole, Pottstown's first casualty of World War I, and Harry Ginther and Bill Wagner, who were also WWI veterans and friends of my father. Finally, a portion of the proceeds of this book will benefit the Berks Military History Museum, 198 E. Wyomissing Ave., Mohnton, PA 19540. *Remembering those who served.*

INTRODUCTION

My grandfather, Thomas Hubert Schalata, was among the first generation of my father's family born in America. He was also the first to serve his country.

Secondly, my grandfather was part of the American Expeditionary Force in World War I. Initially, his unit was mobilized to protect Texas and other states during the Border Conflict with Mexico. Pancho Villa, a Mexican bandit, attacked, robbed, and pillaged small U.S. towns along the border. He evaded capture by the military forces of both countries for quite some time.

Although I was only eight years old, when my grandfather passed away in 1963, he told me many stories about his service time. I have inherited a large number of photographs that belonged to him from this period. Included in this collection is a set of rare glass negatives of German soldiers. Some of them are very high-ranking officers. These images were evidently part of the spoils of war that he brought back with him, and are included in this book.

During his time of service, his primary assignment was with the 108th Field Artillery, Sanitary Detachment Unit, 28th Division, Pennsylvania National Guard. This unit was comprised mainly of men from the Philadelphia area.

My father, Thomas E. Schalata Sr., was a veteran of World War II, a member of the U.S. Army Reserves, and the Pennsylvania Army National Guard. During his four-decade stint, he served in several units, including the First Army, 2nd Army, IV Army Corps, *The Stars and Stripes* U.S. Army Newspaper, the 79th Division, the 42nd Infantry Division (The Rainbow Division), and the 28th Division (The Iron Division, The Bloody Bucket).

These outfits were: infantry, armor, field artillery, and medical. As previously mentioned, he also served with *The Stars and Stripes*, the official U.S. Army newspaper in Darmstadt, Germany.

Of all my father's ties to the service, he was most proud to be part of the 28th Division. The same division as his father.

The title of this book, *"The Bloody Bucket,"* was a moniker given to this famous Pennsylvania outfit by the Germans during World War II. This was a reference to their fierce fighting ability combined with the unit's distinctive red keystone insignia.

Therefore, due to the 28th Division's storied history in *both* world wars, I believe the unit's veterans have earned the right to hang their helmets on the term "The Bloody Bucket."

Many consider the Korean War to be the forgotten conflict involving U.S. troops in the 1950s. It has only been in recent times that Vietnam Veterans have gotten the recognition they deserve.

In my opinion, the horrors that took place during World War I have been grossly overlooked, as well. The world recently paid tribute to the 100th Anniversary of "The Great War,"..."The War to End all Wars." The commemoration recognizing this era in history as one of the world's greatest tragedies was underwhelming.

Over the years, there have been some excellent movies on the subject.

That list includes: "War Horse," "The Red Baron," "Lawrence of Arabia," "Flyboys," "Joyeux Noel (Merry Christmas)," "All Quiet on the Western Front," and "The Blue Max." Another recent release, "1917," also hit the silver screen. These films, however, have been spread out over several decades.

The decision for me to tell my grandfather's story was not only an easy one but a long overdue one. Keep in mind, though, there were many handicaps in recreating life during this era. Less than 10 percent of the population had a telephone, and only one in 50 individuals had access to an automobile.

The motion picture industry was in its infancy. Short films dominated the 20th century's early teens, and silent pictures were just an initial experiment.

Victrolas and record players were only beginning to become affordable for all classes of people. The radio would not become a commercial breakthrough until after the war.

Most of the country had to rely on word of mouth, newspapers, and letter writing to gather information. My goal was to illustrate some of the experiences of those young American men who went to war in 1918. In my opinion, it was also essential to paint a picture of their day-to-day life in the service, whether it be in training or action. They met with atrocities that they never imagined were possible. Some of those men came home, while many didn't. This is their story!

"SPRING'S ARRIVAL IN 1916"

The Schalata Family home - 4445 Thompson St., Phila., PA
Image Source: Unknown

Chapter 1

"Spring's Arrival in 1916"

I was awakened when the distinctive aroma of frying bacon wafted its way to my tiny second-floor bedroom at the back of the house.

It was warm beneath the covers, and I was hesitant to venture out from my haven into the chilly room. Given the position of my tight quarters, heat was at a premium in these parts.

When the second wave of smells followed, fried onions and potatoes, I knew it was time to start the day. Besides, my Waterbury wind-up clock told me the hour was 6:17 am. The loud clanking alarm would force me out of bed in just 13 minutes, nevertheless.

Once I hopped out of my warm cocoon, I quickly slipped into the clothes laid out for me on the chair in my room. I hastily washed up and shaved using the basin and water pitcher that sat on top of my modest oak chest of drawers.

Today, Thursday, April 20, 1916, was a significant day in my life. I was required to go down to the recruiting station at Philadelphia's city hall to update my service registration. I have been a member of the Pennsylvania National Guard since 1914, but now it appears that my service will be that of a greater need. It is rumored that we will soon be assigned to federal forces.

Naturally, I have mixed emotions about the whole thing. President Wilson has his sights set on intervening in the ongoing revolution in Mexico.

Pancho Villa, a Mexican revolutionary general, has been wreaking havoc on the U.S. border and Mexico for quite some time now. He has raided several American towns, and there have been casualties reported. We may be headed to Mexico as part of the expedition to capture the elusive outlaw and to protect our interests in Texas or New Mexico. At least that's what I hear.

The war has been raging in Europe for two years, and it is only a matter of time until we join in the fray. I am apprehensive about getting into something so foreign to me. Yet, I feel compelled to do my patriotic duty. Many of my friends feel the same way, but I shall leave the matter in God's hands.

Finally, as I descended the stairs and approached the kitchen, the tempting aroma I detected earlier grew much more potent.

My 47-year old mother, Jadwiga (Henrietta), was busy preparing my breakfast at the cookstove: three slices of thickly cut smoked bacon from the local butcher, three sunny side eggs, just the way I like them, and fried sliced potatoes with onions. The source of these items was Wasko's Meats and Groceries, located at 4443 E. Edgemont Street. This is the next street over from our house on Thompson Street.

As I drew even closer to the kitchen, the coffee pot came into view, which was a welcome sight. Everything that my mother prepared was on our two-tone gray wood-burning cookstove.

Four of my sisters were getting ready to leave for school; Florence (age eight), Stella and Henrietta (who were 11-year-old twins), and Helen (age 14). I also have two older sisters, Veronica (age 18) and Maryanna, whom we call Mamie (age 21).

Veronica works at a nearby hosiery mill, while Maryanna also lives on Thompson Street but in the Port Richmond section of Philadelphia. She lives there with her husband, Bill Weise. They were married earlier this year.

Although Veronica still lives at home, she sees a fellow by the name of Joe Zivie. His surname was Zwolinski. Joe has since Americanized it and shortened it to Zivie. He seems like a nice enough chap, but he's talking about joining the Navy. The Navy may seem like a safer bet on paper, but after the Germans sunk the Lusitania last year, I doubt that theory. There are many reports about German submarines patrolling the Atlantic.

"Thomas!" My mother yelled, "Grab yourself a plate. Your breakfast is ready! You'll have to get yourself a cup, too. The coffee is there on the stove."

"Let's not dilly dally. You have less than an hour to catch the trolley to get downtown," Mom reminded me.

"Yes, mom. I know the drill," I replied. "I'm up and about every day when I go to work in the morning," I concluded.

I feel like I am contributing to the war effort by working for Baldwin Locomotive Works at Broad and Spring Garden Sts. I am assigned to read blueprints, which isn't a bad job.

After nearly closing up shop ten years ago, business is booming once again. We have a long list of locomotives we are producing for the Allies. I hear the total orders could reach several thousand. Down at the Eddystone Plant, they are making Enfield Rifles for Remmington. This contract came in just last year. That's been a big boost for the company. Baldwin laid off over 10,000 workers less than ten years ago, and now we're back up to strength. The allies are still using steam locomotives to move troops and supplies. However, the trend in the U.S. is moving towards electric power.

1 NOTE: The Baldwin Locomotive Works' main facility comprised about eight city blocks bounded by Broad Street and 18th Street, and Spring Garden St. and Pennsylvania Avenue. The 185-acre Eddystone Plant was located in the suburbs of Philadelphia, was added in 1906.

The girls all got up from the table and gave their mother a peck on the cheek. They said, "Goodbye, mother!" and marched single-file to the front door as if they were in a parade. St. John Cantius Parish School is directly across the street from our home.

I expect that they will be joining their sister, Veronica, at the hosiery mill in just a few years. All of them except Florence. Unlike her sisters, Florence seems to enjoy going to school, and I believe she will someday make something of herself.

The others, well, they complain that the school work is too hard, the nuns are too strict, and they just want to get out in the world and make money. They'll be sorry someday!

In a small way, however, I can understand how they feel. When I was a student in the first grade at Our Lady Help of Christians in Port Richmond, I ran into some tough nuns myself. I was the first in our family to attend school in Philadelphia.

We lived on Thompson Street, just four doors down from Bill Weise. I mentioned earlier that he recently married my sister, Mamie.

It was a German Catholic school, and my first-grade teacher was Sister Benedictus Carmella. She quickly pointed out that my given name of "Thomas Szałata" was not German and insisted that I spell my name as "Schalata." To qualify herself, she stated, "That the *S-C-H* would make my surname German!" My family has spelled it that way ever since. How could a six-year-old Polish boy argue with a 50-year- old German nun with a metal-edged ruler in her hand? She wasn't afraid to use it, either!

The girls often confided with me that the Mother Superior at St. John Cantius, Sister Rozalijia Humilitas, was as tough as nails. The short, rotund sister was about five-foot, three inches tall but had a bulldog's personality.

One Friday during Lent, the entire student body was filing into the church for Lenten Devotions. St. John's Church is adjacent to the school. The large gray stone school building, however, sits back from the church.

My sister, Helen, who is very timid in her own right, was momentarily confused. She entered the wrong door into the church. The Mother Superior was waiting for Helen and slapped her across the face with her hand.

When the girls ran home for lunch, the nun's red handprint was still visible on my sister's face. Mom felt sorry for the poor girl and gave her permission to remain home from school for the rest of the afternoon.

My mother is about five-foot-six inches tall and always wears her hair in a bun. Whenever she's cooking, she dons her favorite apron. It is blue with pink roses on the front. I think pop gave it to her for her birthday one year. The apron was handmade by the wife of one of his friends down at Szczepanski's taproom.

Her mother, Josephine, was slightly taller. She, too, was never seen without a long apron that hung around her neck and went all the way down to her ankles. My grandmother passed away about four years ago.

By the time I got my coffee, mom had grown impatient waiting for me and had already filled my plate with food. She placed it on the table and commented, "I said no dilly-dallying, Thomas!"

When she called me "Thomas," that was a sign that she was cross or impatient, but "Tommy" was her common term of endearment for me.

As I dug into this delicious breakfast, my mother reminded me, "Don't forget, Tommy, to stop at the butcher on your way home and pick up the kielbasa!"

"Yes, mom. I won't forget," I assured her.

"I have a list of things that I need you to pick up at the Reading Terminal Market, as well," she added.

Sunday would be Easter, and we always had fresh and smoked kielbasa for the occasion. Mom made a plentiful amount of food on such holidays.

"We need it for Sunday, and your father is working the later shift today, so he'll be of no help to me," she added.

My father, Stanley, works for the streets department. His job involves the patching and paving of city streets. Usually, he is long gone by this time, but today they needed him to start later. This change of shift meant he would be arriving home late that evening, as well.

When I finished my breakfast, I gave mom a hug and kiss goodbye.

"Be careful, Tommy," she said. "Don't sign-up for anything too dangerous," she warned in her own motherly way.

"Yes, mom. Don't worry," I assured her. "I'll be back with the kielbasa and the rest of your list!"

As I headed out the front door, pop sat in his favorite rocker on the front porch, reading his newspaper.

"Take care, Tommy," pop said as he looked up from the paper.

"I will pop," I answered back. "Have a good day at work," I said while giving him a nod.

"Don't let Wilson push you around," he added. This comment was a reference to the opinion that the president would eventually get us involved in the war despite his talk about world peace.

Pop has a small table next to his rocker, where he keeps his pipe and ashtray. It's also the perfect spot for his cup of coffee or glass of beer.

My father, Stanislas (Stanley), Schalata, has been the unofficial mayor of Bridesburg ever since we moved here from Port Richmond a few years ago. Whenever he is positioned on that dark green rocker, he's available to dish out the latest news, opinions, or gossip. Passers-by rarely fail to acknowledge him when he's there! Many people from the community come to him for advice because they value his opinion.

He is very active at St. John Cantius. Monsignor Bednarczyk relies heavily on pop whenever he has a particular project that needs attention.

He reads every newspaper he can get his hands on. We have The *Philadelphia Inquirer* delivered, but he exchanges his copy with a neighbor who gets *The Public Ledger* later in the day. It is common for him to hang out at Kowalcyzk's Barber Shop. There he has access to other periodicals. He also reads the Polish newspapers, *Patryota* and *Gwiazda*.

I gave my father a final wave as I crossed the street to the schoolyard's wrought iron fence. I paused for just a few moments to watch my sisters and their schoolmates in the playground before the morning bell rang.

In the center of the action was Sister Maximillian Joy. She was joining in with a round of jump rope with the girls. My sisters reported that Sister Joy, as the children called her, was indeed a joy. The tall, young, and slender nun was very down-to-earth and took a completely different stance from Mother Superior on handling these young boys and girls.

Helen looked up from the action and saw me standing by the fence. She coyly smiled and waved. Of all my sisters, Helen is the one who really looks up to me. Sometimes she seems infatuated with me, her big brother. That's unusual because I have always been looked upon as the black sheep of the family.

Mom says I am wild and unruly, but I just don't think she's used to me with all those girls in the family. My mother tried to change me when I was younger, but I believe she gave up on that idea years ago!

I gave Helen a wave, then walked down Thompson Street to Orthodox. I turned onto Orthodox. It was a short distance to the trolley stop.

The familiar green and cream-colored street car was quite crowded at this time of the morning, but I managed to see Will Pfingsten from the neighborhood.

We gave each other a wave from opposite ends of the car. Since we were packed together like sardines, I had to stand in the aisle and grab one of the safety straps whenever the vehicle suddenly lunged forward or backward. At times it would lean to one side when rounding a sharp corner. That generally made the lights flicker on and off momentarily. The steel wheels ground against the equally unforgiving rails, and this made a loud screeching sound that was deafening to the ears.

A woman in her mid-twenties caused a commotion with her babe in arms. The young child, who was ill, vomited on the back of an older man. The senior fellow was wearing a brown fedora and a brown woolen overcoat. The smoke from his cigar added to the carnage. He was outraged over the whole affair and immediately began to scold the young woman.

Several other passengers came to her aid. A grandmotherly-type woman, who was toting a bag of rags, stepped in to assist in the clean-up. When this operation was complete, the scene returned to normal.

Once I transferred to the Market Street line, it was just a short ride to city hall.

As I made my way up Market Street, the gigantic figure of the city's founder, William Penn, came into view on top of city hall. Billy Penn, as the locals refer to him, faces northeast.

I arrived at the recruiting office by 8:50 am and found my place in the already growing line. By the time I reached the front, I was addressed by Capt. Winston Burlholme.

Just as I suspected, the basis of this appointment was to go over my paperwork. The officer also discussed my possible future assignments.

"Private Schalata," he began, "I cannot say for sure, but your assignment will likely have something to do with the Mexican Border Conflict."

"Yes, Sir!" I answered.

"There will be no physicals conducted at this time, but I need to ask you a series of questions regarding your general health, employment and marital status, and the like," he concluded.

"Very good, Sir," I replied. "whatever you require, Sir!"

The captain informed me that I would be mustered into active duty service within the next 60 days. The paperwork that I received from him stated that I was to report to the Pennsylvania Railroad's Broad Street Station at 0700, 24 June 1916. The form revealed that I was to be transported by rail to the military camp at Mt. Gretna, PA. The facility is located in Lebanon County, not far from Hershey.

I left that meeting, at least knowing a few more details about my future. The time was now 10:33 am, and I spent some time browsing in the immediate area on market street.

On my list of things to do was a stop at the Reading Terminal Market. My mother had two essential items on her list. They were horseradish (Chrzan) and red beets. These ingredients are required to make her special holiday relish known in Polish as Ćwikła. Typically, this relish is a spicy condiment primarily comprised of horseradish, red beets, and sugar. Traditionally, it is served with ham or kielbasa.

Since it was Easter week, the market was jammed. There were plenty of shoppers gathering their needed items for the holiday.

Before having my lunch, I stopped at the corner newsstand to pick up a New York newspaper for pop. This enabled me to browse through some of the day's topics before handing it over to him. This small gesture would truly make his day.

I tossed the man at the newsstand three cents, and he acknowledged me, saying, "Thank you, Sir. Good day!"

Since my breakfast was beginning to wear off, I sought out the closest Horn & Hardart's Automat* for some lunch.

With several locations in the area, I opted for the cafeteria located at 909 Market Street.

*   *2 NOTE: Horn & Hardart was a coin-operated dining cafeteria that offered self-serve food through vending machine compartments. You could get three meals per day for about 50 cents.*

I purchased a cup of soup, a ham sandwich, and a coffee for 20 cents with my pocket full of nickels.

It was a short walk to the closest station on the Market Street line, and the ride went quickly to my trolley stop.

There's no way I could forget to pick up the kielbasa at Lachowicz Butcher Shop at the corner of Orthodox and Almond Sts. There was already a long line of customers that spilled onto the sidewalk outside the shop. Once I made it to the counter, my mother's order was ready and waiting for me to pick it up. It's no wonder that my mother sent me on these errands. She very wisely was able to avoid dealing with these crowds.

As I walked home from the butcher shop, the church bells signaled the three o'clock hour, and that indicated the girls would soon be back from school, as well.

From a religious standpoint, this was the busiest week of the entire year. Tonight we would be attending the Holy Thursday Service.

While the girls will have to attend school tomorrow, it was Good Friday, which meant that they would be in church from noon until three o'clock in observance of the Holy Day. My mother would be busy baking bread, babka, and preparing the other foods she planned to serve on Easter.

On Saturday morning, we would participate in another Easter Vigil Service. The priest will also bless the food that each family will be serving on Easter. Parishioners are required to bring their baskets of food to the church for the ritual.

Before heading across the street to the church that evening, we gathered around the table for a quick meal. My mother prepared a large pot of potato soup. Some delicious rye bread and butter accompanied the steaming soup.

"Well, Tommy," pop began, "what did you find out on your mission today?"

"Most of the meeting with the captain was focused on my paperwork and my current status," I answered.

"Did he give you any indication of what may be next?" My father pried.

"He was of the opinion that our assignment might be to Mexico, Texas, or someplace down in that area of the country," I revealed.

"Nobody can catch that bandit, Pancho Villa, my father said in expressing his opinion.

"You're right, Pop," I agreed. "He is one slippery devil," I concluded.

"Do you think it will be dangerous?" My mother asked.

"No, mom. I don't think so. I talked with some of the other guys down there, and they think that we'll be there just to guard the border. They said they expect it to be rather boring," I assured her.

"That's good! Thank heavens," she exclaimed as she began to clean up.

"Come on, girls," she scolded, "let's get these dishes done before we go over to the church."

My sisters scurried like scared rabbits, and the clean-up was completed in short order. A spring chill had settled in for the evening, and we threw on our coats even though it was just a short walk across the street.

Bridsburg, 1901
Image Source: Unknown

Jadwiga, Maryanna & Stanley Schalata
Image Source: Author's photo

Stanley and one of his daughters
Image Source: Author's photo

Schalata breakfast room
Image Source: Author's photo

Schalata dining room
Image Source: Author's photo

Schalata living room
Image Source: Author's photo

2

"A POLISH EASTER"

St. John Cantius R.C. Church on Thompson St., Phila., PA
Image Source: Unknown

CHAPTER 2

"A Polish Easter"

Nothing was quiet or orderly in our house. With me, my parents, and my five sisters, it was always a circus. My mother insisted that the girls had to look just perfect in their Easter outfits. From their hair down to their shoes, there was a lot of fussing, a bunch of giggling, and plenty of effort by my mother to keep them in line.

Mom had spent most of the winter making the girls' outfits. She bartered some cooking and cleaning with another woman from the neighborhood who happened to have a quantity of material leftover from other projects.

Florence, the youngest, wore a long white dress trimmed with a pink collar and some pink ruffles on the sleeves.

Henrietta and Stella also wore white dresses, but small pink flowers were a significant print feature. Helen, who was the shortest of the bunch, wore a pink jumper with a white top, and she looked her Easter best in that style.

Veronica, the tall and mature 18-year-old, sported a pale blue medium-length dress with darker blue trim.

Despite my mother's limited resources, I had to admit that she managed to dress all the girls well.

My mother re-fashioned some bonnets she had stored in the attic from previous Easters. The girls were beaming when they got to show off their outfits for the very first time.

It was 6:30 am. We were finally ready to find our places in church for the Sunrise Service.

According to the thermometer that hung near our front door, the temperature was 47 degrees. The skies were nearly clear, and a sunny day seemed likely.

Once again, the Schalata parade marched across the street to the church.

The edifice was a massive brick structure with two square towers, each with a steeple on top. Three sets of double-paned stained glass windows adorned the towers, while seven steps led to a trio of doors at the main entrance.

The procession was already forming in the schoolyard. The long line of participants was comprised primarily of 73 first-grade students and 67 second-graders. Each one of these innocent-looking boys and girls carried a small candle. The calm morning gave them little trouble keeping them lit.

Monsignor Bednarczyk was flanked by Fr. Ignatius Kuchma and Fr. Piotr Lewandowski. Deacon Don Sopot and approximately a dozen acolytes all had critical responsibilities for the celebration, as well.

As we filed into the church, there was a series of large white wooden columns along each of the three aisles leading to the front. We took our usual pew on the right side, about ten rows from the communion rail. The youngest went first, with mom and pop taking their regular places at the end of the row.

St. John's Church features a large, intricately hand-carved altar and a semi-circular blue and gold dome masterfully painted with several religious figures, including Our Lady of Czestochowa.

The church has always had a familiar essence about it, but today, the overwhelming number of white lilies that adorned the altar took over your senses. The sights, sounds, and smells of this day were unmistakable. It indeed had the aroma of an Easter morning. Soon, the distinct fragrance of burning incense would overwhelm our senses even more.

The choir, combined with the organist, seemed to be at their best. The parochial school students also blended in with the choir quite nicely. Little Florence informed me that except for Good Friday, they had been rehearsing all week long.

While this unique service is always one of the most beautiful and awe-inspiring celebrations of the year, it is incredibly long in duration and quite boring due to the Latin Rite's predominant use.

The older girls were required to keep their younger sisters under control, but I was free to let my mind wander independently.

For a time, I thought about what was in store for me over the next 60 days. I thought about how my life was about to transform.

I would be separated from my family for months, perhaps longer. Holidays such as this would probably no longer exist as I knew it. My routine at the Baldwin Locomotive Works would come to an end, as well.

Taking the place of these familiar aspects of my life would be a variety of new encounters. I would be making new friends, learning new skills, and adding unique experiences to my life's journey. Many, I suspected, would be indeed heart-breaking, while others would qualify as gratifying. The trick would be how to separate one from the other.

It was easy to see how this Easter Sunday would be a turning point in my life, but my prayers to the Almighty sought out the faith, hope, and courage that I would need to see this mission through, whatever it was.

You could see the expressions on my parents' faces that all of this uncertainty weighed heavily on them, as well. The threat of war could shatter their innocent and mostly prosperous life here in America at almost any time.

The fighting was real, and reports from Europe painted an ugly scene. As much as mom and pop tried to deny it, they knew in their hearts that I would soon be a part of it.

When the service drew to a close, the grim outlook of the future was chased from our minds.

Instead, our focus was on celebrating the Ressurection of Our Lord, Jesus Christ.

As a family, we returned home, where my mother and the girls began preparing for our holiday meal in the dining room.

Mom put the finishing touches on the food while the girls set the table. Pop and my sister, Veronica, quietly snuck out the back door to hide a few Easter treats in the yard for the younger ones.

My sister, Mamie, and her husband, Bill, wouldn't be joining us today. They would be spending the day with his family down in Port Richmond. My mother always put on a big feast at Easter and the following day, on Easter Monday. During both days, various friends and relatives took turns visiting each other.

Before we sat down at the table, my father summoned the younger girls to go out in the backyard to search for their treats.

The yard measures a mere 12-feet wide by about 25-feet long. A four-foot-wide slate sidewalk separates the two grassy sections. This gray sidewalk runs down the center. A white-washed wooden fence borders the entire plot.

The gate in the back of the yard leads to a very narrow alley. Wasko's Meats is located directly across this alley.

It was no surprise that the girls quickly gathered all of the treats placed for them to find. They rushed into the house to show off their bounty.

Once everything was in place, my mother made the announcement, "Everybody sit. The food is ready, and your father will give the blessing!"

It took very little convincing for the eight of us to get busy digging into this feast. We were only treated to a spread such as this a few times per year.

My father insisted on a minimal amount of conversation at the table. That was reserved for later when the main meal was cleared, the coffee was served, and dessert was in hand.

Everyone waited for my father to speak first, and not surprisingly, he did!

"Today, my dear ones is my father's birthday," pop began.

"Your grandfather, Tomasz, would be in his eighties if he were alive today. I never really knew my father because he died when I was just a child," he continued.

"He fought in the Polish Uprising in 1848. It was one of the many times we that we tried to win democratic control over the Prussians. As we all know, this really didn't end successfully for the Poles," he explained.

"Tell us the story about our family name, father!" Florence interrupted.

"Yes!" The twins said in unison. They almost always followed that up with, "Mmmm. Yes. That's right. Uh-huh!"

Helen and Veronica also agreed that they would like to hear pop's story. "Really, Pop?" I interjected. "We've heard this story a thousand times."

"But..." he argued, "It's my father's birthday, and all the girls agree that they want to hear it," he insisted.

"Oh well. You tell the story. I'm going out to the kitchen to make more coffee. Is that okay with you, mom?" I asked.

"You'll make a mess, Tommy! I'll do it. If you don't want to sit in on the story, you can come out there and help me if you want," she concluded.

As we left the dining room for the kitchen, my father led right into his story as my sisters attentively listened with complete fascination.

"According to the story," my father began, "your grandfather got mixed up in the Polish Uprising against the Prussians in the spring of that year. Most of the fighting took place around Poznan."

Pop continued, "Polish forces defeated the Prussians in a battle near Mirolsaw on April 30. There were a series of attacks and counter-attacks by both sides, but the Poles prevailed."

"By May 6," pop explained, "the Prussians had regained control of the area and eventually squashed the rebellion.

"Many of the Polish men who participated in the uprising were captured and imprisoned. Several were tortured and branded. Some even had their heads shaved for participating in these treasonous acts." He explained.

"Your grandfather, Tomasz, and a fellow soldier by the name of Wilenty found themselves isolated from their outfit." Pop continued the story with authority. "After walking many miles from the Oder River to the Warta River, they removed their clothing and swam across the river.

"They staged a scene to make it seem as if they had drowned while swimming. The two men were deserting their posts in the army." He noted.

"When they arrived at the other side of the river, they came upon a field. As far as the eye could see, there were crops of growing vegetables, including lettuce. The legend that has been passed down in our family is that my father changed his name to something resembling "sałata" (lettuce) or "sałatka" (salad). As you school girls know, we originally spelled our name "Szałata."

"We know that our family settled in the area near Rogaline, which is just outside Poznań.

My father concluded his long-winded story with the following commentary, "So, there you have it, my little ones. That is the story of our family name, and today we raise a glass to celebrate our founder's birthday! Sto lat!" He exclaimed while raising his coffee cup above his head."

"I love that story, father," Helen was the first to respond. "What happened to our grandfather, pop?" Stella asked next.

"Unfortunately, he died when I was just a few years old. My mother remarried, but she also passed away. So, I actually didn't know either one of them," he ended.

By then, my mother returned from the kitchen with a fresh pot of coffee. She caught the tail end of my father's story and said, "Perhaps, the next time Uncle Aldalbert comes for a visit from Buffalo, we can ask him," my mother suggested.

My mother was referring to my father's half-brother, Aldalbert Mioducki. My parents moved from Philadelphia to Buffalo in 1892 to run Aldalbert's Saloon located there. I was born in Buffalo, but we soon moved back to Philadelphia after that experiment had failed.

The afternoon wore on in a most relaxing way. Friends and neighbors dropped in from time to time, and the temperature grew warm enough in the afternoon for pop to take his familiar place on the front porch.

The next day for the Easter Monday holiday, much of the city was closed.

My mother bolstered what remained of the Easter dinner with more food.

Mamie and Bill sent word that they would drop by about noontime, while Veronica announced that her boyfriend, Joe, was also planning to call.

Pop sent me down to the tavern for a quantity of beer, soda, and ice. It was a remarkably warm day for spring, and my parents had the girls set up some folding chairs in the backyard just in case we had a large turnout. You would be surprised by the stuff that pop had squirreled away in that cellar!

No sooner had the church bells struck noon than our guests began to arrive. First, Mamie and Bill, followed by Joe Zivie.

My mother's brother, Stanley Kubacki, his wife, Mary, and their one-year-old son, Stanley Jr., were next to visit.

Pop had a steady flow of his buddies in the mix, as well. This group included guys from work, men from the church, and drinking pals from the saloon. He smartly arranged for them to pass through the back gate in the alley.

In the yard was a wooden washtub filled with beer and ice. Due to this arrangement, my father obviously kept my mother out of the loop. Smart guy, my old man!

In addition to the beer, liquor bottles such as Krupnik (a vodka/fruit brandy made with honey), Starka (a rye-based spirit), and vodka (produced from fermented grains and potatoes) were being passed around. Sal Lovato, one of pop's Italian friends from work, brought a couple of jugs of his homemade wine, and that, too, was enjoyed by many.

Before long, the talk and the laughter had broken into song as one of the guys, Pawel Stefanowitch, began performing on a small squeezebox. Another, Joe Remko, was strumming on an old beat-up guitar. How the instrument ever held a tune was a mystery to me. The body of the guitar was not only well-worn but had two holes in it. The strings were utterly disheveled around the tuning pegs like a wild bird's nest. Nonetheless, the two sounded great as they belted out one song after another from the old country. Songs such as "Haj Sokoly," and "Karolina."

The music began to pick up steam, drawing a much larger crowd to this tiny patch of green. By four in the afternoon, it was standing room only, and those who couldn't get through the gate began to set up chairs in the alley outside the fence.

It seemed like as the alcohol consumption increased, the merry-making intensified, as well. The scene was getting a little rowdy.

These men worked hard and viewed such holidays as an opportunity to forget their troubles.

An argument broke out between Joe and Pawel over one of the verses in a song they were playing. Just as I finished settling that matter by calming the two musicians down, another fight erupted over a nearly empty bottle of vodka.

Franz Sabulsky and Tiny Treblinka almost came to blows over who should get the final swig. Two other fellows separated the pair before the fists started flying.

Finally, Tiny managed to get to his feet and declared, "I'll settle this! Ima' goin' home to get my bottle of zubrowka. Eeet's a much better than 'dis Śmieci (garbage)."

    *   *3 NOTE: Zubrowka (zu-BROV-ka) is a legendary vodka that dates back to the Middle Ages. It is seasoned with bison grass or zubrowka, a plant that grows in Poland's northern region where the now-endangered European bison graze.*

After that statement, Tiny stumbled to the gate out back and left. I'm not sure if he ever returned that evening!

Looking for a little more peace and quiet, I stepped back inside and found my two sisters, my brother-in-law, and possibly future brother-in-law together in the parlor. It was a perfect chance for me to join in the conversation.

Bill and Joe both stood up to greet me and shake hands, while Mamie and Veronica were also eager to get me involved in their discussion.

"Tommy," Veronica began, "Joe's thinking about joining the Navy. I told him you were an Army man." "Yeah, that's right," I acknowledged.

"I've been in a Pennsylvania National Guard Unit for about two years now, but it seems like I'm being called up for the regular Army,"

"A lot is going on in the world right now," Joe noted. "What about you, Bill?" I questioned.

"I haven't decided yet," he said. "I'm just going to give it some time and see where it goes," he added.

"I just met with the army recruiting officer down at city hall the other day, and he hinted that National Guard Unit might be called up and sent down to Mexico," I explained.

"Is that so, Tommy?" Joe seemed surprised.

"Yeah, he couldn't elaborate, but he gave me some strong hints," I remarked.

"Well, let's all change the subject from all this military talk," Veronica piped in.

"Joe and I are going to a dance at St. Laurentius this Saturday night. Right, Joe?" she stated proudly. "That's right, Veronica. I think the band playing that night is "Chester Pinkston's Ragtime Band," Joe answered.

"I just love doing the Texas Tommy, the Turkey Trot, and the Fox Trot," Veronica exclaimed.

"When do you get out to do all this dancing?" Mamie questioned.

"Joe and I have been to a couple of dances," she assured her sister.

"Say, Tommy," Veronica said, turning towards me, "Joe has four sisters, and I bet you would get along famously with his sister, Stella. What do you think?"

"Oh, I don't know. I'm sure she's nice and everything, but I've never met the girl," I said in an attempt to defend my bachelorhood.

"Yes, Veronica, that's an excellent idea," Joe returned. "I think you two would hit it off," he added.

"What do you think, Mamie?" I pleaded with my sister for an opinion.

"It's just a dance, Tommy. Nobody's asking you to marry her," Mamie asserted.

My brother-in-law, Bill, couldn't resist putting in his two cents. "I think it's a good idea, too, Tommy. Besides, you'll be with Joe and Veronica, and they'll be there to save you if you run into any trouble," he reasoned.

Joe's face beamed with a warm smile.

"That's fine. It's all set. I'll tell Stella all about you. We'll grab a bite to eat at the modest little cafe near our house before the dance. Don't worry, Tommy, we'll make sure you don't get into a flap," Joe assured me.

I'm not quite sure if I fell into some good fortune or an ambush, but I had my first date in a very long time. I had all week to dwell on the matter.

St. John Cantius Church and School
Image Source: Unknown

"LIFE AT BALDWIN LOCOMOTIVE WORKS"

Finishing touches at the Baldwin Locomotives Roundhouse
Image Source: Public Domain

CHAPTER 3

"Life at Baldwin Locomotive Works"

I awoke Tuesday morning at 5:30 to hear the loud clanging bells of my faithful alarm clock. Initially, I did not detect the aroma of breakfast cooking in the kitchen, but as I shook off my morning grogginess, the air permeated with the garlic's distinctly pleasant smell.

Typically, in the days following the Easter holiday, my mother made kielbasa and eggs from the leftovers. She took a couple of hunks of the leftover garlicky sausage, sliced it into about one-eighth- inch thick coin-sized pieces, and browned it in a lard-laden skillet.

Mother scrambled the kielbasa with a half dozen eggs. This dish was a meal in itself, and it could carry you through until the lunch hour. A good strong cup of black coffee made the morning complete.

Today, I would need to leave much earlier than I had the other day. My trip would take me a little over an hour.

To get to Baldwin Locomotive Works, I would take the 73 and the 60 trolleys. Then, I was required to hop on the Broad Street Subway Line to the Broad and Spring Garden Street shops. The official starting time in the blueprint shop was 7:30. Our day ended at 5:30.

My mother already saw to it that my lunch was packed and ready to go, as well. Contained inside the dull black metal box was a ham sandwich made with my mother's homemade bread, plus a slice of her raisin babka, an apple, and a thermos of her famous pepper pot soup.

As I look back on the whole affair, I often wonder where she ever found the time to get these tasks done? I can't speak for my father, but I don't think that my sisters nor I ever really appreciated everything that she did for us!

"Hurry, Tommy. Finish that coffee, or you'll miss your streetcar," she reminded me. "Yes, mom, I'm just about ready to head out the door," I assured her.

My father typically started work shortly after dawn each morning. Therefore, he was on his way to the job site by the time I got up. He told me in passing last night that his crew would be working in the area of Bridge and Salmon Sts. This location was only about a half dozen blocks from home.

As I grabbed my coat, my hat, and lunch pail, I headed for the door. The sound of thundering footsteps told me that the girls were stirring in their rooms, and soon the morning chaos would begin. I was glad to be on my way.

I bid my mother a final goodbye, but she couldn't resist sending me on my way with a few reminders.

"Have a good day! Be sure to eat all your lunch! Don't stop at the saloon on your way home from work. Dinner will be on time tonight!" That was her mantra.

The impressive brick main building of Baldwin anchored the corner of Broad and Spring Garden streets. A large American flag flew from a staff that appeared to be at least 30-foot tall.

As I walked in the shop door at 7:16, I found the boss, Leonardo Gaspari, at his desk already drinking a cup of coffee. Gaspari was our supervisor in the blueprint shop. He was a short Italian man. I suppose that he was about 53 or 54 years old.

Most of the workers called him "Uncle Leo" or just plain Leo. His English was generally very good, but he did have a strong Italian accent.

Twelve months of the year, he ran a small coal-burning stove in one corner of the room. Naturally, during the winter months, the stove's primary function was to supply heat for the room, but its dual purpose was to percolate his large blue and white agate coffee pot.

Above the stove was a four-foot piece of eight-gauge single-strand wire. The wire had a loop fashioned at each end — these loops were attached to the corner walls with a couple of rusty, bent ten- penny nails.

Hanging on the wire was about a half dozen tin cups for the coffee drinkers. Joining these crude and well-worn coffee cups was an old dented A & P Eight O'clock coffee can. The tin can had a hole punched in it near the top. Just like the coffee cups, the can hung on the wire with a hook.

Its purpose was for donations to purchase the coffee. Uncle Leo charged a penny a cup for his coffee, and he watched his precious java like a hawk.

If you wanted to partake in a cup, you had to like it strong, and you had to drink it black. Neither cream nor sugar was provided, and Leo warned you not to ask!

After placing my coat, hat, and lunch in my locker, I had to start my day with Uncle Leo's coffee. The old man drank it all day long, but one cup was enough for me.

I barely got situated at my mechanical desk when Leo barked his first command at me.

"Tommy! Take these prints over to the foundry shop in Building 5. Hank is waiting for them," he said firmly.

"What are they?" I asked.

"They're the spec prints for the Class 10-12-D," he replied. "They're casting the connecting rods and valve gears this week," he replied.

I was very familiar with the 10-12-D's. We had been working with this model for quite some time now. The locomotive is a narrow gauge tank steam engine that has been ordered from Baldwin by the British War Department.

Destined for light rail service in France for the war effort, these engines have a 4-6-0 drive. Basically, that means they have four small wheels on the front, six large driving wheels in the center, and no wheels in the back.

When finished, the locomotive weighs almost 15 tons and has a fuel capacity of about three-quarters of a ton of coal.

*   *4 NOTE: Locomotive Nos. 778 and 794, built by Baldwin in 1916, remain in operation today for the Welsh Highland Railway. There are five engines known to exist.*

"You got it, Leo," I said as I snapped the plans under my arm.

"Get right back here, too!" He ordered quite assertively.

"We have a lot more work that needs to get done today since everybody was off yesterday," he ended.

We were getting quite a bit of work from the Brits, but I was surprised that we didn't really have any French contracts.

According to Leo, the French lost most of their locomotive building capacity in Northern France due to the German occupation.

Leo also explained that Baldwin received three sets of drawings for locomotives from the French with guaranteed financing. Still, we only produced a handful of engines, and the entire project dried up. We never received an explanation. Thank God for the Brits!

The walk from Building 1 to Building 5 took about seven minutes. Hank was impatiently waiting for my arrival. He moved around from building to building to check on the progress of various projects.

"It's about time you got here! What are you guys on one of Uncle Leo's coffee breaks or what?" He bellowed.

Hank is the absolute opposite of Leo. He's a tall, strapping man well over six-foot tall. Most of the well-known characters around the works have nicknames, and Hank is known as "Hank the Hungarian" or "The Mad Hungarian."

He is not only an imposing character, but he's loud, he's gruff, and he's very excitable.

I handed off the plans and was on my way. I saw no need to prolong the visit. Besides, my coffee would be stone cold by the time I got back. I would need to warm it on the top of the stove if I had any inclination to drink it.

Once the plans were delivered, Leo seemed to have settled down. He was already on his second cup of coffee when he broke the silence with some small talk about his tomato plants.

"You know, Tommy, in just a couple of weeks, my tomato plants will be ready to plant in my garden," the old man beamed.

Leo lived in a small row home on Catherine Street in the Italian section of South Philly. Much like our house on Thompson Street, Leo's backyard was probably about 100 to 150 square feet, but he grew about a half dozen tomato plants. They were produced from heirloom seeds brought directly from Italy by his father, Sylvestry.

The old man often bragged about his grape arbor, which produced enough grapes to make quite a few bottles of wine.

"My momma's gravy recipe was the best in the whole world," he said with pride.

That statement was a reference to his mother's homemade marinara sauce. The Italians often refer to it as gravy.

"My Anna's gravy is very close," he explained, "but nobody made it like momma!"

"Sounds great, Leo! I don't doubt that it was the best," I responded with the most positive answer I could give him.

"Do you plan on making your wine again this year?" I inquired.

"Oh, yes," he replied. "I will be sure to give you some," he promised.

The old man's wine was like no other I've tasted... not too sweet, not too dry... and with plenty of flavor!

"Well, if I'm still here, that would be great," I said.

"What's up, Tommy? You find a new job?" He asked.

"No, Leo. I'm afraid the army might have other plans for me. It looks like I may be called up soon," I explained.

"That's too bad," he said while shaking his head. "You're a good boy, Tommy. If you leave, we'll miss you around here."

"Thanks, Leo," I commented. "I am sure that wherever I go, I am going to miss this place, as well," I concluded.

On that note, the small talk quietly went away, and the old man gave me a list of tasks that needed immediate attention. Most of it involved filing drawings and searching for other plans requested by the casting department for this 10-12-D project.

After lunch, the peaceful afternoon was interrupted by another of Uncle Leo's tirades.

"Tommy," he said, calling my name, "We have a problem.

Milton Shomper just called from the boiler shop in Building 2, and they're having issues with the boiler on one of those 10-12-D units.

"They're trying to match-up the boiler to the frame, and it ain't lining up." Leo fumed.

"I need you to take both sets of these plans down to that idiot and straighten him out," he ordered.

"Sure, Leo," I replied. "What should I tell him?"

"Look at this drawing," he began. "See this lip all the way around the boiler?"

"Yeah, I see it," I answered affirmatively.

"He's claiming that the boiler they have is missing that lip, and it won't line up. I think they pulled the wrong boiler. My guess is they have one of those French boilers.

"Tell him to look here," Leo said while pointing to the spot on the drawing, "This is the part number, 10-12-D-2278B."

He further clarified, "The first series is the model number, next is the part number, 2278, and the "B" means boiler. How much easier can it be?" He asked.

"Got it," I acknowledged.

"Here is a copy of the blueprints for the French version. Show this to him, too! See- the numbers are different, and there's no lip around the boiler. Completely different animal!

"It's a wonder that we even stay in business with guys like him around! Oh yeah, Tommy, tell him to get his act together, or he'll be working at the monkey cage down at the zoo!" Leo fumed some more.

The last comment was a close reference to one of Leo's favorite sayings, "It's not my monkey, not my circus." The basic translation is it means "it's not my problem."

Once again, I confirmed that I understood and was on my way to Building 2.

Now, Building 2 was just a short distance away. As I left our own Building 1, a light rain began to fall, and I made my best effort to dart from one building to another. The prints were secure in a canvas bag, but moisture was indeed their enemy. It could take hours for an engineer to copy or repair any damage that may be incurred.

It was interesting to see the entire manufacturing process of these engines. Most of the buildings were very hot, with casting, welding, and other procedures requiring extreme temperatures. Even the grinding room, where I was assigned to work initially, was a hot, dirty workshop. Fresh air and light were a premium, but the men went about their tasks like an army of ants trying to move a morsel of bread just a few inches. Most of the work was hard, the conditions were poor, and the hours were long, but it was good steady work most of the time.

Our building was once the final erecting shop, but when the facility was in dire need of expanding about 14 years ago, a new engine finishing shop was built at 26th Street. That facility, which is only a few blocks away, is the most impressive. This massive shop is home to the final assembly for most of the projects. Giant cranes, heavy-duty hoists, and iron chains worthy of anchoring an ocean liner made these tasks possible.

During this expansion, the company invested one million dollars in electrical drives for tools, cranes, and elevators. These improvements allow the shop to concentrate on heavy work.

After chasing down three different floor workers, I finally located Shomper, who was still baffled over the boiler riddle.

The 25-year-old Boiler Assembly Assistant lived in the Kensington section of the city. Actually, he lived on the 1800 block of East Tusculum Street, just around the corner from Kensington Avenue.

Shomper was another Baldwin hot head. He constantly complained that the entire world was against him. In all of my dealings with the man, he never once gave me the time of day.

With slicked-back dark hair, a matching mustache, and a stubby cigar hanging out of his mouth, he gruffly barked out orders.

Every foul-up seemed to be my fault. His account usually blamed me for providing him with the wrong set of plans, or he often accused me of transcribing the part numbers incorrectly.

After showing him the drawings given to me by Leo, Shomper walked away, red-faced, and yelled to his crew to track down the correct boiler. The word spread quickly about the mix-up, and his team went into action like a swarm of cockroaches when exposed to the sudden light. The whole scene was rather comical, and I couldn't wait to get back to Uncle Leo to give him my report.

The crew assigned to the engine finishing shop worked on a 2-8-0 consolidated engine for the Oneida & Western Railroad.

As I explained locomotive wheel configurations earlier, this locomotive had two wheels, called trucks, on the front and eight driving wheels behind them. There were no trucks on the back. The drive wheels were 50 inches in diameter, while the coal capacity was about six tons. The customer expected delivery of Engine No. 15 sometime in June. At this point, the project was on schedule.

According to Leo, the Oneida & Western Railroad is a short line that runs between Oneida and Jamestown, Tennessee. It mainly serves this area by hauling coal, lumber, and other goods. It also provides limited passenger service and delivers mail and groceries to the locals.

    *   *5 NOTE: Locomotive No. 734, another steam engine of that same class, was built by Baldwin in 1916 and is still in operation with the Western Maryland Scenic Railroad.*

When I filled Leo in on the incident down in Building 2, he didn't know whether to laugh or get upset. He checked his pocket watch and announced that it was 5:15. The old man shrugged his shoulders and walked over to the stove to clean out his coffee pot for the day.

"Well, boys, we get to do this all over again tomorrow," he said with a well-earned sigh.

"If I have to deal with another simp in the morning, someone will be read the riot act," he concluded as he finished cleaning the pot.

"See you tomorrow, Tommy," he said to me, and that was my signal that he was permitting me to go home.

Although the saloon was calling my name, I went directly home. My mother's warning not to stop haunted me as I walked up Orthodox Street.

When I reached our house's front steps, pop was in his usual spot on the porch. After we exchanged pleasantries, I asked father whether he still had any leftover beer down in the cellar.

"Yes, son. There's a bucket of water down in the corner. There should be about two or three bottles in there," he answered.

As I entered the house and put my lunch pail in the sink, my mother informed me that my supper was in the oven. The rest of the family had already eaten.

"I'll get it shortly, mom," I replied. "I'm going out on the porch with pop for a while," I explained.

Sure enough, down in the corner of the cellar, there was a bucket with three bottles of Schmidt's beer. They were obviously all that remained from the recent Easter celebration.

I took one bottle and joined my father on the porch. I sat down on a straight-back wicker chair that was well-worn but painted the same shade of green as his rocker.

"So, Pop," I began, "you fought in the war. What advice can you give me? It looks like I'm heading there eventually!"

"Tommy, I was only 15 years old when the Prussians forced me to fight the French in 1870," he recalled.

"Lucky for me, the war only lasted six months, and the whole thing was a ruse to unify the German states," he went on.

"As I said, it was only a short affair, but I was scared... scared out of my wits," he admitted.

"That story I told the other day about my father's desertion in the previous war? That could have easily have been me. Had the fighting not ended when it did, I would have figured out a way to get out!" He revealed.

"Son, you know I read all the papers. I know what's going on over there, and the reports are that the fighting is one hundred times worse than anything I ever experienced," he said with honesty. I also detected the look of sadness in his eyes.

We both paused to take a swig of beer, and then he said, "I wish I could tell you that you'll be fine, but I'm not in the habit of passing out bullcrap. If you are lucky enough to return home safely, you probably won't be able to talk about things that happened over there," he added. "But they'll stay with you forever," he presumed.

"I know what you mean, pop. I hear about what's going on, too. It's just that the talk keeps getting louder," I observed.

"Listen, Tommy, you're a smart guy. You've got a good head on your shoulders. You don't take chances, and you won't if you are called upon to fight." he said to comfort me.

"Thanks for the talk, pop," I said. "What did mom make good for supper? She said my dish is in the oven."

"Ham and cabbage, my boy. Ham and cabbage. Tell her you want extra. She has some stashed away in the back of the ice box," he said while giving me a wink.

I took my last swallow of beer while my father picked up his pipe and lit the bowl, which had grown cold by now.

My father and I had very few of those talks over the years. He wasn't bashful about giving his opinions to those around the neighborhood, but he preferred to keep it low-key in our home. I knew it took a lot of courage for my pop to open up the way he did, and I was grateful for the opportunity to hear his thoughts on the matter.

Baldwin Locomotive No. 778 Leighton Buzzard Railway UK
Image Source: Ian Boyle

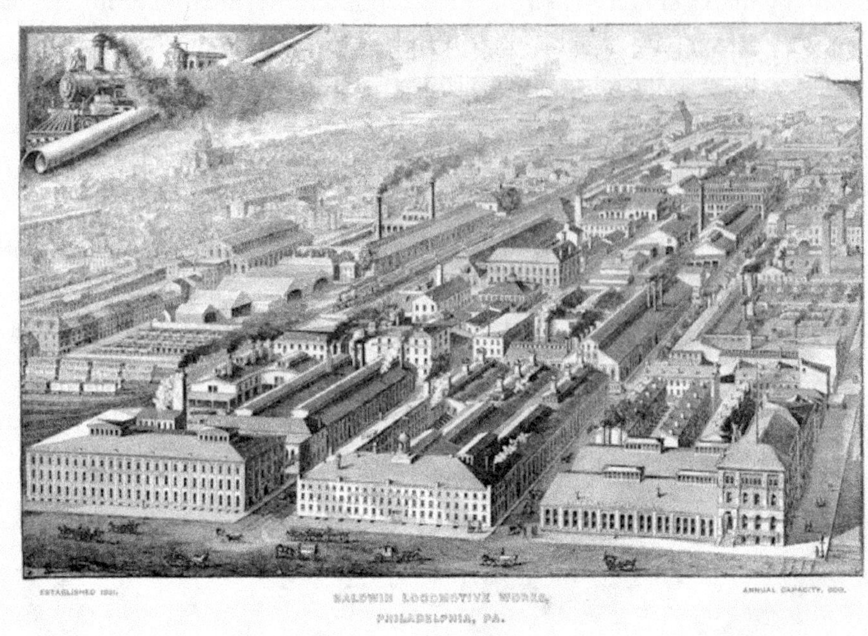

General view of Baldwin Locomotive Works
Image Source: Catskills Archives Photo

Hoisting a Complete Locomotive Baldwin Locomotive Works
Image Source: Author unknown

"Birth of a New Romance"

Tommy Schalata and Stella Zwolinski
Image Source: Author's Photo

CHAPTER 4

"Birth of a New Romance"

When Saturday arrived, it was time for my monthly drill at the National Guard Armory. The fortress- like structure was built in 1901 and is located at 22 South 23rd Street. It's just west of center city. The previous armory was located only a few blocks away, but that structure had collapsed from heavy snow in 1899.

Our monthly drills typically involved:

- Calisthenics.
- Lessons on general military procedures.
- Updates on new policies and scheduled training.

Soon after the company fell in for roll call, it was apparent that today was not going to be just another monthly drill.

Captain Elwood Hawthorne informed us that we would become part of the active army as of June 24th. Therefore, we had less than seven weeks to prepare ourselves for the transition.

"Effective immediately, our orders are to increase our mandatory drills from once per month to every Saturday until further notice," he declared.

"If your employer requires official notice of this change, the proper paperwork will be given to you," he went on to say.

"This morning," he stated, "each platoon, in this company, will have a classroom session. Its purpose will be to provide each and every one of you with the details of what is expected to happen during this period.

"Following the classroom work, we will break for mess at Noon," he continued. "The afternoon session will be devoted to taking a complete inventory of the equipment that we have on hand.

"Future drills will be devoted to the organization and cleaning of such equipment. Suspended until further notice will be all physical training and calisthenics. You will get plenty of that at your next mission," the Captain noted.

"Finally," he announced, "your classroom assignments will be as follows: 1st Rifle Platoon, Room 3A with 1st Sgt. Donnelly; 2nd Rifle Platoon, Room 3B with Staff Sgt. Ulrich; 3rd Rifle Platoon, Room 4A with Sgt. Lingleman, and Weapons Platoon, Room 4B with Gunnery Sgt. Gutkowski. That is all," he concluded.

"Dismissed!" was the order that was given by Lt. Hanahan.

We immediately broke rank, and I joined the rest of my platoon in Room 4B. This development was all new territory for us, but little did we know that this was only the beginning.

Sgt. Gutkowski informed us that we would be part of a complete re-organization. Presently, we were part of the Second Pennsylvania Infantry Regiment.

Sarge revealed that our company would be part of a new division comprised primarily of Pennsylvania National Guard Units.

Before giving us the details of our expected mission, the gunnery sergeant pulled down a map that illustrated the borders in question. The plan outlined the areas of Arizona, New Mexico, and Texas.

"Men," he began, "this conflict with Mexican revolutionary Pancho Villa actually started in 1910 when General Pershing deployed several troops in this area to protect U.S. lives and property. Pershing's initial goal was to ensure that the fighting remained on Mexican soil.

"Hostilities escalated earlier this year when Villa's men stopped a train near San Isabel, Chihuahua. The marauders killed 18 American passengers who worked for a U.S. firm based in Arizona." Our instructor pointed out the area in question on the map.

"Last month, 500 of these revolutionaries went up against 300 of our forces near Columbus, New Mexico. This is very close to the center of the area in question," he said while pointing to the border town.

"The raiders, who were looking to capture American supplies," he stated, "were defeated in the battle. About 60 to 80 of the enemy were killed, while we lost about a dozen soldiers and civilians," he further explained.

"General Pershing was ordered to form an expeditionary force of 5,000 to be sent to the area to capture or kill Pancho Villa.

"President Wilson has issued a second order to station approximately 117,000 National Guardsmen on the border to protect U.S interests," the sergeant said in outlining the plan.

"It is very likely," Gutkowski revealed, "that we will join about 4,800 of these guardsmen at Camp Stewart in El Paso, Texas. The camp is currently under construction. It is a rough desert area located in the foothills of the Franklin Mountains.

"In case you were wondering," he noted, "daytime temperatures in May through October range from the high eighties to right around 100 degrees," he said with a laugh.

"Also," he went on, "the area tends to be very windy and extremely dusty. It is not a very friendly environment," he explained.

The gunnery sergeant also informed us that there are about a half dozen varieties of rattlesnakes in that region, in addition to scorpions, tarantulas, and poisonous spiders.

"Most of these creatures are encountered in the evenings, late at night or early morning hours," he said assuredly.

"Any questions at this point?" he asked.

"How long do you think we'll be there?" was the first question from the floor. It came from Pfc. Quentin Johnson.

"Naturally, it's hard to say," the sergeant tried to answer honestly. "Right now, they're projecting about six months. It could go longer, or things could wrap up rather quickly if they capture this guy," he finished.

"What can we expect once we get there?" asked another.

"After we set-up camp and get organized, we will be used primarily to guard the border. You can expect some of the time will be spent receiving additional military training, with some drilling and formation work besides," he stated.

"Sarge, do you have any more information on this whole re-organization process?" I inquired. "There's a lot to this process," he answered, "but the word I'm getting from the higher-ups is that we may be destined to be converted to an artillery unit eventually."

Before any more questions could be heard from the floor, the alarm sounded, and our morning session was over. As a platoon, we immediately filed out of the classroom and headed for the mess hall.

The smell of turkey was the first thing that hit you when you picked up your tray at the end of the line.

Sure enough, today's menu included a turkey hash. A thick gravy that consisted of turkey and mixed vegetables was flung on top of a large scoop of potato dressing. Rolls, butter, coffee, and juice were also there for the taking.

Our mess table had a handful of regulars in addition to myself. Sitting at my table were: Harry Haeberle, Irvin D. Schweppenheiser, Roy Wilson, and Bernie Halliday. We were all Philly guys, and we naturally gravitated towards each other.

"This is a big deal, guys. Whaddya think?" Wilson was the first to ask.

"I kind of expected this," I responded.

"Ahhhh, I think we're going to become a bunch of glorified babysitters," Haeberle sneered. "We are never going to see any action," he went on, "that's going to be reserved for the regular army, the Buffalo Soldiers, and I heard they even have Indian Scouts involved."

Schweppenheiser, who usually keeps his mouth shut, also chimed in, "I think you guys are right. It's going to be boring. It's going to be dusty, and I think we will be going out of our minds most of the time. However, it beats the alternative of going to France and fighting Jerry's."

"Guess you're right there," I answered.

"Yeah, it could be worse," Halliday said, finally offering his opinion.

"What's up with you, Tommy? I heard you have a hot date tonight!" Haeberle inquired.

"Well, I don't know about a hot date, but yes, I'm going to a church dance tonight. Where did you hear that from? I questioned him.

"My brother-in-law, Gus Smith, works over in Building 2 at Baldwin. He must have heard it from someone else over there," Haeberle revealed.

"I know word travels fast," I responded, "but I really didn't talk to too many guys about it. Uncle Leo must be spreading the gossip around these days," I reasoned.

Wilson continued to push the issue, "So, what's the scoop? Who is this mystery babe you're going out with tonight?"

"It's not a big mystery," I replied in an effort to downplay the whole thing. "My sister and her boyfriend were visiting for the holiday. They invited me to tag along to this dance with the guy's sister. That's all there is to it," I explained.

"Good luck!" Schweppenheiser said.

"Yeah, I hope it works out," Halliday chimed in.

The signal sounded, telling us that mess hall was over. One of the NCOs (Non-Commissioned Officers) instructed us to meet in the gymnasium in the center of the building. The Captain's instructions were to remove everything from the secured lockers and sort it out in piles.

"Each platoon sergeant will pair you up with a buddy, and the two of you will take inventory of everything that is assigned to your area. One of you will have a clipboard that contains the inventory sheets. You will mark down the item, the quantity, a brief description, and its condition. Regarding the latter, you will have three options: replace, repair, or clean. This information will be useful when we move to the next phase of this mission. That is all!" He bellowed.

"Dismissed!" Capt. Hawthorne ordered.

We broke down into our smaller groups, and our platoon sergeants followed through on the orders given to us by the Captain.

Each platoon was also given several colored bandanas. Green indicated the items were good to go, while yellow signified that the locker's articles required some type of repair. If a locker was designated with a blue bandana, the elements contained therein would need to be cleaned, and obviously, red was a sign that the article was beyond repair and should be replaced.

The Captain emphasized that all weapons, such as rifles and such, were to be cleaned and oiled whether they needed it or not.

The men spent the rest of the day going about their work, and there was very little horseplay or distraction. The equipment that had not yet made it through the reviewing process was secured in another locked room. Naturally, this would be our starting point the following week.

We were dismissed at five, which meant that I had but one hour to get home and change for my date that evening.

As I passed the time on the trolley car, I decided that my brown suit with my brown tie would be my choice for the evening.

Getting to St. Laurentius Church was relatively easy. As a matter of fact, my sister Veronica would be traveling with me.

It was about a two-minute walk from our house to Orthodox and Almond Sts., where we would catch the 25 trolley. The 25 would drop us off, and Memphis and Berks Sts. From there, it was just a short walk to the church. The trip would take us about 30 minutes to complete.

Veronica informed me that we would be meeting Joe and Stella at a place called "Andy's Cafe." It was about two blocks from the church hall, she noted.

The quaint corner eatery featured plenty of luxurious cherry wood trim, with about a dozen round tables and matching cherry chairs. Blue and white checkered tablecloths made this small restaurant very warm and inviting.

The four of us were seated by one of the large windows facing Norris Street. Even though it was still early evening, the street was bustling with pedestrians making their way past.

A young man, who appeared to be in his mid-twenties, greeted us warmly and handed us each a menu. He introduced himself as Samuel.

"Our soups du jour are puree of split pea and mock turtle soup," he began, "and our dinner specials for this evening are roast prime ribs of beef with vegetables and roast turkey with oyster dressing and cranberry sauce," he explained. "Does anyone have any questions?"

"No, Samuel. Not at this time," Joe spoke up. He looked around the table to be sure, and we all agreed that we were fine at this point.

A quick glance at the menu revealed that some of the cafe's other menu items included: beef a la mode, roast loin of pork, boiled beachnut ham and cabbage, fried Long Island scallops, and baked sea trout in creole sauce.

Once the task of ordering our meals was out of the way, the small talk business began in earnest. "So, Tommy," Joe began, " I understand you had your guard drill today. Did they tell you anything more about what lies ahead?"

"Well, Joe," I quickly answered, "as you may have guessed, I'm not really at liberty to discuss any details, but suffice it to say that we are preparing as if we are heading to the border of Mexico, and we are busy getting things in order. That's about all I safely say," I concluded.

"I understand," he acknowledged. "Veronica tells me you're leaving June 24th, is that right?"

"Unless something changes in the meantime, that's right!" I confirmed.

"So, how's this band we're going to see tonight?" I asked. "Chester Pinkston's Ragtime Band?" Joe responded.

"They're excellent," he went on. "They call themselves a ragtime band, but they play a lot of popular music. Ragtime is on its way out," he explained.

"They usually perform tunes by Al Jolson, Billy Murray, John McCormick, and other famous singers."

"That's right," Veronica joined in. "They'll do a well-known ragtime song like "Maple Leaf Rag, and then come back with a slow song like "Close to My Heart," she said.

"How many are in this orchestra?" I asked.

"I think it's about seven or eight," Joe guessed.

"What do you think, Stella?" I asked to get her involved in the conversation. "Does it sound like a good time for you?"

She flashed a wry smile and said, "I guess so. I'm not a very experienced dancer, but I'll give it a try," she concluded.

"Me too!" I agreed. "If you're willing, I'll do the same."

Once the ice was broken, the cafe's meal went much smoother, and it seemed like time flew by. Before we knew it, the time had come for us to walk back to the school gymnasium for the dance. The building was located directly next to the church.

We were able to locate some seats that weren't directly next to the band. That allowed us to at least have some form of conversation during the dance.

The band started the evening with "Alabama Jubilee," "Back to Carolina You Love," and "On the 5:15."

After a very rousing welcome by the crowd, the band leader, Chester Pinkston, addressed the full house.

"Thank you all! Thank you very much! It's a pleasure to be here again at St. Laurentius. We hope you all have a wonderful time here tonight.

He said, "I'm sure you all recognized that first number, "Alabama Jubilee." Next, we offered our version of the popular Al Jolson tune, "Back To Carolina You Love," and finally, a train song, "On the 5:15."

"Get ready," he warned, "the fellows and I are ready to play for you the top song of 1915, "Hello Frisco."

"Are you ready, fellows? One-two-three..."

Joe and Veronica were on the dance floor from the very beginning, and they were trying their best to coax Stella and me to join them there.

"Come on," Joe insisted, "once you get up there, you'll forget about everything else and have a good time," he promised.

Finally, we relented and joined the others on the crowded dance floor. As promised, once we got our feet wet, we found the water to be fine.

Punch and cookies were served during the band breaks, but by 9:30, the dance hall became hot, stuffy, and smoke-filled. Stella and I agreed to step out to get some fresh air.

Less than a block from the dance hall was a small park that comprised about one city block. It was a clear, starlit, and pleasant evening. The moon was nearly full, and it cast plenty of light in addition to the handful of gaslights scattered about the park. We found a bench that offered an inviting spot to recoup our senses, and we took advantage of the situation.

Initially, we exchanged small talk about our families and our jobs. I learned that Stella was working at the Frankford Arsenal Munitions Plant. She worked on the inspection line, checking and double-checking for defects in the cartridges as they passed by her post.

I explained my role at the Baldwin Locomotive Works. It seemed ironic that we were both involved in the war effort somehow, but I guess with the rest of the world participating in this conflict, that would be expected.

It also seemed quite a coincidence that her family consisted of her brother, Joe, and four girls, while I was likewise the only male in my family with six sisters. Ironically, we also each had girls named Stella, Florence, and Mary.

Out of nowhere came a question that I least expected from the otherwise shy 18-year-old girl, "So, what are your goals, Tommy Schalata?" she asked.

"My goals? Where do I think I'm going with my future?" I asked.

"Yes!" She came back, "what do you expect the future to hold for you?" She insisted that I come up with an answer.

"To be honest, I have no goals right now," was my initial response.

"This army thing is looming over my head, and while I know that this assignment to the Mexican border won't drastically alter my life, eventually going overseas to fight in The Great War will.

"Not only will it probably change my life, but I may not come back from it. I see no point in setting any goals at this point," I explained.

"Well, maybe I worded the whole thing wrong," she back-tracked. "Let me put it this way," she said, "what would be your dream for a perfect future?" She asked in an effort to pick my brain. This shy young woman wasn't at all bashful about sizing me up on the first date!

"When you put it that way," I answered, "I guess I do have a dream in my head."

"What is it?" she anxiously inquired.

"My dream is to have a small farm in the country. Grow my own vegetables and such," I explained.

"I want to look into a cloudless sky and see nothing but that vivid blue roof above me.

"I want to sit in my own backyard and watch a pair of Mourning Doves settle in for the evening on the branch of a tall Walnut tree. In the background is the most radiant red sky as the sun sinks beyond the next hillside.

"As I'm watching this sunset, I'm nursing a cold beer while my faithful dog lies at my feet. He's comfortably resting, but he has one ear trained on any unusual sounds he detects coming from the darkness.

"Instead of the screeching, ear-piercing sounds of trolley car wheels on the tracks and the blasting factory whistles announcing the shift changes, I hear crickets and katydids. They are orchestrating their own natural symphony in the nearby woods. That's my dream," I concluded.

"So, you can be romantic," she pointed out.

"Romantic? I don't know," I responded, " but I know I would like to escape this life in the city," I asserted.

"How about you? I inquired. "What's your dream?" I asked as I tossed the ball into her court.

"Believe it or not," she began, "my dream is very similar.

I looked at her, and she nodded affirmatively.

"I see myself in a small rural cottage, too. The colors I see are in my many flower beds that I have cultivated on the property.

"In the spring, my yard is blooming with yellow daffodils and red tulips. The forsythia bushes are bursting with yellow, as well.

"I see a large circular flower bed that is filled with Iris of every color. They are as white as snow. They are as yellow as the sun. They are light lavender, deep purple, and as blue as your eyes.

"In addition to Black-eyed Susans and Daisies, the summer brings me roses that are pink, red, and yellow. There is a border of my favorite Tiger Lilies. These tall sentinels show off their orange blooms all summer long, and they will rival your red sunset," she said.

"Wow. That's a lot," I observed.

"In my dream," she added, "a dozen inquisitive chickens are wandering around the property. They spend the day searching the lawn for tasty treats but offer me a bounty of fresh eggs that I can use to make breakfast or bake a giant chocolate cake.

"When I put the coffee pot on in the morning, my lone rooster will let me know if I am on schedule or if I am behind my time. That is my dream, Tommy Schalata," she concluded.

"Sounds like a competition," was my first response. "Which one of us can dream about a more idyllic life?"

"I think we should head back to the dance," Stella stated to bring us both back to reality.

"You're right," I answered. "Your brother and my sister must be looking for us by now."

Together we stood up from the bench. I took hold of Stella's arm and escorted her back to the dance hall.

The night was winding down. We danced a couple more numbers before the band announced the final tune of the evening.

"We would like to thank everyone for coming out tonight. We certainly hope that you all had a good time. Tonight's performance will conclude with our own rendition of Billy Murray's hit song, "Pretty Baby."

"By the way, this is the top song of 1916 so far this year. Have a good night!"

Joe Zivie
Image Source: Author's Photo

Stella Zwolinski
Image Source: Author's Photo

Stella Zwolinski
Image Source: Author's Photo

Stella Z. on Kenilworth Street
Image Source: Author's Photo

"THE DART MATCH"

The local saloon was the place to meet.
Image Source: Unknown

CHAPTER 5

"The Dart Match"

The month of May would fly by. My weekly routine would change very little during this time. Naturally, my job at Baldwin Locomotive Works garners most of my time on Mondays through Fridays.

Though initiated by my father, a new ritual was a trip down to Szczepanski's Saloon on Friday nights. I'm not sure if my pop was trying to make the most of our time together before I went into the service full time or if he was just looking for a reason to get away from the women in the house for a while.

Generally, the two of us headed down to the local taproom at about 7:30 in the evening. Pop was usually ready to return home about two hours later.

As you turn the corner from Thompson Street onto Orthodox, Sochko's Flower Shop is on the corner.

When I passed the shop, I made myself a mental note that Mother's Day would soon be upon us. Another local landmark, Stottlemeyer's Bakery, is located alongside the flower business.

Otto Stottlemeyer, a third-generation baker, runs the local bakeshop. His Persian Buns are the best this side of anywhere. The icing, which tops the round cinnamon rolls, is the perfect marriage of consistency and sweetness. It sounds improbable, but I can tell the difference when the buns are made by Otto, as opposed to his son, Johann.

Next door is The Polish Falcon Bank and Trust Co. The local financial institution has been around since 1874.

Before you reach the saloon, you must pass E.H. Felding's Haberdashery. Gus Felding inherited the men's shop from his father, Edmond, and the business offers everything from hats, gloves, and ties to belts, dress shirts, and suits.

As you peer into the front window on the tavern's left side, the first thing you see is the upright piano against the wall. "Slim Eddy" Pinkos typically tickles the ivories on most Friday and Saturday nights.

Visible from the store front window on the other side of the door are several round tables and chairs. They are covered in thick, black lacquer paint, and it's apparent that they are wearing several coats of enamel.

Next to the piano is a long wooden bench that runs the length of the entire wall. Rectangular tables, also covered in multiple layers of black paint, are placed next to this bench with accompanying chairs. This arrangement produces a large seating area on that side of the room.

The last table in the corner, however is set up with a checkerboard. Frequently, older men gather at that spot in the afternoons and challenge each other over a game or two. The winner of these highly contested checker games will often savor his victory with a nickel beer supplied by the loser, of course.

Running the length of the wall on the right side of the taproom is a dark walnut bar complete with a long mirror and several shelves for bottle storage behind it. The structure is hardly a finely carved work of art, but the local patrons find it more than serviceable.

In the back of the taproom is the dartboard. This is located right near the toilet. A small shelf on the wall offers a place to put your beer during the competition.

Sometimes we sit at the bar with the other regulars, just shooting the breeze. Beer is the standard beverage of choice, but the evening often begins with a shot of Old Overholt rye whiskey. This brand is my father's favorite.

Occasionally, Stosh and Casimir, two of my father's pals, talk us into shooting some darts. Pop has always been a pretty good dart player. I imagine he picked up the talent when working in his brother's neighborhood bar in Buffalo. Notwithstanding, by the fourth or fifth pint of beer, his accuracy begins to suffer. This disadvantage means we have to get off to an early lead if we have any chance of winning the match.

It was evident from the start that this evening was would probably not go as planned. As we sat at the bar drinking that first shot and beer, we could see that a torrential downpour was taking place outside.

Inside, a thick cloud of cigar and cigarette smoke enveloped the room. Rowdy conversations were drowned out by Slim Eddy pounding the keys on the piano.

Pop ordered a second round of Old Overholt before we were midway through our first pint. This second drink did not bode well for us if a dart match was in the cards.

Stosh and Casimir did not attempt to hide the fact that they observed the entire scenario from their vantage point at a table near the piano player.

Sure enough, by the time we finished our second round, the duo approached us with a challenge.

Pop never backed down from such a request, and they knew it.

The stakes were high. The winning team would win four bits from the losers, or a half dollar.

Typically, a match consisted of three games of 701. My father was off to a fast start. Not only did he earn the right to shoot first, but his first throw also doubled in at 13. His next two darts were both singles, 11 and 16. His 53 points gave us an initial score of 648.

By the end of the first round, we were leading by a score of 592-638. Our team won the first game of the match comfortably by 62 points, and our opponents lobbied for a short break to replenish their drinks.

When pop opted to celebrate our victory with another rye shot, I was sure that our good fortune was short-lived.

Our opponents grabbed an early lead in the match's second game, but my father was unstoppable. He hit two straight treble 20's and capped them off with a single 15. That hot shooting spree garnered him 135 points. This gave us the lead, and we never looked back.

Stosh and Casimir made a last-ditch effort to save face by trying to win the third set of our match, but pop remained undaunted and kept his hot streak going. We took the final game of the match by 54 points.

As the losers bought us a round of drinks and tossed two bits at each of us, my father exclaimed, "You tried to take advantage of an old man, but it didn't work, did it?"

By the time we finished our victory drinks, my father was beginning to sway noticeably. I convinced him to hang onto the bar as I searched the room for someone I would be able to enlist to help me get him home.

The pouring rain still had not let up. Therefore, the trek to our front porch would indeed be a hurdle.

Joe Karkowska volunteered to give me a hand, and the 10-minute walk home seemed like an eternity. One factor that I hadn't planned on when we finally dragged my pop up the front steps and onto the porch was the sight of my mother standing in the doorway with a rolling pin in her hand.

"You're not bringing that drunk into my parlor," she warned us.

"You'll have to take him around to the back door and into the kitchen," she decreed.

When we reached the end of our trip, our clothes were dripping wet. I thanked Joe for his efforts.

Mom and I proceeded to get pop out of his clothing.

Once we put the old man in bed, he was able to sleep it off until morning. That is if my mother let him. As for myself, I had to get up early to attend my National Guard Drill.

I succeeded in getting through my drill just fine. Our unit spent most of the day cleaning, packing, and sorting the equipment. There were no classes on the schedule.

It was a quiet evening at home for a change. I spent a relaxing hour reading a few passages from "A Connecticut Yankee in King Authur's Court" by Mark Twain.

My parents were very much in favor of our education and had acquired several volumes of Harper's Mark Twain Collection.

Stella and I agreed not to go out dancing this evening. Instead, her parents invited me to Sunday dinner the following afternoon.

Veronica was going with me for the meal at the Zwolinski's. There were two different methods to get to their home at 2702 Cambria St. We could take the 25 Trolley. This route would get us there in about 24 minutes, including an eight-minute walk. The 73 would get us there in 20 minutes but required a 15-minute walk. There were fewer stops on the 73.

The Federal-style row home was a three-story brick structure with three white marble steps leading to a landing at the front door. A narrow passageway shared with the house next door obviously led to the backyard.

Nearly the entire family greeted us at the entryway with a warm welcome. Joe and Stella's mother, Rozalia, was putting the finishing touches on her dinner.

After going through the introductions and exchanging pleasantries, we were ushered into the dining room for the feast. The air was heavy with the tantalizing aroma of roast chicken.

The first course to be served was Kapuśniak. This is cabbage and sauerkraut soup. It was a delicious meal in its own right.

Two finely roasted chickens on a large platter were the centerpiece for the table. Accompanying the chicken was potato dumplings (KLUSKI ŚLĄSKIE Z DZIURKĄ) and cucumber salad (MIZERIA).

The father, Franz, was a man of few words. He appeared to be quite pleasant, but he merely smiled and nodded when you spoke to him. He was either remarkably shy or grappled with a limited vocabulary of the English language.

His wife, Rose, was a delightful woman. While my mom was of slight build, this mother of six had a round face and more of a stout body frame. Unlike her husband, she took an active role in the conversation.

Lottie, the youngest, was asked to say the blessing before the meal began.

The oldest daughter, Mary, also lived in this large row home with her husband, Joseph Olewnik, and their two daughters, Florentina and Josephine.

Stella's other sister, Sophie, resided nearby. She was married in 1911. Florence, who was 20 years old, still lived at home, as well.

Talk at the table was more acceptable than silence, which was the norm at my own house. The conversation touched on such subjects as my military service, my job at Baldwin, and aspects of my own family.

Since Joe had been dating my sister, Veronica, for some time now, I was asked if I had planned on seeing Stella regularly.

"Well," I countered, "this is only our second time together, and I am still getting to know Stella," I said. "But so far, we seem to be getting along famously, thanks," I affirmed.

As expected, the girls were most interested in all the details, but Stella and I continued to keep the matter at bay.

After dinner, the routine was much the same as in my own house. Rozalia had the girls clear the table, and apple cake (Szarlotka), was served with coffee.

Franz seemed to have a bit of a sweet tooth, as he was the first to dig into the dessert. A large cup of black coffee seemed to be obligatory, as well.

The girls were required to clean up in the kitchen while the rest of us retired to the parlor.

Since the personal fact-finding mission appeared to be over, the conversation shifted to the matters of the weather and current events around the world. The war in Europe, naturally, garnered a wide range of opinions.

The views on the performance of President Wilson varied from a strong approval to an unsatisfactory one. However, of the opinions expressed, most agreed that our involvement in the war was only a matter of time.

Stella suggested that we get some fresh air and take a walk. Our stroll took us about four blocks up Almond Street to a small city park near the Richmond Libary.

There were plenty of trees and benches on this square. The warm sunny day brought out several others looking for an agreeable reprieve on a Sunday afternoon.

Two older men were walking their dogs there. The two pups also appeared most content, judging by the rhythm of their wagging tails.

"Have you given any more thought to your own little patch of paradise?" Stella questioned me once again.

"No. I'm afraid not," was my initial response. "It's a dream, of course, but it's still just a dream. I need to see where this road takes me. Perhaps when all this uncertainty passes, I may have a better plan to fulfill my dreams."

"I just don't want to end up like my sisters," she lamented. "I won't allow myself to be in my twenties and living on the third floor of my parents' house," she explained.

"I know what you mean," I sympathized. "Just about everyone has the same goals," I continued. "Good things come to those who are patient and wait for their time," I cautioned.

"If you put too many dreams into your basket, like a basket of eggs, you run the risk of having those eggs tumble out. Then, what will you have?" I asked her.

"You're right," she admitted. "But I'm not sure I have that patience inside me," she observed.

"You'll find it," I assured her. "Your circumstances will force you to acquire that patience. Hopefully, you will learn to accept that. Otherwise, it will drive you crazy. Don't let the latter happen, Stella!"

She said, "You're right, Tommy," and she hugged me as we stood there in the park.

The hug appeared to be a turning point, and we walked hand-in-hand back to the house.

When we entered the home, we soon discovered that Stella's sister, Sophie, and her husband, Steven, had dropped by for a visit. He brought a bottle of Polish vodka and a couple of bottles of beer. It was like Easter all over again, but Veronica and I decided that we had better start our journey back home as evening approached.

With a workday looming in the morning for both of us, we said our goodbyes, and we were on our way.

It was Monday morning, and Uncle Leo already had a pile of work lined up by the time I arrived at the blueprint room. It was apparent that the situation was more than just a typical stress-filled Monday morning. He was clearly beside himself.

I hated to see him in such a lather and losing his wits. The situation was beyond bad. "What's up, Leo? What's all the fuss about?" I asked.

He threw his arms up in the air, and he was pacing around the room.

"Hank called already this morning, and he was ranting and raving that they have a couple of big projects due in the course of the next two weeks, and they are out of steam pressure gauges and water level gauges!" Leo fumed.

"Which locomotives do they need the gauges for?" I questioned. "They need to finish eight more of the Pennsy L1's," he responded.

*   *6 NOTE: The L1s were a series of 2-8-2 steam engines built for the Pennsylvania Railroad between 1914 and 1916. Baldwin made two hundred and five of the Mikado-type engines*

during that time frame. While Pennsy built three hundred and forty-four in their Juniata Shops, Alco (American Locomotive Co.) constructed another five. No. 520, a Baldwin-made engine, is on display at the Railroad Museum of Pennsylvania in Strasburg.

"First of all, Leo," I began, "that's not even your worry. You are in charge of the blueprint department, not the parts department," I said to calm him down.

"I know! I know!" He acknowledged, "But if I don't get him off my back, he will be sending his people up here all day to bug me."

"What's the other project that requires these gauges," I asked.

"They are two Class 4 locomotives. The contract states that the 4-4-0's are being delivered to Yucatan, Mexico," he revealed.

*   *7 NOTE: Locomotives No. 65 and 66 were built in 1916. They were purchased in February 1969 by the Walt Disney Co. Disney acquired a total of five of these engines. Three are in operation at Disney World in Florida, and two are in use in California's Disneyland.*

"Well, I'm going down to the office to see what we can do about these parts," Leo said as he stormed out of the room.

About 30 minutes later, he returned, and he proceeded to fill us in on the entire story. "Another fine mess," he began.

"Our regular supplier for these gauges is Conshohocken Precision Instruments. Apparently, they recently had a work stoppage, and they are running about three weeks behind in their orders. We are on the list, but they have nothing in stock right now." Leo explained.

"I called Aramingo Gauge Co., here in the city. We usually don't deal with them because of their prices. They run about 30 percent higher in cost." He figured.

"We need the gauges now, and they have about two dozen of each in stock," Leo noted.

"Tommy, I need you to take one of the company trucks and run over there and pick them up, pronto!" He concluded.

"Sorry, boss," I shot back. "I don't drive!"

"Whatta ya mean you don't drive?" he asked, quite surprised.

"I don't have a car," I responded. "I never ever had to drive, period!" I said emphatically.

"Well, grab Paul Larson and have him drive you over there. We need those things ASAP," he barked.

"You got it," I assured him.

Larson was part of the maintenance department, but most of his assignments were in the buildings located in our immediate area.

Paul and I grabbed our coats and hats and headed for one of the company trucks. Uncle Leo instructed us to use the 1914 Model T Roadster Pick-up. The dull black vehicle was so dirty and rusty that it appeared much older than two years old.

Once we turned the crank to start the engine, the truck ran rather steadily. However, the motor was noisy with the constant sounds of fluttering, popping, ticking, and squealing.

He explained that the ticking sound was not coming from the engine but from the coil, which provided the electric spark.

When the vehicle shifted the gears, a definite whining noise was also evident. The bottom line was that we made the trip without incident.

It took us about 25 minutes to navigate the five-mile drive to Aramingo and Tioga Sts. Leo advised us to ask for Edgar when we got there. He had the parts ready for us.

We compared notes on the service, and like my future brother-in-law, Joe, he too was contemplating the idea of signing up for the navy.

"In a few weeks," I told him, "I am being mustered into the army full-time after spending the last two years in the National Guard."

He wished me luck but admitted that he would wait as long as possible before committing to the navy.

When we arrived back at Baldwin, Leo was relieved to see us walk through the door with the two crates of gauges.

"Get them down to Hank before he blows a gasket!" Leo ordered.

Paul helped me find a hand truck to transport the gauges to the engine finishing shop. Hank appeared hot at first, but he too calmed down when he saw the two crates of gauges.

"Thanks, Tommy," Hank said sheepishly.

"Don't thank me, Hank. Thank Leo. He's the one who arranged all this. Give the man some credit," I commented in an effort to put the man in his place.

With that, I turned and headed back to the blueprint room. I shook my head as I walked away, knowing that whatever was in store for me in the service, I wouldn't miss days like this!

"VISITORS FROM BUFFALO"

Wojiech (Aldalbert) & Balbina Mioducki and family, Buffalo NY
Image Source: Polish-American Heritage Society, Buffalo, NY

CHAPTER 6

"Visitors from Buffalo"

The calendar had flipped to June. It was the first Saturday of the month, June 3rd, to be exact, which meant that I had to report for another National Guard drill at the armory.

Business began as usual. Our unit fell into formation, and the captain issued the announcements for the day.

Surprisingly, he remarked that this would be our last drill before shipping out.

"Men," he began, "we were initially scheduled to have a drill next Saturday, June 10th, and the following Saturday, June 17th. These drills have been eliminated."

The captain continued, "Our mission to complete the packing of our equipment should be accomplished today. Therefore, the higher-ups have proposed to give you the extra time to spend with your families before we ship out.

"As per procedure," he directed, "you are to report your platoon sergeants to receive your orders for the day."

Regarding our inventory of weapons, we packed 347 M1903 Springfield rifles. These .03-06 bolt-action rifles were determined to be in good working order. They were cleaned, oiled, and packed. An additional 16 of these weapons were set aside for repairs, while seven others were deemed to be beyond repair.

When we finished packing company supplies and equipment, we went over our own belongings.

Each man was issued a large duffle bag and given a second uniform. The platoon sergeant handed out an inventory sheet and instructed us to double-check everything against the list. If we were missing any of the required items, we had to see the supply clerk and sign for them.

Another pleasant surprise was revealed when we reported to the mess hall at Noon. The cooks served our unit a generous portion of roast beef with potatoes and vegetables.

For dessert, we had a choice of cookies or a slice of Philadelphia cream cheese pound cake. I must say, for army issue, it was pretty darned good!

Our regular lunch table gang gathered one last time. Once again, speculation centered around the future. With our call-up to the regular army just a couple of weeks away, the situation sunk in among us that this was real. It was going to happen.

"Say, I have an idea," said Haeberle. "What's that, Harry?" I questioned

"Let's get together at a taproom sometime before the 24th," he explained.

"That's a good idea," Wilson agreed.

"Where should we get together?" Schweppenheiser inquired.

"Well, my pop and I hang out at Szczepanski's Saloon on Orthodox Street. Why don't we meet there the Friday night before... the 23rd?" I suggested.

"That's not too far for you, Harry? Bernie?" I added.

"No," Haeberle replied. "How about you guys? Does it suit you?" He asked the others.

Everybody seemed to agree that Szczepanski's would work, and the night before we shipped out would be okay, as well. That is as long as we didn't make it a long night.

Friday's were also the usual night that my father and I hung out there. Therefore, he could invite a couple of his buddies, and we could make it a farewell party!

The final session of the afternoon focused on departure day, June 24th. The engineering company was to handle the transportation and loading of all our equipment and supplies onto the train. It was our duty to arrive on time with our personal bags. We were expected to load them on the cars that we were assigned to us.

It was announced that the train that was transporting us to Mt. Gretna would consist of 14 cars. There would be four baggage cars, six combination cars (these cars were set up as partial baggage cars and partial passenger cars), one dining car for officers only, two parlor cars for officers only, and one observation car for V.I.P.'s. Someone at the station would hand us our car assignments before boarding.

When I left the armory, I was relieved that I could put the military out of my mind for the next three weeks.

Next on my list of things to do was get my personal life in order. I had already determined that I wanted to spend as much time as I could with my family before I left.

My first goal was to take my sisters to the Philadelphia Zoo. They were getting older, now, and they have never been there. I thought it would be a nice day out for all of us.

I rushed home to tell everyone the news and discovered that my family had news of their own to share with me.

My father's half-brother, Aldalbert, and his wife, Balbina sent word that they were coming down from Buffalo this weekend for a visit. They, too, wanted to see me before I left for the military.

Our uncle was a huge man. He was well over six-foot-tall and probably weighed about 280 pounds. He also sported a large mustache. His wife, Balbina, was about five-foot-four inches tall. She was also a large woman.

Uncle Aldalbert owned a Ford Touring Convertible. A few years ago, he came for a visit and gave my sisters their first ride in an automobile.

The wealthy uncle also gave each of the girls a gold piece. My wise mother convinced her daughters to trade their gold pieces to her for a shiny new penny. The ploy worked.

Since sleeping arrangements were a premium at the Schalata household, our aunt and uncle typically stayed at the Abraham Lincoln House on Girard Avenue. They would arrive sometime on Friday and leave on Monday.

The girls will be very excited when I tell them my plans for taking them to the zoo. Others told me that the Zoological Gardens contain between eight hundred and one thousand animals. The admission price is twenty-five cents for adults and ten cents for children.

Visitors can get to the zoo on foot, on streetcars, by horse and carriage, and by automobile. There is also a steamboat on the Schuylkill River that arrives every fifteen minutes at the zoo's own wharf.

The week passed by quickly. There were no significant incidents at Baldwin. Uncle Leo was quiet but drank several pots of coffee daily.

My aunt and uncle arrived at the Noon hour on Friday. They told my parents that they left Buffalo on Thursday and spent the night in Scranton, Pennsylvania.

My mother was planning on preparing a meal for Friday night, but pop's brother insisted on taking us all out to dinner at the Abe Lincoln House. I am not sure that we *ever* went to a restaurant for dinner as a family. This evening would be a treat. My parents argued that the whole thing was unnecessary, but Uncle Aldalbert convinced them otherwise.

Mom dressed the girls in their Sunday outfits, and I wore my trusty brown suit. Pop even looked rather dashing in his suit, as well.

My uncle put the top up on his convertible for the sake of the women and their hair. Somehow we all managed to fit in the black sedan. Unlike the old work truck at Baldwin, the car was clean and shiny. He stated that he had a man at the garage clean and service the machine regularly.

When we arrived at the hotel, we were impressed by the three-story brick structure. Each floor had a large wooden porch with a roof on the front of the building. There were plenty of chairs for hotel guests and their visitors to enjoy.

The interior had a Victorian-style decor with coal oil lamps and gaslight fixtures. The fashionable wall covering in each room rendered an elegant look that gave us the impression that the restaurant was not just fancy but expensive.

As was Uncle Aldalbert's nature, he clearly informed us that we were allowed to order anything off the menu that we wished. However, mom whispered down the line that we were to mind our manners and get her approval on what we wanted to order.

Fortunately for my mother, the Abe Lincoln House offered a limited menu. Appetizers included: oysters on the half shell, celery, olives, nuts, and puree mongole. The latter is a creamed split-pea and tomato soup.

The vegetable selections were: Parisienne potatoes, with Hollandaise sauce, roasted young turkey with cranberry sauce, roasted pork loin with apple dressing, Virginia baked ham, and Italian-style spaghetti and meatballs.

My sisters were most interested in the desserts, including raspberry sherbet, ice cream and chocolate cake.

The girls ordered spaghetti and meatballs all the way around and ice cream, of course.

Pop and I ordered the roast pork loin. My mother preferred the turkey. Uncle Aldalbert was anxious to try the filet of sole, while his wife, Balbina, had her sights set on the ham. The pair also ordered the oysters on the half shell and the soup. Uncle Aldalbert asked our waiter if each of the girls could have a fruit cup. Our server stated that the request would not be a problem.

As we awaited our meals, Uncle Aldalbert recognized that the downtime was the perfect opportunity to catch up on the latest family news.

The girls reported to their aunt and uncle that school was going fine. Helen, the shy one, of course, chose to remain in the background. She was much too timid to answer any questions, no matter how much our uncle prodded her.

He was anxious to hear from my father how his job was going. Pop admitted that his time with the streets department was probably winding down.

"I am getting too old to do such work," my father declared.

"Some of the men I work with suggested that I find a job as a night watchman," he added, "I'm not convinced that I want to work nights, but I wouldn't have to put in a full day of hard labor. The work of patching and paving streets is very hot and dirty, and I am soon ready to be rid of that work," he reasoned.

"You could have stayed in Buffalo with me," Aldalbert said with a hearty laugh.

"That was never going to work," my mother joined the conversation. "He wasn't cut out for saloon work!"

"Just a couple of weeks ago, Tommy and one of his buddies had to help him home from Szczepanski's," she responded.

"He came in soaking wet from the rain," she concluded.

It was unusual for my mother to take my father to task, especially in front of the girls, but I guess she wanted to put a quick end to any thoughts of moving back to Buffalo.

Aunt Balbina and my mother began a side conversation on matters of clothing styles and cooking.

Before we knew it, our dinners had arrived at our table.

This sumptuous dinner at such a lavish hotel was quite an experience for our family, and when the evening was over, we all piled into the uncle's car for the ride home.

Before Uncle Aldalbert and Aunt Balbina headed back to the hotel, they made arrangements to pick us up in the morning to give us a ride to the zoo. We agreed that we would all be ready by 8:30 am. I also insisted that I would pay for the girls' admission to the zoo.

"I said from the beginning that this would be my treat before I went away, and I must insist on keeping my promise," I said firmly.

"Fine," my uncle agreed. "We will work out all the details when we get there," he said.

At 8:30 am sharp, I was just finishing a second cup of coffee when I heard the distinct rumbling and rattling of my uncle's Ford Roadster. It was a bright, sunny day. I checked the thermometer on the front porch, and the temperature had already reached 84 degrees.

As you can readily imagine, the girls were very excited as we all piled into the automobile. The drive to the zoo would probably take us an hour or more to complete.

It was nearly 10 o'clock when we arrived at the Zoological Gardens. As promised, I paid the admission fee for myself and my sisters. Uncle Aldalbert, Aunt Balbina, and my parents were also planning on touring the grounds.

To my surprise, once we entered the grounds, we found Stella and her brother, Joe, sitting on a bench waiting for our arrival.

"Wow! I'm amazed," I exclaimed.

"I had no idea the two of you would be here," I added. "We thought we would surprise you," Stella responded immediately.

"How did you get here?" I asked.

"We took a couple of street cars," Stella said while looking in her brother's direction.

"Well, that's great," I exclaimed. "I am delighted the both of you were able to make it. I need to catch up with my sisters. They are so excited about today," I concluded.

A large open area ringed by shade trees proved to be an exhibit that featured deer, elk, buffalo, and even a pair of zebras.

The girls were wide-eyed when they saw all of the animals, but the zebra was most impressive to them.

"Look," Florence yelled, "that horse is wearing his pajamas!"

"Well, that looks that way, Florence," I said, "but that's part of his camouflage when he's in the wild.

It protects him or her from predators such as tigers and lions," I concluded.

Contained within their own separate cages were foxes, wolves, bears, and other similar creatures.

In one fenced-in area was the seal exhibit. Close by was the primates' display. According to one of the zookeepers we spoke with, there were 50 monkeys in that enclosure.

The birdhouse, which was just one of the many Victorian-style buildings on the property, housed more than 67 species.

Some of the more exotic animals on display were antelopes, lions, kangaroos, rhinoceros, and a tiger. Due to compatibility issues, most of these animals were segregated in their own pens.

Not surprising, the girls were most excited to see the giant elephant roaming around its enclosure. The animal was indeed a magnificent-looking beast. The elephant keeper told us that her name was "Bonnie." He explained that she is an Asian elephant, as opposed to an African elephant.

"While puffing on a cigar, the man told us, "African elephants have a flatter head on top, and they are the ones that grow tusks."

The keeper told the girls that Bonnie replaced another Asian elephant, "Bolivar," who died in 1908. "He was a very mean and dangerous elephant. He broke through a brick wall here in the zoo enclosure. He was powerful."

A large iron clock in the center of the gardens informed us that the one o'clock hour was upon us.

My mother packed a picnic lunch for us, and we found a grassy area that was quite suitable.

Naturally, my aunt, uncle, and parents searched for the restaurant on the zoo grounds while Stella, Joe, Veronica, and I cared for the girls. We spread out a blanket on the soft, green grass.

The girls kept themselves busy by discussing the various animals they had seen so far on the outing. "Hey, Tommy!" Joe spoke up first, "Veronica and I are going to another dance next week. I understand you only have two weeks before you get called up. Do you and Stella want to go with us?"

"Sure, that's fine with me. What do you think, Stella?" I asked her.

"I think I'm ready for another night out," she answered.

"Do you know the name of the band for the dance," she inquired.

Joe replied, "It's a popular dance band, Harlan Tucker and his Country Weasels." He added, "They play such tunes as 'Alexander's Ragtime Band,' 'Let Me Call you Sweetheart,' 'Down by the Old Mill Stream,' 'I Love You Truly," and 'Moonlight Bay."

"Sounds like a good line-up for starters. What do you think, Stella?" I asked.

"Certainly, I think it sounds spiffy," she exclaimed.

"Shall we meet at the cafe again?" Joe wondered out loud.

"Sure," I was quick to answer. "It was convenient, the food was good, and the prices were reasonable," I responded agreeably.

By this time, we were finished eating our lunch, and the girls were very anxious to explore the grounds and see more animals.

We concluded the afternoon with a visit to the fish and reptile house. Here my sisters were amazed by the variety of rare and exotic species that were on display. Nearby a pair of hippopotamus were cooling off in a large pond that was constructed just for them.

The large iron clock in the center of the gardens told us it was approaching 4:30. We needed to locate the others before closing time.

Henrietta ran ahead and found the foursome sitting on a couple of benches near the park's main entrance.

"Did everyone have a wonderful time?" Aunt Balbina asked.

"We sure did," Henrietta was the first to reply, "the animals were like none I could have ever imagined," she further explained.

"Yes," her twin sister, Stella, joined in, "I really enjoyed seeing the monkeys. They were so silly," she added.

"How about you, Florence?" the aunt inquired.

"I really liked the elephant, but the fact a big, heavy chain had her tied to the wall made me sad," was her answer.

Before we went our separate ways, Aunt Balbina had a bag of trinkets and souvenirs she handed out to each of the children. They were filled with delight and skipped around the area to display their joy. Then, in unison, they lined up in front of our aunt and uncle and thanked them for their gifts.

I said my goodbyes to Stella and Joe and confirmed that we would get together the following weekend.

The rest of us walked to the parking lot to find the shiny Ford Roadster Convertible. The ride again would be cramped, but it would easily make the journey homeward to Bridesburg.

When I arrived at work on Monday, Leo informed me that the plan was to finish two of the Pennsy 2- 8-2's this week and two next week. It would be the last action I would see at the plant, at least for the foreseeable future.

Leo sent me on several projects involving the distribution of blueprints. It would take me from one end of the facility to the other. He expected the task would require roughly two or three hours.

My first stop was in the offices downstairs, where I needed to drop off some paperwork for the managers.

From there, it was onto Building No. 2, where they required several drawings in the wheel shop for a future design. The wheel shop was located on Hamilton Street, but the department also contained the boiler shop on the second floor and the third floor's brass shop.

Sure enough, I bumped into Milton Shomper again, and he was *pleasant* as always.

"Hey, Schalata, what are you doing slumming around these parts?" he cracked.

"Just making my rounds!" I quipped.

"Oh, I thought Uncle Leo ran out of coffee or something and had you fetch him some more," he remarked with a grin.

"No, no... just business," I assured him.

"You guys got it so easy up there. I just wish I could change places with you for one day. See how'd you like it down in the sweatbox for a change," he sniped.

"So stinkin' hot you can't stand it... so damn noisy you can't think... no goddamn air to even breathe... no 15-minute coffee breaks to sit on your asses... you guys have no clue!" He concluded while shaking his head and walking away. I just shrugged it off, knowing that Milton was just plain being Milton.

Although I had no pressing business in Building No. 3, I stopped for a few minutes to chat with my pal, Franz Golembeski. He was part of the crew in the hammer and smith workshop on the third floor. The six-story structure was also home to the powerhouse, another boiler room, a shed, and what was called the Willow Street Annex. I'm entirely not sure what went on there.

Most of the drawings that I needed to deliver were going to Building No. 4. The facility was also six stories tall. This area of the plant contained the machine shop, the boiler annex, and the pattern shop. There was a large open-air yard in-between the two sections of the building.

My final stop on Leo's list was Building No. 12. The structure, located on the corner of Pennsylvania Avenue and 18th Street, was four floors. Contained therein were the tank shop and the wood mill. Leo directed me to see George Perkins, who was looking for some renderings associated with their current project.

Two other buildings that were not on my list were: Building No. 6, which was the flange shop, and Building 11. The latter was the 17th Street tender shop. The five-story shop was located between Buttonwood and Hamilton Streets. The first floor was devoted to tender assembly, while the remaining four levels were primarily for the painting of the cars.

When I returned, Leo commented that the gauges we picked up at the Aramingo firm were working fine. Though, the order from our usual supplier would be arriving any day now. I informed him that Milton Shomper sent him his regards, as well. We both laughed.

The remainder of the week passed without incident, and I was looking forward to another Friday night at Szczepanski's with my father. If we were going to get involved in another dart match, tonight would be the night.

Next Friday night, I had plans to meet my fellow guardsmen at the saloon. Pop and his friends would be welcome to join us, but I felt that it would be impossible to shoot darts that evening.

When we left for the taproom, mom gave us strict instructions to come back in one piece.

"Eka," pop replied, which translated from Polish basically means "we're just going around the corner." *"Na słowo honoru,"* he added, meaning "you have my word."

With that, I put pop's hat on his head, and we walked out the door. There was no rain in the forecast. So, we had that going for us.

It was another packed night at Szczepanski's, but we found two open barstools. A quick glance around the room, and we spotted Stosh and Casimir at their usual table near the piano player.

My father was determined to be a good soldier tonight. Therefore, he passed up on his usual shot of Old Overholt.

Like clockwork, the pair was on our backs, ready for a dart match by the time pop was midway through his second beer.

The duo shot well from the start, and before we knew it, they had won the first set comfortably. I chalked it up as one of those nights when my father's game was off, but as we turned towards the bar for another beer, pop gave me a wink. This sign soon told me he was holding back and had plans for Stosh and Casimir.

His barroom pals were as happy as clams. They were celebrating the win with a couple of shots of vodka.

Pop opened the second game with a score of 97. Stosh followed with a 37. I managed to shoot 65, while Casimir shot a 53. This round put us in the lead, 539 to 574.

As I stood back and watched the entire affair unfold, I could see that my father knew precisely what he was doing. He was keeping the game close but was waiting for the right time to strike.

In the end, we were in the lead 133-148. With nerves of steel, pop shot two 20 trips and a single 13 to end the contest.

With the match even at one game per team, we paused for another round of beer. At the bar, our competition still felt that the night was theirs.

During this intermission, things were beginning to heat up between pop and Stosh. The bravado was increasing, and the arguing grew louder. Stosh insisted that we had no chance, but pop countered that he could beat his buddy while shooting blindfolded.

When my father issued the challenge, the whole place grew silent. You could hear a pin drop, and everybody turned their attention to the two men.

"I will settle this whole thing," pop shouted. "I will beat you in a game of 301, and I will shoot blindfolded," he stated as he pounded his fist on the bar.

"You couldn't beat me if I handed you a fist full of darts," Stosh answered back.

"No! No!" Pop insisted, "three darts per play is all I need."

The next thing I know, Casimir is walking around the bar with his hat in hand. He's taking bets on the whole thing.

Although he was utterly blindfolded, pop managed to earn the chance to go first. His first throw was a double 10, followed by a single 5 and a single 1 for an opening score of 26.

Stosh garnered a double 14, a double 9, and a single 7 for a count of 53. After one round, the score was 248-275 in favor of Stosh.

As one might expect, pop struggled mightily throughout the match. The game was coming down the home stretch, and Stosh was leading 31-100.

Before his turn, pop called to stop play for a minute. He asked me how much beer remained in his glass. I told him it was about half full. He had me lead him to the bar, where he emptied the pint with one swallow.

He signaled that he was ready. They positioned him on the spot in front of the dartboard. He took a deep breath, then fired a single bull for 25 points. Again, he sighed heavily and fired a second single bullseye for another 25 points.

If the joint wasn't already silent, it was now. One guy in the front of the room hollered, "Geez, it's so quiet we should call the undertaker!"

Several men shot back, "Sssshhhh!!!." The guilty party was grabbed by the collar and thrown out the front door.

When things settled back down, Wojieck, the bartender, murmured in a quiet voice, "Stanley, it's all yours!"

With the pressure on, you could see pop's hand quiver just a little. For a third time, my old man took a deep breath.

He stood there for just a few seconds, but it seemed like an eternity. He raised his hand. He released the dart, and it landed on the inner red circle for 50 points.

The place went wild. Some stranger pulled the blindfold off pop and kissed him on the top of his head.

Wojieck announced that the drinks were on the house while Casimir went back to his corner with an empty hat.

It reminded me of that day last October when the Philadelphia Phillies beat the Boston Red Sox in game one of the World Series. Of course, the Sox went on to win the next four games straight, and the series, but the Phillies were winners for one particular day.

Despite a wild night of celebration, my father kept his word to my mother to make it home safely and relatively sober.

He was a hero at Szczepanski's, and once again, he earned celebrity status not just with the guys at the taproom but also with me. It's a day that I shall never forget. A day that made me proud!

Wojieck (Aldalbert) Mioducki
Image Source: Polish-American Heritage Society, Buffalo, NY

Balbina Mioducki
Image Source: Polish-American Heritage Society, Buffalo, NY

7

"CALL TO DUTY"

Thomas (Tommy) H. Schalata, Author's Grandfather
Image Source: Author's Photo

CHAPTER 7

"Call to Duty"

Saturday, June 17, 1916. It would be my last Saturday in Bridesburg for some time. I told mom the night before that she needn't prepare breakfast for me in the morning. I was heading down to "The Neutral Corner Cafe."

The local dive is on the corner of Orthodox and Edgemont Streets. It opened a few years ago when local boxer, Irish Joe Keegan, finally hung up his gloves.

About 15 years ago, he lost a 19-round bout to another Philly Irishman, Jack O'Brien. The contest was in the middleweight division, but O'Brien eventually moved up to the light heavyweight and heavyweight classes.

The centerpiece of the eatery is its long counter. A few booths run along the wall on the left side of the joint.

Hanging on the walls are various boxing-related photos that capture some of Keegan's memorable boxing moments. Other local fighters are represented with their pictures, as well.

The decor also features fight-related artifacts such as a leather boxing speedball that hangs from the ceiling, boxing shorts, and gloves. Keegan rings a bell whenever he places a completed order at the service window. The bell once signaled the end of a round in a match.

I sat at a stool at one end of the counter, and the regular waitress, Irene, was ready with her order pad in hand. I did not have any doubt that some friendly banter was in store, as was her style.

"So, what's up, Tommy? Mother out of town this weekend?" she quipped.

"No," I answered back, "I just wanted some Bridesburg grub since I'll probably be away for a while."

"Black coffee to start with, honey," she asked as she batted her eyes.

"Well, that's another thing," I replied, "I just want to compare Keegan's hot dishwater with the stuff I'll be drinking in the army soon," I shot back.

"I heard that the coffee they give the soldiers is like that oil you guys drain from the machinery down at Baldwin," Irene countered.

"Coffee it is, sweety. Here's the menu. I'll be right back," she said as she walked off.

Before long, she returned with a mug of coffee and asked me, "So, what will it be? Make up your mind?"

"Yes, ma'am," I said while looking directly at her. "I'll have an order of Joe's flapjacks and a hunk of that sausage."

"No scrapple today, hon?" she asked.

"Nah!" I countered. I'm in the mood for sausage. Besides, Keegan's scrapple is as hard as a brick."
"You got it," the waitress said as she veered towards the kitchen.

A quick glance to the other end of the counter, and I spotted old man Jablonski. His first name is Leonard. Furthermore, I dated his daughter, Sophie, once or twice.

Sophie's a lovely girl, but she isn't the kind of dish that I typically date. I did it as a favor to my mother.

Leonard was peeking over the top of his newspaper, and I could instantly tell that he was giving me the evil eye. I decided to walk down to his end of the counter and diffuse the situation.

"Well, hello, Tommy. How are you doing?" He asked in a most polite tone as if nothing were wrong.

"I'm fine, sir," I countered.

"Sophie still asks about you," Jablonski made sure to inform me.

"Oh, I have been swamped. Next Saturday, I am being called up to the regular army from the National Guards," I explained.

"Good luck with that. I'll be sure to tell Sophie the news," he said.
"Thanks, Leonard. You take care," I replied as I turned away. I had the feeling that the old man was hoping that if I did wind up overseas, there was a bullet with my name on it.

By the time I returned to my place at the counter, I had expected to see my breakfast waiting for me.

When Irene went by, I questioned, "What happened to Keegan? Did he go down for another ten-count? Where's my flapjacks?" I summoned her.

"They're coming," she contended. "Just hold your horses," the waitress said to keep me at bay.

Surprisingly, within the blink of an eye, my breakfast was served, and it was delicious despite the hostile atmosphere. The meal set me back 35 cents, including the tip.

My next stop was about a block away. I stopped at Marvelous Marv's Colonial Jewelers. Marvin Kleimbaum ran the local jewelry store. I had my sights set on purchasing a gold locket for Stella.

The craftsman showed me several pieces from his display case. Although a gold locket shaped like a heart would be a conventional purchase, a round piece bearing Forget-Me-Not flowers seemed to garner my attention.

Marvin quoted me a price of $4.25. When I reacted to the ostensibly high amount, he showed me a similar flowered silver necklace.

"I'll throw in this silver piece that you can give to one of your sisters all for the one price. What do you think, Tommy?" The man said to sweeten the deal.

I thought the matter over and really wanted to give my sister Helen a small gift before leaving. I was confident that she would take my going away the hardest.

"Well, Marvin," I began. "I like the whole idea a lot. Do you mind if I run home to see if my mother has a photograph that I can place inside? If she does, I'll be back and have you wrap it up. Would that be okay?" I reasoned.

"Sure! No problem, Tommy. I close at 4 pm today," he stated.

Excited by my decision, I dashed home and convinced my mother to search through her old shoe box of photographs for one of me that would fit in the locket. I would give the locket to Stella at the dance this evening. However, the other necklace would be my present to Helen next week. That was my plan!

Luckily, my mother found an appropriate photo, and I made it back to the jewelers to finish the transaction by closing time.

As Veronica and I were getting ready to leave to catch the streetcar, it began to rain. It was a cool, steady summer rain. We each grabbed an umbrella from the stand near the front door.

The two of us had a friendly brother-sister chat on the way down to the cafe. She acknowledged that things were getting pretty serious between Joe and herself, but they had both agreed not to rush into anything with such an uncertain future.

I admitted to my sister that Stella and I had come to the same conclusion. Our relationship was moving right along, and we both longed for the same things in life, but this was not the time.

However, since we had grown very fond of each other, I revealed to Veronica my plan to give Stella a locket that evening.

In the past, Stella and I usually took a short walk to the local park during one of the band breaks, but tonight's weather did not cooperate with that plan. I stated that I would probably have to give it to her at the cafe before going to the dance.

Veronica graciously suggested that she and Joe would skip out of the cafe and head to the dance hall to give us a few moments of privacy.

Before we knew it, we arrived at our stop. Now we had to walk the remainder of the way to the cafe in the pouring rain.

Due to the lousy weather, Joe and Stella also arrived early at the eatery. They were already seated at a table. Joe stood up and signaled to us their location in the back of the restaurant.

The specials tonight at Andy's Cafe included potted oxtail, lamb fricassee with rice, and breaded veal cutlet with spaghetti. The regular menu offered roast turkey, baked ham, roast pork loin, and broiled sea trout.

My selection was the veal cutlet dish with a mixed salad, while Stella settled on roast turkey with stewed corn.

The lamb fricassee with rice was Joe's choice. Veronica also ordered roast turkey.

Since many of our previous conversations seemed to focus not only on my work status but also on my impending call up for the service, I decided to steer the conversation elsewhere.

"So, Joe," I began, "we know you're interested in joining the Navy when the time comes, but what are you doing these days? I asked politely.

"I work at the Barrett Chemical Co. The plant is located at Margaret and Bermuda Streets in the Frankford section. The company is engaged in the manufacture of various kinds of coal tar chemicals," he described.

"Mainly, our products are related to the roofing and paving industry," Joe further remarked.

"There's a rumor going around the plant that Allied Chemical Co. may take us over at some point," he revealed.

"If that happens," he continued, "we may be involved more in dyes and chemicals and things of that nature," Joe surmised.

"What do you do there?" I prodded just a little.

"Electrician," he said. "I'm an electrician. My job entails working on the plant machinery or general electrical issues that pop up!" Joe continued.

"That seems kind of handy," I added. "I would like to learn a little about that myself. It never hurts to be knowledgeable on those things," I stated.

"Well," he replied, "sometimes we can get together, or you can go with me on a job, and I'll show you a few things. People from the neighborhood often ask me to take on small electrical projects for them, and I oblige."

"Sounds great," I said appreciatively.

Naturally, the conversation always comes back to me no matter how much I try to avoid it. "This is your last week at Baldwin, correct?" he asked.

"Yes. I'm afraid so," I conceded.

"What's happening down there right now?" Joe followed up.

"This week, we are completing construction of the last two Pennsy Mikado locomotives," I stated. "We had a contract to build 205 of the engines, and as I said, we're down to the last two.

"I hope to go down to the final assembly building on Friday, which will be my last day there. I'd like to see Engine No. 520 fire up for the first time!" I concluded.

"That sounds exciting," Stella said, joining in the conversation.

We all agreed that witnessing a project such as that come to life would be quite a thrill, especially if it was on a person's last day on the job.

As dinner ended, it was unanimous that we would order pie all the way around—two slices of blueberry, one peach, and one apple.

Joe and I took care of the check. From there, it was a short walk to the dance. Regrettably, the rain had not subsided at all.

Veronica gave Joe a gentle nudge in the ribs and whispered into his ear.

Veronica turned and revealed, "Joe and I will reserve a table at the dance. We'll meet you there," she said while giving me a wink.

Since we were alone for the first time this evening, and it may be my only opportunity, I decided to delve right into it.

"Stella," I began, "as we know, next Saturday I leave with the army, and I have no idea when I may be returning. I have really come to enjoy your company during the last couple of months," I explained.

"I think you share my feelings, at least I hope you do?" I looked directly into her eyes. She nodded affirmatively.

I continued, "Since we have no idea what lies ahead, I just was to give you this small token before I leave."

With that, I reached into my jacket pocket and retrieved the gift box.

Stella was already a little teary-eyed as she began to unwrap the item, but she managed to compose herself when she discovered the gold locket inside.

"The flowers are Forget-Me-Nots, and there is a photo of me inside. I hope the message is clear, at least while we are apart. Perhaps, we can think of each other from time to time," I explained.

She said, "Yes! Tommy! It is beautiful! I had no idea!"

At that point, she gave me a huge hug and kiss. The kiss seemed to linger for a relatively long time, though I am sure it only lasted a moment or two.

The two of us recognized that there was not much more we could say at this point, but we took a few extra minutes to let this special moment sink in.

Initially, we held hands tightly when we left the cafe, but as the rain grew more substantial, I wrapped my left arm around her, and we shared just one umbrella on our way to St. Laurentius.

Once we arrived at the dance hall, we joined Joe and Veronica at one of the tables. We had intentionally planned to arrive there early due to the inclement weather, which proved to be a good idea. The extra time afforded us some time to relax and continue our conversation from the cafe.

As I looked around the pale blue hall, I was familiar with the stage, which was flanked by long navy blue curtains, but what I hadn't noticed before was the room's focal point. The sizeable open wall on the left side of the room featured an immense oil painting.

In my estimation, the piece of art was approximately four-foot-wide and about twelve feet tall. An engraved, bronze plaque attached to the ornate gold frame read: "St. Laurentius."

"Who was St. Laurentius?" I asked.

"St. Laurentius (Saint Lawrence) was a third-century martyr of the church," Joe explained.

"He was appointed archdeacon of Rome by the pope," he proceeded. "He was in charge of collecting and delivering alms to the poor," Joe added.

"The Emperor of Rome ordered the execution of Laurentius and many other church officials. His body was placed on a gridiron prepared with hot coals beneath it.

"After the martyr had suffered pain for a long time," Joe stated, "the legend mentions that he cheerfully declared: 'I'm well-done on this side. Turn me over!' From this, St. Lawrence is the patron saint of cooks, chefs, and comedians." Joe remarked.

"Interesting," I said. "I never heard that story before tonight."

Later, the band opened the show, and we were all in a great mood to let loose and savor the evening. Joe and Veronica obviously enjoyed dancing, but Stella and I commenced celebrating the fact that our relationship had gone to the next level. The evening was splendid, and we spent more time on the dance floor than we had ever done before. We both gathered that this was the start of something bigger!

By the end of the evening, Stella and I were pretty exhausted from being on the dance floor nearly the entire time. Topping off a beautiful night was the last song to be played by Harland Tucker and his band, "All I want is a cottage, some roses, and you."

The band leader announced, "This song was recorded by Geoffrey O'Hara and written by Charles K. Harris. I hope you all enjoy it. Good night!"

...and the band closed the show with this most appropriated song:

"Last night while I lay sleeping, dear,
I dreamed you came to me
You promised, dear
To love me through all eternity
I dreamed we'd reached that isle of love Where true hearts never part
I held you close and called you mine
My very own sweetheart

All I want is a cottage, some roses, and you
Won't you come back and make my dream true
I will build you a castle of love for your own
With lilies and heartsease in bloom
I'll fill it with sunshine No care shall you know
And safe from my keeping
You never shall go
Oh, come back to me, sweetheart
And make my dream true
All I want is a cottage, some roses, and you

The dream, it could not last, dear
And when morning came again
My empty arms I stretched to you
And called your name in vain
But dreams often come again, dear
And I know sometimes come true
All that I want in this wide world is love
A rose and you

All I want is a cottage, some roses, and you
Won't you come back and make my dream true
I will build you a castle of love for your own
With lilies and heartsease in bloom
I'll fill it with sunshine
No care shall you know
And safe from my keeping
You never shall go
Oh, come back to me, sweetheart
And make my dream true
All I want is a cottage, some roses, and you."

Monday morning opened my final week at Baldwin Locomotive Works. Leo appeared to be in a cheerful mood to start the day, which was always a good thing.

"Good morning, Tommy!" he began. Are you ready for your final week?" "I guess I have to be, Leo," I answered.

"Listen," Leo said as he took a sip of his coffee, "I'm going to be working most of the time with Charlie Lafferty. He's probably going to be taking your place. I may need you to occasionally show him a few things, but you can take it a little easy for the most part.

"I know you're interested in watching them put the finishing touches on that last Pennsy locomotive No. 520. If you want to ramble down to the engine finishing shop, you can hang out there and catch some of the action; it's not a problem. Just check back with me from time to time," he arranged.

"Okay, boss, whatever you say," I replied happily.

When I arrived at the assembly building, I met with the chargeman, Irving Hinkleman. He's the guy that oversees all the work on a single engine.

"Hey, Tommy, what are you doing down here?" he queried.

"Well, Leo told me to come down here and hang out. He suggested that I watch the final production of this engine. This is my final week before I go into the service," I concluded.

"No problem," Irving came back.

"As you can see," he explained, "most of the assembly work is completed. The boiler and the smokebox are in place, as well as the wheels and axels.

"The springs are on the axle boxes," he added, "and the connecting rods are in place, as well. "We have about 45 hours logged in for this baby's assembly," he pointed out.

"The tender is being completed over on 17th Street. We will bring it over here shortly. That will probably take place on Wednesday," he estimated.

"Homer and Frank are working on setting the valves on the engine. The valves are critical in determining the piston's position when the steam is cut off, the exhaust opens, and monitoring the compression when the steam begins," he affirmed while pointing at the two men dressed in greasy, grimy coveralls.

Before this final check down, Baldwin hired outside contractors who divided up some of the work. These specialized work gangs focused on tasks such as setting up the valves, erecting piping, installing piping, and jacketing. These external jobbers supervised many of the unskilled members of the workforce.

As we walked around the giant locomotive, he emphasized, "Everything has been tested for tensile strength and has passed the bending test."

"I see," I responded after taking his extensive visual tour. "What's next?" I inquired.

"Well," the chargeman responded. "Early on Thursday morning, the plan is to fire it up for the first time. We will check all the systems, pressures, etc. We will inspect for leaks in the boiler, oil leaks, leaks in pressure, listen for any unusual noises, and study for apparent defects.

"Friday, however, will be the engine's trial run. If everything checks out on Thursday, we will take it on a 20 to 25-mile run," he said excitedly.

"During this trial," he further noted, " the performance of its working motion, the springs, the brakes, the injectors, and sand gear will all be closely monitored.

"The axel bearings must run perfectly cool," Irving was insistent, "and there cannot be any leaks at the joints or fittings."

"What happens after all that?" I questioned.

"It will go on a few short runs for further testing to estimate oil, coal, and water consumption. Gradually the locomotive is broken in until it is deemed worthy for service. Small passenger runs are typically part of the process," he reasoned.

"Thanks for the tour," I told Irving, "I'm going to go back and check on Leo to see if he needs anything. I'm sure he's going to be sending me down here from time to time."

When I arrived at the shop on Thursday morning, Leo barked out immediately, "Tommy, grab yourself a coffee and head down to the finishing shop. They're going to fire up that No. 520 this morning," he said with a sense of urgency in his voice.

When I arrived at the building, coffee cup in hand, the engineer, Ralph Lerner, and his fireman, Bobo Grundle, were just starting the process.

Bobo was stoking the fire while Ralph was carefully listening to the various noises that resulted. Most of them were normal sounds, but his job was to direct his trained ear towards those that were not.

Since there were no cars coupled to the engine, the automatic air brakes were in the released position. However, the engineer fully applied the independent brake to the engine and the tender.

I noticed that the sight feed indicator was in the off position, so it would not waste oil. This component supplies oil to the cylinders virtually one drop at a time. Mechanics and engineers treat oil like gold.

The reverse lever, known as the Johnson bar, is centered, and the cylinder cocks are left open. The throttle is just cracked a little. This set-up admits a bit of steam to the cylinders to keep them warm when not running.

During this time, the engineer and his team of mechanics are walking around the giant beast to be satisfied that everything is working as it should be. The fireman is keeping a close watch on his firebox and the water level.

In the meantime, an unorchestrated symphony of noises radiate from the engine. The loud sounds of creaking metal, quick bursts of steam, and a variety of obnoxious knocking and pounding discords remind one of the death-knell of a doomed, sinking steamship.

Ralph looked at my perplexed face and assured me, "Don't worry, Tommy, everything's fine. This action is part of the process.

"It takes about five hours to get the boiler up to temperature and arrive at the proper pressure," he informed me.

"Many of those sounds are part of the expansion process," he reassured me.

"We're going to check everything out today. Tomorrow we'll take it out on its test run. Check with Leo. Maybe he'll let you ride along with us. We'll probably be ready to roll about Noon tomorrow," Ralph said in closing.

"Okay, pal," I said. "I'll let you know."

I finished out the day showing Charlie Lafferty where to file the various blueprints. During this time, I instructed him on the ins and outs of the general filing system.

Before the day ended, I told Leo that Ralph, the engineer, invited me to ride along on the 520's shake-down run tomorrow.

"What time will that be?" he asked. "Around Noon, he told me," I responded.

"That should be fine. I hope Lerner has you back here by four o'clock, though. I want to see you before I leave," Leo noted. By the tone of his voice, it almost seemed important.

I arrived at the shop at the usual time, 7:15 am. Leo and Charlie were sitting in the corner, drinking coffee. It didn't take Leo long to take the young man under his wing.

"I would head over to the shop around 11," Leo shouted across the room in my direction.

"Hinkleman had his crew in here at 5 am firing up that 520. They are pulling out at Noon sharp," he reminded me.

"Just remember," he went on, "be back here by four. Tell that S.O.B. that I said so!" Leo exclaimed. "Okay, boss," I said to appease the old man.

At 11 am on the nose, I grabbed my lunch pail and proceeded to the workshop.

When I got there, the black giant was huffing and puffing. Massive bursts of steam randomly blasted the area at various intervals.

The irregular banging, clanging, rapping, and creaking brought the Iron Horse to life like a fire-breathing dragon. Most sporadically, you could hear a sound that resembled a hissing snake or the intermittent tapping like an incessant woodpecker as various parts of the locomotive sprang to life.

Bobo, the fireman, once again checked the water level. His job was to ensure that the water level was high enough to cover the crown sheet entirely on the firebox roof.

He also had to keep the fire low, so it would not cause "pops," allowing the safety valves to open.

Bobo turned to me and said, "You must have a good bed of coke because you need to be ready to put out a lot of heat the minute the engine starts up."

The chargemaster gave the call over the loudspeaker, "You're clear to depart," and with that signal, a crew of about six opened the large iron doors at the far end of the brick structure.

Ralph acknowledged the order with two short whistle toots and started ringing the bell.

From my vantage point, I could see the engineer release the latch on the quadrant and drop the reverse lever into the full forward position.

Simultaneously, Bobo shut off the blower and threw about three scoops of coal into the firebox.

I could feel the beast come to life. The huffing and puffing and the clanging and banging grew louder. Ralph motioned to me that he was about to turn the lubricator and the sanders on. I watched as he gave a gentle tug on the throttle and then feathered off, meaning he slowly released it.

As the locomotive began to move, Ralph told me that he could adjust the throttle accordingly. "You have to be careful not to slip the drivers," he warned.

Ralph also warned, "An engineer uses four of his senses to coordinate everything. He uses his sight, his hearing, his smell, and his feel," he explained.

Within about ten seconds, Ralph seemed to have the throttle wide open. Before long, the engine was accelerating in the full cut off. That means that the engineer had the Johnson Bar in the corner position. If he feels or hears the engine's acceleration decreasing, he knows that it's time to hook up the Johnson Bar.

Ralph explained that after about 15 to 20 seconds of running, the cylinders are fully warmed and cleared of any condensation.

During the time that I spent with Ralph, Bobo, the fireman, was kept very busy. He has been putting another three or four scoops of coal into the firebox. He generally waits for an additional 15 to 20 seconds, then repeats the process.

Ralph told me that a scoop of coal weighs about 15 pounds.

Between the periods of shoveling the coal, Bobo must check the boiler pressure and the water level.

He must maintain about four inches of water on top of the firebox to cool it.

Once the engine was up to optimum safe speed, I asked Ralph if he was ever "concerned about taking these locomotives out for the first time?"

"We build a thousand of these babies a year, and they always roll out of the building without a hitch.

Why would I worry now?" He replied.

As an amateur, my opinion was that the black beast was running smoothly. The engine seemed to move effortlessly down the track. The pistons' constant chug was occasionally drowned out by the blasts of steam coming from the pressure release valves and the puffs emanating from the smokestack.

As you stick your head out of the cab to catch a glimpse of the track ahead, cinders and ashes from the smokestack pepper your face.

The smell, nonetheless, is unmistakable. It blends the odor of rock dust with the aroma of cigar smoke. Sometimes you can detect a bit of sulfur mixed in, but the wind generally carries most of that smell away.

Ralph explained that we were heading to the P.R.R. (Pennsylvania Railroad) railyards in Paoli. He remarked that there was a turn-around spur at that location.

For miles, this newly created bucket of bolts showed off its power and fury. The unburdened locomotive journeyed from town to town at lightning speed. I was surprised that they tested it so!

"We will stop the train at a junction in Paoli and then back the engine through a switch that leads onto a spur. The brakeman will throw a switch, and we will pull forward out of the spur while heading back to the shops," he stated.

"It's a straightforward operation," he noted.

I recognized that the procedure for stopping the locomotive was similar to starting up but in reverse order.

The crew of the 520 made the entire operation look relatively easy. Within a half-hour, we were heading back to Baldwin.

At exactly 3:38 pm, Pennsy Engine No. 520 pulled up to the facility. Even the engine seemed to offer a sigh of relief when the final chug of the piston, the last puff of smoke, and the concluding hiss of steam signaled that it was the end of the line!

An army of mechanics and their helpers immediately swarmed over the vehicle to check every square inch for any sign of weakness or failure.

On Monday, the 520 would join the other 448 Mikados that were part of the Pennsylvania Railroad's fleet.

I had less than 15 minutes to get back to my own shop and meet Leo's 4 pm deadline. When I arrived, there was a crowd gathered around Leo's desk. As I entered the room, a tremendous cheer sounded, and the group immediately shoved me to the front.

There stood Leo with his coffee cup in one hand a cake in the other. As it turns out, the old man set up a bon voyage party for me, and buckets of beer soon replaced the coffee.

There was plenty of singing and much more back-slapping. I was totally surprised by the number of co-workers who came to see me off.

Everyone knew that I was off to join the service. Therefore, the songs they sang were mostly of military and patriotic nature.

Somewhere between five and five-thirty, the crowd had begun to thin out. The cake was all gone, and the beer was all but spent, as well.

At least for now, it appeared that my time at Baldwin Locomotive Works was also spent. Like the 520, I had reached the end of the line!

Baldwin locomotive No. 520, Railroad Museum of Penna.
Image Source: Derek Ramsey

8

"TIME FOR GOODBYES"

Pennsylvania Railroad Broad Street Station, Phila., PA
Image Source: Library Company of Philadelphia

CHAPTER 8

"Time for Goodbyes"

They say when one journey ends, another begins. It was apparent that this was *that* point in my life. When the alarm sounded at 4:00 am, I dressed and shaved in my little room for the last time.

Perhaps one of the girls would claim my spot after I left.

I would be sleeping on a canvas cot that measured 75 inches long by 26 inches wide and about 17 inches off the ground.

Once I was ready and satisfied that my uniform was presentable, I joined my family in the kitchen.

My mother planned a modest breakfast of scrambled eggs with fried potatoes and onions. Coffee was mandatory.

Most of the girls were excited and cheerful, but as expected, Helen sat in one corner with her elbows perched upon the table. She hung her head straight down towards her lap.

As I went to her side to console her, she shrugged her body away from me.

"Helen, dear," I began, "I know my going away will be difficult for you, but I'll be back. I promise.

Everything will be okay while I'm away," I said, comforting her.

My words did very little to convince her, but when I told my 14-year-old sister that I had a gift for her, Helen seemed to take notice.

I reached into my pocket for the nicely wrapped box that I purchased at the jewelry store. The paper was silver in color and had a matching bow.

Suddenly her eyes grew larger, and she excitedly unwrapped the small gift. When she saw the pretty silver necklace, her mood changed completely.

"The flowers are Forget-Me-Nots," I told her. "I gave my girlfriend, Stella, a locket with those same flowers," I explained.

"Thank you, Tommy! Thank you so much! I will take excellent care of it," she promised. "I will gaze at it every day until you return home," she pledged.

Satisfied that I had at least eased my most vulnerable sister's burden, it was time to make my final preparations to leave.

The entire family would be making the trek down to the Broad Street Station, a massive structure on the corner of Broad and Market Streets in the shadow of Billy Penn.

Naturally, the girls enjoyed the early morning streetcar trip and the subsequent ride on the Market Street Elevated/Subway Line. It was my goal to arrive at the platform by 6:15 am. Our orders required that we be ready to ship out at 0700.

Once inside the massive station, I checked with a railroad worker at the information desk for directions to Platform No. 14.

The man, who appeared to be in his mid-forties, sported a typical brimmed railroad cap. He also had a small mustache that was flawlessly trimmed. His instructions directed me to the lower level, where I would find all the platforms were clearly marked. My family followed me in tow.

Upon reaching the already crowded platform, we saw the impressive troop train for the first time. The brick-colored passenger cars appeared shiny, clean, and ready for their mission. At the lead was the engine. It was obviously a Pennsy Mikado 2-8-2. I dropped my bag and ran to the front of the train to see if it was the 520, but the front plate identified the locomotive as No. 207.

At 0630, a staff sergeant was handing out the car assignments, and I drew number 8177, which seemed like a lucky number. So far, it was a good omen.

It was a long process of saying my goodbyes. My departure involved lots of hugging and kissing, and the moment did not pass without tears.

My parents handed me a prayer book to take with me on this journey. The black leather volume measured about four inches wide and five and a half inches long. With more than 600 pages, it was just over one inch thick.

Just before I was about to board my assigned car, Stella and Joe arrived on the platform. I could readily identify her in the distance. Her brother, Joe, was also sporting his favorite wide-brimmed tan hat.

She was wearing the locket that I gave her, and everyone in the family was anxious to see it. So eager were they with their inspection that I had to wait to hug and kiss her myself.

Before I stepped away to board the train, Stella handed me a small package wrapped in plain brown paper and tied with a piece of twine.

"Here. Take this with you," she insisted.

"Perhaps it will remind you of home while you're away," she added.

Quickly and excitedly, I opened the parcel. The article was also a book entitled "The Poetry of Robert Frost."

"It's a very recent collection of his works, including "The Road Not Taken," she stated proudly.

"Thanks, Stella," I said, giving her another hug. "I am sure it will help me through my travels."

It was an emotional time on the platform inside the huge train shed. Before I knew it, the whistle was tooting the warning that departure was forthcoming. Soon the locomotive's bell would join in the ritual.

Hundreds of uniformed soldiers were all scrambling to find their assigned cars and secure a seat inside. The scene was a familiar one as you looked up and down the platform. Many families were also offering their tearful goodbyes.

Finally, I tore myself away from the others and entered the car that would present me with the next part of my mission.

Even inside the car, you could feel the coal-burner power up and begin to move slowly. The shaking and rumbling of the train grew more intense, and the many sounds associated with that activity increased, as well.

Sitting by the window, I waved at the saddened faces until they passed from view. Their reaction from the platform was the same.

Several of the guys in my car were familiar to me. However, many were not.

The scuttlebutt on the car was that the entire 83-mile trip to Mt. Gretna would take more than an hour and a half.

Surprisingly, about 30 minutes into our trip, dining crew workers brought carts around that contained doughnuts, pastries, toast, cereal, coffee, tea, juice, and ice water pitchers.

Some of the men read books, while others began letter-writing. A handful couldn't resist taking over a corner of the car for gambling purposes.

A card game was in progress in our car, while others reported that dice games were also the norm throughout the train.

The 90-minute trip stretched into more than three and a half hours. We received a report that railroad traffic around Mt. Gretna was so heavy that much of it was at a standstill.

The time was nearly 1100 hours when we disembarked the train. Most of our equipment remained on the railroad cars. The cars sat on a siding near the camp.

Meanwhile, we unloaded our personal belongings and marched about three-quarters of a mile to the center of the installation. At that point, individual barracks assignments were issued.

Before being dismissed, the drill sergeant announced the schedule for the remainder of the day:

1200 - Lunch in the Mess Hall
1300 - Physical Examinations and inoculations in the Hospital Building
1500 - Personal appearance and grooming at the camp barbershop
1700 - Chow in the Mess Hall

The physical examination and medical inoculation procedure was a prolonged ordeal due to the number of personnel needed to be processed. We received inoculations for smallpox and anti-typhoid. The military haircuts followed that.

Luckily, Sunday's schedule was minimal. Chow was served in the Mess Hall from 0600 to 0800. Various religious services were available at the base chapel from 0800 until 1200. Traditional non-denominational worship took place at 1000.

The remainder of the day was open for new recruits to get acquainted with the camp. A limited number of recreational activities were also available such as horseshoes, quoits, and billiards.

One of the other guys, Joe Herbein, announced that he was going fishing that afternoon. Herbein was a country boy from Berks County, PA. His family farm was about 50 miles northwest of Philadelphia.

"I heard there's a creek that passes through the meadow. I am going to see if I can catch a couple of fish," he stated.

"Tommy, do you want to go along?" he asked. "What are you going to use?" I wondered out loud.

"I snatched a couple of extra-long straight pins from the infirmary, and I have a length of a string. All I need is a stick," the private explained.

Joe also mentioned that he saved some corn and pieces of bread from lunch to be used for bait and said that he might dig around the creek bank for some worms or insects.

We learned that the Conowingo Creek was not very far from camp. A trail through the woods provided us with a direct path.

Joe crossed the creek, which was about 15-feet wide at its narrowest point, using some large rocks as stepping stones. He spotted a deep pool of water with a large sunken tree trunk just offshore.

"This is the spot!" He exclaimed. "You'll see!" The self-proclaimed fisherman assured me. My preference was to remain on the opposite side of the stream.

Surprisingly, he began to get a few bites, and within 10 minutes, he caught a few sizable bluegills and one rock bass.

As I watched this country boy enjoy the moment where he was in his own element, about a half-dozen black and white Holstein cows approached him from behind. I tried to warn him, but Joe kept telling me to be quiet. He was getting a few gentle nibbles on his line.

Before I could say another word, the lead cow butted Joe with her head, and he was now flat on his back in the water. The poor guy not only was in the middle of a total panic, but he was floundering like a drowning man.

Just as I was poised to jump in and rescue the unfortunate chap, he righted himself and stood up in only about two feet of water.

Done for the day was our fishing expedition. Now the task was to get him back to camp to get cleaned up and dried off.

Several fellows from the outfit got a good chuckle when they heard about Joe's misadventure. Evening chow time was 1600 through 1800 hours. The food was generally pretty palatable.

At Monday's roll call, the sergeant reported that our stay at Mt. Gretna would only last until Saturday. Our next stop, via another train ride, was El Paso, Texas.

The CO declared that our schedule for the next five days would be as follows:

0545-0600 - Morning Inspection in Barracks
0600-0700 - Breakfast in the Mess Hall
0700-0730 - Calisthenics on the Drill Field
0800-1000 - Marching on the Drill Field
1000-1200 - Military Instructions in the Education Center
1200-1300 - Chow in the Mess Hall
1300-1400 - KP and Latrine Duties (See posted assignments)
1400-1600 - Guard Duty (See posted assignments)
1700-1800 - Chow in the Mess Hall

If we didn't know it before, we knew it now that we were in the army for sure. This week-long regimen was just a prelude to prepare us for our real test in El Paso.

Barney Roth, a private in our outfit, caused a commotion on Tuesday morning when he cut himself shaving. The tall, slender soldier hailed from Philly, Emily Street, actually. His razor took a sizable nick out of his neck, and the sarge asked me to run him over to the infirmary to get the bleeding under control.

I couldn't believe it when the doctor actually had to give him two stitches to close up the wound. It also made me chuckle when the nurse handed him a small booklet on the topic of proper shaving techniques. Barney was not amused, just a little embarrassed.

At Tuesday evening's mess, most of our tablemates from our old guard unit had reunited. Sitting on my left were Harry Haeberle and Irvin Schweppenheiser. On the other side of the table were Roy Wilson and Bernie Halliday.

"Hey guys," Wilson broke the silence, "Has anybody seen or heard from Cookie? You know Cookie Mulligan?"

"Come to think of it, no," I replied.

"The last I saw him," Halliday reacted, "was during the physicals on Saturday. I don't think I've seen him since. Now that you mention it."

The ordinarily quiet Irvin Schweppenheiser finally spoke up, "He's in the hospital. They're keeping him there. He's not shipping out with us," he revealed.

"Did you hear what's up behind the whole thing?" I inquired.

"He has Bright's Disease. It's a serious kidney ailment that's probably going to kill him," Schweppenheiser casually and calmly lowered the boom.

Haeberle jumped in with the snied comment, "So, how do you know this, Mr. Smarty pants? How is it you know everything? You sit back in your chair, all quiet and everything, then, you come out with the know-it-all routine!"

"Yeah, what are you, a doctor?" Wilson joined in the fray. "What makes you an expert all of a sudden?" He quipped.

"First of all," Irvin stood up with his tray in hand and began, "My grandmother passed away from the disease last year. Therefore, I know!" He answered adamantly.

They say that an army mess hall can be one of the noisiest places on earth, but for just a few moments, you could hear a pin drop in that room.

"Sorry, man," Wilson said apologetically, "We didn't know."

"Yeah," Haeberle joined in sheepishly, "We didn't mean nothin' by it!"

I added my two cents, saying, "My grandmother also passed away four years ago of Bright's. She lived with us. I'm aware of its seriousness, also."

"Okay, Schweppenheiser," Wilson followed up. "The floor's yours. Tells us what's up."

"It's a horrible and painful malady related to the kidneys," he began.

"Symptoms include sensations of pain, swelling of various body parts plus vomiting," he went on.

"In plain English," he explained, "it's an inflammation of the kidney that eventually worsens, and the organ no longer functions. Right now, there is no cure," he concluded.

The mood grew immediately somber at the table. I quickly suggested that we visit Cookie in his room over at the hospital later that evening. Perhaps we could lift his spirits a little. From that point on, however, Schweppenheiser was given the nickname "Doc."

    *   *8A NOTE: Many well-known individuals were diagnosed with Bright's Disease during this time, including Rowland Macey Sr., founder of Macy's Dept. Store; Alice Roosevelt, first wife of Teddy Roosevelt; Emily Dickinson, poet; Chester A. Authur, 21st US President; James S. Sherman, Vice President of the US; Ellen Wilson, wife of Woodrow Wilson; Richard W. Sears, founder of Sears Roebuck and Co., and Booker T. Washington.*

All agreed on the idea, and we made plans to meet in front of the barracks at 1900 hours.

Four of us were there and waiting in front of the building. We were delayed because of Haeberle, who was still fussing over his looks in the mirror. Like the rest of us, he had no hair to speak of, so we were unsure what kind of grooming it was that he needed.

The charge nurse directed the five of us to Cookie's bed, and we found him resting comfortably and reading the newspaper.

"Hey, Cookie! How's it going?" We all seemed to yell out in unison. "Fine. Fine," he noted.

"Looks like you're not heading out with us," Wilson said.

"Yeah. The docs say they're sending me back home on a train this Saturday," he replied, but you could hear the frustration in his voice.

"Look, you're probably better off anyway," Haeberle added.

"We're going down to Texas to babysit the Mexicans, and then, it's off to France to fight the Jerry's," he said to cheer him up.

"Would you rather be back in Philly eating corned beef and cabbage or in a trench somewhere eating mush while watching bullets fly over your head?" Haeberle asked.

"I guess you're right," Mulligan agreed.

"Say, Mulligan, how'd you ever get that nickname, Cookie?" I asked while joining in the conversation.

"Well," he began, "when I was just a baby, I didn't speak a word until I was almost two years old.

"My folks thought there was something wrong with me. They took me to the doctor and everything," he went on.

"When I was teething, and they gave me these tough, round biscuits to chew. They were supposed to make my gums feel good. Eventually, from being in my mouth, they got soft, and I was able to eat them.

"My parents say that I loved those crackers so much that when someone walked into the room, I would sit up and say cookie, cookie!"

"That was my first word, and that is what they started calling me. Today, at 21 years old, I am still 'Cookie.'

"Great story, man," Halliday commented. "It was terrific seeing you. We all wish you the best, and we're all pulling for you. Hang in there, chap!"

Fortunately, we had already started our goodbyes when the nurse approached to inform us that it was time to leave.

We all felt terrible knowing what the poor guy had in store for him, but at least we made an effort to cheer him up a little.

On the walk back to the barracks, we all agreed to go back on Thursday night and spend some more time with him before going our separate ways.

By Wednesday, most of us had the routine down, and we were adjusting to this full-time military life just fine!

Thursday's march on the drill field was interrupted at about 0930 when Leo Quigley stepped on a bee's nest hidden in the ground. The swarm of yellow jackets sent the entire formation scattering in all directions, but Quigley was the man who took the brunt of it. He received several nasty stings, especially on the arms and face.

Wilson and Erdley took him to the infirmary for treatment. With his face already swollen, the concern was that this setback could hinder his chances of leaving on the train to El Paso with the rest of us.

Thursday evening, we met again in Mulligan's room. This time our friend was experiencing an unusual amount of pain, and the nurse instructed us to keep our visit brief.

Once again, we all wished him luck with his recovery, acknowledging that it would probably not be the case in our hearts.

However, the five of us did gain some satisfaction that we attempted to comfort the poor guy before shipping out.

It was no surprise that much of Friday's schedule was abbreviated so we could prepare to ship out again on Saturday morning. We needed to be ready to board the train by 0500, 1 July!

We received word from the sergeant that Quigley was recovering nicely from the bee stings, and he would be released from the infirmary this afternoon. We were all pleased to hear that news.

Of course, the poor guy instantly was given a new nickname, "Stinger!"

When we arrived at the railroad depot Saturday morning at 0400, the report passed down the line was that today's train would be double in size of our original 14-car caravan.

There was just enough light to see the engine and its cargo chug around the bend on the mainline. According to the Almanac, sunrise would officially arrive at 0438.

As the mighty locomotive approached our position, it was plain to see that it was another Pennsy L1. Young saplings along its path seemed to bow in honor as the impressive engine provided large gusts of wind when it passed by.

The large headlight on the front temporarily blinded my eyes. I shielded my forehead with my hand. When it approached, I could read the round black plate edged in gold with the matching gold number "520."

My old friend, No. 520, would provide the trip to El Paso! To me, this was another good omen. I was comfortable with the next leg of my journey.

It took nearly an hour for the hook-up of the two sections of the train to be completed. Several of the cars had to be re-arranged to put the officers' units at the tail end. A small yard shifter participated in the operation. I was assigned to ride in car number four.

The CO on our car announced that the trip to El Paso would take about three or four days, depending on stops for coal, water, sand, etc.

In many cases, the train could take on water without stopping. Trenches, built in the center of the tracks, were filled with water. The engine's tender had a scoop underneath that could be lowered to refill the water tank. Whenever these troughs were not available, the train would need to stop at a standard water tower to be refilled.

These stops would allow the troops to stretch their legs and take a break from the long ride.

They say the worst thing you can do is put an engineer behind in his schedule. The jockeying of the cars and the loading of troops forced the 520 to pull out of the Mt. Gretna Depot at 0545. This departure was 45 minutes later than the appointed time.

Due to heavy traffic on the rails, the 32-mile trip to Harrisburg, PA, required an hour and a half. We crossed the grand Rockville Bridge, situated on the Susquehannah River, about five miles north of the city. The railroad viaduct is constructed of forty-eight 70-foot arches. They say it's almost four thousand feet long.

Six hours later, we approached Pittsburgh. The skies grew dark and overcast as an apparent storm was approaching from the west. The clouds combined with the smoke and soot from the area's many steel industries gave the appearance of nightfall.

The 28-car train had to cross two bridges as it passed through the "Steel City." The Fort Wayne Railroad Bridge forged the Allegheny River, while the Ohio Connecting Railroad Bridge traversed the Ohio River.

We made a planned stop in-between to load up on coal and water. This operation required about 45 minutes. The railroad workers brought sandwiches and drinks around during the stop in Pittsburgh. They also served us an assortment of fruit and cookies.

From Pittsburgh to Columbus, OH, was a five-hour trip. At the midway point, the rain began to fall. When we passed through Zanesville, OH, it was time for supper.

The dining attendants wheeled their carts through the cars with trays of steaming food.

Although we had no idea if the food was even tasty, the aroma was very tantalizing.

This evening's selection was a generous plateful of beef and potatoes with a side of green beans or corn. The coach attendants brought us rolls, butter, and beverages, as well.

For dessert, we had a choice of apple pie or chocolate cake. At least for now, the army was treating us well.

Despite the many hours of traveling thus far, the trip was relatively uneventful. The guys spent the time chatting in small groups, reading, sleeping, or staring blankly out the window. As reported earlier, some sort of gambling game took place in nearly every car on the train.

Like many others, I occasionally took a stroll through some of the other coaches just to break up the time and afford myself some form of exercise. There were washrooms on each car, as well.

Columbus, OH, meant another stop for coal, water, and sand. By this time, we knew the routine.

The rain was torrential during this layover.

Nevertheless, there was a passenger station close by, and a few of the soldiers elected to hop off the train and grab a smoke while standing under the platform roof.

Two quick whistle blasts signaled that we were pulling out, and as we left the station, the solitary bell sounded its warning despite the weather conditions.

We were informed when we left Columbus that it would be around midnight when we rolled into Indianapolis, IND. This five-hour trek would take us through the Ohio towns of Dayton and Springfield.

At about 2100 hours, the lights were dimmed to about half their average brightness. This action forced many to catch some early shut-eye. However, that did not deter those involved in the local card game from continuing their gambling operation.

An attendant came around and announced that one of the dining cars was now open for enlisted men and NCOs (Non-Commissioned Officers). Previously, officers were the only personnel allowed in this car.

The railroad worker noted that the dining coach was only serving non-alcoholic drinks and snacks at this time.

I went with Wilson to the dining car for a cup of coffee. We were fortunate to catch a table with a couple of other guys. They were also from Philly, but they were attached to another outfit.

Information flowed a little more freely in the dining car. We learned that our next major destination was Nashville, TN., but the train would be making a stop in Haywood, KY.

At this leg of the journey, we would be outfitted with a new engine. It seems old faithful, No. 520, would not see me all the way to El Paso. I shrugged my shoulders and was glad for the opportunity to ride on my pal from Baldwin. More than likely, our new locomotive would also be a Pennsy L1, which was fine with me, too!

I was back in my old coach at daybreak, which was at 0500. There was no sunshine, however. The rains remained heavy. You could hear the downpour pounding the metal roof of the car. Within the hour, we would be arriving at Haywood to make the engine swap.

The 520 pulled onto a long siding about four tracks to the right of the mainline. Her replacement was idling directly to our left.

As per the routine, we anticipated that the changeover would take about an hour. Although there was virtually no cover from the storm, some of the guys jumped off the train to stretch their legs, catch a smoke, or be a little nosey about the stop.

When we were finally coupled up to the new locomotive, we expected to power up and be on our way. The hour dragged on to an hour and a half. At the two-hour mark, we were still sitting on the siding.

Finally, the first sergeant, Wilbur Ackton, stormed through the door. The NCO was about five- foot-ten inches tall and looked like he was about 30 years old. The man wore a pair of gold wire-rimmed glasses. The lenses were perfectly round. He stood there calmly for a few moments to be sure that he had everyone's attention. If he did hear any mumbling or grumbling, he cocked his head and pointed one of his ears in the direction of those conversations. When he was confident that he had everyone's full attention, he went forward with his statement.

"Gentlemen," he began, "we will probably be here for the next six hours, at least."

The sounds of moans and groans filled the coach. Before the sarge could explain, the men shouted out remarks such as, "Are you kiddin'?"... "You're joking, right?"... "What's the deal, sarge?"... "Six hours? Whatta ya nuts?"

"Listen up," he shouted while trying to maintain order.

"Between here and Scottsville, Kentucky," he explained, "we have to cross the Barren River. Actually, there's a Big Barren River and a Little Barren River, but where we need to pass, there's a railroad trestle that's entirely underwater right now. It's been raining down here for five straight days now," he went on.

"Also, on the other side of the crossing," he added, "fallen trees and debris obstruct the tracks."

"So, what's the plan, Sarge," one of the guys sounded from the back of the coach.

The NCO went on to reveal the plan that the higher-ups devised to resolve the situation.

"The brass has called up two Engineering Companies that will split into two teams, one North and one South.

"The unit in the North will search for anything that may be hindering the flow of the river. Their mission is to open things up to allow the water to drain away from the trestle.

"In the South," he noted, "the team will clear the debris from the tracks to make it passable."

"What's the alternative?" another asked.

"If the rain doesn't let up and we can't open the passage, the train will have to back up about five miles to another spur and bypass this mess," he concluded.

I chipped in with my own question, "What will do to our ETA?" (Estimated Time of Arrival). "Well," the sergeant said while hanging his head and letting out a sad sigh, "this already sets us back six hours, but you're probably looking at another 18 to 24 hours overall." Finally, before leaving the car, the sergeant left us with a little more news.

"There's no depot here in Haywood," he confirmed, "so, there's no place to go in this immediate vicinity.

"However, " he went on, "if the rain lets up, they tell me that there's a little country store down the road about a half-mile to the left. It probably ain't open on a Sunday, though.

"About the same distance down the road in the other direction, there's a baptist church. I understand that their service starts at 0900.

"We could all use a little religion today!" He said as he turned around and walked out of the car.

Mt. Gretna, PA Military Camp
Image Source: Public Domain

"TRAVELING TO TEXAS"

PRR No. 520 leaves Kentucky bound for Nashville, TN
Image Source: Unknown

CHAPTER 9

"Traveling to Texas"

No sooner had First Sgt. Ackton left the coach when the rains began to lift. The dark clouds were starting to show signs of brightening.

The situation went from a complete downpour to a mild drizzle in just a matter of minutes. You could feel the mood change from car to car instantly. Many of the 1,200 troops aboard the train began to disembark to taste their newly discovered freedom.

As quickly as the weather situation changed, the men let out a loud cheer as a Louisville & Nashville RR 4-4-0 locomotive roared by on the mainline. The eight-car train sounded its whistle in warning with several powerful blasts as it passed our position. Dragging behind it were three boxcars filled with men, two cattle cars with horses and mules, two flat cars with heavy equipment, one open gondola loaded with supplies, and a wooden red caboose with its road name "L & N" emblazoned on the side with yellow letters.

As the train went by, the boxcars' open doors revealed members of the engineering outfit hanging out of the cars. The celebrating soldiers were waving and cheering, as well. Their mission was to get the river flowing and get the trestle back in operation.

About 40 of us met on the siding and decided to make the trip to the Oak Grove Baptist Church in Glasgow. The half-mile walk would take us about 20 minutes.

The rain had stopped entirely when we enter the brick house of worship. A sizable crowd had already gathered for worship, but the congregation was more than willing to make room for the visiting troops.

Pastor Calvin Price, a 50-year old preacher who arrived recently from Decaturville, TN, led the Worship Service that Sunday morning.

Amazingly, the local baptists joined hands with these men in uniform who were likely destined to participate in the world war.

Dressed in a black Geneva preaching robe, Rev. Price glanced around the crowded church before beginning his sermon. He spoke directly about the turmoil that was taking place around the world.

"My brothers and sisters, we are witnessing the likes that this world has never seen before. There have been wars and rumors of wars over the centuries, but in these times, it seems like the entire globe is embroiled in this conflict.

"In Luke: 21-25, we are old "And there will be signs in the sun and moon and stars, and on the earth distress of nations in perplexity because of the roaring of the sea and the waves, people fainting with fear and with foreboding of what is coming on the world. For the powers of the heavens will be shaken."

God also sends his message in the process from Daniel 11:41, "He shall also enter into the glorious land, and many countries shall be overthrown: but these shall escape out of his hand, even Edom, and Moab, and the chief of the children of Ammon."

"Here, Jesus Christ, Our Lord, and Redeemer, reveals that he not only wants satan defeated but assures us that his evil ways will be crushed.

"The Good Book has been given to us as a reference for God's plans. Today, He unveils to us His intentions during this current world crisis.

"Our most powerful and loving Savior has sent us his Army of Angels as a sign that His will be done. "I say to you, my brothers and sisters in the Lord Jesus Christ, we must welcome these visitors in our home today. Their mission is to ensure that God's peace reigns on this earth forever and ever, Amen!" He finished.

Deacon Hobbs announced that everyone in attendance was welcome to partake in refreshments in the church hall after the service.

The choir of the Oak Baptist Church led the entire congregation in singing the recessional hymn, "Onward Christian Soldiers."

Because of the enormous turnout, the pastor immediately determined that the refreshments on hand would not be enough to keep up with the demand. Initially, the women of the church had provided an assortment of cakes and cookies. Beverages included coffee, hot tea, iced tea, and punch.

Clyde Higgins, an upstanding member of the congregation, was the proprietor of M. Clyde Higgins General Store & Dry Goods. He grabbed his son, Melvin, and drove to his business for more supplies.

The pair made the one-mile trip down Scottsdale Road in a 1912 Packard delivery truck.

Within 30 minutes, they returned with a galvanized washtub of lemonade, a small barrel of savory biscuits, and a block of cheese.

The congregation welcomed these military guests with open arms, and small assemblages of individuals gathered at various spots in the room for this impromptu meet and greet.

It didn't take Harry Haeberle long to make a play for a couple of the babes in the room. Over in one corner, he was deep in conversation with a cute blonde. The young lass was about 19-years old. She had blue eyes, shoulder-length hair and was sporting a pink gingham dress.

The other gal wore her red hair up in a bun. Haeberle appeared to be focused on her green eyes and pale yellow dress.

Apparently, his charm was working since both girls interacted with smiles, giggles, and body language that went beyond shyness!

The scene at the church earned him a new nickname, as well, "Chickie," due to his interest in chasing women.

Just before Noon, a pair of MPs (Military Police) arrived on the scene and coaxed our men to head back to the train.

MPs and NCOs urged us to get back on the coaches since railroad staff would be serving lunch soon.

The men were all settled in their assigned seats when the dining car workers started rolling carts of food down the aisles. Today's menu was a typical fried chicken dinner complete with mashed potatoes and an assortment of vegetables.

At 1300 hours, Sgt. Ackton returned to our car while we were eating. The NCO was carrying a clipboard and was obviously prepared to make several critical announcements.

"Gentlemen, I have good news!" He began.

"Word has it that we will be moving out at 1500 hours. Both units of engineers were successful. The 201st Engineer Battalion opened a blockage in the Barren River. The water has since receded, and they are in the process of inspecting the trestle for damage. We expect them to give it a clean bill of health by 1430," he explained.

"The 203rd Engineer Battalion was also successful in clearing the tracks of fallen debris, and that stretch of the railway has already been declared fully operational," he added.

A rousing cheer followed the sarge's report, and the men were ready to see the train rolling again. "Furthermore," he stated, "once we are given the green light to move out, it's about 19 miles to Scottsville, KY, and another 66 miles to Nashville. If we don't experience any further delays, we should pass through Nashville at about 1700 hours.

"From Nashville, our anticipated route during the night will take us through Jackson and Memphis, TN, to Winona and Jackson, MS. With our planned stops for fuel, etc., we should reach Jackson, MS. Monday at about 0900," he said, wrapping up the itinerary.

Not long after the sergeant left our car, the Louisville & Nashville train carrying the engineers roared by on the mainline. Once again, the troops had their cars' doors open and were cheering as they passed by. Our men quickly opened the coach windows and returned the yells. The men also whistled and hollered as if they were watching a vaudeville show.

Within a short time, we were moving for the first time in many hours. As we approached the wooden trestle that spanned the river, we reduced our speed to a crawl for safety reasons.

We surpassed the first hurdle by traversing the river bridge. Then, we passed through the areas that had been obstructed by debris. We could see the remains of the devastation. Large piles of fallen trees and their branches were stacked on the hillside to the left.

When we traveled beyond both checkpoints, the guys in our coach let out a huge victory cheer. I am sure similar actions took place in other cars, as well.

Both the railroad and the Army generally run like clockwork. Keeping on schedule is vital to every mission. The balance of the trip seemed to go as planned. We were making good time heading south and making our scheduled stops for fuel and maintenance.

During the night, I was awakened when one of the railroad porters was making his rounds, cleaning the coach, and sweeping the floor.

He was a colored fellow by the name of "Sedrick." By my estimation, the man was about six-foot-three inches tall and of slender build. His facial features included a tiny mustache and a two-inch scar on his left cheek.

As I grew more acquainted with Sedrick, I soon learned that he had a very mild and friendly personality. It was easy to strike up a conversation with the man.

"So, how are you this evening? Sedrick," I asked.

"Very well, Sir," he replied. "What are you doing awake at this hour of the morning, sir?" he asked.

"Cannot sleep. You can just call me Tommy. The sir isn't necessary," I insisted.

"Whatever you say, sir," he said out of habit, I suppose.

"Where are you from, Sedrick," I questioned.

"Actually," he replied, "as the crow flies, not too far from here.

"I grew up in Fayette, Mississippi. It's southwest of Jackson," he explained.

"My family worked on a farm there. Unlike most of Mississippi, we didn't grow no cotton," he declared. "our plantation owner planted corn, sweet potatoes, and oats, mainly."

Sedrick proceeded, "Mister Vernon Sinclair didn't want no parts of that cotton crop. It was way too much trouble, he maintained."

"What was that like, Sedrick?" I asked the man.

"It was hard work, especially out in the hot sun, but we were treated as about as fairly as we could expect given the times," he declared.

"How did you end up working for the railroad?" I asked out of curiosity.

"Pappy died of pneumonia when I was around 20 years old, and mammy died a few years later of the fever," he remarked.

"Fever?" I asked.

"Yes, Sir. Yellow fever," the man clarified. "I see," I lamented.

"With the folks departed, I headed up North. I would end up in Philadelphia and made friends with another colored fellow by the name of Bo Buford. He arranged for me to get this job with the railroad," he concluded.

"Interesting," I commented.

"Well, sir," he interrupted, "it's been nice chattin' with y'all, but I need to get back to work, or I'll be diggin' taters again."

Once the porter left, I managed to get a little more shut-eye before daybreak.

The serving of breakfast between 0600 and 0700 was the only thing that broke up the monotony during this long stretch.

Things changed drastically, however, when a considerable commotion took place around 0837. The entire train came to a screeching halt, and dozens of NCOs and MPs were running from car to car.

We sat dead on the tracks for a good 20 minutes when word began to filter up and down the line. One of those card games got out of hand. The CO's told us one of the guys was stabbed in the process.

Eventually, further news about the incident began to filter about the train. As the story was told to me, Tony Cariello, an Italian from Dauphin County, PA, accused Joe Kozlowski, a Polack from Wilkes Barre, PA, of cheating in the card game. They were in car No. 3552.

Though Cariello warned the Polack twice, Kozlowski ignored him and continued his play again.

Kozlowski raked in the pot at the end of the last hand without showing his hand or saying a word.

The Italian produced a six-inch knife and slashed his opponent across the stomach. With blood spilled everywhere, the Polish fellow lay sprawled on the floor. Somebody summoned the MP's immediately.

It was at that time that the train came to a screeching halt. In addition to the MPs and NCOs, several officers were called upon to assess the situation immediately.

Cariello was handcuffed and taken to an individual jail cell located in one of the baggage cars.

Kozlowski was placed on a stretcher to one of the officers' combination cars.

An Army medic attended to him until we could make an emergency stop at the hospital in Jackson.

There was a civilian ambulance waiting for our arrival at the railway station.

Within about 15 minutes, the wounded soldier was on his way, and he would probably require surgery. Our train, though, was being detoured to Camp Shelby, MS.

This military installation was located about two and a half hours south of Jackson. The prisoner would be transferred to the pokey there. Eventually, Kozlowski would be moved there as well if he indeed recovered from his wounds.

We arrived at the camp at 1200 hours and were back on the mainline headed for Baton Rouge, LA, by 1238.

The railroad staff served us lunch just before 1300 hours, and the schedule called for us to arrive in Baton Rouge around 1800 hours.

We received an update that the train would not actually be passing through Baton Rouge. The stop would take place in Anchorage, LA. Once there, we would again switch engines.

At 1830 we arrived in Anchorage, and as the yard workers were performing the critical task of making the engine swap, the staff served us dinner. Tonight's meal was a type of Louisianna Gumbo.

Our new locomotive is from the New Orleans, Texas, and Mexico Railway. The engine, which has the front of its boiler and smokestack painted silver in color, is a Baldwin 2-8-0. Baldwin built the unit in 1911, which was before my time there. The railroad line was now part of the Gulf Coast Lines.

* *8B NOTE: The Gulf Coast Lines was the name of a railroad system comprising three principal railroads and some smaller ones that stretched from New Orleans via Baton Rouge, LA, and Houston to Brownsville, TX. Chartered initially as subsidiaries of the Frisco Railroad, the system became independent in 1916 and was purchased by the Missouri Pacific Railroad in 1925. The Independent Gulf Coast Lines' parent company was the New Orleans, Texas, and Mexico Railway incorporated in Louisiana on February 28, 1916, which bought the property and assets of the Frisco-owned New Orleans, Texas, and Mexico Railroad.*

The railroad personnel told us that they expected the one thousand-mile trip from Anchorage to El Paso to take about 22 hours.

Surprisingly, we were ready to roll and begin our trek across Texas by 1915 hours.

According to the sergeant's map, our train would pass through the Texas towns of Beaumont, Houston, Hallettsville, San Antonio, Hondo, Del Rio, Sanderson, Alpine, and finally, Socorro before arriving in El Paso.

A member of the dining car staff came through the coach at 1930 with a cart of soft drinks and candies. The colored fellow was much shorter than Sedrick and had an average build. The name badge on his railroad uniform read, "Hiriam."

"What do we have here, Hiriam?" I asked.

"Well, sir," he quickly replied, "we have an assortment of fountain sodas and fine chocolates," he noted.

"Soda and chocolates," I commented, "that's quite a treat!" I exclaimed.

"We is the Pennsylvania Railroad, Sir. The finest in the world. We's like to treat our passengers as the best in the world! too!" He stated proudly.

"Tell me what you're serving, my fine man," Wilson inquired of the railroad worker.

"Sir, here we has Coca-Cola. It comes from Atlanta, Georgia, and it's one of the best soda waters there is," he began.

"Dis' is Dr. Pepper," he explained. "It's a blend of 23 flavors and was invented by a pharmacist right here in Waco, Texas. It **sure** is good!" He declared.

"Now this," he went on, "is Ginger Ale. It's a tasty soda water dat's just a wee bit spicey, and here we got just plain club soda that you can have with a splash of lemon or lime," he ended.

"That's swell," Haeberle commented. "What about the candies?" he questioned. "Sir," he replied, "Deez candies come all the way from *New O'lins (New Orleans),* and they are of the finest quality," he assured us.

"Gent-men, you're lookin' at chocolate creams, caramels, and nougats, all from down on Bourbon Street," he beamed proudly as if he had made them himself.

We gave the man our orders, and he dished out these unexpected treats in short order. When he was finished, he tipped his hat and made his way down the car's remaining section.

As we enjoyed our snacks, Haeberle surprisingly broke the silence with an ice-breaker.

"So, what are you guys planning to do after this whole army thing is over?" He threw out there.

Nobody answered at first, so he went on, "You first, Schalata. What are you gonna' do when you get out of this outfit," he said, putting me on the spot.

"I'd like to get a little place in the country, like Herbein over there," I began in reference to my fishing buddy Joe Herbein, who was sitting across the aisle.

I continued, "I want a couple of acres of land to farm. Smell the fresh air, and be as far away from the crowded, noisy city as I can be."

Since he brought up the subject, I knew that Haeberle had his own opinion ready to go.

Harry began, "My lady and me are going to buy a bungalow just outside Atlantic City, and I'm going to get myself a fine little boat for down there.

"I'm going to spend the mornings in the back bay fishing and crabbing, and in the afternoons, my baby and me are going to cruise out to one of those cozy private beaches to bask in the sun and sip cocktails," he proclaimed.

"We're gonna have about three or four kids, and life is going to be a ball," he added. "What about work?" Wilson questioned in an effort to provide the guy a dose of reality.

"My old man taught me a lot about construction. I'll either get a job down there or start my own business," he said, sounding most sure of himself.

"Maybe I'll even talk to my brother. Billy into going down there and joining me," he concluded. "And you, Wilson..." Haeberle asked while looking in his direction.

"I may go to school to learn to be an optician," he noted.

"My old man keeps telling me there's money in eyeglasses, and there are no shops right now in Bridesburg," he reasoned.

"Schweppenheiser, it's down to you," Haeberle said, putting Irvin on the spot.

"Somehow, I don't think whatever you say will surprise us, Schwepp. Tell us what you're going to do," Harry pushed.

"Well," he began. He was muttering at first. "I have almost enough money saved to go to medical school. I want to go to Penn," he added.

"I want to learn how to help guys like Cookie and others who have to deal with the variety of diseases and illnesses we have today." Schweppenheiser revealed.

"Like I said, " Haeberle crowed, "no surprise there. Mr. Smarty Pants is going to save the world!" He quipped.

"Come on, Haeberle," I chipped in. "Give the guy a break. He wants to do something good with his life," I said in an attempt to shut him up. The others all nodded in agreement.

In an attempt to deflect the attention suddenly thrown on him, Haeberle quickly countered by engaging Emilio Manicotti in the conversation.

Manicotti, who was sitting in the same seat across the aisle with Herbein, was an Italian from South Philly.

The dark-haired boy looked up from the book he was reading and said, "Huh? Whatta ya want?"

"What's your plans when you get out of the service, Emilio?" Chickie shouted across the aisle.

"Me? You talkin' to me?" He replied.

"Yeah, you, Manicotti? Who'd you think I was talking to?" He shot back.

"What's your plans when we're done with this army life?" Haeberle insisted on an answer.

"I'm going to get my own place in South Philly. Probably around Mifflin Street... Passyunk. Somewhere around there, I guess," he began.

"Then what?" Haeberle continued the inquisition.

"I guess I'll probably work at my pop's barbershop. My grandfather, Valentino, started the shop. It's on 18th Street. My father, Val Jr., runs it now," he explained.

"That's what you want to do? Spend your life giving haircuts and shaving old men?" Haeberle sounded surprised.

"Yeah! I like it there. It's home to me, and I have everything I could want in South Philly," Manicotti concluded.

"More power to you, I guess," Harry sighed. "You guys are in for a boring life, I'll tell ya'. You guys have no sense of adventure; that's all I have to say," he went on.

Haeberle continued to ramble on, but most of us just ignored him. Gradually, most of the guys drifted off to sleep. Although, Schweppenheiser and I snuck off to the dining car. I searched for another glass of that Dr. Pepper, while Irvin, I believe, just wanted to get away from Chickie for a while.

The two of us each had a couple more sodas, and the dining car server brought us some cheese and crackers left over from a little gathering held earlier by the officers.

I never doubted Irvin's intelligence, but when he opened up to me about the importance of his interest in medicine, I was indeed impressed.

He went into great detail about how his grandmother's affliction affected his life and his experiences with other medical conditions. This smart young man was determined to make a difference in the field.

In my mind, it was clear to me that when the time came for us to serve overseas, Irvin's interest in medicine would be quite valuable.

As our train drew closer to El Paso, Texas, I realized that our ultimate destination would eventually be the already blood-stained soil of France, Belgium, and Germany.

"ARRIVAL AT CAMP STEWARD"

Mexican Border: Camp Stewart, El Paso, TX
Image Source: PA National Guard Museum

CHAPTER 10

"Arrival at Camp Stewart"

By sunrise, it had finally begun to sink in that this was our last day on the train. Besides, it had never occurred to me that today, Tuesday, was Independence Day, the Fourth of July! Ironically, the 1,200 men aboard this train would be gaining their physical independence on this very day.

Gone were the lush forests and meadows that had passed by our windows over the previous four days.

The dozens of small towns and villages disappeared from view, along with the rural farmhouses and rolling fields of corn and wheat.

The cities that we passed through with their bellowing smokestacks of industry and sprawling acres of railyards were nothing more than a memory at this point.

Replacing these images of middle America was a barren landscape. The ground, instead, was littered with sand, dirt, and dust. Yuccas, Creosote bushes, and agaves grow there, along with prickly pears, tarbush, and Honey Mesquite. Not much of anything else.

In the distance, small mountain peaks break up the generally flat terrain. The landscape, which goes on forever, appears to be a blend of mostly beige, brown, red, and gray. Only wisps of green offer a slight contrast.

By mid-morning, the temperature in the coaches was approaching 95 degrees. With the windows open completely, soot and cinders from the engine's smokestack were a constant menace. Finding a happy medium was a challenge.

The anxious anticipation of seeing this journey come to an end overshadowed the men's boredom.

Knowing we would be in El Paso by afternoon was all the relief that was needed.

Following breakfast and lunch, our next major maneuver would be leaving the mainline and switching to a spur belonging to the El Paso and Southwest Railroad. This line would take us directly to Camp Stewart.

Before we arrived at the spur, we needed to stop at a remote outpost to take on water and coal. Unlike our previous layovers, which took place in major cities and towns, this repository was literally in the middle of nowhere. The time was 1530.

Devoid of any civilization, aside from the railroad facilities, the only distinguishing feature was a rock formation situated roughly 100 yards from the track, *Roca del Desierto, or The Desert Rock.*

The ruddy-colored natural landmark was approximately forty-foot tall and resembled a chimney or smokestack. Two distinct bends in the tower provided the configuration with its unique crooked appearance. A heap of rubble surrounded its base.

The fuel stop appeared to be taking longer than usual, and before long, the men were growing impatient already.

Once again, the first sergeant came into our car to be the bearer of bad news, "An inspection of the train shows that we have four hot boxes that need to be repacked."

*   *9 NOTE: Each truck on a railroad car contains a journal box on the wheel. Inside the journal box is an axle bearing. When these bearings overheat, it is called a hot box. The box is packed with oil-soaked rags or cotton to reduce the friction of the axle. When this oil leaks or dries out, it could cause a fire and severely damage the bearing. Hence, if caught in time, it needs to be repacked. Railroad workers refer to the term "All Black" to signify there are no problems with the bearings and "Red" if there is an indication of fire or smoke.*

He went onto reveal, "The two front boxes on the right side of car No. 6076 will need to be repacked, and two on the back left side of car No. 1006 needs the same treatment. Fortuitously, this will only put us about 30 minutes behind schedule. The railroad has two crews working on this immediately," he concluded his briefing.

"So, sarge," one of the guys challenged, "when do we actually expect to get into El Paso?"

"I am told we should be rolling in there at about 1730," he said with confidence.

After four days of traveling practically across the country, we could finally see the depot at Camp Stewart, El Paso, Texas, just ahead.

The fidgety men were highly anxious, and a crescendo of cheering and applause was quietly building inside the coach. The tension continued to grow until the engine made its final screeching, jerking stop at the platform. Then, it was possible to hear all the cars in the train erupt in jubilant pandemonium.

As we disembarked the train, NCOs, officers, and MPs were standing by to dish out orders. Our mission was to gather our personal belongings and march along the dusty trail to camp. Supply companies loaded our equipment onto mule-driven wagons and into a handful of motorized trucks.

When we arrived at the camp, we were instructed where to set up our tents. Fortunately for us, we would bivouac near the mess hall, the latrines, and the field hospital. How convenient!

Our outfit had a deadline of one hour to complete the task. The mess hall would remain open for us to catch some chow. If we missed it, that was on us.

Once we pitched our tents in the designated area, we constructed a make-shift sign designating our newly created pathway as "Broad Street." This reference paid homage to Philly's main thoroughfare.

Each tent was capable of accommodating eight men. Bunking with me were Harry Haeberle, Irvin Schweppenheiser, Jimmy Rafferty, Alfred Gray, Roy Wilson, Barney Roth, and Elmor Hutchinson. How I got stuck with Haeberle and Schweppenheiser in the same tent was beyond me. I accepted the fact that it would make for some rather interesting nights.

Our unit was called to formation by our new NCO, Sergeant First Class Charles E. Vogan, after chow.

"Men," he began, "Welcome to Camp Stewart, El Paso, Texas. You are now part of the military forces protecting the border of the great United States of America. There are 110,000 National Guardsmen taking part in this operation. From Brownsville, Texas to Yuma, Arizona, our mission is to secure 1,200 miles of boundary that abuts Mexico," he explained.

"Tomorrow," he went on, "we will all rise at reveille, which will be at 0545. The mess hall will be open for you from 0700 until 0745. After that, we will assemble here where you will receive instructions on your daily routines. Taps in the evening will be sounded at 2300 hours.

"Is that understood?" He roared.

"Sir, yes, sir!" We replied in unison.

"That is all! Dismissed!" he barked.

As promised, the bugler's playing of "Reveille" broke the silence on Wednesday morning at 0545. Everyone scrambled from their cots and got ready for the day. Each soldier is required to police their area before leaving. This practice was necessary to pass unannounced inspections that are sprung on us from time to time.

There are always long lines at the latrines, especially in the mornings. That is the primary reason that our schedule allotted us an hour before chow time.

It was the first day in camp, and some of the guys were already beefing about the morning routine. "Be happy with what you got," I said.

"I spoke with a guy last night from the 106th Mobile Veterinary Section, and he said that those guys have to get up at 0400 and tend to the horses," I went on.

"He told me that they have to feed, water, and groom the animals. Then, they must get them ready by putting on their harnesses by candlelight," I concluded.

"I guess you're right, Tommy, " Wilson yielded.

Following mess hall, our outfit met SFC Vogan in front of our encampment, and he proceeded to outline our daily routine for the next three weeks.

When chow is over, we will participate in a half-hour of calisthenics. From 0830 until 1200. This routine involves training in the following areas:

- Target range practice
- Extended order drill
- Basics of scouting
- Laison procedures
- Weapon instruction (rifle, pistol, bayonet, grenade)
- Essentials of signaling

The company will break for lunch in the mess hall from 1200 to 1300 hours. In the afternoon, there is training in advanced guard duty and outpost duty. For the remainder of the day, we will pull guard duty at various positions along the border. Horse-drawn wagons and the few motorized trucks we have will transport us to some outlying areas.

From a drilling standpoint, we quickly learned what it was like to march with a nine-pound Springfield rifle and be capable of moving it from one shoulder to another in a fluid motion.

Bandoliers containing rifle ammo in five-round clips also hang around our waists. They are attached to a separate web belt.

    *   *10 NOTE: A bandolier is a specialized belt capable of holding special equipment such as rifle cartridges, hand grenades, etc.*

Also dangling from this belt is a bayonet and sheath, a first aid pouch, canteen with cover, and a machete with scabbard. Most NCOs even tote a heavy Colt .45 pistol.

Our previous training did not include marching and going on extended hikes with a backpack. This home-away-from-home usually is outfitted with the following: a can of bacon, a can of condiments, a mess kit with a spoon and knife, one blanket, a water-repellent poncho, a cake of soap, two pair of socks, extra drawers, a towel, toothbrush, a spare undershirt, rifle-cleaning kit, and a housewife kit.

    *   *11 NOTE: A housewife kit generally consisted of the following: needle, thread, extra buttons, indelible pencil, a few postcards, and supplies for making smokes (cigarettes).*

For the duration of that first week, the routine was an exercise in improvisation. Days of sweltering heat in the neighborhood of 110 to 120 degrees also resulted in several passing summer rainstorms.

The approaching disturbances often issued a warning to us in the form of unrelenting gusts of wind and violent sand storms.

When the resulting downpours ensued, the tent cities were awash with pop-up rivers in the unpaved streets. Despite the weather, infantry patrols remained on duty slogging through the mud and mesquite. The filling of sandbags was another chore that was handed out to some units when time permitted.

During the evening downtimes, the men resorted to their typical gambling games such as playing cards, shooting craps, and tossing pennies. Surprisingly, most of these games operated without incident, and the MPs were rarely called upon to settle disputes or break-up fights.

As a result of sheer boredom, a group of guys often tossed one of the fellows back and forth with blankets. The act would require the use of two blankets and the action of four men.

Our entire sector was awakened in the early hours of Saturday morning by the sounds of explosions, ensuing screams, and the commotion of men running in different directions.

The disturbance began at 0300 when several loud bangs shattered the otherwise tranquil darkness.

The noise seemed to come from a tent about 30 yards from our position.

When officers and MPs arrived on the scene, they found Pvt. Clarence Becker, of the 103rd Ammunition Train, Company B, on the ground next to his cot in an apparent daze.

After interviewing the others who bunked in the same shelter, those in charge of the investigation determined that two guys crept in and planted a couple of lit fireworks under Becker's bunk.

Within 30 minutes, the MPs had everything under control and all that could went back to sleep. Saturday morning, however, the higher-ups did not sweep the matter under the rug. The Regimental Commander, Col. Hamilton D. Turner, ordered a full assembly of the troops on the camp's main street.

He addressed the formation, saying, "The military police will carry out a full investigation, and those responsible for today's early morning disturbance will be punished."

Col. Turner also made a plea, "The military code requires anyone with information regarding this incident to come forward."

Sunday, I found myself out of sorts with my schedule, and by the time I reached the mess hall for breakfast, I was unable to join my regular tablemates.

I found an open seat next to another guy who was already midway through his morning meal. He was sipping on his coffee and finishing the last of his toast bread.

Naturally, I struck up a conversation with the fellow and soon learned that he was one of May's early arrivals. He introduced himself as just plain Sam.

"So, you're one of the new guys!" the man stated matter of factly.

"Yeah, that's right," I answered. "We've been here about a week."

"Anybody show you the ropes, yet?" he asked me.

"Not really," was my reply.

"Well, the first thing you want to do in the morning," he explained, "is bang the heels of your boots on the ground and then turn them over and give them another good whack. Scorpions are always looking for a dark, cool, quiet place to spend the night.

The first time you run into one of them critters, you'll know it," he warned.

Sam continued his diatribe, "Don't forget to clean and polish those boots. The NCOs are always on the look-out to find ways to pile extra duty on unsuspecting guys."

"That's good to know," I said appreciatively.

"On the subject of KP (kitchen patrol), get to know the cooks over in the mess hall. They can give you a heads up on the menu a few days ahead," he explained, "and you can volunteer to take an assignment before it's assigned. That way, you don't work as hard," he confided.

"I've only been here a few months," Sam noted, "but it doesn't take long to figure out the system. There's always a system. Don't let them fool ya!"

"Anything else I should know about?" I figured I'd ask as long as he was handing out free advice. Why not pick his brain?

The veteran gave me some additional pointers to keep my area in tip-top shape for inspections and warned me about which places to avoid if I did venture into El Paso for some fun.

"If you're not used to tequila," he stated in his final warning, "you're better off passing on the stuff. It will mess you up fast."

He elaborated his point, saying, "When I first got here, I wandered into *Bebida del Diablo.* There's a reason they call the place, *Drink of the Devil.*

"After seven beers and seven shots of tequila, the barkeep told me if I drank one more, he would give me a free sombrero. I did and found myself passed out in the doorway several hours later," he remarked.

"Take my advice, my friend, pass on the tequila and *Bebida del Diablo!*" He finished his unmistakable warning.

I politely thanked the fellow soldier for his sound advice. He tipped his hat, got up from the table with his tray in hand, and left.

As I finished up my breakfast, I allowed the stranger's counsel to sink in, and I was determined not to allow what he said to fall on deaf ears.

On Monday, July 10, the regiment witnessed a special cavalry drill and inspiring talk on the regiment's esprit-de-corps and our commanding officer, Col. Turner.

* *12 NOTE: The term esprit-de-corps is French, and it literally means "the spirit of the body," with the body in this case meaning "group." Originally, esprit de corps was a description of the morale of military troops. It should be pronounced with a hint of a French accent: "Espree de core."*

On the asphalt street in front of the Regimental Headquarters, Major George T. Langhorne began the presentation with a squadron of his own Eighth US Cavalry.

With hundreds of enthusiastic troops looking on, the imposing Langhorne sat tall in the saddle while wearing his wide-brimmed hat, Teddy Roosevelt-style. He garnered everyone's attention and spared nothing in the execution of this sophisticated exercise.

The squadron began the ceremony by performing an intricate timing drill at full gallop on their chargers. At the conclusion of the exercise, Col. Langhorne had his mount stop poignantly in front of the American flag floating in the breeze.

The colonel saluted the Star-Spangled Banner and rode to the center of the circle that was formed by his squadron. Then, he delivered his most inspiring speech. The 10-minute address was an attempt to rally the troops of the regiment behind the newly appointed Col. Turner.

His discourse resonated favorably with the men, and they responded by cheering most thunderously.

By Tuesday, rumors were beginning to circulate regarding the fireworks prank. The news coming out of the 103rd was that the two guys behind the caper were Ray Crawford and Jimmy O'Donnell. They were also members of B Company, but their bunks were located elsewhere.

The pair supposedly went into El Paso and got smashed on tequila and beer at one of the local cantinas. O'Donnell allegedly bartered for the fireworks earlier with a Chinaman working on the local railroad. When they returned from a night of drinking, they conceived the scheme to scare the wits out of Becker.

Within 24 hours, details of the incident began to get back to the authorities. The MPs brought Crawford and O'Donnell in for questioning.

Both men went before Col. Turner. SFC Ralph Bowman, the NCO for B Company, was also summoned by the colonel.

The commanding officer looked at the evidence, heard the testimony, and then made the following decision.

"Sgt. Bowman," the colonel began, "first of all, these two soldiers will be assigned extra duty for the next two weeks, KP, Latrine Duty, etc."

"Secondly, Sergeant, you are to give them the Jack and Jill treatment," he added.

"Jack and Jill treatment, sir?" Crawford asked.

"Yes," the colonel explained to the pair, "Tomorrow at 1200 hours, you will be escorted by Sgt. Bowman to the base of Mount Franklin. With full packs on your back, each of you will take turns carrying two buckets of water up the summit. It's about 100 yards, and you will complete the task 50 times. Should you spill any of the water, Sgt. Bowman will gladly refill your bucket, and you may start over," he concluded.

The men were dismissed. As they left the colonel's office, the perpetrators couldn't decide if they had gotten off easy or if they were the victims of some cruel punishment. Either way, there would be no visits to El Paso for a while, and fireworks would be reserved for Independence Day and New Year celebrations.

By July 25th, most of the newly created camp was set up. The expanse of tents, wagons, and equipment had doubled in size since we arrived a few weeks ago. Quarters for the officers were upgraded to actual barracks, while stables and mess shacks replaced their temporary counterparts. The desert city appeared to make the Franklin Mountains even less notable.

During this construction period, the men built a movie theater, and when it was completed, volunteers conducted minstrel shows and talent contests.

Sunday Mass's celebration was a regular occurrence when the small chapel went up next to the movie house. Sometimes, an army chaplain conducted the service, while other circumstances often required that one of the local padres come over from El Paso.

One of the improvements made to our quarters was the placement of wooden floors in our tents. However, the ground was extremely hard, and it was almost impossible to drive the stakes back into the ground.

No alcohol was permitted in camp, but some of the locals set up make-shift cantinas and booths selling their wares on the installation's edge.

As we moved into August, food supplies were running low. Nearly every meal consisted of beans supplemented by some sort of small ration of meat.

Members of the Apache tribe that were assigned to the US Scouts for the expedition often passed through the area. The troop spent a great deal of time hunting while they were out on patrol. Whenever they had surplus meat from their hunts, they would share it with our cooks.

During this period of un-Godly heat, the rocks in the desert were radiators of heat. Many of our men fainted from the extreme temperatures when we were on one of our typical six to seven-mile marches. During the nights, however, it was downright cold. Many of the guys complained that the one standard- issue blanket was not enough to keep warm. Those types of items were in short supply, given the sheer number of troops bivouacked in this region.

We relied on mule-driven wagons and pack trains to deliver supplies to the outlying areas with no train service available.

Each wagon was drawn by four mules and could haul three thousand pounds of cargo over flat terrain. As you can imagine, the territory did not always cooperate.

Not surprisingly, one day in the mess hall, I chatted with one of the guys in a machine gun battalion. He was attached to another regiment.

"How are you guys making out?" the soldier asked.

"Not bad, and you?" I replied, "By the way, the guys call me Tommy," I said, introducing myself.

"Phil. Phil Marcus," he responded.

"I'm with a machine gun outfit. We're from out near Pittsburgh," he clarified. "and you?" he queried. "Infantry, Philly," was my response.

"Do you know that we don't even have machine guns?" he informed me most astoundedly. "They gave us wooden ones to drill with... unbelievable!" He exclaimed.

"Wow, that's rough," I concurred. "How do they expect you to learn anything from that?" I agreed.

Despite all the construction activity and other duties that were designed to keep us occupied, boredom among the troops was on the rise. General John T. "Black Jack" Pershing, commander of the entire operation, issued a new order, fearing increased gambling activities and alcohol consumption.

In addition to Camp Stewart's other physical improvements, Gen. Pershing ordered the construction of a boxing ring for the men.

"Where is Joe Keegan when you need him?" I wondered to myself.

Under Pershing's direction, the engineers cleared an area in the open range for sports events such as baseball and football.

It took no time at all for these new improvements to be put to use. Most outfits had no trouble recruiting their own guys to compete against other companies.

The top two fighters from our regiment were Frank Muezenberger from Supply Company and Danny Deegan from Company B.

Muezenberger was a well-built young lad from the Kingsessing section of Philadelphia. Word has it that he gained some boxing experience at the YMCA (Young Men's Christian Association).

The tough-looking Irishman, Deegan, was fearless. If he gave you the stare, you had better step aside. Both of the chaps fit into the middleweight class.

Deegan came down with the mumps and was scratched from the card. Wilmont P. Rapine replaced him.

There must have been five hundred on-hand all crowded around that boxing ring when Muezenberger, wearing olive green trunks, took on Rapine of Headquarters Company. His trunks were white.

The two were evenly matched in terms of height, weight, and reach. The competition would be an amateur bout, purely for entertainment purposes. The fighters would compete in five three-minute rounds with a two-minute break in-between. It went without saying that the gambling elements were out in full force, as well.

Rapine came out swinging from the outset while Muezenberger played it cool. He spent the first few rounds sizing up his opponent.

Each man threw their fair share of punches, but most of the action was relegated to jabs, some cross punches, and a handful of rare combinations.

In the first few rounds, it appeared as though the combatants were relatively evenly matched. In the fourth round, however, Rapine seemed to be making his move. The Norristown native hit Muezenberger with a flurry of punches before landing a solid right hook to his opponent's jaw.

Muezenberger was beginning to sway a little, and he shook his head momentarily to come out of the stupor.

Rapine followed with another burst of punches, but this time Muezenberger remained unfazed. He evaded another potential deadly blow from Rapine before countering with his own left hook.

The 159-pound fighter went down in a heap, and Muezenberger just stood there as the referee issued the count. It was our outfit's first win in the ring.

Several other companies took advantage of the ring over the ensuing days. Finally, it was time for another match-up between two guys from our infantry regiment.

There was still plenty of daylight at the 1900 starting time. Although the temperature remained around 85 degrees, the crowd was elbow to elbow around the boxing arena.

In one corner was Connie Dougherty, a wagoneer from Headquarters Company. The Philly boy weighed in at 169 pounds, very close to the light-heavyweight class. The blonde-haired lad was wearing blue trunks.

His challenger for this match was a Clinton, Iowa farm boy, Carlton Williams, of D company. Although Williams, a southpaw (left-handed), was slightly shorter than Doughtery, it seemed like he may have had a couple of pounds over his opponent. His trunks were bright yellow.

Round one got off to a slow start. Both fighters danced around the ring and seemingly played cat and mouse. The purpose of this feeling out period was to establish a strategy against the other opponent.

The two boxers exchanged a few short flurries of punches. Doughtery landed a cross punch and a combination before Williams landed a sucker punch to Doughtery's gut when he left himself exposed.

Neither fighter had the advantage when the bell sounded, ending round one.

In round two, Doughtery managed to block several punches the southpaw directed at his face. Frustration began to show from both men.

The referee had to stop the action several times when the combatants were guilty of throwing illegal blows.

First, Williams landed a kidney punch that required a quick warning from the referee. Not to be outdone, Doughtery tried to sneak in a rabbit punch to the back of Williams' head. The referee signaled that this would not be tolerated, either.

Since this was the first bout for each of the men, both fighters were tired and clinching or holding onto each other too much, so the referee told them to "break."

In rounds three and four, the crowd grew immensely louder as both men rallied. Initially, Doughtery brought on a barrage of blows. Opening with several jabs, then following with a combination. His best combination proved to be a left jab followed by a right cross and finishing with a left hook.

He quickly followed that assault with another hook and a deadly uppercut. The farm boy appeared in trouble as he languished near the ropes. Doughtery resembled a shark who had smelled blood. Sensing he may be winning the battle, he was determined to keep the punches coming. Williams, meanwhile, stood by the ropes with his gloves up. He did his best to resist the blows as they pummeled his body.

Close to exhaustion, Williams attempted to wrap Doughtery up with his arms to buy some time. After a warning was issued to the struggling fighter for holding, the bell rang to signal the end of the round.

Nobody was leaving the arena when the bell clanged to begin the fifth and final round.

Williams evidently regained his composure and came out on the offensive to open the round. The lefty threw several jabs with his right and followed those with numerous power punches with the left.

With Williams issuing a relentless attack, Doughtery did his best to evade those punches.

The experienced fighter tried a move called *slipping.* He turned his body slightly from the hips to let a punch "slip" past.

Next, Doughtery tried a tactic called *swaying.* In this instance, he sought to dodge blows to the head by swaying backward.

His evasive moves were an attempt to buy himself some time, regain some composure, and mount his own counter-attack.

However, no matter what he tried, it was apparent that he was having difficulty adjusting to the left- hander's unorthodox style. Williams continued to come after him until the two were tied up in the corner of the ring.

After the referee broke them apart, Dougherty looked for an opening. Without giving Williams a chance to establish his footing, the city boy took on the farm boy with his own barrage of blows.

Instead of sticking to sound, conventional boxing techniques, he relied solely on his instincts and unleashed a salvo of unorthodox punch combinations of his own. Doughtery used everything in his bag of tricks in order to regain the advantage, and it seemed to be working.

You could see it on his face and read it in his body language that Williams was struggling. Although he was holding his arms up to guard his face, his legs were growing rubbery.

Doughtery managed to slip in a hook, and the stunned boxer went down to his knees.

The referee began the count, but Williams somehow managed to right himself by standing back up, and the fight continued.

Although the match was outdoors, the noise of the crowd grew deafening. Sensing this bout was nearing its conclusion one way or another, the troops went utterly wild.

Williams continued to evade his opponent's assault, but Doughtery was determined to finish him off before the bell.

The Philly fighter teased the Iowa lad with a series of jabs but selected just the right moment to unleash his deadly blow, an uppercut to the jaw.

The southpaw fell to the canvas like a 50-pound bag of potatoes, and there was no doubt that this bout was over.

All the day's complaints about lousy food and 100-degree weather vanished when the guys walked back to their individual campsites bragging about the greatest boxing match they had ever seen in their lives. Perhaps, General Pershing knew what he was doing when he ordered the engineers to build this 16- foot by 16-foot square arena.

Col. Hamilton D. Turner
Image Source: The 28th Division in World War 1

US Army armored military vehicle, El Paso, Tx
Image Source: Author's Photo

On the Mexican border
Image Source: The 28th Division in World War 1

"THE BALLGAME"

Baseball games between outfits at camp
Image Source: George Grantham Bain Collection

CHAPTER 11

"The Ballgame"

When September 1916 arrived, it became clear that we were being re-organized into an artillery corps. They informed us that we would be part of the Second Field Artillery Regiment of the Pennsylvania National Guard. Later, we received the official designation of the 108th Field Artillery Battalion.

The battalion consisted of Headquarters Company, Supply Company, Sanitary Detachment, Veterinary Detachment, and Batteries A, B, C, D, E, and F.

In the artillery batteries, the men were initially equipped with 4.7-inch howitzers. These guns had an effective firing range of 6,600 yards and a maximum range of 7,300 yards.

Although we only received a partial shipment of the pieces, the entire regiment went out to Mount Franklin to drill on the plains. Originally, the troops merely practiced their formations with horses, caissons, and guns, but target practice would follow.

 * 13 NOTE: A Caisson is a two-wheeled horse-drawn wooden box used primarily to transport ammunition.*

Due to a shortage of these weapons, the battalion also used 2.95-inch Vickers-Maxim Mountain Guns. These howitzers, though, only had a maximum effective range of 500 yards. They required four mules to haul one gun, unassembled. Pulling a wagon load of ammo for these field pieces required six additional mules. The weapons, though, could fire eight rounds per minute with a good crew.

In this re-organization, my assignment was with the Sanitary Detachment unit. Fortunately, all of the guys in my guard unit transferred with me.

Technically, we were part of the medical branch of the army, but we were not medics. The main focus of our duties would be in the areas of infection, sanitation practices, and preventive medicine. We would receive formal schooling at our next stop, Camp Hancock, GA. In the meantime, our orders were to report to the field hospital and gain some on-the-job training.

Camp Stewart actually had two field hospitals, one at each end of the installation.

They were designated as No. 1 in the east end of camp and No. 2 in the west. There was an aid station in the center. Both of these portable hospitals contained about 40 beds.

*   *14 NOTE: Typically, a field hospital had a staff of about 30 to 35: a captain or major, four medical officers, three general surgeons, 25 enlisted men including two surgical and eleven medical technicians, and four nurses. All of the unit's equipment, medical and surgical supplies, and rations could weigh no more that what 29 men could personally transport.*

Captain Newhart was the CO on duty when we reported to Field Hospital No. 1. His instructions were to divide us into four groups, and each group would report to one of the nurses on duty. He stated that the nurse would assign us to shadow various personnel in the unit. Our mission at this point was one of observation.

In addition to myself, our group consisted of Bernie Halliday, Irvin Schweppenheiser, and Barney Roth. Our trainer was Medical Technician, Jacob Vanderslice of Phoenixville, PA.

The thirty-something-year-old man was of average build. He gave us a thorough tour of the facility and explained general operations and procedures.

"As you can imagine," he began, "most of the cases we get here are mild illnesses and wounds.

"Insect bites, such as scorpions," he went on, "and secondary injuries from sprained ankles and broken arms to contusions and minor cuts.

"From out on the range, we may get a soldier in here who was injured during the recoil of his weapon, or we may need to treat an artilleryman who received a severe burn from mishandling a hot shell casing," he further clarified.

"As I said," Vanderslice reiterated, "you never know what you're going to see, but most of it is minor and manageable. Any questions?"

"What's the worst case you've seen since you've been here?" Schweppenheiser asked.

"The worst," he said, pausing for a moment, "it's probably a toss-up between the unlucky guy who got kicked in the head by a mule or the soldier that got sacked by four of his buddies in a crap game that went sour," he recalled with a slight chuckle.

It was evidently a quiet afternoon. Our trainer took us through the ward, and we chatted with a couple guys. One was recuperating from a gout case, and the other unfortunate chap was the victim of a rattlesnake bite.

At 1600 hours, we were told to grab some early chow and call it a day. The nurse ordered us to report to the hospital the following day by 0800.

Like the brand-new boxing arena that quickly became popular with the men, the athletic fields were getting put to good use.

Most evenings and weekend afternoons, pick-up baseball games were going on. Football was not nearly as popular as baseball. Occasionally you would see a handful of men tossing around a football, but baseball was king.

A half-dozen of the fellows took it upon themselves to build a backstop behind home plate. A quantity of scrap wood was discovered, and it was suitable to assemble a bench for each team to sit upon.

Before you could blink an eye, there were dozens of teams being formed. My unit, the 108th Field Artillery, enlisted players from the Philadelphia area primarily. We called ourselves the Philly Quakers.

Although I made several attempts to sit out this endeavor, I was goated into joining the team as a fill-in. Should I be needed, my position would be first base.

Several of my pals were also on the squad, including Jim Rafferty, Roy Wilson, Al Gray, Bernie Halliday, and the Haeberle brothers, Harry and Billy.

Also from the 108th were: Edwin Ferguson, Carl Knauer, and Ben Short, all of Headquarters Company. Add to the roster Clarence Dunlap and Art Kitson of Battery B., Joe Polensky, and Ray Slater were both Battery C members.

Our first game was against the 103rd Ammunition Train. Most of the guys in this unit were from the Pennsylvania Coal Regions area, mainly Shamokin. The team monicker was the Shamokin Gray Legs.

Their roster was as follows: Paul Fegley, Harry Warfield, Charlie Berry, Daniel Kehler, Donald Reid, and Bill Ryan.

Also playing for the Shamokin Gray Legs were: John Taby, Neveille Wilson, Harrison Witmer, Peter Milchalavage, Charlie Erdman, David Brown, John Yost, and James Kistler.

There was virtually no equipment provided to the troops. The supply master managed to secure a box of baseballs and about a dozen bats.

Since we had no gloves or other protective equipment, the games were limited to five innings each. The men fashioned bases from materials they could scrounge up around camp. "Tubby" Bleakmeyer, a cook from the mess hall, served as the lone umpire. He was also in charge of supplying each squad with a large pail of water and ladles for drinking.

After flipping a coin, it was determined that the Gray Legs of Shamokin would be the visiting team, and we would bat in the bottom half of the inning as the home club.

It was a Sunday afternoon without a cloud to be seen. Although the sky was a brilliant, piercing shade of blue, the unimpeded sunshine would undoubtedly be a factor. The temperature felt like it was about 83 degrees. At game time, the air was still, meaning that we wouldn't have to contend with dust blowing around the field from the outset.

About one hundred curious men had gathered around the ballfield, hoping to witness an entertaining contest. There was little doubt that gambling was also on many of their minds.

Billy Haeberle would be on the mound, while his brother, Harry, was the catcher behind the plate.

Not an easy job without a glove or padding. Harry also designated himself as the team manager.

Filling out the remaining positions on the field were: Gray at first base, Rafferty at second, Wilson at shortstop, and Slater on the hot corner at third. This was another tough spot to play without the protection of a leather mitt.

Playing the three outfield positions were: Halliday in right, Dunlap in center, and Polensky in left. The Gray Legs sent Charlie Berry up to bat in the lead-off position.

Somebody started the rumor that Berry played two years of minor league ball with the Langford Red Hats in Iowa.

Billy's first two pitches were off the mark, and Berry took both for balls. The count was 2-0. Harry gave his brother a sign on the mound, and his next pitch was over for a strike.

With the count 2-1, Haeberle went into an unorthodox wind-up and unleashed a breaking pitch that damn near beaned the batter in the head.

The batsman and the hurler exchanged words immediately, but the ump ran out to settle things down quickly.

It appeared that both the cat and the mouse composed themselves, and each player was focused on the next pitch. Haeberle chucked it right down the middle. Berry reached back and smacked it over Dunlap's head in centerfield. Initially, we thought that Dunlap lost the ball in the sun, but as the play unfolded, it was clear that Berry hit the ball squarely, and it was a case of good hitting on his part.

The Gray Legs' slugger rounded those makeshift bases and scored the game's first run with an inside-the-park home run.

It was evident from the start, with this being the first game ever at Camp Stewart, combined with the lack of proper equipment, that the contest would be a high-scoring sloppy affair.

The visitors scored seven more runs in the first frame before Haeberle struck out Charlie Erdman for the final out. We were down 8-0.

Ray Slater, our third baseman, was said to be a fast runner, and he led off for the home team. Joe Polensky mentioned to me that Slater was a stand-out ballplayer in high school.

Nevielle Wilson, a lefty, was pitching for the Gray Legs. After completing a few warm-up tosses, he gave the umpire a sign that he was ready to go.

Slater sat on the first offering. It was a called strike one, but then, Wilson hurled a nice fat pitch that Slater was able to hit. The ball squirted between the first and second basemen for a single.

Jim Rafferty followed at the plate and ran the count to 2-2. Slater took off for second and stole the base easily.

Wilson was slightly rattled, and his next pitch was way outside for ball three. Working without a mitt, the catcher had to knock the ball to the ground when he extended his reach. As the ball rolled away in the dust, Slater moved to third.

With the count at 3-2, Rafferty smacked Wilson's next pitch directly over second base. Slater scampered home untouched, while Rafferty rolled into second base because the centerfielder had trouble handling the ball. The Quakers were trailing 8-1 with nobody out.

Similarly, as the Gray Legs were able to take advantage of the playing conditions, the Quakers bounced back with five additional runs in the inning. The Haeberle brothers each chipped in a hit, as did Wilson, Halliday, and Polensky. The visitors maintained an 8-6 lead.

It was a see-saw battle for the next three innings. Both teams seemed to score at will, and the lead changed several times.

However, when the game went to the fifth and final inning, the Gray Legs were on top by a score of 17-16. An occasional burst of wind would kick up some dust in the infield, but this didn't significantly affect the play.

Art Kitson replaced Billy Haeberle on the mound, and it was his job to hold the visitors in check so we could mount a comeback in the end.

Charlie Berry, Pete Michalavage, and Harrison Witmer all tagged Kitson for hits in the top of the fifth.

The Gray Legs increased their lead to 18-16 and had men on first and third with nobody out.

Kitson followed that disaster by hitting Paul Fegley with a pitch on the arm and walking Harry Warfield on four straight balls. Haeberle trotted out to the mound to settle him down.

"Hang in there, Art," Harry began the conversation.

"We're still only down by three runs, and anybody can score in bunches on a day like today," he added assuredly.

"Got it?" He asked Kitson.

The pitcher nodded affirmatively, and Haeberle ran back to his position behind the plate. The umpire gave the signal to resume play.

The score was now 19-16, but the visitors still had the bases loaded. There were no outs.

Finally, Kitson struck out Charlie Erdman for the second time in the game. Next, the Gray Legs sent John Yost up to bat. The bases remained loaded with only one out.

The Quaker hurler mixed up his pitches and managed to get ahead in the count, 0-2. You could see Kitson sweating even from the bench as if it were the World Series's final game.

He got the signal from Haeberle and checked the runners to make sure they were not going. Kitson stopped and took a deep breath. You could see his chest rise and fall as he let out a huge sigh.

The pitch was on its way, and Yost hit a soft liner to Slater down at third base. Without a glove, the fielder managed to trap the ball on his chest with his arms. Slater took two steps towards the bag and got Witmer on the double play. The Quakers survived the inning but needed three runs to tie the game and four to win.

While most of the team gave Slater a round of cheers and whistles for his masterful play in the field, Harry Haeberle couldn't resist making one of his patented snied remarks.

"Who do you think you are out there, Eddie Collins?" Haeberle asked of Slater. "No!" Slater came back.

"No?" Haeberle returned.

"No!" the third baseman insisted.

"No?" The manager repeated unrelentingly.

"No!" Slater yelled emphatically.

"Then, who the hell do you think you are making a play like that?" Haeberle asked while laughing out loud.

"Frank Home Run Baker," Slater quipped with a broad smile on his face. "Collins is a second baseman, Baker played third for the A's," he answered matter-of-factly.

The exchange between the two players would prove to be typical team banter during most of our games, but it was almost always initiated by Haeberle.

*   15 NOTE: Eddie Collins and Frank Home Run Baker were Hall of Fame player for Connie Mack's Philadelphia Athletics. The pair often led the American League in several offensive categories.*

With John Taby, now pitching for the visitors, Joe Polensky led off the bottom of the fifth inning with a single to right. Harry Haeberle called on me up to pinch-hit for Gray.

"Schalata! Get up there and bat for Gray," he yelled from the other end of the bench.

"Me? Come on, Harry, I'm just supposed to be a fill-in on this team," I responded.

"You're on the team, and I need you to hit, Tommy. I'm playing a hunch. We're just trying to win a ballgame," he explained.

Reluctantly, I walked over to the pile of lumber on the dust-filled ground and selected a honey-colored ash bat. The bold markings on the barrel read Louisville Slugger, King of the Field - No 13. It felt comfortable to me. I was confident that it was the right length and weight.

Slowly I walked to the plate. After taking a couple practice swings, I turned to the ump and signaled that I was ready.

I tried to conceal my nervousness, but I'm not sure how successful I was in that endeavor.

Immediately, the guys began to cheer me on.

"Come on, Tommy, let's see you get things started, " I heard one of the guys yell.

"Yeah, let's go, chap! We could use a hit here," another cheered.

Taby threw the first couple of pitches, and I let them pass for balls.

However, the next pitch was right down the pike, and I took it for the first strike. A sudden calm came over me, and I decided to relax and make the best of the situation. After all, it was just a friendly game with the guys. Nothing was indeed on the line but our pride.

Fortunately, I avoided embarrassing myself by walking on five pitches. I casually trotted down to first base, trying to appear confident.

Since the home team was down by three runs with two men on and nobody out, Haeberle called on Edwin Ferguson. The six-foot-three-inch Philly guy was a giant of a man but not well-known for his athleticism.

The pinch-hitter flailed wildly at the first pitch missing by more than a foot. Taby's next throw was nearly in the dirt. Ferguson wisely held up on his swing. The catcher managed to block the ball, and neither Polensky nor I tried to advance.

Taby followed with some kind of trick pitch, and Ferguson went after it, missing once again by a mile. With the tension mounting, the Gray Legs hurler threw the 2-1 pitch towards the plate. Much to our surprise, Ferguson connected by hitting a ball down the third baseline. The umpire ruled the ball fair, and Polensky crossed the plate making the score 19-17. I had to stop at third, while Ferguson was on first with a long single. The big bull had power but absolutely no speed.

Slater batted next and hit a grounder to short. Ferguson was an easy out. I succeeded in scoring on the play. The score was now 19-18.

With one out, Slater on first, and Rafferty at the plate, the Quakers needed just one run to tie and two to notch the victory.

Taby was keeping an eye on Slater, who had stolen a base earlier in the game. The base-runner started to snatch second, but he attempted to go back to first. He got only about eight feet when he was picked off for out number two.

With our team down to its final out, we seemed to have lost our steam. Rafferty battled away, holding on to a 3-2 count. Taby kept tossing pitches, but Rafferty managed to foul them off to keep his at-bat alive.

Evidently, the Gray Legs' hurler grew impatient. He stepped off the mound several times. The visitors' pitcher even walked in a circle around it to gain his composure.

Rafferty, however, remained undaunted. He stepped up to the box and took a couple more swings to relieve his tension.

Both the pitcher and the batter were ready. Our guys began cheering wildly, hoping that Jim could keep the comeback going.

Taby completed his wind-up, and Rafferty was ready, but much to our dismay, he struck out to end the game.

The boys were down after the defeat, but considering the playing conditions and the fact that it was our first game, we were proud that we could hang in there until the end.

12

"VISIT TO EL PASO"

Downtown El Paso, Tx., near Camp Stewart.
Image Source: Unknown

CHAPTER 12

"Visit to El Paso"

Since most of us had been in Camp Stewart for about three or four months, we settled into the situation. The men were not only familiar with the layout of the installation, but our daily routines had become just that, routine!

The Third Pennsylvania Artillery, an outfit from Wilkes Barre, formerly the Ninth Pennsylvania Infantry, arrived by train in El Paso on September 30. As part of the reorganization, they now became part of the 109th Field Artillery.

Meals in the mess hall were a great place to exchange information between the outfits. The new troops told us that while they were issued their horses, guns, and caissons, most of them had never handled a horse in their lives.

Archie Cohen, a wagoneer from the 109th, stated, "We have to learn how to harness and handle these animals right after morning chow. It's a painful learning experience," he added.

"Cavalry troops are required to go one step further," he explained. "Their duties are to break the animals, then harness, saddle, ride, and love them. In very short order, they are expected to go out to the plains and learn how to walk, trot and gallop their mounts," he concluded.

As part of the reorganization process, the 103rd Ammunition Train now consists of 12 companies. Unlike most other battalions with alphabetical company designations, this unit's companies have numerical labels from one through twelve. Each company has 55 enlisted men, and new recruits are primarily young men who are familiar with automobiles, both as drivers and mechanics.

Although it began as a humble outpost, the border installation presently extends from Camp Stewart past El Paso and beyond Fort Bliss.

By October, the supply trains had caught up with the influx of troops. The arrival of rations and much-needed military equipment was keeping up with demand. The meals were improving, and the forces stationed here in El Paso commenced training with real guns and artillery pieces. A new YMCA (Young Men's Christian Association) building provided another recreation facility for the troops.

Throughout the entire summer, I never found the time to venture to El Paso. I was starting to believe that I was missing out on something.

One day while working in the field hospital, the captain came to me and stated that he needed a couple of volunteers to pull duty on Saturday afternoon. He explained that if Schweppenheiser and I stepped up, he would issue us a pass to go into town plus an extra afternoon off duty.

Later in the mess hall, I broached the subject with Irvin. Logic told me that the trip to the border town would be safer if I had an accomplice.

"What do you think, Doc? Do you want to make the trip with me?" I asked.

"I'm not sure, Tommy," he replied. "I hear there's a lot of bars, drinking, and rowdiness in the streets.

You know that's not a primary interest with me," he emphasized.

"No, Irv," I promised him, "we'll go in the afternoon. Check out the town. Maybe have a few beers, a bite to eat, and then head right back here," I said convincingly.

"It'll be fun. You'll see!" I ended.

"Okay," Irv finally gave in. "You set it up, and I'll go with you."

A short conversation with the mess sergeant and I had the whole matter arranged.

"I have a wagon going into town tomorrow to pick up supplies. You guys may have to ride in the back with some wooden crates and sacks of potatoes. Meet my guys here at 1200, and you can ride with them," he said.

"How long will they be in town?" I inquired. "About three hours," was his response.

"Perfect! See you then," I said of the arrangement.

On Friday, October 13, Doc and I met the wagoneer and his helper at the appointed hour, and we were on our way.

Most military equipment is dressed in a drab, olive green color, but this Studebaker wagon appeared to be more of a faded seafoam shade.

A canvas canopy, in a much paler tint of the same color, draped the frame overhead. In bold, black letters, the covering was clearly marked, "U.S. Army."

Pulled by a team of four mules, the wagon had two smaller wheels on the front to allow more play in the axles during turns. The larger rear wheels were designed to negotiate bad roads, especially under wet, muddy conditions.

The driver informed us that the vehicle was made from hickory and seasoned ash.

"We can haul 2,500 pounds of supplies or ammo with this wagon and this team," he bragged.

As we approached the top of a rise in the road, El Paso's municipality became visible in the distance. The town was more developed than I had expected. My vision was one of a small cluster of rudimentary shops and dwellings, but several significant structures that came into view quickly changed my opinion.

A closer look revealed that these buildings represented banks and hotels, as well as other commercial enterprises and industries. A business district with paved streets gave me the impression that this sleepy border town had quickly evolved into a small city.

The driver left us off at the majestic White House Department Store and Hotel McCoy. Located at 109 Pioneer Plaza, the six-story building is an architectural work of art. More specifically, we found ourselves at the corner of South Oregon & South Santa Fe Streets.

One final warning," the driver added, "be careful while you're in town. El Paso is 44 percent American and 52 percent Mexican. At least that's what they tell me. It seems that way to me," he concluded.

Doc and I tried to get the lay of the land by walking around this main business disctrict.

My first goal was to obtain a couple of newspapers. There were two in El Paso. *The El Paso Times* hit the streets in the morning, while *The El Paso Herald* was an afternoon edition. Since it was mid- October, I wanted to check on the status of the baseball World Series. Back issues of the newspaper would be required if I wanted to learn how the season ended for the two Philadelphia teams, the Phillies and the Athletics.

I stumbled upon the Rio Grand Cigar and News Stand on one of the city's busy corners. The man in the booth could provide me with yesterday's copy of *The Herald* and this morning's *Times*. I purchased one of each for a penny a piece. For back copies, I would have to go to the newspaper office on El Paso Street.

Once I found the newspaper office, the desk clerk suggested I buy a copy of the October 6 and 7 editions since the season ended on the fifth. It cost me another two cents.

The hub of the downtown's central region was around Second Street and San Francisco Avenue. A sampling of the establishments that we passed included: Kelly & Pollard Druggists, Elite Confectionery Co., El Paso Phonograph Co., and the American National Bank.

Other interesting business places were: A. N. Lombardi Co., Jewelry & Watch Repair; Gem Cigar Shop; El Paso Sunset Eating House; The Cactus Barber Shop, and Barela Marguerita Cafe.

I suggested to Irvin that we try the latter. Its appearance gave me the impression that it was a clean, well-run local business that not only served local cuisine but also had an outdoor seating area with tables, etc.

The weather was ideal. The temperature was a comfortable 80 degrees. The day was sunny and bright. A sizeable mature Cedar Elm tree provided us with a shady spot for lunch and furnished us with a cool breeze on occasion.

Just before the waitress arrived, I tried to assure Schweppenheiser that I spoke a little "Mex." "Where'd you learn that?" he asked.

"Just from the guys around camp," I stated.

Our server was a young, 20-year-old, unmistakably Mexican girl, and she was not only cute but very polite. She informed us that her name was "Eleena."

"Buenas tardes! Como puedo ayudarte?" She quickly asked if she could help us. "Two beers and a couple of menus, please," was my response.

The charming senorita returned with our beers and left. As the girl returned to the bar, she turned slightly towards us and flashed a warm smile.

Apparently, the two of us were looking a little perplexed as we studied the menu, and an elderly Mexican gentleman dropped by our table to lend a hand.

"You hombres look like you could use some help," he commented while leaning in between us."

"Si! Por favor!" I acknowledged.

"Steak is what you gringos need and want," he said with conviction.

"You," he said, placing his forefinger directly into my chest, "Carne Asada is what you want," he insisted.

"What's that?" I inquired.

"It is a delicious combination of spices added to strips of beef and served with rice, beans, grilled onions, and potatoes. It is Excelente!" he concluded.

"And for you," he said while turning to Irvin, "I recommend Arrachera steak. It is another of our favorite dishes here in the area."

He explained, "This special meat comes from the abdominal muscles of the cow. It's tenderized and marinated, making it as soft as butter. I guarantee it!" The old man said convincingly.

Going with the stranger's recommendations, we ordered each of the dishes.

"How do you think it's going so far, Doc?" I asked my friend to get a conversation started.

"Oh, as I expected," he replied.

"It's been an adjustment, but thus far, it's nothing that I haven't been able to handle," he added.

"Me, too!" I concurred.

"The weather is hot every day, but it's not that stinking, unbearable humid stuff we're used to in the city," I noted.

"I know what you mean, there," Schweppenheiser agreed.

Just then, another soldier walked up and interrupted our meal. "Hey! Youse guys with the 108th?" He asked loudly.

"Yeah! What's up?" I came back.

"Well, I'm with the 109th, and we're going to kick your guys' asses when we play ball against you." He roared.

"Listen, pal. That's all well and good. You can boast all you want about how good you guys are, but we don't care right now. We're here to have a little lunch and a few beers. Why don't you be on your way?" I recommended.

"Are you going to chicken out on me," he asked, obviously looking to pick a fight.

"No!" Schweppenheiser shot back.

"You see those two MPs standing across the street in front of the cigar store?" Irvin asked while pointing to the other side of Seventh Street.

"What about them?" the bully questioned.

"Well," Schweppenheiser responded, "the tall guy is my brother-in-law, and all I have to do is take off my hat and wave, and he'll be over here in a flash!"

On that note, the loudmouth waved his arms in disgust, shook his head, and stormed off. Crises averted.

"Where did you come up with that line?" I asked Doc in amazement.

"Oh, I'm generally the quiet type, but I can surprise you once in a while," he replied. "Sometimes, I even surprise myself," he stated while taking a sip of his beer.

"How's your food?" I questioned him.

"Not bad!" He acknowledged. "How about yours?" Irvin asked, looking for my opinion.

"It is a little on the spicy side, but the flavor is truly amazing," was my response.

When we finished our meals, Eleena came to check on us and suggested some coffee and dessert.

We both agreed and asked her to bring us something that she thought we might enjoy.

Our server returned quickly with a tray containing two cups of coffee and two plates of some sort of cake.

"This, fellows," she began, "is Pastel de elote!"

"It looks excellent, Irvin commented, "what is it, cake or bread?" he asked her.

As she leaned over the table to place the items in front of us, she explained, "It is not really cake nor bread. This dessert is a blend of cake and pudding.

"It is a traditional dish here in our area, and this is very much like my momma used to make," the woman continued.

"She always used a combination of the juiciest corn and condensed milk. This mixture gives it an almost custard-like texture and density." the server concluded.

"I hope you both enjoy it," she commented while flashing another one of her smiles.

Schweppenheiser dug right into the dessert while I casually sipped my coffee and turned one of the newspapers directly to the sports section to catch up on the latest news.

"Damn!" I exclaimed as I studied the newspaper. "What, Tommy? What's up?" Irvin questioned.

"Look at this headline: Red Sox down Brooklyn Robins, 4 games to 1, Capture second straight series," I read aloud.

"Last season, they beat the Phillies, 4-1, and this year they did the same to Brooklyn," I commented while shaking my head in disbelief.

"Listen to this," I said while trying to maintain Irvin's attention, "With Boston leading by a score of 4- 1, Casey Stengel singled to lead off the Brooklyn ninth, but Ernie Shore, the pitcher, buckled down and didn't let the ball out of the infield. He struck out Wheat and got Cutshaw to ground out to second, forcing Stengel. Mowrey was up.

"While the band was playing 'This Is the End of a Perfect Day,' Shore induced Mowrey to hit a pop fly to Everett Scott at short for the third and final out," I continued to read from the newspaper account.

"Shore, who pitched the entire nine innings, walked off the mound triumphant as the Red Sox won the game, 4-1, and captured their fourth world championship," the description closed.

"I didn't realize this," I said to Irvin when I read one of the game's side-bars.

"What's that?" Schweppenheiser asked.

"Ernie Shore's contract was purchased by the Red Sox on July 9, 1914, the same day the Red Sox bought Babe Ruth," I quoted from the story.

"According to the newspaper," I continued, "the clincher saw the biggest crowd of the series, and the game was held at Braves Field in Boston because the ballpark had a larger capacity than Fenway.

"It also states that it was a very cold Columbus Day for a baseball game," I noted.

Doc and I agreed that our dessert was a nice treat. We finished our coffee, and we were on our way. Because it was about 30 to 40 minutes until we had to meet the supply wagon's crew, we explored the business district.

My first stop was across the street at the cigar shop. I wanted to pick up a couple of smokes to take back to camp with me. There was also a stationary store and the end of the street where I could purchase some writing paper. Writing a few letters to the folks at home was also a priority.

At the agreed-upon time, we met the guys at the wagon, and we were soon on our way back to camp. Just as we were warned, the vehicle was packed with wooden crates and numerous sacks of supplies. The unmistakable smell of fresh meat was also evident.

Saturday, Irv and I worked our shift at the Field Hospital. The nurse on duty asked us just to make the rounds with the patients. Our instructions were to check on them to be sure they were comfortable.

Should anyone complain that they were having any discomfort or if we observed anything out of the ordinary, we would report it to her immediately. Otherwise, we were free to spend some time chatting with the fellows to lift their spirits.

Most of the afternoon passed without incident. At approximately 1500 hours, one of the guys broke the ward's silence with some loud yelling and moaning. Upon closer examination, we found the poor guy in a state of delirium.

Doc went to get the nurse while I tried to calm him down as best I could. The patient in question was Charlie Baver of headquarters company. He was admitted for influenza-like symptoms.

The nurse took his temperature and revealed that his fever had reached 103 degrees. Irv and I were told to summon the doctor on duty and make ourselves busy elsewhere. By the time our shift was over, the medical staff had appeared to have the matter under control.

On Sunday morning at 0900 hours, nearly 100 of us crowded into the tiny camp chapel. The ringing of church bells broke the silence of an otherwise peaceful morning. This solemn signal meant that Padre Pérez was about to begin Mass.

About a quarter of a mile down the road, Sgt. Howard Merkle of Supply Company was still under the covers in his bunk when he heard a familiar whine in the distance.

He sat up and recognized the sound immediately. The noise was unmistakable. There was no doubt in his mind that roaring down the dusty road at a very high rate of speed was a 1910 Indian Roadster.

You see, Merkle was a mechanic for four years at the Hendee Manufacturing Company in Springfield, Massachusetts, where Indian motorcycles were produced.

The soldier thought to himself, "It's not the Powerplus V-twin flathead they're putting out today, but the sound of the bike's engine combined with its two-speed transmission is distinct."

As the commotion drew closer, Merkle could visualize the motorcycle's distinguished deep red paint scheme that left no doubt that it was an Indian.

The vehicle roared past his tent, and he could quickly tell that the cyclist had spun around the corner. He imagined the rear wheel fish-tailing as the motorcyclist made an effort to maintain control.

From the corner, the rider sped up Grant Street to the church.

He drove the bike up the two steps of the white clapboard building. The front doors burst open from the impact of the motorcycle. The driver, who was obviously intoxicated, stopped his vehicle at the back of the chapel and hollered, "Well, Padre! Did I make it here in time for service?"

The men inside were utterly startled. Several ran to the back to apprehend him, but the MPs were there almost immediately, and the perpetrator was taken away. The Mass began shortly after the matter was cleared up.

According to the story that was passed around, the motorcyclist was identified as Sgt. Rodney Becker, of the 107th. He spent a week in the Brigg for his stunt and was busted down to corporal.

In early November, Camp Stewart was abuzz when we received word that a contingent of General Pershing's Expeditionary Forces would be passing down the installation's four-mile-long Main Street.

Hundreds of troops lined the thoroughfare, hoping to catch a glimpse of this highly regarded outfit that included Cavalry troops and Indian Scouts assigned to capture Pancho Villa.

When the parade of nearly one hundred of these forces went by, it was easy to recognize Col. George S. Patton, Jr. leading the way. The newspaper accounts all painted him as a soldier who had no fear but packed plenty of ego.

One of the stories that I read reported that Patton led a foraging expedition of about a dozen men in three Dodge Touring cars. Their job was to buy food for the American soldiers. One of the interpreters recognized a man that was a senior member of Villa's gang at one of the stops. Patton began a search of nearby farms.

At San Miguelito, the men noticed someone running inside a home. Col. Patton ordered six men to cover the house's front and sent two around to the southern wall. Three riders tried to escape, and they rode right at Patton, who shot two of their horses as the third attempted to flee. Several soldiers took shots at the gang member and managed to knock him off his horse. This third rider was a senior leader of Villa's forces, Julio Gardenas.

The first two riders were dead, and Gardenas was killed when he pretended to surrender and then reached for his pistol. Patton ordered a withdrawal when the Americans spotted a large group of riders headed to the farm. They strapped the bodies to the hoods of the cars and went back to camp.

The men were cheering wildly as the troops proudly passed through the reviewing area. Their horses were finely groomed, and the parade participants seemed to enjoy their moment of glory as much as their leader.

When Col. Patton rode past my area, one of the guys behind me called out to him, "Where are you heading, Colonel?"

Patton smiled, tipped his cap, and replied, "I'm trading in my horse for a tank and going over to Germany to kill krauts!"

"CHRISTMAS IN THE DESERT"

Men waiting to be served Christmas Dinner in chow line
Image Source: State Archives North Carolina

CHAPTER 13

"Christmas in the Desert"

It didn't take the U.S. Army long to realize that while the expedition wasn't successful in capturing the Mexican outlaw, Pancho Villa, the operation was, however, a big test in training procedures and utilizing trucks and motorized vehicles for use under battle conditions. In many briefings, the higher-ups emphasized that the army's air service gained valuable experience.

Under the old methods, a mule with a pack-saddle could only carry a maximum of 200 pounds of supplies. When we began using mechanized vehicles during the Border Conflict, trucks could move ten times that amount.

Initially, two truck companies soon expanded to 17. By the end of November, the U.S Army had 588 cargo trucks, 57 tanker trucks, 12 mobile machine shops, and six wreckers along the border.

In addition to the many new roads built by the engineers, the Signal Corps erected two wireless telegraph stations and a battery-operated telephone system to manage communications when the telegraph system went down.

November 26 marked my 24th birthday. It would be my first ever away from home. Birthdays are such a trivial matter, but when you're more than two thousand miles from home, separated from your family, it seems like a big deal.

Before we realized it, the Christmas season was upon us. Many of the guys were homesick since they found themselves away from their loved ones for the first time in their lives.

During the week leading up to Christmas, Col. Turner managed to have entertainment arranged for the men every day.

Sunday's feature movie in the camp theater was "The Perils of Pauline." The three-hour silent film kept our attention for most of the afternoon.

Monsignor Alvarez from St. Patrick's Cathedral in El Paso sent the children's choir to the post on Monday and Wednesday evenings. The boys and girls performed on the theater stage. The program began with a short Christmas play, complete with various religious costumes from the bible.

The group ended the presentation by singing a selection of Christmas Carols such as "Away in the Manger," "O' Little Town of Bethlehem," and "Jingle Bells," Sister Norine Francis directed the little children from the floor in front of the stage.

Rev. Gossemer of the Trinity Methodist Church in El Paso provided two evenings of holiday entertainment on Tuesday and Thursday. The church's adult choir rendered an excellent performance.

About 15 chorus members, dressed in festive red robes with gold trim, sang many seasonal songs. The presentation lasted nearly an hour and featured the following Carols: "Go Tell It on a Mountain," "Rise Up Shepherds and Follow," "We Three Kings of Orient Are," "God Rest Ye Merry Gentlemen," and "The Holly and the Ivy."

Friday evening's program featured three short films for the men to enjoy. The evening began with a brief monologue by Bert Higgins, a member of the 108th Field Artillery Battery F. The young soldier acted as an emcee and loosened the guys up with a few jokes.

"When I took my physical to get into this outfit, they gave the guys in my group a test. Did they give you guys an exam?" He asked.

"Well, they gave us a test. I think they called it an aptitude test or something like that," Higgins explained.

"Me and another guy were fillin' out the questions. We're all farm boys from Iowa, you know," he went on.

The fellow next to me leaned over and asked, "Old MacDonald had a what?"

"I whispered, had a farm!"

Next, he questions, "How do you spell it?"

"I told him, E-I-E-I-O!"

"I never did see that guy again. Maybe they sent him to officer's school," he said with a shrug while rolling his eyes.

That first joke was enough to get the guys in the crowd laughing.

"You know, just yesterday morning when our outfit fell into formation, the sarge addressed the squad and said: 'I have a nice easy job for the laziest man here. Put up your hand if you are the laziest,' he commanded.

"All the men raised their hands, but one. The sergeant asked the other man: 'Why didn't you raise your hand?'

The man replied: "Too much trouble raising the hand, Sarge."

Higgins went on with his act once the applause and cheering had died down.

"In case you guys haven't noticed," Higgins followed up, "they're starting to replace those horses and mules with motorized trucks and other vehicles.

"I swear, the other day, when I was on my way out to the plains for training exercises, I saw two of my buddies driving a truck down a muddy back road. They encountered another vehicle stuck in the mud with a red-faced Lieutenant at the wheel.

"When they pulled alongside the stranded vehicle, one of the sergeants got out of his truck to render assistance.

"Your car stuck, sir?" asked the sergeant.

"Nope," replied the Lieutenant, meeting him halfway and handing him the keys. "Yours is." Again, the guys roared with approval.

Higgins continued, "How many of you guys have had the pleasure of meeting a scorpion down here at Camp Stewart?"

"Go ahead, raise your hands," he urged the guys to weigh in.

"They are nasty little buggers, aren't they?" he asked, hoping the majority would agree.

"You ain't been here until you ran into one of them little fellers, am I right?" Higgins continued. "If a corporal, who's been here three or four months, finds a scorpion in his tent, he kills it.

"A sergeant, however, when he spots one of those little devils, calls the corporal and has him kill it. "Now, when an officer happens to run across a scorpion in his tent, he calls the sergeant and asks why is there a tent in my room?" He concluded.

"Did you guys noticed that they moved the latrines about fifty yards from where they used to be when the camp opened?

"It's further to walk now to take a leak, but I noticed that the coffee tastes better!" He shook his head and laughed.

When the comedian finished his bit, the troops brought the house down with laughter. They were yelling and screaming for more.

Higgins went on to introduce the three films we would watch that night.

"Our first film tonight," he began, "is a French short, "The Christmas Dream." It was made in 1900 and is about 13 minutes long."

When the first movie ended, Higgins came out to introduce the next show.

"In the spirit of the holiday," he noted, "we are pleased to present Charles Dickens' 'A Christmas Carol.' This classic story was filmed in 1910 and is about the same duration as the French film that you just saw," he remarked.

Higgins came out on stage for the final time of the evening and announced, "Tonight's feature is a 20-minute Charlie Chaplin production, 'The Tramp.'

The well-versed emcee further explained, "Chaplin made this film just last year, and his character is a childlike, bumbling and good-hearted vagrant, who behaves like a well-heeled gentleman. I hope you all enjoyed the evening," he concluded as he walked off the stage.

There was no doubt that the evening was a smashing success.

On Saturday morning, December 23, several crews volunteered to go out into the desert and dig up small mesquite bushes and other shrubs.

The guys planted these make-shift Christmas trees on the corners of the tent city's dusty streets. Others scavenged around the camp for items that could be used as decorations: tin cans, rags, string, cardboard cartons, even empty shell casings.

In the morning, any last-minute mail that arrived in the camp was handed out to the lads. Letters and packages began to arrive from home earlier in the month. The American Red Cross sent many trucks to make these shipments. Anything and everything from home was a welcome sight to these guys.

To my surprise, the sarge had two parcels and two letters for me. I grabbed them and rushed back to my bunk to open them.

When I opened the first package, I found a small box of Christmas cookies and a note from my sister, Helen. It read:

" *Dear Tommy, I hope everything is going well for you. We miss you very much. I helped mother make these cookies just for you. I look at my necklace every day. We are all just waiting for you to come home. Merry Christmas! Your loving sister, Helen.*"

In a separate envelope was a letter from the rest of my family. Veronica wrote it.

"Dear Tommy, mom, pop, and all of us girls wanted to send you a special message for Christmas. We try to continue our day-to-day activities as if nothing is changed. Although, believe it or not, we miss having you around, big brother.

Mother has been cooking and baking all the time. However, it's not the same without you. Pop still goes down to Szczepanski's. You can tell that he misses you too! He won't say it, but you know he does. All of us are waiting for the day you return home. Mom says we will have a big party and invite all the family and neighbors.

Take care of yourself. We hope you have a Merry Christmas where you are. With love, Veronica, Stella, Henrietta, Helen, Florence, Mamie, Mother, and Father."

The second package, I could tell right away, was from Stella Zwolinski, just based on the wrapping and the hand-writing. She wrote:

"My Dearest Tommy, I hope this letter finds you well wherever you are. The family is busy making all the necessary holiday preparations. Veronica and Joe are still seeing each other and have been to a few dances. I haven't joined them for any of the outings. Enclosed, please find a box of my mother's Polish Teacakes. The recipe for these special cookies belonged to my grandmother from Poland. They are my favorite. I hope you enjoy them! The weather has been quite stormy, with rains and blustery winds earlier in the month. However, we did have about three inches of snowfall here in Philadelphia when I wrote this letter. I wish you were here to celebrate.

I am looking forward to your return. Please hurry home. With love, Stella."

I was totally shocked to discover that the last letter came from Uncle Leo at Baldwin. When I left Baldwin back in June, I was under the impression that it would be my last contact with anybody at the firm. To get a letter from Leo was most surprising. He wrote:

"Tommy! Consider yourself lucky to hear from me. I am not big on letter-writing, but I do miss having you around. You were one of the most dependable guys that I had working for me. The new guy is doing fine, but he's not you! Hank is still Hank, and we are still putting out locomotives for the Brits. I know what it's like to be away from home, your family, and friends, and just wanted you to know that the gang here at Baldwin is thinking about you. PS? The coffee's always on when you get back. Take care, Leo."

Uncle Leo surprised me with his sentimentality, but I very much enjoyed receiving the note from him. The collection of cookies combined with the touching letters would see me through this Christmas away from home. I needed to find a good hiding place for them because the vultures I bunk with are always looking to steal whatever they can get their hands on.

From an entertainment perspective, the week's highlight was a self-produced talent show put on by the troops in the camp that night.

The two-hour program featured many gifted guys from several different outfits. A couple of guys hung a hand-made banner on the front of the theater building: *"Camp Stewart's Amazing Holiday Revue."*

Remarkably, the show reminded one of a vaudevillian production. The evening presented a series of acts of all descriptions. One would never realize that a group of men, assembled from all parts of the country, could possess such a wide range of talent.

By popular demand, Bert Higgins returned to the stage to be the show's emcee. He introduced such acts as Bobby Jones, from Bowling Green, Kentucky, who sang and played guitar throughout the evening. Leon Cherneski, who hailed from the northwest side of Chicago, entertained with his accordion. The guys went wild with his lively polkas.

Next up was a colored fellow, Elija Boison, from Blakeslee, Alabama, who displayed some superior tap-dancing while playing the mouth organ.

One of the surprising acts of the evening was George Clementine from the 103rd Engineers. He dressed in a borrowed officer's uniform and did an impersonation of Teddy Roosevelt.

Complete with his rough-riders hat and trademark Roosevelt spectacles, Clementine looked and played the part to a "T." He impersonated the famous miliary figure and former president by throwing out various quotes attributed to the legendary American hero:

"If you could kick the person in the pants responsible for most of your trouble, you wouldn't sit for a month."

"Speak softly and carry a big stick. You will go far."

"When you get to the end of your rope, tie a knot, and hang on."

And the one that brought the house down with laughter was, "If you got them by the balls, their hearts and minds will follow!"

Two other acts that stood out during the show were a magic act performed by Donald Yost of the 109th Field Artillery and Frank Ash from Headquarters Company, who showed off his prowess as a strong man.

Yost did some card tricks and other amazing stunts that thoroughly entertained the men.

Ash was impressive, as well. First, he tore a very thick book in half with his bare hands. Next, he took, not one but two, horseshoes and bent them entirely out of their standard shape.

The show ended with Ash asking for 15 volunteers from the audience. Once the men assembled on the stage, he engaged in a tug of war against all 15 soldiers. As hard as they tried, they could not budge the well-built, towering man. When the guys were near exhaustion from the effort, Ash gave one final pull, and the entire group came tumbling across the stage in his direction. The strong man received a standing ovation, and Higgins closed the event by bringing all the entertainers out for an encore. The night was a rousing success!

Even the mess cooks got into the act. As gruff as those guys could be at times, it was evident that the Christmas spirit had hit them, too!

A few days before the holiday, the regiment dispatched several details to dig enormous pits. Many of us suspected that it was some trench warfare training, but large spits were put in position when the holes were completed.

A cattle train rolled into the depot, and it was soon apparent that the livestock was being slaughtered and butchered in anticipation of a large barbeque.

Negro cooks of the 10th Cavalry did much of this preparation work.

The tantalizing smell of the smoking pits permeated the entire camp. Also, coming from dozens of large cast-iron kettles was the pungent aroma of sweet and sour sauce.

On Sunday, December 24, many other mess hall sections were busy cooking up the troops' perfect Christmas dinner. Just a walk past the mess shack elicited the smells of sweet potatoes, collard greens, and fresh-baked biscuits.

Our cook from the baseball game, Tubby Bleakmeyer, told me that the mess sergeant purchased some supplies from the local Mormons. He provided a little Yuletide eggnog from the extra milk and eggs and a few bottles of whiskey that he hoarded.

These dedicated cooks remained awake all night long with large pots of coffee on the wood ranges. Others stood watch over the roasting barbeque pits. Everything was fine until an unrelenting wind blew through the camp and created a catastrophic dust storm. Even though the meat in the pits was believed to be safely under blankets, it was inedible.

The mess company tried valiantly, but the dirt and sand completely ruined the meat. The Company CO issued an emergency order and sent six wagons into El Paso to secure whatever meat was available. Beef, pork, ham, turkeys, and chickens were now on the menu. Dinner may be delayed, but the colonel was determined to serve us a Christmas Dinner one way or another.

The camp chapel was the gathering place for several religious services throughout the morning. However, since the windy conditions had passed, and the weather was a bright, sunny 86 degrees, Padre Pérez held Christmas Mass out on the drill field. Several hundred men attended the service.

By 1600 hours, the mess hall's dedicated cooks managed to pull off the most amazing Christmas meal, despite the weather's cruel trick. The staff served a diverse selection of courses that they could cobble together under adverse circumstances. No one complained. All enjoyed it!

For the remainder of the holiday week, the officers rewarded our efforts with a hefty dose of light- duty. Naturally, assignments to stand guard on the border and KP jobs were mandatory, but no orders were handed out for marching, drilling, or target practice.

Passes to go into town were given generously, but they were limited to four hours only during daylight hours.

The men were encouraged to participate in many recreational activities planned in the camp that week.

The NCOs organized competitions in horseshoes, billiards, darts, and baseball to keep the guys occupied. You could easily find something to do anywhere on the installation.

Also, the movie house had films showing Friday, Saturday, and Sunday nights.

Friday's films were: " *The Werewolf" and "The Battle at Elderbush Gulch."* The latter was a 1913 American silent western film featuring Mae Marsh and Lionel Barrymore. The third film was *"The Keystone Cops in The Stolen Purse."*

Featured on Saturday evening were: " *A Study in Scarlet,"* the first British film to feature Sherlock Holmes, plus two westerns, *"An Apache's Gratitude,"* and *"Chip of the Flying U,"* both of these films starred cowboy, Tom Mix.

Sunday's films were: *"The Girl of the Golden West,"* another western, *"The White Pearl,"* a tale about a sea captain's daughter, and *"Right off the Bat,"* a baseball story.

Colonel Turner even disbanded his strict "no alcohol policy" and arranged for a local business to set up a beer garden near the recreation hall on New Year's Eve for four hours. Beer and soft drinks were served under a large tent from 1900 to 2300 hours.

The year 1916 drew to a close that New Year's Eve at Camp Stewart, Texas. It is customary to look forward to the new year with the promise of hope and optimism. However, if I do not hold the future to such a grand expectation, I most assuredly will not be disappointed.

14

"MISSION OF MERCY"

U.S. First Aero Squadron Lt. Edgar S. Gorrell (Left)
Image Source: history.net

CHAPTER 14

"Mission of Mercy"

With the holidays over, the officers began the push to get us back to our standard routine. It was time to resume drilling on the field, marching on the plains, and firing artillery on the range.

Doc and I continued pulling duty at the field hospital. Our experiences remained unchanged. Most of the patients in the ward encountered minor issues such as a stomach virus, a cold, a sore throat, an ankle sprain, or the gout.

On Friday, January 5, once the company fell into formation, SFC Vogan issued the following directive:

"Men, the entire regiment has been ordered to assemble on the drill field at 0900 hours. At that time, Col. Turner will address the troops," he started.

"I don't believe that I need to remind you that a full uniform with all standard elements is required. You are soldiers, and you must look the part. Should any of you be singled out by the colonel's staff, you will feel my wrath for even the most minor infraction. That is all. Dismissed!" Vogan warned as he laid it on the line.

At the designated hour, the 108th Field Artillery, Sanitary Detachment Unit, advanced in formation to the parade field. The entire Second Field Artillery Regiment passed in review before the colonel and his senior officers. The space between each company was six steps, and twelve steps separated each formation from its company commander.

Mounted on his famous dapple gray horse, "Dutch," Col. Turner paced back and forth in front of their view. He sat straight up in the saddle and held his riding crop under his left armpit.

The well-groomed animal was wearing a black saddle blanket, trimmed in gold, with a visible gold star in the rear corner. The saddle had a deep chocolate-colored seat and wooden stirrups with a much lighter brown leather skirt. The apparatus also contained a rifle boot that held the officer's Winchester rifle.

Once everything was in place and to his liking, the commanding officer was ready to address the troops.

In addition to his imposing presence on his mount, the colonel had a bellowing voice that easily reached the men at the rear of the formation.

His distinctive and effortless delivery clearly annunciated every phrase, every word, and every syllable. There was never a doubt when he spoke. The troops gave the commander their full attention, and he began as follows:

"Men, it has been my pleasure to command this regiment over the last several months. During this expedition, I have observed this outfit perform its duties in every phase of the operation. You have excelled not only in training but in the execution of our mission.

"We are witnessing the transition from a dependency on mules and horses to a modern mechanized army that utilizes vehicles such as armored cars, trucks, and motorcycles.

"Here in this region, we have also introduced the First Aero Squadron and have effectively used these airplanes to conduct valuable surveillance from above. This expedition has allowed us to test new equipment and new methods of warfare.

"Men, you are a witness to this new era in American Military History, and you are better today because of it.

"Now, you may be wondering why I ordered you to assemble here this morning. It's not to give you a pep talk."

A few laughs from the troops broke the silence momentarily, but the colonel continued with his monologue.

"At precisely 0800 hours, the Second Field Artillery Regiment of the Pennsylvania National Guard has been officially re-organized as part of the new 28th Division, "The Keystone Division.""

"Adjutant," Col. Turner commanded, "I order you to announce to the troops the new 28th Division Order of Battle!"

"Yes, sir!" The adjutant replied and began reading from the list.

"55th Infantry Brigade: 109th Infantry Regiment, 110th Infantry Regiment, and 108th Machine Gun Battalion; 56th Infantry Brigade: 111th Infantry Regiment, 112th Infantry Regiment, and the 109th Machine Gun Battalion; 53rd Artillery Brigade: 107th Field Artillery Regiment, 108th Field Artillery Regiment, the 109th Artillery Regiment, the 103rd Trench Mortar Battery. The 107th Machine Gun Battalion, 103rd Engineer Regiment, 103rd Field Signal Battalion, Headquarters Troop 28th Division, 103rd Train Headquarters and Military Police, 103rd Ammunition Train, 103rd Supply Train, and the 103rd Sanitary Train.

"Additional units are 109th, 110th, and 112th Ambulance Companies and Field Hospitals, Sir!" the adjutant concluded with a salute.

"Thank you!" Col. Turner nodded and returned a salute. He briefly turned his mount to face the adjutant but soon resumed pacing his horse back and forth in front of the troops. He continued his address.

"Presently, we are now part of this new 28th Division, but we trace our lineage as a military unit back to Benjamin Franklin's battalion, *The Pennsylvania Associators*, in 1747. I know your service to your country will proudly honor this storied military tradition.

"Finally, for the news, you have all been waiting to hear. Commencing February 5, 1917, the troops assigned here at Camp Stewart will withdraw from the area."

Spontaneously, the entire formation began to cheer wildly. Some men even threw their hats in the air and could be seen hugging each other while breaking rank. The colonel allowed the guys to have their moment of celebration without interruption. He continued once order was restored.

"Your individual CO's will reveal your departure date to you and provide you with further details. The evacuation process will continue through March," he explained.

"In conclusion, I expect every soldier to carry out his duties to the best of his ability for the remainder of your charge here at Camp Stewart. That is all," he concluded.

Adjutant, "DISMISSED!"

It was the news we had all been waiting to hear. At least we knew that our assignment here in El Paso was about to be over. There would be no official news until our CO addressed the matter, but nearly every one of us believed that we would be returning home temporarily.

Perhaps there was a reason for optimism in the new year, after all.

SFC Vogan had us march back to our area and then proceeded to give us the details for our unit. "Gentlemen, I am pleased to announce that the 108th Field Artillery will be among the first outfits to ship out," the sarge began.

"Once again, we will board the train at the depot and be transported back to Philadelphia. At this point, we have no particulars regarding the exact time of departure, etc. I will keep you posted as the circumstances become available," he concluded.

I dashed back to my tent upon our dismissal and immediately penned a letter to my family, informing them of the news. Most of the other men did the same.

Irvin and I continued our duties at the field hospital, and everything appeared to be routine there, as well. That is until we arrived for our shift on Monday, January 15.

The nurse specified that she wanted us to devote our attention to one corner of the ward.

"These six patients," she explained, "are all suffering from acute appendicitis, and we must keep a close eye on them until Capt. Peroni takes them in for surgery. Let me know if you observe anything out of the ordinary," she instructed us.

"What are their symptoms?" Schweppenheiser asked the nurse.

"They all are experiencing nausea, vomiting, and diarrhea," the RN described, "this is accompanied by loss of appetite, fever, chills, and severe stomach distress."

"Okay, " Doc acknowledged, "we'll keep an eye on them."

At various points of the morning, each of the men experienced multiple symptoms. We supplied them with extra blankets for the chills and applied cold compresses to keep their fevers at bay.

Finally, Capt. Peroni arrived at about 1130 hours and instructed the nurse to send word to Major Sullivan that the appendectomies would begin within the hour.

At that point, Schweppenheiser spoke up.

"Sir, I don't think you have a situation of appendicitis cases here," he offered his opinion. "Who the hell are you?" the captain barked.

"PFC Irvin Schweppenheiser," Irvin replied.

"Like I said," the captain questioned a second time, "Who the hell are you? Are you a medic?"

"No, Sir. I'm in the Sanitary Detachment Unit, but I'm assigned here at the field hospital," he explained.

"Listen, soldier," the captain said with frustration in his voice, "I don't have time for this nonsense.

We have six lives that we need to save," he added.

"But... but... Captain, Sir," Irvin was insistent, "My opinion is that you need to rethink this whole matter with six cases. Don't you think that this sends up a red flag?" the private persisted.

"I am one of the best surgeons that the army has, and I have been practicing medicine for 17 years. I don't have time for this. Nurse get this man out of here and summon Major Sullivan immediately," he ordered.

To avoid a confrontation with the doctor, the nurse ushered us out of the hospital. She told us to make ourselves useful and find Major Sullivan.

We encountered the major at the mess hall and notified him that Capt. Peroni had directed us to deliver him to the field hospital.

Irvin, however, took the opportunity to bend the officer's ear.

"Sir, Capt. Peroni is confident that these six patients all have appendicitis, but I'm not convinced of his diagnosis," he gave his opinion.

"My Uncle Bill drives a milk wagon in Philadelphia," Irvin revealed, and last summer, about eight people on his route began showing similar symptoms. They were all taken to the Stetson Hospital on Orianna Street.

"It turned out," Schweppenheiser further noted, "they all contracted a bacterial infection due to *Staphylococcus aureus* from the milk.

He added, "Their symptoms mimicked that of appendicitis." "Is that so?" the major questioned.

"Yes! Not only that," Irvin continued, "There was a case in February 1915 at the Culver Military Institute in Indiana, where eight cadets also came down with similar manifestations. In that case, however, the infection did develop into appendicitis," he admitted.

"Well, young man," the major responded, "why do you think this is happening here?"

"Sir, where do we get our milk?" Irvin asked, "Local farmers and half of them are over in Mexico where they don't abide by the same health standards as we do. The average temperature here ranges from 80 degrees to over 100. Don't you think that the conditions are right for spoiled milk? I don't know about you, but I would bet on it," he concluded.

"Sir, if I may," Schweppenheiser suggested, "if you do nothing else, send a messenger down to the field hospital at the other end of camp. If they have similar cases, you know that this can't possibly be a coincidence," he pleaded.

"You make some interesting suggestions, private," the major observed. I will look into it, I assure you," Major Sullivan added.

"By the way, why does this matter interest you so, and how is it you are so well-versed in this subject matter?" he inquired.

"Sir, it is my goal to attend medical school someday. I'd like to go to the University of Pennsylvania," Irvin revealed.

"Based on this conversation, you'll make a fine physician eventually," the major commented. "Keep up the good work!"

As our conversation with the major ended, we both saluted the officer. He turned away from us and headed for the field hospital. He knew he would have to deal with Capt. Peroni, next.

Since we were already at the mess hall, Irvin and I decided to grab some lunch.

When we sat down at the table, I asked Doc about his uncle's story and the milk wagon. "Yes! It's all true," he assured me.

"My Uncle Bill has been working the milk route at Harbinson's Dairy for years. Most of his customers reside essentially in the Fishtown and Kensington neighborhoods of the city. His horse, whose name is "Lucy," has been doing it for so long that she knows all the stops.

"When my uncle has been out drinking the night before, Lucy walks the route on her own. She even stops at the customer's homes along the way. They grab their milk, butter, etc., and she's on her way.

"When I was a kid, my uncle would pull up to our house on Lawrence Street, and I would give her a carrot from the open window," he recalled.

"Interesting. That's quite a story," I remarked.

Later in the day, we heard that Major Sullivan had convinced the captain to hold off on performing the surgeries. The patients were still showing signs of the infection, but their conditions had not worsened.

Capt. Peroni agreed to send a messenger to the other Field Hospital, and they reported that they had five patients with the same symptoms. Several other men complained of similar stomach discomfort, but their cases were considered mild. That brought the total to 11 confirmed diagnoses plus the other mild conditions.

However, there was no treatment for bacterial infections, aside from bloodletting and leeches. Physicians did not perform bloodletting treatment. Barbers implemented the practice. Those methods, though, were losing favor in the medical profession.

The following day, the doctors' consensus was that some sort of treatment would be required, even if it was an experimental approach.

Since Major Sullivan was more receptive to the process, he took the lead in finding a suitable treatment for our patients.

The physician first sent a telegraph message to one of the army's chief medical officers for advice.

A telephone connection was set up to facilitate a practical course of treatment.

According to the army's top experts, the only known compound that was somewhat effective in fighting a bacterial infection was Manuka honey.

Capt. Sullivan was informed that this type of honey was native to New Zealand. When bees pollinated the manuka bush, they produced honey that had antibacterial effects. Studies showed that the compound had antiviral, anti-inflammatory, and antioxidant benefits. It seemed worth a try. At this point, the honey had positive results both as a topical compound and when ingested internally.

The next problem was that the honey's closest source was at St. Joseph's Sanatorium and Hospital in Albuquerque, New Mexico. It meant that somebody needed to travel 265 miles from Camp Stewart. Time was of the essence.

The camp's medical officer was a problem solver, and he inquired to the 1st Aero Squadron to see if one of their pilots was willing to make the trip to Albuquerque.

He soon learned that the squadron was ill-equipped to make any substantial flights. The unit began service with a handful of Curtiss JN-3s (Jenny's). These canvas-winged planes flew with 100 horsepower engines and had severe problems.

Pilots experienced engine problems and control issues between 4,200 and 6,000 feet. Besides, they were not powerful enough to make it over the mountains. Most of their missions were a distance of 30 to 36 miles, strictly on reconnaissance or mail delivery. The record flight for the aircraft was 315 miles, but on that particular mission, Lieutenants Edgar S. Gorrell and Herbert A. Dargue had to make a forced landing 100 miles from any American forces. The planes were not reliable for such a task.

The squadron just received 12 new aircraft. These planes were Curtiss R-2s. The hastily constructed flying machines boasted a 160-horsepower engine but were missing parts such as compasses, locking rings, bracing wires, screws, bolts, propeller hubs, and assorted wrenches and specialized tools. They also had faulty wiring and leaky fuel tanks. The mechanics did their best to make them airworthy.

Because there were problems with the engines overheating, the mechanics had to install new water pumps and larger radiators.

Due to the hot, dry climate along the border area, the glue holding blades of the wooden propellors together dried out and caused them to warp and split. Squadron personal also found the Curtiss Control system to be deficient and often replaced it with a universal stick system. It would be a dangerous undertaking.

Despite these deficiencies, the group's major in command was willing to go ahead with the mission.

He just needed to find a pilot who was willing to volunteer.
Gorrell and Dargue were the only flyers with long-distance experience. The pair stepped up and proposed that they fly the mission.

Although the Curtiss R-2 was capable of a top speed of 86 miles per hour, the trip would require at least three and a half hours in each direction. In the interest of safety, each pilot would operate his own machine.

At 0630 on Wednesday, January 17, with the sun barely peeking over the Franklin Mountains, two Curtiss R-2s appeared very low on the horizon. The temperature at that time of the morning was 71 degrees, and the forecast was for clear, blue skies.

Nearly 300 men lined both sides of the main street in Camp Stewart. You could hear the sound of the roaring engines increase dramatically as the aircrafts approached from the west.

Initially, the cheers of the men on-hand to witness this unusual event began as a low decibel rumble, but when the pair of flying machines touched down and came to a halt in front of Col. Turner and the other officers, the yells became deafening. The clapping, cheering, hollering, and howling lasted for a good seven minutes. The two pilots' reception was comparable to that of returning heroes, and they hadn't even left for their mission yet! Gorrell's plane had the number 71 painted on the fuselage, while Dargue's craft had the No. 43 designation.

The colonel handed the adjutant the pilots' orders. They saluted and were on their way.
During the 20 minutes that the pilots had touched down, the now blazing sun draped a scarlet blanket over the mount range.

Everyone stood there, mystified until the aircrafts disappeared from view. Should the two brave airmen return safely with their precious cargo, the welcoming committee would be in an even higher frenzy state.

Touch down for their return was expected at approximately 1500 hours. All we could do was wait.

The pair's real test would be following the Rio Grande River north through the Rio Grande Rift river valley. Visible from the air midway on the course would be the settlements of Rock Canyon, Elephant Butte, and Truth or Consequences.

The two pilots encountered some severe turbulence whenever they climbed more than 4,200 feet. Albuquerque sits at 5,300 feet, but the airmen managed to maintain adequate control throughout the flight.

Gorrell and Dargue would have little trouble identifying St. Joseph's Hospital and Sanatorium on the Albuquerque approach. The sprawling brick complex looks like a giant "V."

Without much of a welcoming delegation, Nos. 71 and 43 landed on the u-shaped driveway in front of the hospital. Two nurses were waiting on the front steps of the facility for the craft to arrive. The women appeared to be in their mid-twenties and were wearing white uniforms with light blue sleeves. A large red cross was visible on their chest and a white armband with a red cross on the left sleeve. The nurses were also wearing their appropriate white caps, which were an essential part of the uniform.

As the aircrafts rolled to a stop on the driveway, the two carried a large wooden box with rope handles to the first plane. The pilot jumped out and carefully placed the box in the compartment behind him. Inside this crate was a pair of one-gallon jugs containing the precious Manuka honey. Securely swaddled in bedsheets, there was little doubt that the vessels would survive the mission.

Lt. Gorrell handed over the paperwork, and within minutes the two aircraft were taking off for their journey back to Texas.

On the return trip to El Paso, the pair of aircraft experienced no problems until they reached the two- thirds mark. Gorrell's plane encountered some engine problems, and the expert pilot, who had been in this predicament before, decided to look for a place to set it down.

According to his map, the closest landing spot was the White Sands area. This action would require climbing to a higher altitude to cross over the San Andres Mountains, but there was no other option.

With the misfiring of the engine occurring more frequently, locating a suitable landing point became critical. Dargue, unaware of Gorrell's situation, followed closely behind. There were no radios aboard these planes.

After clearing the San Andres Peak, the White Sands quickly came into view. Luckily the pilot spotted a suitable flat area that was not too sandy, below on his left. The highly concentrated sand basin would be enough to hopelessly bog down his machine if he did not choose wisely.

The ground was stable enough for both planes to land effortlessly. Gorrell taxied to a stop and immediately analyzed the situation.

"What's up?" Dargue asked.

"I think some of the plugs have fouled, causing the cylinders to misfire,' Gorrell assessed the situation.

"Is it overheating at all?" he asked Gorrell.

"No. Just misfiring," he replied.

It was a common practice to carry tool kits and spare parts in these planes. Many pilots flying these airplanes even had a spare propellor on board.

Gorrell replaced three fouled plugs, and the plane started right up without a misfire. The two airmen turned their planes around and took off bound for El Paso. At this point, they were about 45 minutes behind schedule.

The time was 1600 hours, and once again, hundreds of soldiers had assembled along the camp's main street. They had been waiting for over an hour, and still, there was no sign of the planes.

Finally, a single plane approached the camp as it crossed the Franklin Mountains. It was No. 43, which belonged to Lt. Herbert A. Dargue. The cheering began, although apprehensively, when only one aircraft appeared.

As the pilot circled the landing area to ensure that he had a clear approach, the crowd recognized that the rear cockpit seat was vacant.

A million thoughts were going through their minds as a result of this observation. Where's the other plane? If Gorrell had to sit it down, why isn't he riding in Dargue's machine? Which pilot was carrying the medicinal honey? Did he crash somewhere along the way?

When the wheels of Dargue's plane touched down on the asphalt of Main Street, the signalman in the guard tower on the northern-most point of the camp observed a second plane with his field glasses.

The soldier quickly signaled the second incoming flight, and the cheering accelerated to a frenzy status.

Gorrell also circled the camp before landing, and it was evident that his flight was not without problems. His approach was much slower than Dargue's and slightly erratic. Eventually, No. 71 descended and landed safely. The pilot was swarmed by the crowd and almost removed bodily from the cockpit.

The MPs cleared the area, and the medical personnel was allowed to remove the precious honey from the craft and took it immediately to the Field Hospital.

As for Lt. Gorrell, he relaxed in a chair, smoked a long cigar, and described the details of his mission for the fellows.

According to those within earshot, after replacing the spark plugs at White Sands, the plane developed rudder issues. Gorrell was forced to reduce his speed and baby the aircraft for the remainder of the flight. That is why he arrived a good five minutes behind Dargue. We were all exhilarated that the mission had a fortunate ending.

By the weekend, all of the patients had shown signs of improvement. The treatment called for a cup of tea with a tablespoon of Manuka honey three times per day. If needed, an extra tablespoon of the honey could be administered by itself in-between the other doses.

Within one week, the physicians discharged them from the hospital. The results were the same at the other field hospital.

My buddy, Schweppenheiser, should have earned a promotion to sergeant for his role in the matter, but he was passed over. I was confident, however, that he was on his way to one day becoming Dr. Irvin Schweppenheiser.

Our outfit basically all came from the same part of the country, including the Philadelphia area. We represented 14 different nationalities, including Irish, English, Welsh, Polish, German, Lithuanian, Italian, and Slovak.

We came from all different walks of life and had skills in 70 distinct trades. The army did its best to determine how it could best utilize those skills.

We were thrown together in a border camp and shared a hundred common experiences - experiences of hardship and pleasure.

As individuals, we didn't know what to expect when we arrived here, but now that we were leaving, we knew that we could count on each other no matter what the future had in store for us. I guess that's what the commanders tried to teach us from the beginning, and I think it worked!

Curtiss R2 aero plane No. 71
Image Source: Public Domain

"THE HOMECOMING"

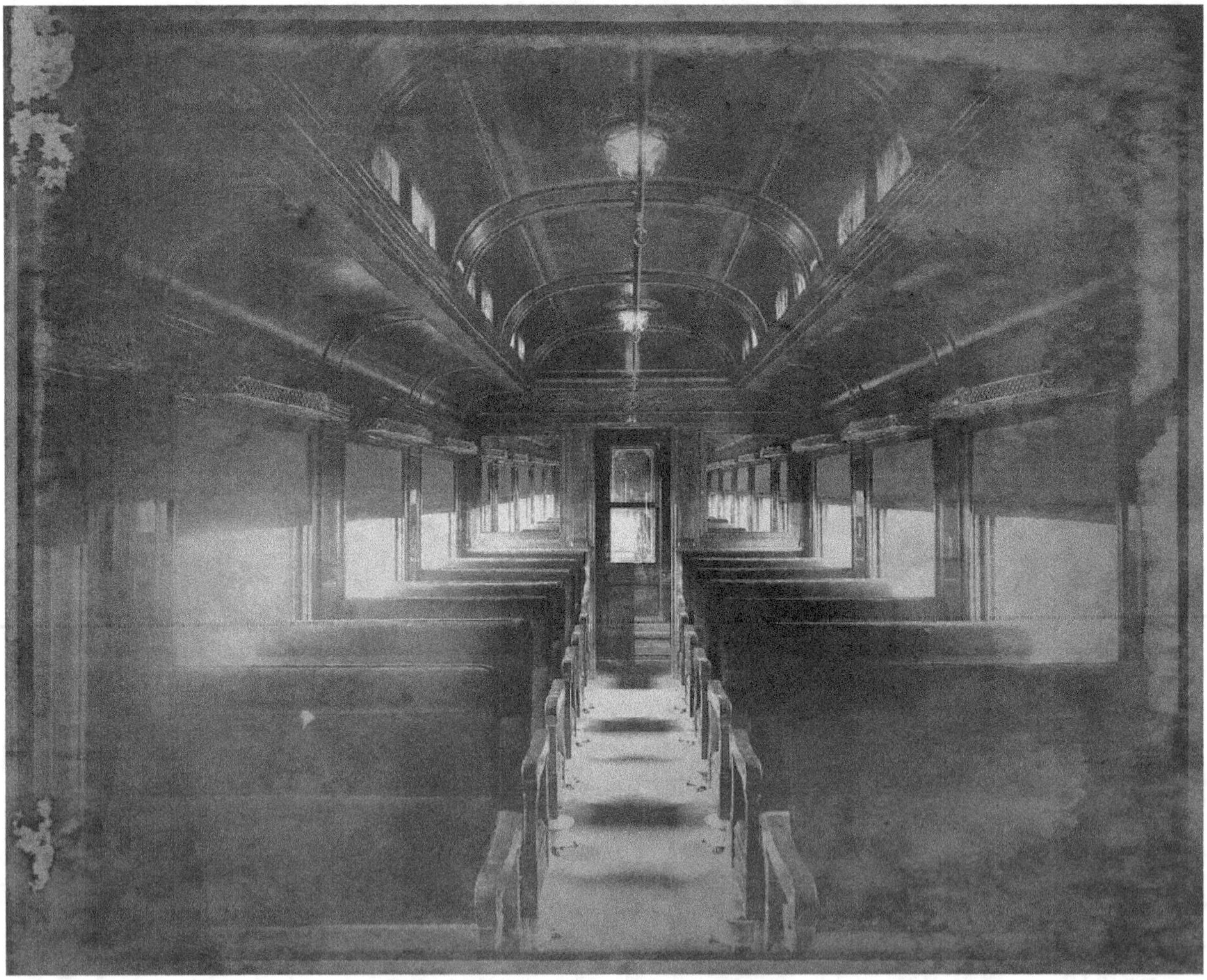

The journey home from El Paso, Tx to Philadelphia, PA
Image Source: Unknown

CHAPTER 15

"The Homecoming"

By 0700, on the morning of Monday, February 5, the troops had finished boarding. The road name on the side of the 18 cars that made up the train was Gulf Coast Lines, but the engine assigned to the first leg of the journey belonged to the El Paso and Southwestern Railroad.

As I sat in car number 837, my seat faced the rear of the train. When we left the depot, there was a sharp curve in the track to the right. This course furnished me with an excellent view of Camp Stewart. This sight stirred many memories of my time there, even though it was only about seven months.

Eventually, the massive installation faded away, but from my window, I could see an occasional cactus, dozens of mesquite trees, and many other small bushes.

The small green shrubs that dotted the landscape would forever remind me of Christmas because of the men who placed them on the street corners in camp and decorated them.

As I gazed across the railroad car's aisle, the Franklin Mountains were another reminder of the 219 days that I spent there. They represented countless days of marching on the plains under the hot sun or the many trips to the firing range to hone in our rifle skills.

My most lasting memory would probably be the image of the two airplanes from the 1st Aero Squadron, as they rose above those mountain tops when they returned from Albuquerque.

Gorrell and Dargue put their own lives on the line for the dangerous mission that saved nearly a dozen others.

Today, the summits rise in the distance, showing off their blue crevices, but the peaks are wearing a cloak of white snow from my vantage point.

Despite this hot, sandy, and unforgiving dusty desert region in El Paso, we created a survival mechanism.

We devised our own entertainment through boxing matches, baseball games, and talent shows. Before long, however, I was now was ready to put the past behind me and prepare myself for the future.

They informed us that our route home would be pretty different than that of our arrival. According to the sarge, we would once again journey across southern Texas, but instead of heading north from Baton Rouge, LA, we would pass through New Orleans and travel through Mississippi.

Our trip would take us through Birmingham, AL; Atlanta, GA; Spartanburg, SC; Charlotte and Greensboro, NC; Charlottesville, VA; Washington, DC; and finally, arriving in Philadelphia.

Once again, the expectation was to make the trip in three or four days. The reports this week called for excellent weather.

We learned early on that this was *not* the Pennsylvania Railroad. Most meals consisted of beans with various meats, beef stew with vegetables, or Hungarian Goulash.

Bacon and eggs were not part of the breakfast menu. In their place were cold cereal, hot porridge, and burnt toast. As far as the coffee went, I would have given anything for a cup of Uncle Leo's strong brew.

The men learned the ropes regarding fuel stops and engine changes on the first trip. Therefore, the operation had become mundane and was largely ignored on this excursion.

By Wednesday evening, I was tired of the train ride and not interested in the small talk with other soldiers. All that was on my mind was getting back home to see my family again.

The rhythmic rocking back and forth of the railroad car, combined with the steady cadence of the wheels when they passed over the joints of the steel rails, lulled me to sleep.

When I awoke, it was early Thursday morning, February 8. I recalled having the most vivid dream. In this illusion, I played in a baseball game at the Baker Bowl, located at Broad and Huntington Sts., Philadelphia.

The contest pitted the fellows of my unit against the Philadelphia Phillies, National League Champions, in 1915.

Naturally, they wore their cream-colored uniforms with a red "P" on the left side. Their baseball caps were the same color with a red pinstripe and a red "P" on the front. Our uniform consisted of our military-issued khaki pants, a white undershirt, and an olive green baseball-style cap with the red Keystone on the front.

In my dream, the game had already progressed to the ninth inning. The Philadelphia squad led by a score of 1-0. Grover Alexander, who would probably be one of the greatest pitchers of all time, was on the mound for the Phillies.

Their line-up featured Fred Luderus at first base and Bert Niehoff at second, with Dave "Beauty" Bancroft playing shortstop. The third baseman was Bobby Byrne, and Bill Killefer was the catcher behind the plate.

In the outfield, the Phillies played Beals Becker in left, Dode Paskert in centerfield, and Gaavy Cravath in right.

Bill Haeberle led off for our team, and Alexander struck him out in short order. Roy Wilson was the second batter of the inning.

I stood with my bat in hand, in the on-deck circle in front of our dugout on the third-base side. The grass was a brilliant shade of green, and the double-deck grandstands went down to the foul pole down the first baseline.

On the third-base side, stands stood about two-thirds down the line. Behind our dugout, I clearly saw my entire family cheering me on. My parents were there, and next to them were my sisters. Likewise, in this cheering section were Stella and her brother, Joe. Even Uncle Leo was part of the crowd.

Although, sitting behind the Phillies dugout were: Leonard Jablonski and his daughter, Sophie, Stosh, and Casimir from the saloon, Hank, "The Mad Hungarian," and Sister Benedictus Carmella. That was a little scary.

Roy Wilson followed Haeberle with a blooper over the first baseman's glove. It was then my turn, and if I thought I was nervous in that game back at Camp Stewart, this trumped that feeling by a longshot.

On the second pitch from Alexander, I connected with the ball, and it landed in centerfield at the feet of Paskert. Haeberle scooted to third as the fielder hesitated momentarily before throwing the ball back to the infield.

With runners at first and third, Al Gray struck out on another series of brilliant pitches by Alexander.

Leo Quigley, a well-built guy who appeared to be well over six-foot tall and around 265 pounds, was the next batter for our team. Alexander made him look bad on the first two pitches. However, Quigley launched a ball over the 261-foot mark in right field. The 108th led the Phillies in the top of the ninth inning by a score of 3-1.

Now for the strange part of my dream. Before we could finish the game, a hot air balloon descended onto the field and carried us all away. I don't know where the airship took us, nor did I ever determine if we won the game. That was probably one of the strangest dreams I have had.

A year ago, when I was still at home, I either had a vision or a dream about my grandmother, Josephine.

My grandmother was standing at the foot of my bed. She was wearing her long apron, and she had a lit candle in her hands. She said, "Thomas, I will watch over you." When I sat up in bed, she disappeared.

To shake off these thoughts about dreams, I made my way to the dining car. It was 0600 hours. I met one of the porters while traveling between cars, and he told me that we would be passing through Washington, D.C., very shortly.

Initially, I sat at a table by myself and ordered a cup of coffee. Within a few minutes, another soldier asked if he could join me. I nodded affirmatively.

The man extended his hand to shake and introduced himself, *"Haya doin'*, pal. Collin Cassidy here from headquarters company."

"Tom Schalata, 108th Field Artillery," I responded as I shook his hand.

"What *was your* assignment back at Camp?" he asked.

"Sanitary Detachment. I spent most of my time at the Field Hospital," I replied. "And you?"

"I'm what *dey* call a cook," he noted. "Third-generation, you know, *yeah*," he stated proudly.

"Is that right?" I questioned. "By the way, is that a New York accent you have there?" I asked.

"Brooklyn, Sir! 333 Chauncey Street, Brooklyn, USA!" He answered proudly. "Where *yous* from?" He asked.

"Bridesburg, Philadelphia," was my reply.

"Bridesburg, yeah? My cousin, Pat, lives in Fishtown. Maybe *yous guys knows* each other, yeah," Cassidy suggested.

"Louie McNamara, ever hear of *'em?*" Cassidy questioned.

"No, pal, I don't think I do," I answered, hoping to put the matter to bed.

"Yeah, *ahrite ahready*. So, let's get back to my *stawry*," he said.

"My *grandfadda'*, Cameron Cassidy, was a cook in *duh* Civil Wawr. He was with the Fighting 69th, *duh* Irish Brigade.

"If that outfit wasn't a *bag 'o nails. Dey* fought in so many battles and lost so many men," he explained, "that by the end of the *wawr*, Ulysses S. Grant ordered his outfit to move up with him at Petersburg and Appomattox. He was there for Lee's Surrender, ya know!"

"Dat's how my *grandfadda' got ta* cook for *duh* general. He could drink his fill; the old general could. God rest his soul."

"Did ya know *that* he had a cucumber soaked in vinegar and a cup of *cawfee* every morning?" Cassidy noted. *"Doncha know that's* what they called pickles in those days?" he added.

"Know, I don't believe I ever heard that," I responded.

"He told me *that* the general also loved broiled Spanish mackerel, steak, bacon with fried apples, and flannel cakes.

*   *16 NOTE: Flannel cakes are very similar to pancakes, and it is an Appalachian term for a pancake. Due to Scottish influence, they are also known as flannen cakes. The Scottish called them flannen biscuits and flannen banococks. These cakes could be any of the following: a "coarse oat cake," a fluffy wheat pancake, thick flapjacks, fat hotcakes, or griddlecakes. The specific term, "flannel cake," probably originated in Pennsylvania and was carried by the "Scotch-Irish down through the Shenandoah Valley.*

Cassidy continued, "According to my *grandfadda'*, Grant hated chicken but loved pawk an' rice puddin'."

"Right before the surrender," the cook continued, "duh general came down *with* a cold. My *grandfadda'* butchered a couple o' chickens and made a big pot *o' chicken zoup*. When he tried to serve the *zoup* to Grant, the general responded, 'Get this son of a bitch out of my tent, and if he ever tries to give me chicken soup again, string the bastard up and hang him from the closest oak tree you can find.'

"When my *Grandfadda' Cam* told me that *stawry*, I said... I said, *'get outta here* I said," Cassidy recalled.

Now, my *fadda'* on *duh* other hand, Conner Cassidy, was in *duh* Spanish-American *Wawr*.

"My pop was assigned to cook for Roosevelt an' his Rough Riders when *dey* fought *duh* battle o' San Juan Hill. He *tawd* me many times, *dat* Teddy made sure *that* his favorite comfort foods were a priority. Pigs in blankets, turtle soup, an' fried chicken smawthered in white gravy. *That* kept *'im runnin'—that and plenty of cawffee*. Col. Roosevelt mostly sweetened his *cawfee* with seven lumps of *suga'*!" He concluded.

"Wow! That's pretty amazing," I commented. "What about you?" I asked.

"I *tawt* I'd get my chance when General Pershing was in *da'* area down at Camp Stewart, but I was in the *terlet* when he stopped by. *Cudja'* imagine th*at*, huh?" He said disappointedly.

"That's too bad," I said to console the man.

"Dollars to doughnuts, I'm *gonna* cook the general a great dish, and I'm not *tawkin' scoumbaish*," Cassidy exclaimed.

"What's scoumbaish?" I asked him.

"*Wella*' let's see," he began, "back in Brooklyn *dats sumptin,'* we say that *yous gonna'* cook enough food to eat. No *scrimpin.' yous know whatta mean, huh?*"

"I see," I acknowledged.

Soon we shook hands and said our goodbyes. I wished Cassidy good luck with his mission, and he said that he hoped that someday we might run into one another again.

*   *17 NOTE: Portions of the previous text were set in italics to denote a typical New York/Brooklyn through accent's phonetic spelling.*

Our conversation took us well beyond Washington, DC, and when the conductor passed through the dining car. He announced that we would be arriving in Philadelphia in about 45 minutes.

As the train entered the outskirts of Philadelphia, I began to see many familiar sights. Before long, the mighty steamer chugged closer to our destination. The famous statue of William Penn atop the city hall building came into view, and that is when I truly felt like I was home.

At precisely 11:35 am, the locomotive carrying its precious cargo rolled into the Pennsylvania Railroad's Broad Street Station.

Slowly we felt the engine grind to a halt, and when we heard that final burst of steam, it seemed like all onboard let out a collective sigh as well.

On the platform, we collected our belongings and were on our way. Some of the guys exchanged goodbyes with each other before they left.

After climbing the steps to the street level, it was apparent that snow had fallen here recently. Piled up on the sidewalk near the curb lay several inches of the white stuff. The rest of the pavement had an inch or two of slush. The footsteps of hundreds of pedestrians created this semi-frozen muck. It was a good thing the army had provided me with a winter uniform and overcoat because it felt like the temperature was in the twenties.

There was a 5 & 10 Cent store on market street, and I thought I would pick up a few things for my sisters. From there, I grabbed some lunch at Horn & Hardart's and a newspaper for pops. A vendor was selling bouquets on the corner, so I bought one for mom.

Before long, I caught the Market Street Line and the trolley home. It was about 2:30 when I turned the corner from Orthodox Street onto Thompson Street. I was glad to get in the door before my sisters made it home from school. I wanted it to be a surprise.

My mother was fussing in the kitchen, but my father was not home from work yet. "Tommy, I'm so glad to see you! And you made it home safely, yes?" my mother inquired. "Yes, mom, I made it home safe and sound," I assured her.

"Why don't you go upstairs and take a hot bath and change before the girls and your father get home," she suggested.

Yes, mother, that really sounds good. Thanks."

Being at home in the family bathroom was like living a whole new experience. I was able to soak in the tub as long as the water remained warm. No worries about standing guard duty, working in the field hospital, or pulling K.P. in the mess hall!

Soon the time had come when I had to get out of the tub, dry off, and get dressed.

By the time I got downstairs, my mother had a cup of coffee waiting for me and a slice of pound cake. The buttery, creamy cake was one of my mother's prized recipes, and it was delicious.

The front door clanged open, and the girls rushed into the house, ignoring their usual single file practice. They ran to the kitchen like an excited flock of chickens.

I was smothered with hugs and kisses as if I were gone for years. They were jumping up and down and even hugging each other.

"Tommy's home! Tommy's home," they shouted with sheer delight.

I handed out their small gifts from the 5 & 10, and more hugs and kisses followed their thankyous.

Naturally, after this reception, a series of questions ensued. Questions about my adventure, but mother quickly interfered, "Now, girls, let's give Tommy a chance to rest from his journey. Perhaps he'll tell us all about it after dinner when your father comes home," she said.

When Pop came home, we all washed up and sat down at the dining room table. My family asked me to say grace before the meal since I had been away for so long.

Mom had cooked a beautiful pot roast with roasted vegetables, and it was a feast like I haven't had for such a long time!

As usual, there was no conversation permitted until the dishes were cleared from the table. Mother treated us all with a slice of that delicious pound cake and a glass of her homemade iced tea.

It didn't take long before the inquisition began. The questions seemed endless.

"What was it like, Tommy?"

"Was it hot down there in Texas?"

"How was the food?"

"Did you have to do a lot of hard work, like marching?"

"What was the weirdest thing that happened down there? Did you have to shoot anybody?"

"Did you have any fun while you were away?"

"What was the most interesting thing you experienced while at Camp Stewart?"

The interrogation seemed to come to a close while everyone waited for my responses.

"Well, the weather was hot during the day but cold at night. There were poisonous snakes and scorpions that you had to keep an eye on all the time," was my first response.

I went on, "The food was generally pretty bad. The army served us a lot of beans, goulash, and mush.

"We did a lot of marching and guard duty initially, but eventually, I was assigned to work in a Field Hospital. I helped the nurses and assisted the patients when needed.

"I suppose the weirdest thing that happened was when a soldier drove his motorcycle into the chapel one Sunday morning during services.

"They hauled him away and put him in jail. He was drunk, they say.

"As far as fun goes, we played baseball and other games. There was a movie theater where they showed picture shows on occasion. The soldiers also put on a talent show once. That was very entertaining.

"The most interesting thing that happened was about a dozen soldiers got gravely ill, but none of the doctors could figure out their ailment. Initially, they thought it was appendicitis, but Irvin suggested it was a bacterial infection caused by spoiled milk.

"Two airmen had to fly to Albuquerque for a special medicine. It was a dangerous mission. One that had never been attempted with this type of plane.

"The two made the trip safely both ways, even though one of the planes had some engine trouble on the route back. The patients all recovered to full health. My friend, Irvin, should have been promoted to sergeant but wasn't!

"By the way, folks! I was promoted to corporal on my birthday," as well! I concluded.

That calls for a toast," my father said, who sat there the entire time soaking in my stories, "Na Dzrowia! To my son, Thomas, on his safely completed mission in the service. May he always have success in the future," he concluded.

We all clanked our glasses together in celebration. My mother asked if anyone wanted seconds. This gesture was entirely out of character for her.

While it was a great feeling to be back home with my family, I had to admit to myself that my experience in the service clearly broadened my view of the world.

Grandmother Josephine Kubacka standing with child
Image Source: Author's Photo

"THE WAR LOOMS CLOSER"

New recruits prepare for military life
Image Source: U.S. Dept. of Defense

CHAPTER 16

"The War Looms Closer"

After finishing my first home-cooked breakfast, Friday morning, February 9, I took my usual route to the Baldwin Locomotive Works to see what was happening down there.

Uncle Louie was sitting at his desk drinking his coffee, but when he saw me enter the office, he jumped up and gave me a big hug and a hearty handshake.

"Tommy! So glad to see you! We weren't sure we'd be seeing you again. How's the army?" He asked.

"It went well," I replied. "I'm back home now, but I don't know for how long."

"Don't suppose you have any work around here, do you?" I inquired.

Louie rubbed his chin for a moment and replied, "Well, I think I can scratch up some work for you. I need a guy to run blueprints around the complex, and I need a courier to pick up parts and other items in the truck once in a while."

"But you know very well I can't drive that thing!"

"We'll get Paul to show you. You'll have plenty of time to learn. Plus, it's easy. You rode with him before, remember?" He challenged.

"What about the bosses? Will the big shots approve this?" I questioned.

"Ahhh!" Uncle Louie shot back, "they owe me so many favors for money that I saved the company. They won't dare say a word to me," he assured me.

"You'll start Monday, your usual time," he informed me.

With that, we shook hands again. I left Baldwin and headed back home.

That evening, Veronica informed me that Stella received the news that I was home. In her message, she noted that I would probably be too tired to go out dancing on Saturday night, but I was welcome to come for family dinner on Sunday. I told Veronica to reply that the idea would be excellent. Just give me the time that I should arrive.

Later, she informed me that 2 pm would be perfect but warned me that it was expected to snow Saturday night and into Sunday morning. Welcome back to Philadelphia!

Just as predicted, about four inches of snow had fallen during the night and early morning hours. It was an annoyance, but the white stuff's fresh blanket looked quite beautiful. The branches on the trees twinkled and glittered in the sunlight. Icicles hung from the porch roof and the wrought iron fence. The temperature registered 30 degrees.

I shoveled the steps and walkway before we all headed across the street for Mass.

Attending the service would be another welcome experience for me. Slowly I was adjusting to civilian life again. For how long that was the unknown!

With everyone dolled up in their Sunday finest, we made our way over to St. John's. The church was packed, despite the weather. Monsignor Bednarczyk and several parishioners embraced me with handshakes and hugs after Mass.

Mom made a quick breakfast and a fresh pot of coffee. Pop and I shared the Sunday newspaper. This ritual was another excellent reason to be back home!

Before we realized it, the time had come for Veronica and me to catch the streetcar to make the journey to the Zwolinski's home. This time we had to bundle up warm and put on our goulashes.

The trip lasted a little longer than usual, but surprisingly, we arrived right on time at 2 pm.

As soon as we walked in the front door, and before we could unbundle our winter clothes, I could detect the tantalizing aroma of roasted pork in the air.

Mrs. Zwokinski made a delicious pan of pork chops, served with potatoes, and fried cabbage with bacon. It was all delightful.

For dessert, the special treat was a platter of Rozalijia's homemade Pączki or Polish doughnuts. Confectionary sugar dusted the doughnuts. Stella's mother offered two flavors: raspberry jam and custard-filled.

While all enjoyed the coffee and dessert, the inquiry about my assignment in Texas was underway.

I was compelled to repeat politely the tales and experiences that I had relayed to my own family just a few nights before. My explanation seemed to satisfy even the most curious minds, and we relaxed in the parlor.

Joe, Veronica, and Stella filled me in on the latest developments in the news, while Franz quietly sat in the corner, smoking his pipe while smiling and nodding occasionally.

Veronica quickly pointed out that her brother, Joe, had recently purchased a phonograph machine. She asked him to show me how it operated. Joe demonstrated the device by playing French Composer Claude Debussy's recording of "Sonata for flute, viola, and harp."

The piece was beautiful, elegant, and full of fantasy. It was a peaceful and most relaxing way to end our visit.

Veronica and I decided to start our journey home since the weather had not improved, and it was beginning to ice over. I assured Stella that I would be in touch to make plans and was so glad to see her once again. With that, we were on our way.

Monday morning, the snow had begun to melt, with the temperature reaching the high thirties. The sidewalks and streets were starting to clear, and the trees were dripping as the sun was radiating its warmth.

My first day back at Baldwin, Uncle Leo had me go slow from the outset. Coffee and chit-chat started the day. When the boss felt the roads were clear enough, he called on Paul to give me my first driving lesson.

We grabbed the same company truck that we used when Leo sent us for the gauges. The old 1914 Model T Roadster pick-up didn't seem any worse for the wear when we drove it the last time.

Paul instructed me how to turn the engine's crank, and the old bucket of bolts started rather quickly. Like before, the motor was rather noisy with its continuous sounds of fluttering, screeching, and popping.

My first driving lesson required that I learn all the vehicle's instruments, the clutch and shifter procedures, and other basics.

Initially, we took the driving exercise slowly. Paul directed me to practice in one of the large open lots owned by the company.

From there, we traveled several blocks around that section of the city.

It was challenging at first, navigating traffic signs and signals while operating the controls. Maintaining an awareness of the other vehicles on the road also required a keen sense of focus. This endeavor proved to be the most stressful.

While driving south of Broad Street, a large produce truck from Levinson & Albright Produce Co. pulled directly in my path from Callowhill Street.

In a panic, I managed to slam my foot on the brake pedal but failed to push in the clutch. Although I was able to avoid a crash, I obviously stalled the pick-up. The maneuver unquestionably frightened Paul but clearly embarrassed me. In the end, it was a learning experience and did no real harm.

Before we realized it, lunchtime was soon approaching. Paul noted that he had a few maintenance chores to handle before the break. He advised me to head back to the office to see if Uncle Leo had any last-minute duties for me, as well.

The rest of the week proceeded as usual. The streets were clear, and Leon interspersed my driving lessons with a variety of office tasks. It was great to be back at work, but I realized more than anything that I had missed Uncle Leo's coffee the most!

Spring produced some mild weather in 1917, and those warm days enabled pop to read the newspaper and drink his morning coffee on the front porch.

Occasionally he would toss a few tidbits my way as I left work.

For instance, "Hey, Tommy! It says here in the paper that the Piggly Wiggley Markets ere opening the first self-service grocery stores," he noted.

He added, "There's also an article here that the breakfast cereal companies are now proclaiming, 'Breakfast, the most important meal of the day,' whattya think about that?"

"Well, that could be true, pop, but I'll still settle for a couple of mom's eggs and toast," I replied.

Since the street department had moved him to the later shift, he was obviously hunting for a less tiring job, such as a night watchman or as a security guard during the day.

"Okay, pop," I said, "have a good day!"

"You, too! Son," he said while never lifting his eyes from his newspaper.

With Easter approaching, April 8, the winds of war appeared to be picking up, as well. I received another letter from the military on March 25 that I was being called upon for active service.

Sure enough, just two days before Easter, on Good Friday, April 6, the US officially declared war on Germany. The winds were growing stronger.

Last year, I faced an uncertain future, but the outlook appeared much grimmer during this holy season. It was only a matter of time before the call to action would be genuine.

As one might imagine, this year's Easter celebration would have a somber tone. Our family went through the motions, but the mood was anything but joyous.

Nearly two months would pass, however, before any more news arrived. My War draft card had arrived on June 5, 1917, and included with that were orders to report to the recently built Camp Wanamaker in Jenkintown, Pa. on Sunday, July 15. This facility was located just outside the city of Philadelphia.

*   18 NOTE: Department store magnate John Wanamaker also created a summer camp for his young employees in 1902 known as the John Wanamaker Commercial Institute Summer Camp.

The 250-acre site was bounded by Hillside Avenue, Jenkintown Road, Highland Avenue and Old York Road. The orders stated that I would be temporarily stationed there with the rest of my National Guard unit.

We expected that this stay at the camp would be a short one. The general sense seemed to be that the army had other plans for us.

In addition to morning calisthenics drills, we spent most of our time re-packing and re-organizing our equipment.

If military life taught us anything, it was the fact that redundancy reigned supreme. The officers ordered us to do things over and over until we could do them in our sleep.

Once we completed that mission, we loaded the gear onto railroad cars parked on a nearby spur.

This task could only mean one thing; we were shipping out. Where? That was the question, indeed!

Since postage only cost two cents per letter, regular correspondence with the family was sent and received quite frequently. From the camp to home and vice-versa, delivery typically took place within a day or so. Rumor had it; however, the war effort would require a postage increase to three cents in November.

A proclamation came down that Sunday, July 28, was designated as "Family Day" at Camp Wanamaker. An open invitation permitted family and friends of the personnel to participate in a picnic on the grounds.

Mom and pop made the trip with the girls, and I just knew that my mother would pack a bountiful bushel of food.

It was a delightfully sunny day. At noon, the comfortable 79-degree weather was further enhanced by a cloudless blue sky.

On two large blankets was spread a feast consisting of a basket of fried chicken drumsticks, ham sandwiches on rye bread with horseradish, a crock of her homemade dill pickles, plus a bundle of plum cake. Two sizable bottles of freshly-squeezed lemonade were made by my mother, as well.

At the picnic, Stella made one final appeal to change my mind about committing our future. "Tommy," she began, "I wish in my heart that you weren't leaving me behind with such uncertainty.

Nothing would make me happier than if we could get married or least engaged before you leave again," she went on.

"I know, Babe. I know," I began, "but you know exactly how I feel about the situation at this time. "There are only three possible outcomes to all this. When I finally get drawn into this war, and you know that it's going to happen eventually, one looming possibility is the fact that I may never return," I explained.

"Where will that leave you?" I asked

"What kind of future would you have? Will you be able to pick up and just go on with your life?" I questioned further.

"The other likely event is that I would survive the war but return severely injured. I could lose an arm or a leg. I could be confined to a wheelchair. Should I be blinded or lose my hearing, or whatever, we could never have a family. I could never support you. Once again, it would be no life for you. A very gloomy outlook, indeed," I went on to say.

"Finally, the best of all possible scenarios would be if I returned without any harm.

"The fact is, the odds are two-to-one against that. I've seen enough dart games and seen my share of card games, and I am well aware of the odds.

"I want the same things you do, but my mind tells me this is not practical. The future doesn't bode well for that little farm in the country right now," I concluded.

"I know... I know you're right, Tommy," she responded, "but I can't help the way I feel," Stella countered.

At that point, I suggested a break from our little talk. "C'mon," I urged. "Let's go for a walk."

There was a small pond on the shaded grounds of the picnic grove. Probably the size of an acre or less. The scene revealed other soldiers and their families enjoying their picnics together, as well.

I spotted Joe Krause, a buddy from the 109th, along the water's edge beneath a tall oak tree with his wife, Irene, and their seven-year-old son, Joey Jr. The young boy was learning the fine art of catching bluegills from his father. A string containing several of the freshly caught panfish seemed to suggest a successful day.

As we passed by the young family, Joe looked up and nodded. He then turned to his son and said, "Daddy will clean those up for you and wrap them in a newspaper. Mommy will cook them up for you later!"

Sitting on a green wooden bench under another mature tree was my pal, Doc. Visiting him today was his brother Calvin.

Irvin's 15-year-old brother didn't have an undeniable passion for formal schooling like his big brother. The teenager abandoned school earlier this year to become an apprentice in his uncle's plumbing firm.

As we approached the midway point around the pond, a small family of wood ducks was enjoying a swim around the water's banks.

Beneath the water's surface, one could see schools of small fish creating their own ripples as they scurried out of the way of the passing ducks.

Our footsteps occasionally startled a wary bullfrog who was probably trying to enjoy the afternoon, as well.

One of the ducklings lost his way in the pond's reeds and promptly sounded the alarm for his momma. She swiftly retreated to perform the rescue. All was right with the world, once again!

Upon our return from our stroll, there was very little time left except for the tearful goodbyes. The remnants of the picnic were gathered and packed up. Hugs and kisses were handed out in bountiful servings because one never knew when the next one would be, if ever!

During the night, it seemed like all hell was breaking loose at the barracks next door.

It was well after midnight when I first heard the disturbance. A scarcely detectable glow of moonlight peeked through a nearby window, and according to my watch dial, it was 12:43.

Despite the muffled sound of footsteps and the crescendo of approaching voices, I preferred to stay put in my bunk and mind my own business. Several others, however, scrambled outside soon after the disturbance began.

Those who witnessed the incident stated that a mob had gathered outside the door of a nearby barracks. About a dozen individuals made up the group. It included two Military Police members, two Philadelphia policemen, a middle-aged couple, and a half dozen civilian men and soldiers bearing torches and lanterns. The lawmen had billy clubs in hand and guns drawn.

One of the MPs yelled, "Private Daniel Doughtery, this is the police! Come out now with your hands in the air!"

After several minutes, the officer warned the soldier a second time, "Private Doughtery, you have two minutes to come out here, or we will come in and remove you by force!"

With no response, the mob grew agitated and urged the law to take action. In addition to pushing and shoving, there was plenty of grumbling and yelling.

Those in charge patiently waited for a response, but none came. Except for some heavy breathing, the night air was deadly silent.

Finally, the authorities stormed the building and were led to the very last bunk in the back of the room.

There on the cot, they found Doughtery. He was motionless under the blanket. They shook him, grabbed him by the arms, and physically stood him on his feet with some effort.

According to witnesses, the soldier stood motionless and spoke not a word. He was either dumbfounded or drunk. Possibly both.

Beneath the bunk, they also discovered the scantily clothed Mercy Hanlon, his 18-year-old girlfriend. She was wrapped in one of the U.S. Army-issued olive drab wool blankets. The police escorted the young girl out of the barracks and into her parents' custody, who were waiting outside.

As for Doughtery, the authorities took him to the camp brigg for confinement. News of the incident quickly circulated the base, and it was evident that "Dandy" Dan Doughtery, as his friends knew him, tried to sneak the girl into his barracks one last time before shipping out.

The next day, a hearing resulted, and the punishment for the guilty party of two weeks in custody. Our CO announced that our unit would ship out to Camp Hancock, GA, on Saturday, August 11.

Doughtery, our CO told us, would eventually join us in Georgia once he completed his confinement.

Mark Twain once said, "God created war so that Americans would learn geography."

Sister Benedictus Carmella would be so proud!

Zwolinski's first residence, 138 Kenilworth St., Phila., PA
Image Source: Author's Photo

Rozalia Zwolinki portrait
Image Source: Author's Photo

Rozalia Zwolinski with Lottie on Kenilworth St.
Image Source: Author's Photo

A young Rozalia Zwolinski
Image Source: Author's Photo

"JOURNEY TO GEORGIA"

PRR Locomotive No. 7002 was built by Baldwin in 1902. RR Museum of Pa.
Image Source: Mike Huhn, flickr

CHAPTER 17

"Journey to Georgia"

We were blessed with another bright sunny day that Saturday morning. Assigned to our trip to Georgia was the Pennsy locomotive #7002.

> *   *19 NOTE: The Pennsylvania Railroad engine No. 7002 was a 4-4-2 E2 Class. It was built in 1902, and three years later, it was clocked at 127.1 mph. The locomotive was initially named The Pennsylvania Special, but in 1912 it was renamed The Broadway Limited. In August 1916, the engine was refurbished as an E7sa. A similar locomotive (No. 8063) was restored and donated to the Railroad Museum of Pennsylvania in 1979. It bears the 7002 number plate.*

As the massive Iron Horse chugged its way onto Camp Wanamaker's siding, more than 300 troops waited for the beast to screech to a stop. The engineer sounded the shrill whistle several times while the bell tolled its own warning. The familiar sounds of banging, hissing, and puffing seemed to create a bizarre mechanical symphony.

Once we were given the signal, the loading began. Army engineers loaded the essential equipment while we took on the responsibility of securing our personal gear.

We were on our way at 0700 hours, and initially, the trip went relatively smoothly. We passed through man familiar sights around Philadelphia and Chester before heading South. I took one final glance back towards the city. The Billy Penn statue atop city hall soon faded from view.

At 0853. the train reached Wilmington, DE. Our route would then take us through Dover, DE. This was followed by Aberdeen, MD, with our sights set on Baltimore.

Seventeen miles from Baltimore, near Essex Junction, at 0944, we encountered a problem. You could feel the train slowing down. The cars began to jerk back and forth as the locomotive decelerated to that of a crawl. Eventually, we stopped dead in our tracks and remained so for 37 minutes.

At that point, one of the NCOs went from car to car with the following announcement:

"Men, we have just received word that a Norfolk and Southern train with 54 cars from the Stone Mountain Coal Co., near Matewan, W. VA, has derailed up ahead. Initial reports are that the damage is extensive, and it could take three or four days to clear."

"Great! What now, Sarge?" one of the guys asked.

"Well... we are just waiting for clearance, but we will be re-routed through Columbia and eventually onto Washington, DC. The detour shouldn't delay our trip more than an hour or so," he concluded.

Apparently, the coal train wreck turned everything into a bottleneck, and nothing was moving. Our one-hour delay turned into an 11 and a half hour layover.

The railroad porters managed to feed us two meals during the setback. Lunch consisted of ham and cheese sandwiches with dill pickles, while the staff served us meatloaf, mashed potatoes, and green beans for dinner.

By 2200 hours, some movement was finally taking place, and our train switched over to another line. Eventually, we rejoined the mainline near Washington, DC. Some of the sights in our nation's capital were visible from our vantage point as we passed through the city around midnight.

We were relieved that there were no further incidents over the next 24 hours. Even though the Pennsy 7002 had high-speed capability, travel was prolonged due to the rails' substantial volume of traffic.

Our journey took us through Richmond, VA, and Winston-Salem, NC, but as we approached Rocky Mount, the seemingly dependable locomotive developed mechanical difficulties. The train was about three-quarters of a mile from the Rocky Mount depot when the engine began to slow down considerably.

The great puffs of white smoke turned a dark gray, almost black color before the massive engine came once again to a standstill.

Immediately after we came to a complete stop, the engineer, dressed in his grimy, well-worn blue coveralls, jumped from the cab's left side and ran to the front of the locomotive. He examined the piston, the connecting rods, and the drivers. Everything appeared to pass his inspection.

His fireman emerged from the cab, and he, too, conducted a visual analysis. Simultaneously, the engineer went to the other side of the track to check the right side. It only took a few seconds for him to recognize that the locomotive had a shattered piston. The fireman seemed to concur as the two men pointed at the engine and nodded their heads affirmatively.

The engineer took a red bandana out of his right rear pocket and threw it to the ground while stomping his foot. Since I had my head hanging out of a window in the second car, I could easily hear him rant for several minutes. His frustration boiled over as he cursed and waved both hands in the air while throwing his hat on the ground. It landed right beside the bandana.

Initially, the bald man began to bend over to pick up the items, but he quickly changed his mind and kicked the hat with his big, black boot. It flew in the air about four feet off the ground, and he nearly caught it, but as luck would have it, the hat landed almost at the original spot.

The fireman merely shook his head and walked away. At the same time, the brakeman and two conductors participated in a conference held trackside. The railroad workers all had a look of frustration on their faces.

Within minutes, two army officers, accompanied by two MPs, navigated their way from the rear of the long train to the front while walking on the uneven ballast between the rails.

Word spread quickly through the cars about the engine's troubles, and we all knew immediately that our arrival at Camp Hancock would again be delayed.

I was beginning to have my doubts about this train travel. We experienced two significant setbacks on our way to Texas, and now our trip to Georgia was much of the same. Seeing many of these iron horses roll off the assembly line at Baldwin, I never dreamed such mechanical issues existed.

Due to the heavy demand for locomotives to relocate troops around the county, it took five hours to get an engine from the Augusta and Summerville Railroad. To clear the tracks, it required another two and a half hours to remove the disabled locomotive.

As usual, card games and other gambling activities filled the downtime. Some of the men walked the distance to the depot to pass the time, as well.

Once the entire operation was complete, we were on our way. Our itinerary took us through Charlotte, NC, Spartansburg, SC, and finally through Augusta, GA.

The Georgia Railroad constructed a special spur that ran directly into Camp Hancock, and at 0623 on Wednesday, August 11, our train rolled into the main depot at the military installation.

After unloading the railcars, we walked to the entrance of the base. While much of it was still under construction, we observed it to be a sprawling complex already. Much more massive than our dusty accommodations at Camp Stewart in El Paso, TX.

Wrightsboro Road ran through the middle of the installation. About midway through the camp, our NCO, Sgt. First Class Charlie Vogan informed us that we would need to cross the drill field on our left.

He reported that we would find the area for the 108th Field Artillery on the other side. Vogan notified us that it was on Tyler Avenue, but we couldn't miss it.

Vogan headed to headquarters to meet with Capt. Mercher. He explained that he would join us later.

We pitched our tents in the specified area. One of the other NCOs told us that wooden floors and sides would be added later.

Sharing the eight-man tent with me were: SFC. Charles Vogan, Sgt. Richard Conolly, Sgt. William Haeberle, PFC Roy Wilson, PFC Harold Dohner, PFC Carrol Kline, and "Doc" Schweppenheiser.

I noticed that the YMCA building was adjacent to our section on the right. However, on the left side, were the tents for 107th Field Artillery, 109th Field Artillery, and the 103rd Ammunition Train.

Beyond that was the Base Hospital Complex, which included the Red Cross Hospital Building and a field hospital.

The 103rd Sanitary Train maintained quarters across the road from the YMCA building. Just south of the 103rd was the camp bakery.

I was indeed looking forward to waking up in the mornings with the aroma of freshly baked bread in the air.

Once we unpacked and organized our gear, Doc and I went on an exploratory mission to get familiar with the rest of the camp.

Across Wrightsboro Road was the MTD. Range Camp (Mobilization and Training Dept.). This field was a large bivouac section comprised of hundreds of tents and temporary structures.

To the north was Pennsylvania Avenue and the location of the 56th Infantry Brigade, Division Headquarters, and the Cavalry. Adjacent to them was the 55th Infantry Brigade and the mess area.

"This place is huge," Schweppenheiser said.

I agreed with him, saying, "Yeah, it makes El Paso resemble a scout camp."

As we looked over the grounds, some large, more mature, shade trees were purposely left standing during construction. The perimeter appeared to be heavily forested, as well.

At the northwest corner of the drill field was another YMCA building and the K of C building (The Knights of Columbus, a Catholic organization).

From there, Stewart Avenue led us past the stables and the 103rd Regiment Engineers' area.

Another YMCA building stood at the end of the road.

Doc and I stopped to chat with one of the other soldiers walking towards us to ask him a few questions regarding the camp.

He was a tall, slender man, and his uniform was in tip-top shape.

"Say, pal," I began, "we just got here, and we were trying to get the lay of the land. We just walked through the main area here, but we wondered about the rest of the place."

"Sure," the corporal replied, "over there," pointing southwest, "is the storehouse, the latrines, the pistol range, and the airfield."

"The trenches are out in that area, as well," he noted. "Okay," I responded.

"There's a couple of ponds out that way, too," he noted while pointing in a more westerly direction, "that's where the rifle range is located and the Remount Depot. You'll know it when you see the railroad spur leading to the depot," he concluded.

*   20 NOTE: During World War I, the US Army established Remount Depots to buy and sell horses and mules. These facilities were generally located near the railroad for their transportation. Camp Hancock had 1,980 animals used as draft, riding, and pack animals. The army also used them for pulling wagon trains, guns, and field ambulances.*

"How big is this place," Irvin asked.

"Well," he began while rubbing his chin with his hand, "let's see," he paused again, "they tell me it's 1,777 acres, and there are 1,300 buildings. So far, it cost a couple of million bucks, but they ain't done yet!"

"Geez," Irvin exclaimed, "that's something else!"

At that very moment, three large trucks loaded with fresh lumber rumbled down Wrightsboro Road, which was just a stone's throw from our vantage point.

"Thanks for the info, pal," I responded. "Maybe we'll see you around."

"See ya' fellas," he replied as he continued on his way.

Most of that first week involved indoctrination into camp life and orientation. Each morning began with the camp band playing a composition entitled "Kahki Bill" or "Number 9." as they call it.

Following morning mess and calisthenics, it's onto the drill field. I thought it was peculiar that each company had its designated place on the drill field.

Still, I soon learned that it was done in this fashion so that any officer could determine where each company in the regiment was during the daily training.

During the balance of the morning, our orders require us to drill around the main areas of the base as part of the process of orientation.

Classroom indoctrination is a significant component of our afternoons. The main focus is on the camp's layout, schedules, and not only what we can expect during our stay but what is expected of us.

In addition to the specialized instruction designed for our outfit, we would undergo extensive training in all areas of military work and warfare, including trench construction, rifle practice, maneuvers, and bayonet use.

My specialized training would be medically related with the Sanitary Detachment, and most of my work would take place at the field hospital just as it was in Texas.

"In essence," our instructor noted, "it was the army's job to teach us how to fight as a team and inspire us to respect the sacredness of the American cause."

Our CO announced that we had the weekend off, but come Monday, our training would begin. "Get ready for a rousing performance of 'Kahki Bill,' at daybreak," he warned us.

Saturday night, as I laid in my bunk, I just couldn't fall asleep. My mind drifted away from my present situation, here in Georgia, and focused almost entirely on Stella back home.

Initially, I envisioned her face. It's a kind face with soft, brown eyes and a captivating smile.

Those brown eyes are deceiving. They feel like they are not just looking at my face but also searching beyond my appearance, delving into my heart and soul.

Her smile is almost Mona Lisa-like. I am not comparing Stella to Leonardo Da Vinci's masterpiece of 400 years ago, but there is something in her smile, as well.

I am always wondering, "What is she thinking? Is she trying to read my mind? Sometimes it seems so. Is she trying to figure out a way into my heart, or is she just happy living in the moment?" I can't tell.

It often appears as a warm, loving smile, while other glances reveal a wry, mysterious, and analyzing appearance. It's a smile that lingers in my mind even when I look away. It is in my mind when I close my eyes to go to sleep at night, and it is there when I awake in the morning.

I constantly wrestle with my decision to hold off on marriage until we see what happens with this war. My mind tells me it is a logical decision based on practicality, but my heart desperately tries to say that it is an opportunity that may never come again. It's no wonder that I cannot sleep.

They say a smile can turn a person's day around, but the voice inside my head is telling me that Stella's smile may turn my life around. Finally, I closed my eyes and slept on it!

Sunday morning, I joined Irvin and a couple of the other guys for a morning worship service. From there, a visit to the mess hall for breakfast was in order. Afterward, I returned to my bunk in the barracks. Reflecting on my insomnia last night, I decided to pen a letter to Stella while it was fresh in my mind.

Camp Hancock, Georgia August 14, 1917

Dear Stella,

> *I survived my first few days here in Georgia. It's just as hot here as it was in Texas, but we have trees to make it somewhat bearable. They say yesterday it was 111 degrees. Not sure if that was in the sun or the shade. Does it matter?*
>
> *There's no electricity here, so I have a candle sitting in an old soup can that I can use for light. My suitcase serves as my writing desk. You should see that sight!*
>
> *I tried to talk to some of the southern boys down here, but they're hard to understand with their accent. Nobody seems to know anything about Augusta. I'm sure we'll find out.*
>
> *There's a couple of colored companies here at the camp, also. They keep them separate, though. I see several working in the mess hall.*
>
> *We had two calamities on our trip down here. One was a coal train wreck, and later our locomotive shattered a piston. We had to sit idle until another engine arrived. I can't wait to tell Uncle Leo that the 7002 left us sitting in Rocky Mount.*
>
> *I hope all is well with you and your family. Tell my sister, Veronica, to let mom, pop, and the others know that I'm getting along just fine.*
>
> *What's new with your brother, Joe? Did he sign up for the Navy yet?*
>
> *Tomorrow, Monday, they warned us that we would get down to the actual work. We'll see how that goes.*
>
> *I often think of you, and if you could send me a photograph of yourself, it would make my time here more bearable. It's not that I need an image because I have every inch of your face memorized. Send me one just the same. Take care, babe!*

With Love, Tommy

* *21 NOTE: Like all southern military camps, those in Georgia operated under the Jim Crow separation laws. Federal prohibitions of Black troops in combat meant that African American recruits trained and served in engineer service or labor battalions under white officers.*

Sunday afternoon, I joined Joe Herbein and Doc for an exploratory mission. Joe wanted to investigate the ponds we were told existed in the remote areas of camp by the soldier we passed on the street.

Herbein was the chap who took me on that wild fishing excursion at Mt. Gretna. I'll never forget the image of him getting pushed into the creek by that renegade cow.

Initially, we discovered two tiny ponds. Herbein referred to them as mud puddles, but eventually, his persistence paid off because we stumbled upon a larger body of water capable of sustaining a variety of fish, including sunfish, bluegills, bass, catfish, and black crappies.

He was very good at identifying fish and their habitats, unlike a city boy like me, who only spent a few summer afternoons fishing in Pennypack Park with some of the other lads from school.

Joe's mission was to scout the area and return early in the morning on one of our days off. I had little doubt that he would be successful but conceded that the odds were good that it would turn into an adventure. I made myself a mental note to be busy that day and reminded Schweppenheiser that it would probably be best for him to do the same.

"We are serving no one man, we are serving our country." - **General Winfield Scott Hancock**. (Union General, who served in the Civil War, and the namesake of Camp Hancock.)

Bakery at Camp Hancock
Image Source: Unkown

Base hospital at Camp Hancock
Image Source: Unkown

Camp Artillery
Image Source: Unkown

Camp Library
Image Source: Unkown

View of Camp Hancock
Image Source: Unkown

Medical trucks in use at the camp
Image Source: Unkown

Red Cross Building
Image Source: Unkown

YMCA building
Image Source: Unkown

"BIG TIME BOXING"

Boxing champ Benny Leonard brings fights to Hancock
Image Source: Unkown

CHAPTER 18

"Big Time Boxing"

The first real excitement at Camp Hancock was the announcement of a boxing match set for Saturday, October 13.

Although the base had three YMCA buildings and several recreation areas, the Commanding Officer ordered the construction of a boxing ring with bleachers in one of the open fields. This arena was much like the one the engineers erected for us in Texas.

News circulated around the camp that the bout's headliner would be none other than World Lightweight Champion Benny Leonard.

Leonard, a Jewish-American boxer from New York's Lower East Side, defeated Featherweight Champ Johnny Kilbane on July 25 at Philadelphia's Shibe Park baseball stadium.

He also defended his Lightweight title against Leo Johnson, September 21. Leonard won convincingly with a technical knockout of Johnson in the first round.

One of the guys commented, "That was hardly worth the effort of putting on his trunks."

Since the fight was so effortless, the champ needed a tune-up before facing Frank Kirke on November 28. That match was scheduled to take place at the Stockyards Stadium in Denver, CO.

At Camp Hancock, Leonard would face the "Camp Champ" as they billed the event. Every Saturday afternoon, two soldiers on the base would square off until a local champion was crowned. That lucky guy would climb into the ring with Leonard.

There were some exciting contests over the four weeks, but Bert Arromanches earned the "Camp Champ" honors.

In the first contest, Arromanches defeated Tommy Reed, from the 103rd Ammunition Train, in four rounds. "Bert the Bulldog" was in total command throughout the fight.

He notched his second victory the following week when he knocked out Patrick O'Hara, of the 56th Infantry Brigade, in Round 3. The challenger hung tough for two rounds before Arromanches flattened him with a left hook. It took several minutes for the loser to come around. They say the Irishman was in a stupor until the following day.

In week three, German-born Hans Schnickelfritz attempted to stop the favorite, but he also lost his bout in the seventh round. This fight was the most competitive of the four. Arromanches appeared to be unstoppable.

In his fourth and final bout to become Camp Champion, Arromanches knocked out Hungarian Andor Palinkas in the first round.

It only took the victor two minutes and thirty-four seconds to deliver the winning punch - a right uppercut that almost took the Hungarian's head off.

The French-born boxer immigrated to the United States about ten years ago and was living in Maine.

No stranger to boxing, Arromanches, won a handful of amateur bouts before joining the service.

The 133-pound fighter is five-foot, six inches tall, and has a 70-inch reach—a perfect match-up for Leonard.

Thousands gathered around the ring for the contest. Wooden barrels, supply wagons, and the high branches of trees served as vantage points for soldiers who were anxious to get a glimpse of the action.

Some stood on the roof of a nearby supply shack, but MPs had to chase many guys away out of fear that the structure may collapse from the weight.

Arromanches stepped into the ring, wearing red, white, and blue trunks. The colors were a tribute to his new life in America as well as his French heritage. Rumor has it that some of the lads in his outfit chipped in to have them made especially for him.

Wearing solid black trunks, Leonard stayed in his own corner. When he was introduced, the boxer received a mix of cheers and boos.

Half of the camp's troops applauded out of respect for the World Champ, but the rest shouted various obscenities and ridiculed Leonard. They were hopeful that one of their own would land a blow that was capable of putting the champion down on the canvas.

The stakes were high for Leonard. He was risking his World Championship reputation by taking on an amateur boxer who had spent the last two months scrubbing pots in the mess hall.

Arromanches, however, had nothing to lose. He had already reached his pinnacle of success by winning the camp crown. Taking a shot at the World Lightweight Champion was a bonus. A good showing in the ring and he would never have to pay for a drink again!

The long-awaited showdown began with Round One!

The referee gave the two men their instructions in the center of the ring. Although the contest was outdoors, the crowd's noise was deafening in anticipation of the competition's start.

Leonard agreed to a ten-round fight, but nobody actually believed it would go that far.

Since I'm not an enormous boxing enthusiast, I didn't know much about the famous fighter. Barney Roth, one of the guys in my company, told me that Leonard had lightning reflexes and could think fast on his feet.

The opening bell sounded, and the fight was officially underway. Both men started slowly, but midway through the first round, the punches started flying.

Barney turned to me and said, "There's some brilliant boxing going on here from both sides."

The score was even in the first few rounds, and it looked like Arromanches might have a chance. However, in Barney's opinion, "Leonard was just waiting him out, letting his opponent tire from putting up a constant defense."

"I think Leonard wants to get a full workout before his next fight. He could've knocked "Frenchy" out in the first or second round, but he's working on some of his techniques," Roth commented.

"I see what you mean," I replied.

"It's a dangerous plan," he went on, "all Arromanches has to do is land a lucky punch, and it's curtains for the champ."

In the fifth round, Leonard landed several punches to his opponent's jaw, which clearly weakened him, but Leonard allowed him to recover.

Arromanches dodged several of Leonard's punches in the sixth and mounted a comeback. The challenger managed to land more punches and better blows in the effort.

While the French boxer out-pointed Leonard in the sixth, very few watching the fight felt like the World Champ was ever in danger. None of Arromanches' blows were devastating to his opponent.

The seventh round, however, was a different story. Arromanches landed only one clean blow to Leonard's face. The famed boxer's dark hair, which he always parted in the middle, remained unfussed.

Leonard looked as if he caught his adversary's punches in the air and blocked Arromanches return blows with ease.

At that point, the World Lightweight Champ mounted a massive assault and knocked the challenger down onto the canvas twice.

Leonard delivered a crossing right punch to put Arromanches down the first time.

Though the "Camp Champ" rose after the referee's brief count, Leonard attacked with a series of rapid rights and lefts. Arromanches went down a second time.

Clearly groggy, Arromanches tried to drag himself to the ropes to get up but was unable. The referee made the mandatory ten count while the beaten boxer sat on the canvas. With sweat pouring down his face from his brow, the fighter looked dazed and exhausted.

Just as the fight began, the mob offered a mix of cheers and jeers. Although Camp Hancock's reigning champion lost the battle, his supporters carried him off on their shoulders in celebration.

Bert Arromanches went toe to toe with the World Lightweight Champion and delivered a remarkable effort. Win, lose, or draw, the mess hall cook had no reason to be ashamed.

As for Benny Leonard, the referee raised the winner's hand as a sign of his victory, and only he knows how tough Bert Arromanches was as an opponent.

Apparently, the champ's visit to Camp Hancock made him no worse for the wear. On November 28, Leonard defeated Frank Kirke with a convincing first-round knockout, just one minute and twenty seconds into the fight. A right hook to the jaw that Kirke never saw coming put him down for the count.

The men talked about the match for weeks throughout the camp, and Bert never had to wash a pot again. His red, white, and blue trunks hung over his bunk with pride. Benny Leonard even autographed them, writing, *"Best of Luck to the Camp Champ - Benny Leonard, October 13, , 1917!"*

Sunday evening, I decided to write a letter to Stella. It was long overdue since it had been a while since I have done so.

Camp Hancock, Georgia October 14, 1917

Dear Stella,

Yesterday, we had some real excitement as one of our boys fought a boxing match against the World Lightweight Champion, Benny Leonard.

Bert Arromanches put up a good fight, but we all knew in our hearts that the champ would prevail.

The big fight was the climax of a series of bouts here in the camp. Several of our lads competed to go up against Leonard.

Today, some of us fellows took a walk to the pine forest at the camp's edge. On the hike were Jimmy Drake, Howard Munson, Jack Boland, and Larry Dunlap. My friends Irvin Schweppenheiser and Harry Haeberle didn't feel up to tagging along.

There was a refreshing stream running through the area, and we sat around a clearing near the shore, talking about home, our families, and girlfriends.

Drake mentioned that he got married right before we left for Georgia. He married a Jersey girl named Thelma. In comparison, Munson revealed that his mother was extremely ill, and he worried about her condition. He told us that his mother was suffering from TB.

You would be surprised by the things you learn about others when you're just having a bull session.

Boland told us he played the accordion back home, and Dunlap chimed in that he was a fiddle player. Both guys noted that they could play almost any music style but lean more towards the Irish tunes they learned over the years.

I asked Larry what the difference was between a violin and a fiddle. He replied, "If you're playing a piece by Frédéric Chopin, it was a violin, but if you're playing an Appalacian folk tune such as "Cripple Creek," or an Irish number like "The Kerry Polka," it's a fiddle." Interesting!

How are things at the arsenal? I bet they're pretty busy. I'm glad you enjoy working there. There's nothing worse than hating your job.

The food around here is no better, but the weather has cooled off considerably. Fall in Georgia is not like fall in Philly. I'll take it over the unbearable weather of El Paso, however!

Please give my regards to everyone. I hope they're doing as well as I am. I will write again when I am able.

Well, babe, it's time that I signed off for now. Take care of yourself.

Sending You My Love, Tommy

During my two months here at the camp, our company usually shared the mess hall with the Hospital Corps.

The mess hall was a wooden structure that was about 50-feet long. The building doubled as a social hall, and the recreation center went not in use for dining.

On Monday evenings, the hall was turned into a canteen for the fellows. There was a Victrola in the room, and it was used heavily by the guys. We may not have the most up-to-date records, but it's pleasant music just the same. Beer is readily available, but the hard stuff is hard to come by.

I have made some new friends and acquaintances. It's always a good idea to have some contacts in the mess hall. Those guys give you a heads up on the food, whether it's good or bad or if there's something exceptional coming up.

One of those associations was with a black fellow that I saw every day in the chow line. I only know him as Clay.

He is of average height and build, very dark-complected, but he always has a smile on his face.

Private Clay invariably greets me as, "Sir, Tommy, Sir."

Naturally, I always return the greeting with a hello and a smile, also. However, this evening, the mess hall worker called me aside and asked if I could help him out.

He motioned to one of the other guys to take his place, handing out the chow, and took me to an area nearby.

"Sir, Tommy, Sir," he began, "I know you don't really know me, but I wonder if you could help me out?"

"I'll try, pal. What can I do for you?" I asked.

"Well, I just got a letter from my grandmama, and she says that my grandpappy is very, very ill, sir. They live on a farm just outside Augusta," he explained. "I'm lookin' for someone to go with me to visit them," Clay went on.

"What do you need me for?" I asked.

"Down in these parts, it's not always safe for black folks to be out and about on their own," he added.

"We was warned not to travel alone," Clay continued.

"Why me, Clay?" Was my next question.

"*YOU* are one of the few guys in camp that greets me every day with a smile, and I just feels like I can trust you," the young man responded.

"I'm very flattered to hear that," was my comeback, "but I'm not so sure that I'm your guy. I've never been outside the camp!"

"You probably should be looking for someone more familiar with the area... the people... the customs of the South," I reasoned.

I could tell the young man was in a desperate situation, and he appeared to be a nice guy, but I wasn't sure I was ready to make such a commitment.

"Listen," he said convincingly, "I'll make all the arrangements. My mess sergeant will see to it that we both have weekend passes, and we will get a ride into town with one of the supply clerks."

"Okay, Clay," I replied, "let me think about it over tonight, and I will give you my answer in the morning, fair enough?"

"Yessir, yessir," he said, smiling from ear to ear while shaking both my hands. "Thank you, Sir Tommy, Sir, Thank you!"

We both walked back to the chow line, and he relieved the other mess worker. On this evening's menu was pork chops, and he put an extra one on my tray and gave me a wink.

Clay turned to the man in the next spot and said, "Give my friend, Sir Tommy, Sir, a big ole helpin' o' beans, Nate. Give him a big ole spoonful o' them beans!"

I wasn't sure I wanted to be wandering around Georgia with a colored fellow, but I needed to make my determination by morning.

The pork chops were mighty fine, and I always had a soft spot for beans, so Clay had the advantage thus far in my decision-making process.

In September, someone from engineering installed a wood-burning stove in our tent because the nights were growing colder.

Now, in mid-October, the heater was in use day and night. I went back to my tent for the evening.

Sgt. Vogan informed those in the tent that Liberty Loan Day would be observed in the camp next week. Although the day would be celebrated as a camp holiday, we were required to participate in a regimental parade.

While we were sitting around the fire, I mentioned to the guys my dilemma with Clay, the black fellow from the mess hall.

"I don't really know the guy that well, and I am not sure how I feel about going to some stranger's house, even if they are his grandparents," I confided.

"Well," Conolly began, "I've found most people in Augusta to be rather friendly and accommodating to us."

"Yeah, but you're white," Haeberle interjected. "They're not all that friendly when it comes to coloreds," he went on.

"That's what I'm afraid of," I admitted.

"Listen, Tommy," Irvin, the level-headed one, began with his opinion, "only you can decide what's best for you, but he obviously sought you out for a reason. He's put his trust in you to help him out."

"Not me, pal," chimed in Wilson, "you wouldn't catch me volunteering for anything like that!"

"Yeah, Tommy, I know you're the friendly type, and you're always looking to help others out," Haeberle explained, "but it's just askin' for trouble to get involved with something like that. There's a reason the army puts those coloreds in their own units," Harry argued.

"Do what you want…" he uttered before stopping in mid-sentence.

The conversation continued for nearly a half-hour, but no one actually convinced me which direction I should take in the matter. How do I get myself in these predicaments?

At morning mess, once again, Clay called me aside. "Did you decide anything, Sir Tommy Sir?" He asked.

Before I could answer, he put up his hand and said, "Wait! Let me tell you what I arranged before you give me y'all answer."

"I talked to my Sarge," he explained, "and he stated that he could arrange for you and me to be off Friday and Saturday. We will ride with the supply clerk into Augusta. The driver will drop us off just outside the city, and we will walk the rest of the way to my grandpappy's farm."

Clay continued, "We'll stay there Friday and Saturday. The supply truck will pick us up and get us back to camp Saturday night. I have to cook morning mess on Sunday. Whattaya think, Sir Tommy, Sir?"

I stood there, contemplating for a minute or two. The man seemed so desperate to see his ill grandfather. I could see it in his eyes as he waited for my response. I'd feel the same way if I were in his shoes.

Finally, I relented, "Okay. You can count on me. I'll help you out, Clay."

"Thank you, Sir Tommy, Sir, I's really appreciate it," he said with excitement while shaking my hand. The two of us went back to the chow line, and he rewarded me with a generous portion of SOS.

* *22 NOTE: SOS is a military reference to cream-dried beef on toast. The acronym stands for Sh*t On a Shingle.*

With that item settled, it appeared that I had plans for the weekend. My only concern was if I would regret my decision later.

I consoled myself by recalling a quote from Charles Dickens, *"No one is useless in this world who lightens the burdens of another."*

Camp Hancock. Schalata on the right
Image Source: Author's Photo

Camp officer on horseback
I Image Source: Author's Photo

Soldiers at Camp Hancock
Image Source: Author's Photo

Camp Calistetics
Image Source: Author's Photo

Schalata on right with assistant
Image Source: Author's Photo

"THE LEGEND OF OL' SNEAKY PETE"

The visit to grandpappy's farm
Image Source: North Carolina Museum of History

CHAPTER 19

"The Legend of Ol' Sneaky Pete"

Friday morning arrived, and I met Clay at the mess hall at 0930. The supply clerk had already fueled up his truck, and we were ready to head to Augusta.

The ride would take us about 30 minutes, and the two of us spent the time genuinely getting to know one another.

Clay told me that his full name was Clay Amole Jefferson, and he lived most of his life on his grandparents' farm. His grandfather's name is Amole Elias Abraham, and his grandmother just goes by Bessie.

As he told the story, his grandpappy and grandmama were former slaves. They worked the land of their owner, a Mr. Clayton T. Bohnefield. Unlike much of the south, Bohnefield was not in the cotton business. He preferred to grow mainly corn and other vegetable crops.

Once slavery was finally abolished, the wealthy landowner rewarded Clay's grandfather for his years of service with a small patch of land at the plantation's edge.

They lived in a modest farmhouse, and he noted that his grandpappy could grow just about anything. People in the area marveled at the variety of crops the old man raised on that small parcel of land. They had a milking cow on the farm and about a dozen chickens.

Clay told the story of a puppy he had when he was a boy.

"The pup was a black lab mix," he began, "and there was a terrible commotion out at the henhouse one day.

"Terrible commotion," he repeated. "Just a God-awful sound we could hear from a distance."

"My grandmama was the first to reach the coop," he went on, "and there was the pup, sticking his head out of that little wooden shack holding a white chicken in his mouth."

"First, my grandmama yelled for him to drop the darn thing, but grandpappy soon followed totin' a shotgun in his hands," he recalled.

"That's the last chicken that mangy mutt will ever see,' grandpappy hollered. He had a horrible, horrible scowl on his face, and his eyes were bulging with anger," Clay stated as he described the scene. "But, my grandmama put up her hands and defended the dog. She argued, 'Poor Boy don't know no better. He's jus' doin' what he knows. I'll make sure it don't happen again. Just leave it to me, old man. Go 'bout whatever it was you was doin' I'll handle it,' she said."

Clay noted, "From that day forward, we called the pup, Poor Boy."

"Grandmama tied a leather strap around the dog's neck, and on that strap was a small brass bell," he explained, "and whenever Poor Boy went near that henhouse, the bell would alert the chickens. One of the hens would sound the alarm, and grandmama put an end to the pup's interest in them. It took him a while, but that rascal soon learned that the chickens were off-limits. Grandpappy never did give Poor Boy another taste of chicken. Not even a scrap," Clay concluded.

"How long did you live there?" I asked.

"The whole story is, my momma and me lived there until I was goin' on 15, I guess. My daddy ran off when I was just a baby," he confided.

"One day, my momma, her name was Marabelle, packed up and says we was movin', her and me," Clay explained.

"Momma and I made our way north. She took on various jobs such as cookin' and cleanin' for white folks," he revealed.

Clay continued, "When we got as far as Baltimore, she found herself a boyfriend, and we settled down somewhat.

"One day, I woke up, and there was a note on the kitchen table, 'Dear Clay, my son, me an' Everett are going west. He thinks he has a job in Kentucky. You're a big boy now. Take care o' youself, momma.' That's how I found myself on my own," he told me.

His mood changed to a melancholy one almost immediately. The ordinarily cheerful fellow became somber as he reflected on that dark time in his life.

"What happened then?" I continued to probe.

"I continued working my way north to Philadelphia," Clay responded.

"The railroad was always lookin' for someone to paint their depots," he noted. "I think I painted every station from Baltimore to Philly," he admitted.

"Once I got to Philly," he continued, "I shined shoes at the Reading Terminal for a while before landing a job as a porter for the railroad."

"How did you wind up in the service?" I inquired because I was merely interested in knowing.

"I was walkin' by a recruiting office one day, and a feller in uniform jus' called me in and asks if I thought about joining the service?" Clay recalled.

My new friend explained that 20,000 blacks had enlisted in the military since May, and it was an opportunity for us to show our patriotism.

*   *22 NOTE: During World War 1, African Americans were eager to show their allegiance. They hoped that in doing so, it would help their cause of being recognized as full citizens.*

Our truck came to a screeching halt by this time, and the driver dropped us off at a dirt road that ran to the right.

"Don't forget," the driver yelled out the window, "I'll pick you two up at 'Cuddy's Place' tomorrow night at 1900 hours. Got it? If you're not there, I go back to camp without yous."

"We'll be there," Clay acknowledged.

The first leg of our journey was over. My traveling companion informed me that it would take about an hour and a half of walking to get to the farm.

Once again, Clay rambled on about his life growing up on his grandparents' farm.

"Not only did my grandpappy teach me a lot about farmin', but he also taught me all he knew about fishin'," he said proudly.

"Fishing?" I asked.

"Yes, Sir, Tommy, sir," he responded emphatically.

"Grandpappy showed me 'bout roundin' up nighthawks, (earthworms), and catchin' hellgrammites."

"Hellgrammites?" I questioned, "What are hellgrammites?"

Clay carefully explained, "They are an insect that lives for two years in the water. When their time is up, they get wings on them and turn into a dragonfly. You find them hidin' under flat rocks in a stream. They have pinchers too, so you have to be careful. Bass love 'em," he concluded.

"Interesting," I acknowledged, but what else did he teach you about fishing," I queried.

"Grandpappy used to take me down to Brussel's River fishin'," he began. "You could say it was either a small river or a large creek. It was called Brussels River 'cause one of the early landowners was from Brussels, Belgium, and it reminded him of his homeland.

"The two of us would go night fishin' for catfish. We'd take a coal oil lamp, our fishin' poles, bait, and stuff down the river around eight, nine o'clock in the evening.

"First, we tried worms, an' if that didn't work, we'd use grandpappy's secret weapon," he noted.

"Secret weapon? What kind of secret weapon?" I pressed on.

"Pieces 'o chicken soaked with chicken blood and a lil' bit of corn whiskey. We'd mix it all up in an old tobacco can and sit it in the sun a couple 'o hours to get good and stinky. I means to tell you that bucket had a nasty smell to it. Catfish likes that a lot!" He exclaimed.

Clay went on, "We always caught three or four nice size catty's, but we never could catch that big 'ol monster that grandpappy called, Sneaky Pete!"

"Sneaky Pete, huh?" I questioned.

"That fish was uncatchable," he remarked. Then, Clay lowered his voice to just above a whisper and confided real quiet-like, "Some nights, you could just get a glimpse of him lurking in the edge of the lamplight or if the moon was real bright that night. The water would ripple, and he'd give that big ol' tail a splash. Then, he was gone."

"Sneaky Pete would play wit' your bait and tease the livin' devil out of you, but nobody could ever catch him. Nobody. No way. No, how!" He stated emphatically.

"Grandpappy and I would take home the fish we did catch, and grandmama would fry them up the next day," he reminisced.

"She'd use some buttermilk, cornmeal, flour, and her special seasoning. Mmmmm, Mmmm, boy, was that good! Can't get much finer than a big plate o' fried catfish and some greens from the garden!" Clay fondly recalled.

By the time the man finished his catfish story, we could see the farmhouse in the distance. As we drew closer, the dwelling appeared to be more like a glorified shack. The wooden frame building was patched up with scraps of wood and appeared to be quickly losing its battle with time.

A large stone chimney anchored one side of the home, which looked like the most substantial part of its construction. Whisps of smoke emanated from the chimney top. A pitiful barn-like structure and a rickety chicken coop stood on the left side of the property. They, too, seemed likely to become a pile of rubble should a strong wind blow through the area.

The porch attached to the front of the house, however, seemed inviting. Several handmade tables and chairs, including a carefully preserved rocker, provided me with a perception that the family gathered there most evenings.

Before long, the chickens sounded a warning that we had arrived, and a young boy sat with a black dog at the top of the steps leading to the porch.

The lad jumped up and ran towards us at once, but the dog merely raised his ears out of curiosity.

He seemed indifferent and preferred to remain in his comfortable spot.

The boy, who appeared to be about seven or eight years old, greeted us, saying, "Are you Uncle Clay? Who are you, mister?"

"Well, yes. I guess I am your Uncle Clay, and who is you?" Clay responded to the young man. "My name is Dayo. I lives here with my grandpappy and grandmama!" he proudly exclaimed.

"Nice meetin' ya', Dayo, 'dis is my friend, Tommy. I calls him Sir Tommy, sir," Clay said to introduce me.

"Tommy's fine, young man," I interjected, "just call me Tommy. That will do," I concluded.

By then, Bessie, the grandmother, appeared at the door and exclaimed, "Clay! Clay! Is that you, my boy? Come here and give your grandmama a big 'ol hug. Well, look at you in that uniform. Yo' looks so handsome I could jus' squeeze yo' to death for lookin' so fine!"

The woman had a very kind grandmotherly face and appeared to be somewhere in her seventies. She was about five-foot-seven inches tall with a stocky build. Her snow-white hair was a stark contrast to her very dark complexion. Her heavily wrinkled face not only validated her age but was a reflection of her many years of hard work.

She wore her hair up in a bun, but it was capped with a blue and white kerchief. Her long dress was also blue, although a well-worn white apron covered the front.

As she approached the porch's top step, the woman gave the dog a nudge with her foot and hollered, "Poor Boy! Move out o' the way!"

It took some effort, but the old dog slowly relocated away from the foot traffic.

Clay and his grandmother embraced as the boy, and I just stood there watching the poignant reunion.

Bessie turned to me and said, "I guess yous met Dayo. Who's this other soldier you brought with you, Clay?"

Her grandson answered, "Dis is Tommy. He's stationed in the camp with me, and he volunteered to come with me to visit you and grandpappy."

"Nice to meet you, son. I'm glad you fellas came. Yo' grandpappy will be so happy to see you!" The old woman stated.

She ushered us into the house and said, "I'm just cookin' up a fine dinner for y'all. I hopes yous brung your appetites."

"While I'm finishin' yo dinner, yous jus' go in there and visit wit' yo' grandpappy. He's been wantin' to see y'all, now! You too, Tommy. Amole might be a tough old bird, but he don't bite none," she insisted.

Clay and I entered the bedroom, and the grandfather was lying in bed with his eyes closed. His hair was snow-white as well, and he had a matching beard. A pair of wire-rimmed spectacles lay on his chest and a pipe, which appeared to be hand-carved, was clenched in his left hand. His breathing was slow and labored.

"Grandpappy! Hey, old man, is yous awake?" Clay shouted.

At the sound of his voice, the grandfather stirred and slowly opened his eyes.

"Clay! Clay, my boy! If you ain't a sight for sore eyes!" The old man responded.

He reached down in an attempt to hug his grandfather and gave him a soft kiss on the forehead. His face was worn and deeply wrinkled. It was apparent that the gentleman was frail, and when he moved, he often winced from the pain.

"That uniform makes you look fine, son," the grandfather commented.

"Yo' son," the grandfather commented. "Yo' grandmama and me are so proud o' you boy!" he added.

"Dis is my friend, Tommy," Clay began. "He's in the service with me at Camp Hancock," he explained.

"Very fine to meet you, Tommy. You take good care of my boy, Clay, won't you?" He begged.

"Sure will, sir," I replied. Glad to meet you, sir."

"You can just call me Amole, or you can call me grandpappy; whichever you want is jus' fine with me," he insisted.

After a short conversation, the old man drifted off to sleep, and we returned to the kitchen to see if Bessie was done cooking.

The three of us took our places at the table, and the grandmother had a big pot boiling away on the cookstove. She filled each plate and brought them to us. Actually, they were more like very shallow tin bowls.

When I looked at my bowl and raised my eyebrows, Clay graciously explained what we were eating. "Well, Tommy, I hope you like grandmama's cookin'. We have ham hocks, collard greens, cabbage, navy beans, and sweet potatoes. She sure knows how to cook, and this will fill your belly, but good!" He said proudly.

"Hold on! Now, hold on, now, boys! I gots a big ol' batch a cornbread comin' out o' the oven. Y'all need to sop up that good juice with somptin'," she insisted.

The woman brought a cast-iron skillet of cornbread and a big pitcher of lemonade to the table and sat down with us.

"Dayo, you can give the blessin'," she ordered.

"Yes, ma'am," he replied.

"Lord, Jesus, we thank you for this food made by the hands of my grandmama and asks you to bless all o' us sittin' at this table. Amen!" The young lad prayed.

It was my first real southern meal, and I was pleasantly surprised, considering I never had anything quite like it. Back home, naturally, I was no stranger to cabbage, navy beans, and sweet potatoes, but mixed all together with ham hocks and collard greens was a brand new experience for me.

My grandmother, Josephine, always taught me that the best way to compliment any cook was to ask for a second helping, and that's what I did.

Bessie noticed and quickly commented, "Tommy, here, must be likin' your grandmama's cooking, Clay, he's a-goin' back for more!"

"That's what I like to see," she added. "I didn't spend all mornin' over this hot stove for nothin', the woman concluded.

"Yes, ma'am," I replied. "This is the best food I've had since we've been here in Georgia."

Clay responded with, "You means that grub we hand out to y'all at the mess hall ain't this good?"

"Not like this," I countered.

The rest of the meal was spent exchanging small talk and other news. The young boy asked to be excused from the table once he was finished and ran outside.

At that point, the conversation shifted to more serious matters, particularly the grandfather's health concerns.

"I's afraid your grandpappy has just' been hangin' on 'cause he had a feelin' that you was a-comin,'" she revealed.

"You're all he talked 'bout over and over," the woman informed her grandson.

"What about Dayo, grandmama? What's the story with him?" Clay inquired about the boy.

"Well, son," she began with a deep sigh, "that poor boy reminds me a lot of you when you was his age.

"His momma, your Aunt Charmaine, had the boy right after you left. The father was Moses Greene," she went on.

"Charmaine wanted her son to have a bonafide negro name, and he was named after my great-grandpoppa, Dayo Onyemeke. The two fools never got married that I's know of.

"They done told me they was goin' to the church picnic one Sunday afternoon, and we ain't never seen them since!" She said, raising her voice.

"Some says they heard they was in Pennsylvania, while others was told they'd be goin' to New York. Lord, Almighty, who knows," she concluded.

Bessie cleaned up the kitchen, and we were chased out to that front porch. Just as I pictured in my mind, we sat around most of the evening just talking.

Clay and his grandmother exchanged stories about their past, and Dayo often interrupted his own questions. Many of those memories were centered around the grandfather.

Before long, it was time to turn in. Clay, Dayo, and I shared a bedroom in the back of the house. "My momma slept in this bed, here," Clay began, "and that was mine where Dayo's sleeping." "Such a long time ago," he said regarding his own childhood.

"By the way, Tommy," he added, "thanks for comin' along wit' me. I really do appreciate it," he concluded.

"No problem," I responded. "Not only am I happy to do it, but I'm glad I came along, as well. It's been an interesting experience," I admitted.

Just like home, Bessie's cooking is what woke me in the morning. When I glanced around the room, I saw that Clay and Dayo were already up and gone from the bedroom.

Bessie was busy at the stove in the kitchen while Clay walked through the door with an armload of wood, and Dayo was right behind him carrying a basket of fresh eggs from the chicken coop.

"Tommy," the woman said, "get yourself a cup o' coffee and sit. I's makin' ham wit' red-eye gravy, eggs, grits, and biscuits!"

"Yous better be hungry, 'cause I ain't cookin' all this for my health," she exclaimed. "Yes, ma'am!" I answered.

The old woman leaned over towards me, put her hand up to the side of her mouth, and said, "Clay an' dem soldier boys don't give you no eats like this back at that camp!"

Halfway through my coffee Bessie sat a plate filled with food in front of me and commanded, "You eats all dis,' and I have more in the pan for ya!"

Dayo seemed to gobble his food down and announced, "Can I be excused, grandmamma?"

"Where you off to in such a hurry, boy?" She questioned the young man.

"I'm going fishin','" he explained, "I'm gonna catch Sneaky Pete for grandpappy and Clay," he revealed.

"Okay, boy. You be careful pokin' 'round that river," she cautioned.

"You fall in, and there ain't no one to pull you out. Don't expect Poor Boy to save ya. Dat mutt's too old for dat!" She warned him.

"Yes, ma'am," he nodded. "I'm usin' grandpappy's secret weapon, and I'm gonna catch him for sure!" The lad said assertively.

As he ran out the door, Bessie yelled, "Be sure y'all back in time for lunch, boy. You knows what'll happen if you don't!"

Clay and I took breakfast into the grandfather, and he talked while the old man did his best to eat. He took a few bites of the eggs and a small portion of the grits. Poor boy was waiting beside the bed for his share of the ham.

Within a half-hour, the old man had dozed off again, and we retired to the front porch.

It was about 10:30 when Bessie checked on her husband, and a few minutes later, she came to the door.

"Clay. Clay," she said in a soft voice. "I's afraid your grandpappy is gone. He's with Jesus," the woman stated calmly, but her eyes began to well with tears.

Immediately, Clay jumped up from his chair and cried, "No! No! It can't be! We were just talkin' with him!"

He went running into the house, but his grandmother held him back. She placed her arms around him and hugged him tightly as he, too, broke down in tears.

The grandmother took a few minutes to calm him down. Then, the two went into the house while I remained on the porch.

A few minutes later, I could hear someone yelling in the distance. As the shouting grew nearer, it was apparent that it was Dayo.

When he finally came into view, the young lad held up a large fish on a rope. The catch was nearly as big as he was.

As Dayo approached, he exclaimed, "It's Sneaky Pete! I got him! I finally got him!"

The boy's face was beaming as he smiled from ear to ear. He was totally out of breath when he boasted, "Grandpappy is going to be sooo proud! Wait 'til he sees ol' Sneaky Pete! He won't believe it!"

Before I could say a word, Bessie and Clay came to the door when they heard the commotion. Still trying to catch his breath, the boy held up the fish and gushed with joy, "I caught Sneaky Pete, Clay! I caught the ol' devil! Wait 'till grandpappy sees him!"

The two congratulated the young man on his great success but kept him from entering the house. "Yo' right, Dayo," the old woman began, "yo' grandpappy will be so proud, but he's a restin right now.

"You take that fish down to the butchering' table under the grape arbor, and I'll be straight down there to help yous clean him!"

Although he was disappointed, the young lad took the giant catfish down to the spot where his grandmother ordered and waited for her to come back.

When they finished, Bessie came to the house with a large pan containing the catfish. Dayo followed closely behind her.

Once inside, the grandmother told the boy that while she was preparing to cook the fish, he was to go into town to fetch the doctor.

"Now, listen, son, you take the horse and wagon and go fetch Dr. Beckett," she ordered him as she placed a silver dollar in his hand.

She continued, "Hissin' is dat big house on the corner of Silver Creek Road and Willow Street, yous remember?"

"Yes, ma'am," he replied while nodding his head affirmatively.

"Now, hurry on back an' I'll have dat Sneaky Pete all cooked up for ya, hear me?"

While the boy was gone, they explained that the doctor was really the undertaker for the colored families. He took a few medical courses before he became a mortician. Beckett helped some of these poor folks with simple medical treatments, as well.

In less than an hour, Dayo returned and informed his grandmother that Dr. Beckett would be here by and by.

"Okay, yous all get your places, and we's gonna try some o' dis Sneaky Pete. We's fixin' to find out if dis big ol' catfish is worth all that hoop an' hollerin' yous guys keep talkin' 'bout," she said.

Bessie fried up that battered catfish just how Clay described and served it with a large portion of sweet potatoes and greens.

"Hey, grandmamma," Dayo spoke up and asked, "did you save some o' that Sneaky Pete for grandpappy?"

"Yessum' boy," she replied, "now you eat up that fish before it gets cold."

Midway through the meal, the undertaker and his helper showed up at the door, and Bessie showed them to the bedroom. About fifteen minutes later, the helper went out to the wagon and returned with a stretcher.

The two men emerged from the room with the grandfather on the litter. He was completely covered in a white sheet. Quietly they carried him out of the house and loaded the body onto their wagon.

Dayo looked up from his plate. At first, his mouth hung wide open. Then, he realized what was happening. He lowered his head and began sobbing uncontrollably.

His grandmother stood up, put her arm around him, and tried to console the boy, but he jumped up from the table and ran out the door.

First, Clay stood up to go after him, but I put my arm out to stop my friend, and I told him that I would talk to the lad.

Still overcome with sorrow, the boy sat at the top of the porch steps. Dayo had one arm around Poor Boy as the dog lay beside him.

I sat with him on the step, and before I could speak, he murmured, "I just wanted grandpappy to see that I caught Sneaky Pete. I wanted him to finally taste that ol' catfish!"

Finally, I was able to talk to the boy, "Dayo, I know it's hard for you right now. You feel so sad that you think you'll never get over losing your grandpappy, but believe me, you will," I explained.

I went on, " I lost my grandmother a few years ago. I think about her every day, and every day it makes me sad, but I think about all the beautiful things she said to me and taught me. When I remember those things, it makes me smile. She's always there for me, still." I added.

"But... but... what about Sneaky Pete? The young man looked up at me and asked. "He never got to see me catch that ol' fish," he lamented.

"Oh... that's where you're wrong, son," I argued. "You're wrong about that," I went on.

"How's that, Tommy?" He looked at me quite puzzled.

"Well, I can tell you as sure as I'm sitting here, your grandpappy saw the whole thing. He's up in heaven, smiling down and saying, ' Atta boy, Dayo. Atta boy! I knew you'd be the one to catch him,' "

"You think so?" He asked, looking for some assurance from me.

"Sure! Not only that but there will be another fish just like Sneaky Pete. You might call him Big Jim or Mighty Mick or whatever name you choose," I promised him.

Suddenly, the boy wiped his tears and ran back into the house. He sat down at his plate, took a fork full of the catfish, and returned to the steps.

Dayo sat down with Poor Boy and offered the dog a bite of his fish, and said, "Here, Poor Boy, this is for you! You can have the last bite of ol' Sneaky Pete. It may not be chicken, but believe me, the way grandmamma cooks it tastes as good as chicken!"

With that, the old hound dog looked over the offering and gave the fork a good sniff. Hesitantly, Poor Boy gobbled up the catfish piece, and a huge smile came over the boy's face.

Bessie and Clay were standing in the doorway, watching the whole thing. Dayo looked up at the two and said, "It's okay! I checked with grandpappy first, and he told me it was okay if Poor Boy ate his piece.

We all exchanged hugs on that front porch, and Bessie turned to me and said, "It musta' been an angel that sent you along with my boy Clay, Tommy. If ya ever wants some real cookin', you come back. I's gonna fix you up some catfish or ham hocks or whatever you wants!"

The old woman smiled, gave me a wink. Clay and I headed back to Augusta to meet with our ride to camp.

Clay
Image Source: Author's Photo

"TROUBLE AT CUDDY'S PLACE"

There was a heap of trouble at Cuddy's Place.
Image Source: Unknown

CHAPTER 20

"Trouble at Cuddy's Place"

We arrived at Cuddy's Tavern well before our appointed time to meet the driver who would take us back to camp.

The watering hole was a three-story brick structure with white shutters. It sat on the corner of Wrightsboro Road and Simone Street.

Several vehicles lined the curb on both streets, and a large wooden sign hung at the top of a long white porch. It read: "Cuddy's Place - Jerome Cudberth, Proprietor - Established in 1897."

Clay informed me that the owner was a tall, husky man with a balding hairline and a bushy mustache. He judged the guy to be about 55 years old, six-foot-four inches tall, and weighing roughly 325 pounds.

I was in for another eye-opener when we walked into the bar. The place was extremely crowded, but the left side was full of whites, and the right side seemed to be reserved for black folks. We managed two find two seats at the bar.

Typical of most drinking establishments, a massive 40-foot wooden back bar anchored the room. At its base were sixteen drawers with matching cabinet doors below.

Resting on top was an eighteen-inch column at each end with a very ornately carved top piece connecting the two. Four large plate glass mirrors separated the top from the bottom. Various liquor bottles lined the countertop: Jim Beam, Wild Turkey, Four Roses, Jack Daniels, Kentucky Gentleman, Old Crow, Old Granddad, Old Overholt, and others.

In the center of the back bar was the cash register. The machine was cast-iron with a copper finish and had the word "National" emblazoned in script on the drawer's front. The drawer had a one-inch marble plate fitted on the top. The register had embossed on it dozens of Fleur-de-lis, a French symbol of heraldry.

The barkeep, who looked remarkably like Cuddy's description but much shorter in stature, waited on us and served us two beers.

Clay began to tell more stories about his grandfather, but the subject left him feeling sad over the matter. I assured him that it would take time before he would feel better.

Gradually, he talked himself through it. Before long, recalling some of those memories brought a smile to his face once again.

My black friend stated that his grandmother did a lot to earn her keep on the plantation. She cooked, cleaned, did the laundry, and was a midwife.

"Mrs. Bohnefield had six children, three boys, and three girls," Clay recalled, "and my grandmama helped deliver 'em all," he said proudly.

Regarding his grandfather, Clay noted, "My grandpappy often told me that come Christmas time, Mr. Bohnefield sometimes gave them two-bits and an extra quantity of food."

He continued, stating that the master would give them a week off during Christmas and some extra eats, but they had to do their regular chores.

"I remember grandpappy telling me, 'Sometimes we had dances, and they'd asks me to play de fiddle. They liked my playin' whether dey was white folks or colored folks. I'd play all night long if dey let me, but yous knows that they wouldn't let me!' "

"That fiddle had me mesmerized as a little boy," Clay recalled.

"Made o' spruce and maple, my grandpappy said of the fiddle. However, it had a distinctive dark finish to it," Clay noted.

"Along the side was hand-painted the words, *I sang in the woods until the angry ax cut me down. Now I sing again!.'* "

"He could play that thing until his fingers turned blue," the soldier recalled. "Man, did that have a sweet sound to it. He was good with his hands; I can tell you that!"

Clay remembered that his grandpappy often sat in that rocking chair on the front porch and talked about his days of slavery.

He said that the work was often hard, but Mr. Bohnefield was a fair man. Many of the other plantation owners worked their slaves to death. He knew many others in the area whose hands were cracked and bleeding from picking cotton.

If a slave was suspected of lying to his master or stealing food, they were tortured or hung, but Mr. Bohnefield always treated his people well, and they respected him for it.

"We's never hadda' steal or nuthin' because Mr. Bohnefield was good ta' us. He was a good man!" Clay remembered his grandfather saying.

He noted that his grandfather could grow so many crops and provide plenty of food for his family because he bartered with the master.

According to Clay, in addition to corn, his grandpappy grew tobacco, tomatoes, collard greens, carrots, pole beans, sugar beets, indigo, rice, okra, potatoes, yams, sweet potatoes, peanuts, and watermelon.

Bessie maintained an herb garden to supply her cooking with the necessary spices.

Clay also recalled his grandfather's description of the life of the slaves on the plantation.

"We were lucky," he remembered his grandfather saying. "Our house was away from the rest o' the colored folk who lived there."

Not too far from the main road and closer to the master's house was a much more cultivated district.

He stated that a large forest of pines stood on one side of the road, but some vast fields were on the other side. He said the soil was rich because it was initially swampland.

Beyond those fields were flat lower lands. Not far from there is where the Brussels River flowed.

About a quarter of a mile from the road were the residences of most of the other workers. They lived in little villages of slave-cabins. The outside of these frame-built cottages had poorly made crude wooden boards, with shingle roofs and brick chimneys.

His grandfather described them as being about fifty feet apart. They had small gardens, chicken coops, and pig yards.

In a garden looking down the street, at the head of this village, was the overseer's house. On one side of the road were the barns and other outbuildings. Straight ahead was a landing on the river, while the other side of the road led to the master's house.

After two or three rounds of drinks, we looked up, and standing next to the bartender was Cuddy himself. The owner had an eighteen-inch club in his hand, and the two of them were staring at us. Both had scowls on their faces.

"Clay!" Cuddy said, "what do you think you guys are doing?"

"What, Cuddy? What's wrong?" he asked the bar owner.

"See the sign? You know the rules! You've been coming in here for years," Cuddy responded while pointing to the sign behind him with that intimidating club.

There, above the mirror, was a white cardboard sign with bold, black letters. It read: "Whites" (with an arrow pointing to the left), and below that "Coloreds" (with an arrow pointing to the right).

"Y'all know that we can't have no whites sittin' over here in the coloreds' section," the man bellowed. "How did this happen, Bert?" he asked the bartender.

"Well... we were busy boss, and I didn't take notice 'til now," he replied.

"You know we don't stand for that around here, Clay. You do know that, don't ya, boy?" Cuddy asked while pounding the club on the top of the bar.

"Yessir, Mr. Cuddy. Yessir," Clay acknowledged.

At that point, Cuddy gave a signal, and two men grabbed Clay by the arms while another began punching the defenseless black man.

They let go of his arms. He fell to the floor like a sack of potatoes. Cuddy came out from behind the bar and also gave him a few whacks with the club.

I wanted to jump in and help Clay, but I was clearly outnumbered. For all I knew, they seemed prepared to drag us both out to a tree and hang us on the spot.

Just when I was looking for a hero to come in and intervene on our behalf, the driver from camp, whose name was Hal, strolled in the door.

"What's going on here?" the man asked.

"Your two soldier friends here seem to have gotten themselves into a heap of trouble," Cuddy shot back.

"Why? What did they do?" He questioned.

Cuddy quickly pointed to the sign with his club and emphasized, "They broke the rules. Here in these parts, we don't take to that too lightly!"

The driver argued, "I thought Abe Lincoln freed the negroes 50 years ago!"

"Well, if Abe Lincoln walks through that door, we'll let him handle it," Cuddy answered, "but I guess we'll allow Judge Higgins to settle the matter. He's a stickler for the law around here," he warned.

"Look, pal," Hal pleaded, "let me take them back to camp, and we'll make sure there's no more trouble."

Cuddy wasn't budging much on the matter and was determined to impose his own ruling. "First, of all, you're a Yankee, and no Yankee has earned the right to call me pal," he began.

"Secondly, this is the way it's gonna be. You, *my friend*, are leaving in your truck. You will go back to your camp and bring me two MPs. They will haul your soldier asses outta' here. You have an hour to do so. If you're not back within that time, Judge Higgins will lock them up. We have our own rules here in Richmond County," he concluded.

Hal left the bar with his tail between his legs. While he was gone, the men tied us each to a chair with a heavy length of rope. Judging by their demeanor, it's about as close I wanted to be to any rope. I never prayed so hard to see two MPs walk through that door!

As the minutes ticked by, most of the bar's patrons went about their business, but Cuddy's men stood guard over us while still drinking their beers. They mocked us and called us names. The men even spat on the floor near our feet and laughed over our predicament.

Moments before the time was up, Hal entered the establishment with two MPs behind him. I was glad to see the Army saw fit to send two of the biggest and nastiest MPs I ever saw.

"You're damn lucky, fellas," Cuddy bellowed, "the boys here were just waitin' to use those ropes for other business!"

The officer on the left spoke first, saying, "You are hereby ordered to release these soldiers into our custody."

Cuddy immediately responded, "Nobody..." but stopped talking when both officers reached for their guns.

He turned away and shook his head, saying, "You don't bring a club to a gunfight!"

Then, Cuddy went back behind the bar and shouted, "Bert, give everybody a drink on the house, and salute these fine, Yankee soldiers when they leave!"

As Bert passed out the rounds of drinks, the entire tavern broke out in the song, "God Save the South."

When the MPs escorted us to the door, the chanting seemed to grow louder with the words:

"God save the South, God save the South,
Her altars and firesides, God save the South!
Now that the war is nigh, now that we arm to die,
Chanting our battle cry, "Freedom or death!"
Chanting our battle cry, "Freedom or death!"

*   *24 NOTE: The song is said to be the unofficial national anthem of the confederacy. "God Save the South." Written early in the war by George H. Miles. He was a Marylander writing under the pseudonym Earnest Halpin. The song was set to music by composer Charles Wolfgang Amadeus Ellerbrock (the arranger of "Maryland, My Maryland"). Some argue, however, that the minstrel song, "Dixie Land," deserves that distinction.*

Although it was only 22 miles, it was a long drive back to Camp Hancock that evening. Clay, Hal, and I had to ride in the truck's back, an area reserved for prisoners.

The incident did get us in some hot water. However, the Army merely issued us a warning to avoid such places. The two of us "volunteered" for a couple of extra days of latrine duty, and the matter was resolved.

Many of the guys in camp boasted about how friendly the people were in Augusta, but I learned a hard lesson that day: friendliness doesn't extend to Cuddy's Bar, especially when a white man travels with a black man.

A few weeks later, Clay received a letter from his grandmother.

Bessie wrote:

"Rev. Lucius Pritcher conducted a lovely service for yo' grandpappy at the Brussels Brethren Baptist Church."

"He's a restin' peacefully in the Pine Hill graveyard," she added.

"Poor Boy passed as well, soon after yo' grandpappy," she noted, "but Dayo has his self a new pup, a white one, he named, "Tommy!"

"HELEN'S CHRISTMAS TREE"

Helen Schalata (circa 1917).
Image Source: Author's Photo

CHAPTER 21

"Helen's Christmas Tree"

The calendar flipped to November, and so did the weather. It was cold and damp during most of the first week of the month. Intermittent rain turned most of the camp into a muddy mess. I seemed to spend most of my free time near the tent stove. I was not only attempting to keep warm but needed to make an earnest effort to dry my clothes and boots. I could handle most of the discomfort, but wet dogs were another story.

Space was at a premium around the stove, as well. I had to share the area with my bunkmates.

By week number two, however, a warm spell was a welcome relief. I spent most of my days off doing my wash.

Time passed by quickly, and before I knew it, Thanksgiving at Camp Hancock was upon us. As usual, the mess company served the men a fine holiday meal. The main meal consisted of a heaping plate of roasted young turkey, olives, celery, and a hot vegetable.

There was tenderloin of beef, cranberry sauce, bread, and cheese in addition to the bird.

For dessert, the offerings included: mince, apple, and pumpkin pie, plus bananas, oranges, apples, mixed nuts, coffee, cigars, and cigarettes.

I was able to sit at the table with most of my friends from my early days in the National Guard.

To my surprise, Irvin Schweppenheiser offered the blessing before the meal, while Harry Haeberle supplied the toast.

"To friends that never part, may we always have a sunny smile upon our faces, the feeling of Thanksgiving in our hearts, and fond memories of the times we spent together," Haeberle said as he raised his tin cup of coffee above his head.

We all smiled and joined him by raising our drinks, as well. It was one of those special moments that stays with you. It was like a photograph captured in your mind.

Monday, November 26, was my 25th birthday, and what a special day it turned out to be. Capt. Mercher called a special meeting of our unit and announced that men who intended to put in for leave for the Christmas holidays needed to have their requests submitted by Friday, November 30. I figured, what the hell, I may as well go for it and submitted my request the very next day. Now, it was a waiting game to see if the captain granted my furlough.

Also, I received a special letter from home on my birthday. It was a note from my sister, Helen.

Dear Tommy,

How is my big brother doing? I hope you are getting along well in the army.

By the time this letter gets to you, it will be your birthday. Happy birthday, brother! I wish you were coming home for Christmas. We all miss you very much. I am making a special Christmas tree for you. Pop is helping me with the construction.

He has made a trunk and branches from scraps of wood that he had down in the cellar. Father has also painted it green with the leftover paint from the front porch chairs.

Mother is providing me with a variety of items to use for the decorations, such as ribbons, scraps of tinfoil, and pieces of cloth. When it is finished, I will put it on your dresser, where it will stay there until you return home for good.

The old Walnut tree in the backyard has produced a good crop this year. Mother has shelled the nuts already for her holiday baking, and pop uses the shells to make a stain.

It is already very cold here in the city, and I wouldn't be surprised if we got some snow before Christmas.

My school essay about William Penn earned me an A-plus in history. Did you know that Philadelphia had initially been an Indian village called Shackamaxon?

I am still wearing the necklace that you gave me. Please write to me when you have a chance. Love, Your sister, Helen

My sister's letter was a most pleasant surprise. I wanted to sit down and scribble out a reply but decided to wait until Saturday to see if my leave was approved. I was no better than my sister, Helen, at keeping a secret. A surprise trip home for the holiday would be the ultimate Christmas gift for my family, but I knew that I would never be able to pull it off.

The week dragged on slower than molasses in January, but at roll call on Saturday morning, Capt. Mercher read the names of the men who were granted leave. Cpl. Thomas Schalata was the last name on that list.

I felt as though I had just won the Irish Sweepstakes. After morning chow, I immediately dashed back to my tent to pen a letter home because I wasn't scheduled to start duty at the field hospital until 1100 hours.

In a matter of a half-hour, I was able to write three letters; one to Helen, one to my parents, and one to Stella.

The trio of letters basically contained the same message except for personal references. Here is the gist of my correspondence:

I hope this letter finds you all well back in Philadelphia. I am writing this letter to inform you of my good fortune.

The captain notified me this morning that I have made the list of men who have been granted a furlough over Christmas.

My train leaves Georgia on Sunday, December 23, and I will arrive in Philly on Christmas Eve. Unfortunately, I must return by rail on Monday, December 31, as I am required to be back on the base by midnight on January 1.

I am genuinely looking forward to seeing all of you at this time.

Love, Tommy

Besides packing for the trip, I needed to do a little Christmas shopping before leaving for home. Doc and Harry agreed to go with me to Augusta on Saturday, December 15. I was apprehensive about going into the city after my horrible experience with Clay a few months ago. Still, the guys convinced me that the excursion would be without incident.

Also on my list was to send a letter to Marvin Kleimbaum at the jewelry store to order an engagement ring. Apparently, all of this good fortune put me in a celebratory mood, and I made an "about-face" on my decision to get engaged to Stella.

I gave Marvin instructions to select a diamond ring approximately one-third to one-half carat in size, and my budget was about $68.

My sister, Veronica, would be in to select the style for me, and she would discretely determine what size the ring should be.

Harry, Doc, and I hopped a streetcar that ran from camp to downtown Augusta on Saturday morning, the fifteenth.

Some of the guys in my tent, who were familiar with Augusta, gave me a list of businesses to visit.

My first stop was Lemar P. Simpson Book Co., located near Eighth and Ellis Streets. There I was able to purchase some pencils, crayons, and a tablet for Helen. For my sister, Veronica, I selected some writing paper. I also decided that a book would be a good selection for my sister, Florence. The sales clerk recommended "The Lost Princess of Oz" by Frank Baum.

The next stop on my list was Hackman and Peabody on Broad Street. The business sold Columbia gramophones and records.

I selected "I passed by Your Window" by Walter Glynne for my girlfriend, Stella. For her brother, Joe, I chose "For Me and My Gal" by Van Schenck. The records cost 65 cents each.

Finally, the last of my shopping would be done at Old Injun Tobacco Shop - Purveyors of Cigars, Tobacco & Candy, on the corner of Reynolds and Seventh Streets.

Shopping for my father was easy. He would be happy with a can of pipe tobacco. A selection of fine chocolates for my mother and my sisters Stella and Henrietta finished out my list.

At noon, I met up with Doc and Harry, and we had lunch in a small cafe on Walker Street in the Old Town section of downtown Augusta. The day went without incident, and the three of us caught the streetcar back to camp in the afternoon.

On Sunday, December 23, I boarded a Southern Railroad train bound for Philadelphia. My ten-day furlough required that I return to Camp Hancock by midnight on New Year's Day.

I boarded the rail car with just a small duffle bag, and we pulled out from the depot at 1007 hours.

Since there were no substantial delays, the train rolled into the station in Washington, DC, at 0900 the following day. I needed to transfer to a Pennsy RR train. Departure time was 1237, and we arrived in Philly just before 1500 hours.

Upon reaching the street when exiting the station, a light snow began to fall. It was already growing dark outside, and as I walked up Market Street to catch the subway/elevated line, a brisk wind made the trek even more unpleasant. I told myself that I would be home in time for our family's traditional Christmas Eve supper, Wigilia. My father insisted that the meal began at 5 pm sharp when the evening's first star appeared in the sky. On such a cloudy night, such as this, however, that appearance was in doubt.

On my way to the subway, I picked up tonight's edition of The Evening Bulletin newspaper. During my commute, I was able to catch up on the local news here in Philly.

One headline that grabbed my attention was: City set to celebrate war-time Christmas Holiday.

The article read in part: "The army recently announced that 25,000 soldiers from the area had been granted Christmas furloughs to come home and visit their families.

The early and unexpected gift was deemed to be good for morale, to allow these servicemen to be reunited with their mothers, wives, sweethearts, and other loved ones before shipping out for Europe."

Also on the subject, the report noted "that four cornetists (coronet players) would stand at the four corners of Independence Hall at four o'clock and play Christmas Carols. The musicians will also perform at Rittenhouse Square. A grand community gathering with singing and refreshments will follow. Similar events are planned in almost every neighborhood in the city."

The newspaper went on to say, "Sailors and Marines from the Philadelphia Navy Yard will play Santa for the children of the Northern Home, St. Joseph's, and the Presbyterian orphanages.

"The servicemen will turn one of the ships into a Christmas Wonderland with Santa Claus himself as the captain. The children will be recipients of a day of fun, food, and gifts," the article went on to say.

When I transferred from the elevated train to the streetcar, it was about 4 pm. That meant that I would arrive home just in time for the celebration of Wigila.

As I made the turn from Orthodox Street onto Thompson, my heart was beating wildly in anticipation. Oddly, the temperature had risen slightly during my trip, and the snow had stopped.

When I reached the top step and walked across the front porch, I observed through the window my family scurrying from room to room, making final preparations.

I stood at the door for a moment just to catch my breath and then made my entrance. Naturally, there was a great deal of yelling and screaming with joy, and my mother ran from the kitchen while holding her hands high above her head.

Everyone took their turn, smothering me with hugs and kisses. Even pop emerged from his favorite chair in the breakfast room with a bottle of beer in one hand and his pipe in another.

A small Christmas tree stood on a wicker table in the front window. I could see the dining room table was impeccably set, featuring my mother's best white tablecloth.

Once the excitement had died down, my father was anxious to begin the evening's celebration. Traditionally, he always began with a short speech. On that Christmas Eve, 1917, he said, "Tonight, we not only commemorate the birth of Our Saviour, Jesus Christ, but we also celebrate almost thirty years since we came to America. Let us give thanks that we are blessed to celebrate this sacred night together, and may God protect us all in the coming year. Na dzrowia!"

The sharing of the oplatek (pronounced opwatek) was next. My father began by breaking the wafer with my mother and then continued to share it with everyone at the Wigilia table. In turn, we offered each other wishes for health, peace, and prosperity.

*   *25 NOTE: Partaking of the oplatek is the most ancient and beloved of all Polish Christmas traditions. Oplatek is a thin wafer made of flour and water, similar in taste to Communion hosts*

during Mass. The Christmas wafer is shared amongst those in attendance before the Christmas Eve supper with good wishes for the new year.

For days, my mother spent most of her time in the kitchen. Her meatless dishes included fish, generally carp, beet or mushroom soup, and various courses made from cabbage, mushrooms, or potatoes. Two different pierogi flavors were her specialty. One consisted of a farmer's cheese filling, while the other was filled with sauerkraut.

She followed the main meal with dried fruit and cake, such as babka, for dessert.

After the meal, the girls finished decorating the Christmas tree, and pop retired to his chair to read the newspaper I had brought home for him.

Helen was anxious to take me upstairs to show me the special Christmas tree she had made. "Come, Tommy! Come see your tree! I hope you like it," she said.

Sitting upon my old chest of drawers was a green wooden Christmas tree. Sporadically placed on its branches was an assortment of nails, screws, and cup hooks to hang the ornaments upon. Ribbons, bows, and strings of popcorn filled the tree's limbs. My father even crafted scraps of wood into various shapes, and Helen vividly painted these ornaments to resemble angels, snowmen, candy canes, and animals.

On top of the tree was a gold-painted star with a photograph of me affixed in the center. She creatively cut fragments of tin foil into strips for homemade tinsel.

My mother also purchased a tiny wooden Nativity scene from Kresge's Five and 10-cent Store on Frankford Avenue. She lovingly placed it beneath its wooden boughs. The magnificent tree, however, was devoid of lights or candles.

"How do you like it, brother?" She asked. "Isn't it wonderful?"

"Yes, it is, my dear," I replied. You are quite the artist! Very imaginative!"

"It is going to sit here on your dresser until you come home for good!" She exclaimed. "Thank you, Helen. It's exceptional," I acknowledged.

"It's a little cold in here, don't you think?" I asked. "There's a coal shortage," Helen explained.

"Between the frigid temperatures we've had and the war effort, there's a scarcity of coal these days," she went on.

"We already have meatless Mondays, and pop says the president may force us to cut off the heat one or two days a week. Here in the city, they're even talking about closing the schools after the holidays," Helen concluded.

"Gee, I don't think I knew that," I admitted.

When we returned to the parlor, I had my sister, Florence, pass out the gifts that I brought with me, and before long, the room was full of excitement. Everyone was excited to open their gifts, and pop sported a huge grin when he opened the can of pipe tobacco I purchased for him. Mother knitted each of us a hat, scarf, and a pair of gloves.

Before we left for Midnight Mass (Pasterka), The Shepherds' Mass, our parents insisted that we sing a few Christmas Carols while standing around the tree. These melodies, which are called Koledy, in Polish, include the beloved, "Gdy sie Chrystus rodzi "(When Christ is Born), "Lulajze

Jezuniu," which is a lullaby to Baby Jesus, and "Przybiezeli do Betlejem" (The Shepherds Arrive in Bethlehem).

At 11:30, we crossed the street to attend Midnight Mass. Fifteen minutes later, Horace Krolowski, the lector, announced that the procession would begin shortly. He also requested that all servicemen in attendance report to the Communion rail at the front of the church.

The men lined up along the railing in a single file from the Nativity scene on the left to the center aisle. I joined 26 other men in uniform, and due to my height, I was instructed to take the first spot on the far left.

At the stroke of midnight, the church bells' tolling signaled that it was time to begin. The organ started playing "Wśród Nocnej Ciszy (In the Night's Stillness), a Polish Carol traditionally sung at the opening of Midnight Mass. Soon the choir and the parish faithful began singing, and the lovely music filled the air.

Leading the procession were 16 students from the parish school, a boy and girl from each of the eight grades. At the front of the group, a girl from the first-grade class was dressed as Mary. She carried the figure of the infant Jesus on a white pillow. A classmate representing Joseph was at her side. The remaining students followed close behind, each bearing a lit candle.

Behind the children were seven altar boys dressed in their red cassocks and white surplices. The lead server was carrying the crucifix, while the others were bearing candles, as well.

An integral part of the pageantry was the distinguished honor bestowed upon a handful of men from the parish to carry the very ornate religious banners. Monsignor Bednarczyk followed the procession, accompanied by two of his assistants.

The procession proceeded up the center aisle, turned left, and circled to the back of the church. It then proceeded down the aisle on the far right and finally came to a halt at the center of the Communion rail.

The priest began, "R. Alleluia, alleluia.

I proclaim to you good news of great joy: today a Savior is born for us, Christ the Lord.R. Alleluia, alleluia... And Joseph too went up from Galilee from the town of Nazareth to Judea, to the city of David that is called Bethlehem, because he was of the house and family of David, to be enrolled with Mary, his betrothed, who was with child. While they were there, the time came for her to have her child, and she gave birth to her firstborn son. She wrapped him in swaddling clothes and laid him in a manger because there was no room for them in the inn.

Now there were shepherds in that region living in the fields and keeping the night watch over their flock. The angel of the Lord appeared to them, and the glory of the Lord shone around them, and they were struck with great fear. The angel said to them, "Do not be afraid; for behold, I proclaim to you good news of great joy that will be for all the people. For today in the city of David, a savior has been born for you who is Christ and Lord. And this will be a sign for you: you will find an infant wrapped in swaddling clothes and lying in a manger." And suddenly there was a multitude of the heavenly host with the angel, praising God and saying: "Glory to God in the highest and on earth peace to those on whom his favor rests."

When he had completed the reading, the monsignor made his way to the front of the procession and took the Christ Child from the girl. He turned and handed the infant to the first soldier. Each man in succession passed the baby to the next man in line until it came to me. I was instructed to turn and place the Baby Jesus in the creche. It was an honor that would be with me always.

Everyone involved in the procession took their appropriate places in the church, and the Mass celebrating the birth of Christ continued.

As I sat in the pew with my family, I couldn't help but feel that this was the most moving religious experience of my life thus far. There was no way of knowing what the future had in store for me, but I was comforted by the fact that this would always be a spiritual inspiration for me.

As usual, the Mass proceeded this Christmas Eve, but when the time had come for the monsignor to deliver his sermon, the message was anything but ordinary.

"A savior has been born for you who is Christ and Lord. Yes, my brothers and sisters, tonight, we celebrate with joy the birth of Jesus, the King of Kings, and Prince of Peace, but our joy is tempered with sadness.

Sadness because we must recognize that the world is without peace at this time. Our young men will soon be engaged in this great and terrible war.

So, this Christmas, let us remember in our prayers those who will take up the fight against the enemies of freedom and make this world safe for democracy. Let us also pray that all who are sent to join in this battle return safely. May our hearts not be burdened with even more sadness.

Tomorrow at 9 am, here at St. John's, around the city of brotherly love and across the nation, we will sing the song, "America," as a sign of patriotism. If you cannot join us tomorrow, we ask that you sing at home with your family.

Wesołych Świąt i niech Bóg błogosławi!"

At the Holy Mass's conclusion, all rose to sing the most famous Polish kolęda, " Bóg się rodzi" (God is born).

22

"THE CHRISTMAS AMARYLLIS"

Christmas Amaryllis arrangement
Image Source: Unknown

CHAPTER 22

"The Christmas Amaryllis"

Christmas morning in our home was as typical as any other household across America. An extensive breakfast consisting of kielbasa and eggs, fried potatoes, and mom's homemade bread. It was one of the rare occasions when mom made hot cocoa for the girls. Several pots of coffee were required, as well.

While the morning meal was being prepared on the stovetop, my mother had a ham in the oven. By noontime, a small turkey with Chestnut stuffing replaced the ham. Everything operated like clockwork.

Mother spent a little extra on such holidays. Her preference was to cook up an extensive breakfast and a bountiful feast at dinner. In this manner, she could skip the mid-day meal altogether.

Pop and I retired to the parlor in-between meals, and my father told me that the war in Europe already had produced some food shortages and price increases.

"That hasn't deterred your mother, however," the old man reported.

"She has scrimped and saved to make sure it's Christmas as usual around here," he went on. "Is that right?" I asked, quite surprised.

"I guess it will only get worse from here on in," I reasoned.

Pop took a puff from his pipe. Then, he looked directly at me and declared, "You could get two pounds of onions for six cents. Now, they're charging 40 cents. 40 cents!" he said while raising his voice.

"Not only that," he persisted, "a pound of cabbage used to be two cents, and now it cost 20 cents. Last year, four pounds of potatoes were just eight cents, and now they're gouging us for 28 cents! The same with butter and everything else. Meat! Forget about it. You either find it hard to come by, or you must pay through the nose for it!" He reported.

"Gee, Pop! I had no idea it's hit here already," I sympathized. "Plus, there's a coal shortage going on," he interjected. "Yeah, I heard that from Helen last night," I acknowledged.

At five o'clock on the nose, we gathered at the dining room table for Christmas dinner. Despite my mother's busy schedule, she managed to instruct my sisters on how she wanted the table set, and the girls came through. The setting rivaled that of the Abe Lincoln House, where we had dinner With Uncle Aldalbert and Aunt Balbina.

I can't recall a holiday dinner or a special occasion that didn't include a speech from my father.

"We gather around this table today to celebrate the birth of the Baby Jesus. Last night we commemorated the arrival of the Messiah first with our Wigilia meal, and then, we welcomed Our Saviour at Midnight Mass, just as the shepherds did that Christmas Eve many years ago.

We are thankful for this bounty, and we are indeed blessed to observe this holiest day together.

As Monsignor Bednarchyk reminded us last night, this joyous celebration is tempered because of the future's uncertainty. Nobody understands this more than Tommy. Let us join together and pray that should he be called to serve in this great war, God returns him to us safe and sound.

Heavenly Father, we ask that you send your angels to fly with him wherever he roams and guide him back safely to our home. Protect him, Oh Lord, and give us the strength to endure these troubling times.

Znak Krzyża świętego

W imię Ojca i Syna, i Ducha Świętego. Amen."

(The Sign of the Cross. In the name of the Father and of the Son and of the Holy Spirit. Amen).

When he finished, he instructed my sister, Florence, to give the blessing. One final tradition before the meal was raising our glasses and giving the Polish toast "Na dzrowia," meaning that here's to your health.

Following dinner, our family spent a peaceful evening together, interrupted only a few times when small groups of carollers dropped by to sing for us on the front porch.

Relatives and friends came to call throughout the remainder of the week, and we did likewise. Plenty of eating, drinking, and merriment filled the holidays despite the frigid weather.

Temperatures in the city that week ranged from two below zero to minus 29. The mercury climbed into the single digits sparingly, usually in the afternoons.

Even though we kept a busy schedule, it was most unusual not having to run off to work nor to rise at dawn at the sound of revelry.

Mother, however, would not allow us to sleep the morning away. We had to be ready to eat breakfast at the appointed hour. Besides, she always seemed to have a list of chores that pop never seemed to get accomplished.

After lunch on Wednesday, Pop found me sitting in his favorite rocking chair on the front porch.

I had a glass of blackberry brandy in one hand and a Chesterfield cigarette in the other. It was a balmy six degrees that afternoon.

Also keeping me warm was my woolen winter overcoat and mother's handmade knitted gloves and scarf. My father looked at me and put me on notice, saying, "You're in my chair!"

"I know, pop," I responded. "I just wanted to see if this magic chair had any words of wisdom for me. You seem to pass out advice freely when you're sitting here. I thought some of it might rub off on me," I grinned, and then I took another sip of the brandy.

"There's no magic to the chair, son," he replied. "It's years of experience and plain old common sense I've discovered."

"What's troubling you?" he asked, getting right to the point.

"Well, pop," I began, "Stella and I have been talking about getting engaged, and my heart tells me one thing, and my head is trying to convince me to do something else," I revealed.

"Decisions are never easy," he explained.

"Naturally, there are two sides to every issue, and only after careful deliberation, weighing all the prospects, can you resolve the matter. Even then, sometimes you're right, and sometimes you're wrong," my father went on to explain.

"I know, pop. I know," I agreed.

"Do you think it was easy for me to come here to America?" Pop asked.

"I had to leave my family and everything I knew in East Preussen. I had to cross the ocean and come here to a land where I knew nothing... knew no one... spoke no English," he reminded me.

"You think that was easy?" he added. "Of course not!" I acknowledged.

"Before. I met your mother; I was married to a woman named Josefa," he admitted.

"She died giving birth to your half-sister, Agniska, who also perished," pop went on to say. "Really?" I asked astonishedly.

"Yes!" The old man confirmed.

"Your sister, Veronica, was playing with her cousin, Stella Sweda, in St. Peter's Cemetery on Belgrade Street. She saw a tombstone bearing the name "Szalata," he continued.

"When she returned home, she questioned what she had seen, and we merely told her that it was just another relative. We didn't dare reveal the truth," he revealed.

"Do you think it was easy for me to tell your mother when we first met? I told her. She understood, and that's the way it was in those days," he concluded.

"When you were born, we moved to Buffalo to work in a taproom owned by Uncle Aldalbert. Do you think it was simple to pick up and move 380 miles away? Hell no!" He exclaimed.

"Only you can decide what's best for you, but Tommy, as I have said before, you're no dummy. You'll reach the decision that's right for you," my father insisted.

I took another gulp of the brandy, finishing what remained, and extinguished my cigarette in the ashtray.

I turned to my wise old man and declared, "You're right, pop. I know you're right!" "Right about what?" my father specifically wanted to know.

"It's not the chair. It seems to be getting colder, though. I'm going in," I said while standing up to go back into the house.

My father let out a hardy laugh and noted, "Tell your mother that I'll be a few minutes longer."

He lit his pipe and took my place on the rocker. Just as I turned for the door, Walter Kazlowski approached. He, too, was seeking advice, and the office of the mayor of our neighborhood was open for business.

On Thursday morning, I had breakfast at The Neutral Corner, and then it was off to the jewelers to pick up my engagement ring. By this time, I was genuinely excited to see it for myself.

I sent Stella a message that we would be spending the day in the city on Saturday, December 29. It was, after all, her birthday!

When I stepped out the front door onto the porch, there was no need to check the thermometer because there was no doubt that it was biting cold. Out of curiosity, however, I examined the thermometer, and it was indeed zero degrees.

By 8 am, I caught the streetcar for Stella's. I promised her that I would arrive before 9, and we would head into center city.

At 8:40, I reached Rosenstein's Florist on Salmon Street. The business was just a couple of blocks from the Zwolinski residence.

I had ordered a fresh bouquet. Wrapped in green tissue were three Amaryllis with bursting red blooms. The arrangement also included red and white Geminis, boughs of pine branches, and several sprigs of holly with red berries. I found it to be quite dazzling, and I hoped that Stella would also.

Just before 9 am, I reached her doorstep with flowers in hand. I could quickly tell by her reaction that the Amaryllis was a most pleasant surprise. My choice of flowers was obviously representative of the holidays as well as a sign of my love.

After the usual "How do you do's," we were on our way.

During our travel time, we spent most of the trip catching up on the latest news. When we arrived in center city, our day began with a stroll up Market Street, marveling at the magnificent Christmas window displays of the department stores of Strawbridge & Clothier, Gimbels, Lit Brothers, Snellenburg's, and Wanamaker's.

We agreed that they were all fantastic, but most impressive were the holiday decorations at Wanamaker's.

Highlighting the store's Winter Wonderland was a concert performance from its mighty organ. Installed in Wannamaker's, at Broad and Market streets, in 1911, the great instrument contains 28,000 pipes. It made its debut at the World Exposition in St. Louis in 1904.

Our next stop was a trip to the top of the city hall tower to see the William Penn statue. The 37-foot figure of the city's founding father gazes Northeast so he can view Penn Treaty Park, where he negotiated peace with the chief of the Lenape Turtle Clan.

An elevator took us to the observation deck at the base of the statue. This is 500 feet above the street level. From there, we were treated to views of the city in every direction.

Stella and I were genuinely amazed by the sights below. People walking on the streets looked like ants from our vantage point. Streetcars and automobiles resembled children's playthings. The city and its surrounding landscape beneath us appeared to be a giant toy railroad display engineered by a team representing one of the local department stores.

For a moment, I recalled the daring flights made by Gorrell and Dargue in their Curtiss R2 aircraft back in El Paso. Their view from the air must have been just as remarkable.

Next on my list was the highlight of my plans, a visit to the Philadelphia Museum of Art.

*   *26 NOTE: The Philadelphia Museum of Art began as Memorial Hall for the nation's Centennial Exposition in 1876. Plans to construct a new larger building began in 1907, although construction did not start until 1919. Due to material shortages resulting from the First World War, it was not until 1928 that the museum was completed.*

For almost an hour, Stella and I wandered from room to room, enjoying the many works of art that the museum had to offer: oils, watercolors, impressionism, expressionism realism, and others. This included sculptures and other representations.

When our visit was nearly complete, we found ourselves at a hall situated in an alcove that appeared to be about 20-foot square. The three walls of this gallery contained about a dozen works of art.

Facing each wall was a large, ornate, red leather sofa flanked by additional chairs and tables. The centerpiece of the display at the far end of the gallery was a 26 by 32-inch oil painting.

I took Stella by the hand and led her to the artwork. A two-inch by six-inch bronze plate noted as follows: "Summer on the Farm" Oil on canvas by Philadelphia Artist Alfred P. Handfinger (1897}.

The painting featured a two-story farmhouse with an addition of the left side. Completely dressed in white, a red tin roof topped the structure.

A small front porch comprised three ornate wrought iron posts that were also white and a matching red roof. A pair of wicker chairs seemed to be quite inviting, as well. On the porch, a black dog was napping in the afternoon sun.

While a tall oak tree towered over the home from behind, it was the front lawn that garnered the most attention. A sea of color dominated the scene: pinks, reds, whites, oranges, blues, and purples. A large lilac bush stood at one corner of the house.

A well-worn dirt footpath crossed through the flower bed on an angle leading to the porch. Its brown color was a stark contrast to the vibrant green lawn and the garden's intense color.

On the side of the house was a bare patch of lawn. A woman, clad in a blue dress and a white apron, held a wooden bucket as she fed about a dozen chickens. Approaching from the back of the house near the towering oak tree was the faint figure of a man.

"What do you think?" I asked Stella as we gazed at the painting.

"It looks just like the farmhouse I envision in my mind. The flowers, the trees, the chickens, the dog on the porch... they're all there," she said in amazement.

I looked at her and confirmed, "When I first saw it, that's what I thought.

I went on, "Stella, do you still want that country cottage as much as I do?" "Yes, Tommy. Yes, I do, and I still want to share it with you!" She exclaimed.

"Well, Stella," I began, "you know how I feel about the war and everything, but during my time in Georgia, I've had some time to think about it all. The truth is... I've had a change of heart."

She took me by the hand, and I continued, "Honestly, I do want to marry you. I want that with all of my heart. I know that I was trying to protect you from an uncertain future. I wanted what was best for you, and I still do."

"I finally realized that I don't want to live the rest of my life worrying about what may happen. It is, however, my desire to spend the rest of my life with you!

"That's what I really want. Stella, will you marry me?" I asked as I took the box out of my coat pocket.

By then, Stella was getting a little teary-eyed, but I could tell they were tears of joy. She put her arms around me and answered, "Of course I will, Tommy! I can't think of anything else I'd rather do!"

She added, "I'm not sure why you changed your mind, but I'm so glad you did."

At that point, I took the ring out of the box and placed it on her finger. She beamed when she looked at it for the first time.

We kissed to seal the deal, and it was the most romantic kiss of the times we spent together. It seemed like our hug lasted an eternity, but I'm sure it was just a moment or two.

Before we got up from the sofa, I exclaimed, "Oh, by the way..." "What? What is it, Tommy?" She asked.

"Happy Birthday, Stella!" I remarked.

When we left the museum, it was mid-afternoon, and we realized that we never stopped for lunch. I mentioned that I wanted to celebrate our engagement by taking her to a nice restaurant. My suggestion was The Three Threes.

"The place comes highly recommend," I began. "It's located at 333 Smedley Street, just off Pine Street."

"No. No, Tommy," she argued. I appreciate it, but I know a great place, Schlorer's Delicatessen on Mifflin and Water Streets. The food is outrageous, and I am dying for a great pastrami sandwich."

*   *27 NOTE: According to various sources, Mrs. Amelia Schlorer began producing the first commercial mayonnaise in Philadelphia in the early 1900s. The condiment was packed in glass jelly jars and sold initially in her husband's Philadelphia deli. The Schlorer Delicatessen Company was established in 1913 to meet the product's growing demand. Before that time, all mayonnaise was made by hand using published recipes. The condiment originated in 1756 in the town of Mahon, on the Island of Minorca, during the Seven Years War. A French chef, lacking ingredients to make his own sauce borrowed a recipe from someone in the village and dubbed the new egg and oil dressing Mahonnaise.*

Initially, I was somewhat disappointed. After all, I wanted to celebrate our engagement in a big way, but Stella, apparently, was being the practical one this time!

"Are you sure?" I asked with a puzzled look.

"Yes, I'm sure. It's on our way back to the train. It will be much cheaper, and I'm anxious to get home to tell my family the news."

"Well, if you say so... but your father already knows!" I hinted. "You talked to my father? What did he say?" She wanted to know.

"Oh, when I asked him for his permission, he just smiled and nodded affirmatively," I revealed. Stella admitted, "He doesn't say much. I don't know what I expected."

We hopped on the Broad Street Subway and then walked a few blocks to the deli. Even though it was barely ten degrees, it felt much warmer.

Actually, all the way back to Stella's house, things were warm and cozy. I'll never know why I resisted the whole idea of getting married before, but as they say, the water is fine.

Philadelphia city hall with William Penn Statue
Image Source: Unknown

"THE ROAD NOT TAKEN"

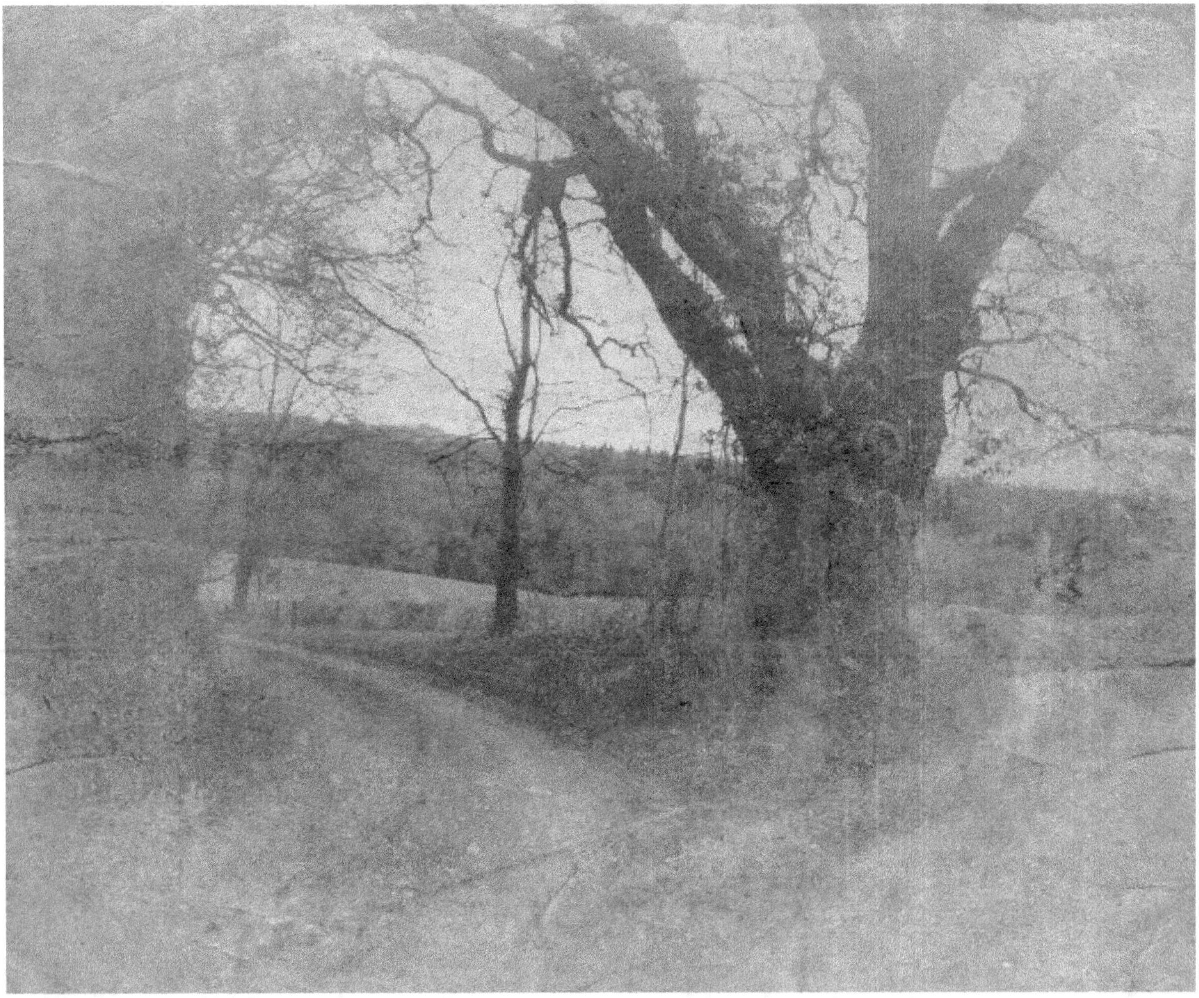

Two roads diverged in the woods...
Image Source: Unknown

CHAPTER 23

"The Road Not Taken"

Stella and I spent some time browsing around the large department stores in center city before heading back to her place.

The subway-elevated line was very crowded with post-holiday shoppers.

When we reached the Zwolinski house early that evening, her family was extremely excited.

Evidently, the news of our engagement had leaked out.

It seemed like the entire family met us at the door—everyone except her mother, Rozalia. We learned that she was just reaching into the oven to retrieve a large pan of Gołąbki.

28 NOTE: Gołąbki is a Polish dish, often referred to as "Little Pigeons," and is comprised of ground hamburger meat mixed with rice and wrapped with cabbage leaves. These cabbage rolls are baked in the oven with a tomato-based sauce.

Although we had a relatively late lunch at the delicatessen, the freshly made Gołąbki were irresistible.

"I hope you have room for Grandmama Szczepanski's chocolate cake!" Rozalia exclaimed as she placed the festive-looking dessert on the table after the meal.

"We have two celebrations," she went on, "It's Stella's birthday, and we're celebrating your engagement, of course!"

In a surprising twist, Franz raised his glass, and his soft voice accompanied by a heavy Polish accent he offered, "To Tommy, I know you will make our Stella very happy! Best wishes and welcome to our family! na drzovia!"

"I know he will," Joe chimed in. "I know he will!" He repeated while looking directly at me. He also flashed a warm smile and a wink in my direction.

Everyone joined in, and there were broad smiles all the way around the table.

Somehow, someway, Stella and I managed to consume a piece of that delicious cake even though we were bulging at the seams.

Since it was already dark, I excused myself, saying, "Well, I guess I best be getting home!"

Stella immediately chimed on, "I want to go with you, Tommy. I want to be there when you break the news to your family."

"Do you really think you should, Stella?" her mother questioned.

"It's getting late to be going out there and coming home alone," she added.

"I'll go with her," her brother, Joe, responded. "That way, I can see Veronica, as well," he reasoned. "Well, okay," the woman relented. "If Joe goes along, I suppose that will be fine."

She glanced at her husband, and as per usual, Franz nodded in agreement.

Our arrival at our house met with much the same reaction as we experienced at the Zwolinski's.

Plenty of hugs, kisses, and congratulations to go around. The girls, naturally, wanted to see the ring.

Before we could even get settled, mom came from the kitchen with a magnificent rum cake for the occasion. Florence was right behind her with a fresh pot of coffee.

On the other hand, Pop had a bottle of brandy in one hand and some Polish vodka bottle in the other.

"You crazy if you think we drink coffee when my son plans to get married," my old man hollered. "We drink real drink," he insisted.

Helen carried a tray of glasses into the dining room, and my father filled the larger glasses with brandy and poured vodka in the shot glasses.

"These glasses come from my cousin, Whitey, and this is what they're for... drink... drink," he ordered.

My mother passed out some very weak wine for the younger ones, and when we raised our glasses, pop toasted, "na drzowia!" meaning, "to your health."

Sunday, December 30, meant attending Mass in the morning and dinner in the afternoon. The skies were clear, but the temperature still hung around zero throughout the day. This was indeed quite a cold spell.

The newspapers reported that the temperatures across the river in New Jersey were even colder. The Mercury registered two below in Cape May and -29 at Culvers Lake in Sussex County in the Garden State. Other cold spots were Mercer County and Monmouth County. Temperatures there were -15 and -14, respectively. Due to the extremely harsh conditions in Barnegat Bay, the oyster and fish industries ceased operations.

My mother roasted a large chicken since we had ham and turkey on Christmas. Unfortunately, I would miss the traditional pork and sauerkraut on New Year's Day.

Naturally, Stella and Joe joined us, as I would need to catch the early train back to camp on Monday morning.

The dinner went famously. Pop even relaxed his 'no talking rule" at the table during dinner since it was my last one before shipping out again.

Despite the frigid weather, Stella and I bundled up and took a walk to Most Holy Redeemer Cemetery. I wanted to visit the grave of my grandmother, Josephine Kubacka. She had passed away about five or six years ago.

This was the last opportunity for Stella and me to have a meaningful conversation before I left for Camp Hancock.

"I wish you didn't have to go, Tommy," Stella began.

"Yes, I know what you mean, babe. That's what was so hard for me to go down this road. I realized how much I love you during my months in Georgia, and I couldn't stand to be without you.

"The more I thought about it, the more I knew it was the right thing to do, not just for me, but for us," I reasoned.

When we reached the massive gray stone entrance to the graveyard, I led her into the center archway for shelter from the cold. I reached into my coat pocket and pulled out a small, folded piece of paper. I then read aloud a few words that I had written down on the note:

"Fair one, I can see thee now,
Aye, how sweet thy snowy brow,
Never since the eve, we met,
Never those brown eyes could I forget.
I have found thee, by my side,
Ever shall my heart abide."

"Oh, how wonderful, Tommy," she gushed, "those are the most beautiful words I've ever heard!"

We hugged and kissed to celebrate the moment. Then, we walked to the far end of the cemetery to find the grave.

"It was a cold, snowy day the morning we buried her here," I remarked, referencing my grandmother. "The black funeral wagon, trimmed in gold, was pulled by two beautiful black horses," I remarked as I described the scene.

"Something spooked the horses during the graveside service, and the two mares reared up on their hind legs," I continued.

"When they jumped, they gave out a deafening roar. The sound scared my younger sisters.

"I remember that Henrietta and Stella clung to my parents, while Helen naturally ran to me, and I picked her up in my arms. Florence and Veronica ran behind a tree to hide. Mary, I believe, was unaffected," I added.

"That night, I sat up in bed and saw my grandmother standing by my feet. Dressed all in white, she told me that she would always watch over me. Then, she disappeared," I explained.

"Wow, Tommy. I had no idea," Stella remarked.

"Yes. It's true. I just wanted to make sure she's with me when I go overseas," I confided.

"It's not only comforting, but it makes me feel protected knowing she's looking over me," I admitted.

Stella gave me a reassuring hug. By now, the cold was chilling to the bone, and we walked hand in hand back to the house.

Monday morning, I was up by 4:30, and mom had breakfast ready for me, hot oatmeal, and hot coffee. Just what I needed on a cold morning like this.

Since my train was scheduled to depart the PRR Station at 6:34, I had very little time to spare. My trip downtown went relatively smoothly, and before I realized it, I was on my way back to Georgia.

Once the train left the city limits, I took out the book of Robert Frost's poetry that Stella gave me when I first shipped out. I flipped through the pages until I came to his work, "The Road Not Taken."

Two roads diverged in a yellow wood,
And sorry I could not travel both
And be one traveler, long I stood
And looked down one as far as I could
To where it bent in the undergrowth;

Then took the other, as just as fair,
And having perhaps the better claim,
Because it was grassy and wanted wear;
Though as for that the passing there
Had worn them really about the same,

And both that morning equally lay
In leaves no step had trodden black.
Oh, I kept the first for another day!
Yet knowing how way leads on to way,
I doubted if I should ever come back.

I shall be telling this with a sigh
Somewhere ages and ages hence:
Two roads diverged in a wood, and I—
I took the one less traveled by,
And that has made all the difference.

Upon reading the poem, I couldn't help but compare it to my own situation. A few months ago, I had determined that I had selected the proper road for me, and now here I was traveling down a completely different one.

Was my journey the road less traveled? Should I have stayed the course? Time would tell if I made the right decision. I placed myself in God's hands and drifted off to sleep.

I found myself in what appeared to be the middle of a battlefield. It was barren and desolate. Devoid of trees or shrubs of any kind, the landscape was mired in mud, covered with craters, and littered with bodies and abandoned equipment.

My orders were to drag a three-foot by four-foot wooden cart through the carnage. The wagon had two large steel wheels and a wide u-shaped handle that was attached to each end of the axle.

The purpose of my mission was to collect the bodies and body parts of our fallen men: arms, legs, torsos, heads, and other gruesome elements. At a distance of about 30 to 40 meters, my cart was full, and I would then return to the field hospital and exchange it for another.

When I entered the hospital, I observed the staff of more than a dozen surgeons and nurses, both French and American, in the operating room. These men and women were diligently piecing the body parts together in an attempt to make them whole once again.

Several teams of men were also scurrying back and forth with patients on their litters. Soldiers wearing armbands bearing a red cross transported the living wounded, while those donning black armbands carried the deceased. Those who were able to be revived went to post-op for recovery, while the latter were placed in a hastily dug mass grave.

As I left my wagon near one of the operating tables, a doctor shouted, "We need blood! Bring me a bucket of blood!"

I turned in his direction, and he repeated, "We need blood here, soldier! Go get us a bucket of blood!"

"Yes, Sir!" I acknowledged.

When I turned away, one of the dismembered arms in the cart reached out and grabbed me by the leg. I panicked and screamed, "No! No! Let me go! Let me go!"

The next thing I knew, I felt someone shake me. I heard a voice calling, "Mister! Mister! Wake up! Are you alright?"

Finally, I opened my eyes. I realized that I was still in the railroad car, and standing over me was a thirty-something-year-old man dressed in a red, plaid flannel shirt, blue coveralls, and a beat-up brown felt hat.

"You were dreaming, sir! Having a real bad dream, I suppose, he said. "Are you okay?" He asked.

"Yes. Yes. I'm fine," I responded.

"I guess it was just a bad dream... is all."

"You had me worried for a while," the stranger explained. "Are you coming back from the war?" He queried.

"No... no. I haven't gone there yet," I revealed. "What day is it?" I asked.

"It's New Year's Day, sir! January 1, 1918! What day did you think it was?" The man asked. "Awww... I don't know. Actually, I have no idea," Was my response.

"My name's Clem, by the way, Clem Haefferschmidt," the man said to introduce himself. "My real name's Clemson, but everyone just calls me Clem," he added.

"Tommy, Tommy Schalata," I returned.

"So, Tommy, where ya' headin'?" He inquired. "Georgia. Camp Hancock, actually," was my answer.

"No, foolin'!" He exclaimed. "I'm a Georgia boy myself, and a singer and musician, too! Just comin' back from Richmond. Had a real payin' job with an or-ches-tra over the holidays," he emphasized.

"Is that right?" I asked.

"What instrument do you play?" I questioned further. "Well, I sing an' play the fiddle," he noted.

"I can play a little guitar, as well," Clem added.

"I performed for two full weeks with Joe Fromm and The Pleasant Valley Boys," the man boasted.

It was about three in the afternoon, and since there were only a handful of passengers in our car, the stranger insisted, "Listen, let me play you a tune. These folks won't mind, will ya'?" He asked as he looked around the car.

Two passengers responded with light applause, one let out a whistle, and the fourth individual appeared to be resting. He never looked up, keeping his eyes closed.

The man reached under his seat for his fiddle case. He took the instrument out, gave the strings a couple of plucks, and went right to work singing and playing.

The longest train I ever saw
Went down that Georgia line.
The engine passed at six o'clock
And the cab passed by at nine.

In the pines, in the pines
Where the sun never shines
And we shiver when the cold wind blows

I asked my captain for the time of day
He said he throwed his watch away.
A long steel rail and a short cross tie
I'm on my way back home.

In the pines, in the pines
Where the sun never shines
And we shiver when the cold wind blows

Little girl, little girl, what have I done
That makes you treat me so.
You caused me to weep, you caused me to mourn
You caused me to leave my home.

In the pines, in the pines
Where the sun never shines
And we shiver when the cold wind blows

My father was an engineer
Died a mile out of town.
His head was found in the driving gear
But his body was never found.

In the pines, in the pines
Where the sun never shines
And we shiver when the cold wind blows

Again, the Georgia musician received a nice ovation from those in our car, and as expected, he tipped his hat and took a bow.

"You might have imagined," he noted, "that song is called, In the Pines. Thank you all very much."

Clem tipped his hat one more time, then he put his bow and violin away, and our entertainment was over.

I was skeptical about going back to sleep after that horrid nightmare. Therefore, I got up to stretch my legs. The next stop for me would be the dining car, where I got a bowl of fish chowder and a cup of coffee.

Later, the conductor made his rounds and announced that the next stop was Augusta. Since it was New Year's Day and nearly 7 pm, no trains were running directly into camp at that time. I would need to collect my bags and hop a streetcar back to the installation.

I met some of the guys in my outfit, and we compared notes about how our holidays went. I revealed that Stella and I officially became engaged, and the fellows showered me with a rowdy round of congratulations.

The boys told me that there was quite a New Year's celebration here at Camp Hancock. They reported that the colonel had arranged for several bands to perform for the men. The entertainment took place on Pennsylvania Avenue, near Wrightsboro Road.

I also learned rather quickly that much of the camp was under quarantine due to a measles outbreak. Entire companies were under lockdown because of the number of cases reported.

Then, it was time to turn in for the night. I suspected that everything would return to normal the following day.

Doc informed me that things were quite busy down at the field hospital. Typhus is going around, as well.

Our instructions at the Field Hospital revealed that the latter is spread by parasites, such as body lice, fleas, and chiggers. Symptoms include fever, headache, and a rash. It can also lead to meningitis.

Just what I needed to hear, measles and typhus. I should have stayed in Philly.

As I drifted off to sleep, I looked back on all the events from my trip back to Philly. I was satisfied in knowing that I made the right decision in regards to Stella and me.

I took the road less traveled, and time would tell which would have been the better choice!

"THE BIG LEAGUES COME TO PLAY"

Walter Johnson and the Washington Senators pay a visit
Image Source: The Sporting News

CHAPTER 24

"The Big Leagues Come to Play"

On Saturday, January 5, a Divisional Dress Parade and Review took place at three o'clock. The pageantry of such an event is a much-celebrated tradition in the army.

This formal ceremony gathers the troops in formation, assesses their appearance, conducts a roll call, and announces essential orders.

The standard practice has been to hold a dress parade in the morning, but for some reason, the colonel chose to schedule it in the afternoon.

Typically, a drum signal is given one-half hour before the troops assemble. In our case, it was at 2:30. The Division band then fell into formation on the parade field. Each company organized its own parade for roll call and inspection.

At precisely 3 pm, the spectacle began, and for nearly one hour, the men went through a systematic series of maneuvers, marches, drills, and reviews by the officers. Even from a civilian perspective, the parade is a remarkable display of disciplined training. The fellows, however, are quite thankful that such exercises are few and far between.

As we stood at attention for inspection, all in our perfectly aligned rows, Bob Kerr, who was standing directly in front of me, began to sway.

Initially, it appeared to be a gentle movement on his part, but his lack of balance became more apparent. Finally, he fell back into my arms and collapsed.

Several of the others came to my aid, and we carried him away from the formation. Two medics ran onto the drill field with a litter and transported him to the field hospital.

Later, we learned that Kerr was dehydrated because he was suffering from Typhus.

Another reason that we were grateful was the fact that the parade did not take place the following day was that Sunday brought with it a terrible rainstorm. So tremendous was the downpour that many men had to move their tents due to flooding.

Many routine drills and activities were scratched from the duty list because of the measles and typhus outbreaks. Reading and writing filled the days during the next several weeks. Those of us assigned to the field hospital and those involved in other essential tasks still had to report to our posts, but the rest of the camp was mired in a kind of perpetual quarantine.

I found myself writing several letters to the folks back home, and for that reason, I appreciated the downtime.

The cold, damp, rainy weather continued for much of January. The worst of which took place on Sunday, January 13. High winds and driving rains caused a great deal of havoc around Camp Hancock that day.

The storm uprooted many trees around the installation, and most of the electric power was down as a result. Extensive flooding forced many men to abandon their tents and run for cover, and many fled while dressed in just their underwear.

Throughout the camp, the higher-ups suspended all regular activity and dispatched details of men for clean-up duties and repairs. On my way to the field hospital, I passed one such detachment at the corner of Wrightsboro and Division Roads. They were repairing the Chautauqua Amusement Tent.

January continued to be gloomy and wet. The rainstorms remained frequent, and flooding continued to be a problem. The disagreeable weather also hampered our efforts to improve the measles and Typhus outbreaks.

By the first week of February, the quarantine was lifted, and the camp was beginning to return to normal. The weather was improving, and for the first time in several weeks, the men were involved in outdoor activities.

On Wednesday, February 20, the colonel granted the camp a half-day holiday, and a massive boxing tournament took place at Division HQ.

The men were treated to over 200 bouts put on by a contingent of amateur and professional fighters.

The following day, the 412-piece Divisional Band performed for the troops. It was a rousing presentation enjoyed by all!

By the weekend, the playing of baseball started up once again. Sunday saw a contest between Co. G and Co. H of the 112th Infantry Company. G Company shut out their opponent 5-0.

The "G-Men" had the advantage on the mound, sending a former pitcher from Connie Mack's Philadelphia Athletics, Bill Hart, to the hill.

> *   *29 NOTE: Bill (William Franklin) Hart played eight years in the majors. As a pitcher and part-time outfielder, Hart was with the following teams: Philadelphia A's (1886-87), Brooklyn Grooms (1892), Pittsburgh Pirates (1895, 1898), St. Louis Browns (1896-97), and Cleveland Blues (1901). His best season was 1895 with the Pirates, where he was 14-17 with 24 complete games while striking out 85. Also, Connie Mack (Cornelius McGillicuddy), was a former big-league ballplayer and manager/owner of the Philadelphia Athletics for more than 50 years.*

The Haeberle brothers resurrected our ball team from El Paso to play once again. They recruited most of our old gang for the squad. Practices and pick-up games were held strictly on the weekends.

In addition to Harry and Bill Haeberle, the roster consisted of Jimmy Rafferty, Elmor Hutchinson, Roy Wilson, Harry Dohner, Barney Roth, Al Gray, Bernie Halliday, Bob Kerr, Leo Quigley, and me.

Several Major League ball teams held their Spring Training Camps in Georgia and neighboring states.

A number of these clubs would stop at Camp Hancock to play exhibition games for the boys.

The men had high hopes that the Boston Red Sox new sensation Babe Ruth would visit the camp.

The Red Sox spent the Spring in Hot Springs, AK.

On St. Patrick's Day, Boston needed Ruth, a successful young pitcher, to make an emergency start at first base.

The Babe launched two home runs against the Pittsburgh Pirates that day. The second shot traveled 573 feet and landed across the street from the ballpark in a pond at the Arkansas Alligator Farm and Petting Zoo.

The American League's Washington Senators, who trained in nearby August, GA, took on our 108th Field Artillery team on Sunday, March 23.

Our poor lads had no prayer going up against Walter Johnson, who won 23 games the year before.

The Senators won 7-0.

Washington outfielders Frank Schulte and Clyde Milan had two RBI's each. Johnson pitched seven innings while striking out 11 players.

Eddie Matteson tossed the final two innings for the Senators. He fanned three while walking just one.

Jimmy Rafferty and Harry Haeberle each garnered one hit for the home team, while Elmor Hutchinson embarrassingly struck out five times. Mercifully, I never got into the game. We also committed three errors in the process.

Naturally, the boys hung their heads a little after that loss but were consoled by the fact that they played their hearts out against some of the best ballplayers in the country!

The Senators returned to Camp Hancock the following Saturday, March 30. Their opponent would be the 112th Infantry.

It was a nearly perfect Spring afternoon at game time. The piercing blue sky was marred by only a few wispy, white clouds. One of the guys told me that the transportation company provided 243 wagons to carry the men to the ballfield.

Washington would once again send Walter Johnson, known as "The Big Train," to the mound to pitch, while the 112th Infantry pinned their hopes on the 53-year-old former big leaguer, Bill Hart.

It had been 17 years since he threw in his last Major League game, but the Louisville KY native was up for the challenge.

Adding to this big game's pageantry, the Washington team walked single-file onto the field, holding their bats over their shoulders like rifles. This gesture was a symbolic tribute to all the servicemen in attendance.

Fellow members of G Company on the team with Hart were: Harry Bishop (First Base), Clarence Bodine (Second), Raymond Rutherford (Shortstop), Fred Scheetz (Third), Nick Bradley (Catcher), John Mooney (Rightfield), Sidney Stuckert (Centerfield), and Bob "Big Bob" Weckerly (Leftfield). Filling out the squad from other companies were: Lenny Garfield, Elvin Bickerson, T.J.

Gratz, George Doughtery, Stan Muskowicz, Amole Harris, Sal Giansante, Elmo Sheplock (Black Elmo), and Buddy Pisianki.

*   *30 NOTE: Black Elmo was not a member of the colored troops. He was a very dark-complected Slovak with jet-black hair.*

More than 5,000 troops and civilians were treated to quite a contest on that day, as Johnson appeared to be in mid-season form. The Washington hurler struck out the first five batters he faced.

Hart seemed to find the fountain of youth because he went toe to toe with Johnson. He kept the 112th right in the battle, giving up just one hit and one walk while fanning three for the first two innings. The score was 0-0.

Base runners were few and far between for the first seven innings. Walter Johnson still had a no- hitter going to that point. He walked Harry Bishop, hit "Big Bob" Weckerly on the knee cap, and increased his strikeout total to 12.

The seemingly ageless Hart conceded three hits and two walks while fanning seven batsmen.

In the bottom of the eighth inning, however, with one out, Elvin Bickerson batted for Weckerly and reached base on an error by the Senators' shortstop, Doc Lavan. The infielder bobbled the ball momentarily, and the speedy runner for the 112th beat his throw.

Trying to capitalize on the situation, Captain Mull, the Hancock squad manager, sent Buddy Pisianki up to the plate.

The fleet-footed Pollack ran Johnson's count to 3-1 before he bounced a ball deep into the hole at third base. Washington's Eddie Foster had no chance at getting Bickerson at second, and much to the delight of the crowd, Pisianki was safe at first, as well.

Bickerson and Pisianki attempted a double steal, with two strikes on the batter, Lenny Garfield. Senators' catcher, Eddie Ainsmith, nailed the lead runner at third, but Pisianki slid into second safely, or so it seemed.

Buddy's momentum took him past the bag, and Lavan put the tag on him for the final out of the inning. The rally died.

Little did anyone know that the eighth inning would wind up being the midway point of the game.

The two teams would do battle for eight more innings.

Johnson continued putting up zeroes, and while the game was a marathon, the Washington pitcher's performance appeared to be effortless.

Seventeen batters from the 112th came up to the plate to face the legendary hurler, and seventeen batters carried their bats back to the bench. The side-arm fast-baller just kept mowing them down.

Hart, on the other hand, was obviously tiring. Although he matched his counterpart's goose eggs, he scattered several hits and free passes over 15 innings. His strikeouts had all but disappeared, as well. He was sweating profusely on the mound, and his shoulders drooped noticeably. After all, he was 23 years older than his counterpart.

Senators' manager, Clark Griffith, went to his bench to break the deadlock in the top of the 16th inning.

Patsy Gharrity led off the inning with a double over the head of centerfielder Sidney Stuckert. Hart managed to strike out Joe Judge for out number one, and Ray Morgan hit a pop-up that was caught in foul territory by Bradley for the second out.

Pinch-hitter, Val Picinich, smacked a liner down the third-base line to score Gharrity and break the scoreless deadlock. Foster grounded back to Hart to end the inning, but the Senators took a 1-0 lead into the bottom of the 16th.

Johnson noticeably embarrassed that a ragtag outfit of recruits, led by a 53-year-old has-been, took him and his team to 16 innings. Therefore, he buckled down and struck out Bickerson, Pisianki, and Black Elmo to end the game.

Naturally, around the camp, the men were disappointed at the outcome, but they took satisfaction in showing one of the best pitchers in the Major Leagues that the men of Camp Hancock were no pushover.

Baseball games among the outfits continued as long as we were there. In addition to the Washington Senators, the New York Yankees, who trained in Atlanta, visited Camp Hancock. The Pittsburgh Pirates traveled from Columbus, GA, to our camp, also.

We saw one final baseball game at Camp Hancock, and that was an exhibition contest between the Philadelphia Athletics and the Pirates on April 8. The scoreless game was suspended in the fifth inning because of rain.

It was quite a sight to see one of the players holding an umbrella over the head of A's manager, Connie Mack.

     *   *31 NOTE: Officially, the majors began to play regular-season games on April 15. Due to the war, it was announced that the leagues would play a reduced schedule in 1918.*

Charlie Chaplain, the famous film star and comedian, arrived by train in Augusta on Tuesday, April 16. The date happened to be Chaplain's 29th birthday. A Southern Railroad train from Columbia, South Carolina, pulled into Augusta's Union Station at approximately 1:35 pm.

According to sources, he reportedly went directly to the Albion Hotel, located on the 700 block of Broad Street.

After freshening up, he walked directly across the street to the Wells Theater at 2:30.

     *   *32 NOTE: The Wells Theater was later renamed The Imperial Theater.*

The world-renown entertainer recently inked a $1 million film contract with First National Company, and his latest motion picture, "A Dog's Life," had just been released.

He spoke to an overflow crowd to promote the sale of Liberty Bonds for the war effort.

"I didn't come here to be funny," the comedian announced, "I've come here to sell Liberty Bonds," he stated.

The Augusta Chronicle noted that he did both. Chaplain acted out several hilarious stunts while directing the 110th Infantry Band from Camp Hancock.

The newspaper reported, "He almost made the audience believe they were at the movies paying their nickel."

From there, Chaplain rode in an automobile to the Camp Hancock Hospital, where he passed out cigarettes throughout the wards.

Local Judge, Henry Hammond, held a birthday dinner for the star at the Augusta Country Club that evening, and at 9:15 pm, Chaplain boarded a train bound for Macon, GA.

Our Company CO told us that in thirty days we would be leaving Camp Hancock, destination unknown. We were certain, however, that our involvement in the war would be forthcoming.

By the beginning of May, we began taking inventory of our clothing and personal articles. The CO also confirmed that we would be heading overseas.

The Quartermaster went over our lists and issued various items such as clothing, socks, and toilet articles. Most personal items that would not fit in our packs had to be shipped home, or we were required to dispose of them. Those men, who were of German descent, were being sent to an installation in Kansas.

Many of us spent a good deal of time at the recreation center during the end of our stay in Georgia. Four of us spent one Sunday afternoon there, shooting pool. In addition to myself, there was Roy Wilson, Harry Dommet, and Bill Haeberle. None of us were incredibly skilled in the game, except for Wilson. I preferred shooting darts.

Dommet and I paired up on one team, while Wilson and Haeberle were the opposition.

It turned out to be a completely casual afternoon, and we made sure to steer the conversation away from the topics of politics and religion.

Instead, the focus was on family, jobs, and non-controversial subjects.

Wilson lived on East Thompson St., in Philadelphia, not far from Lehigh Avenue, while I lived at the other end of Thompson, in what is called the Bridesburg section. However, our family was originally from nearly the same neighborhood as him. My sister Maryanna still lives there.

The Haeberle's, on the other hand, reside on Ridge Avenue in Philly, and Dommet hails from Lancaster, PA.

"So, what do you do out there in Lancaster, Harry? Are you a farmer or what?" I asked Dommet. "No," the 18-year-old responded, "I work for the National Novelty Co., on Fulton Street. We make mouse traps, cookie cutters, and paintbrushes. Things like that," he explained. "You like it there?" I pressed on.

"It's okay. It's a job, you know!" Dommet added.

Just then, Wilson made a bank shot of the five-ball in the side pocket amongst a lot of traffic, and that raised a few eyebrows.

"Wow! Where'd you learn to shoot like that, Roy?" Billy Haeberle questioned. "Countless days of a misspent youth," he replied.

"How'd that happen?" I begged to know.

"Well," Wilson began, "I spent many days down at Krausemeyer's Pool Hall, over on Mercer Street.

You know, right around the corner from Kapinski's Funeral Home?" "Yeah, I know the place."

"Every Thursday night, Ol' man Fogarty came into the place to shoot a few games. He always reserved the same table, number four.

"He was a short, stout man, about fifty-something, I guess. He had a large wart on the left side of his chin. I think he worked in the office down at the shipyard.

"I recall that he always wore a dark blue suit with a light blue tie. I never saw the man without a yellow carnation on his lapel or a matching yellow hanky in his breast pocket. He typically had a big, fat, smelly cigar in his mouth, as well.

"Mr. Krausemeyer paid me 25 cents a week to sweep up, and I got a penny apiece for racking the balls in-between games.

"Fogarty occasionally sent me on errands like fetching him a quart of beer down at Gus's Taproom on Belgrade Street or running down to Fleischmann's Delicatessen, right there on Lehigh," he recalled.

Wilson further noted, "The old man always got a salami sandwich with sharp provolone cheese on a hard Italian roll. Geez! That thing must have been over a foot long and loaded with garlic and hot peppers! The man always had the man at the deli slice it into four pieces."

"No kidding!" I exclaimed.

"Yeah, and he had a special handkerchief in his coat pocket that he used for things like that. I asked him once about the one in his breast pocket, and the old man replied, 'That's for showin'... not blowin'!"

"Usually, Fogarty paid me a nickel to do his running, too!" Wilson continued.

"I learned a lot about shooting pool from that old guy, but the topper was one night when a young punk came into the pool hall. You could tell right off the bat that he thought he was a hotshot! Fogarty sized him up immediately.

"The skinny, little redhead was shooting over at table three, and the old man was watching out of the corner of his eye.

"Fogarty faked a couple of poor shots and even whiffed on the cueball once. He damn near tore a hole in the felt on the table.

"Krausemeyer came out of his office and gave him hell... 'you know better than that, Fogarty. Put a tear in that table, and it's comin' out of your pocket,' the owner warned.

"The kid jumped on the opportunity and challenged the old guy to a best of three match," Wilson continued his story.

"The first game was close, but Fogarty managed to beat the kid. Next, the old man played like a novice, missing shots, overshooting the pockets, etc. He looked awful.

"Smelling blood, the redhead convinced Fogarty to up the ante and even let his opponent break. "Fogarty chalked up his cue stick... looked around the room... and broke the rack. The balls scattered upon impact, and three went in immediately, the seven ball, the thirteen, and the two.

"The old fellow stood there expressionless for a few minutes while chewing on the stub of his cigar.

He walked around the table clockwise. He stopped and bent over. He surveyed the table.

"Next, he stood up and walked around the room in the opposite direction and did the same.

"Fogarty took the cigar out of his mouth and set it on the edge of the pool table. He chalked up again and waved his stick under the light fixture.

"He paused... he thought... he bent over and shot. The cueball rolled between the one ball and the fifteen like a piece of thread through the eye of a needle. It kissed the five ball, which dropped into the corner pocket like a hard-boiled egg without a crack.

"He continued to shoot, and I continued to put up fresh racks. Finally, the young man knew that he was beaten. He laid six one-dollar bills on the table and walked out of the hall without saying a word," Wilson concluded.

"What happened then?" I asked.

"Well," our storyteller noted, " Fogarty took a puff of his cigar, gave me a wink, and tossed a Buffalo nickel on the table. Then, he said, 'get yourself a bag of candy, kid!'

"Wow! That's quite a story," Dommet exclaimed.

It was getting close to chow time, so we packed things up at the rec hall and headed back to our tents.

On the morning of May 11, we assembled our heavy packs, and then the Sargent inspected each one. Finally, we received permission to go to the Mess Hall.

After breakfast, we began loading all our property on railroad cars, and the troops commenced boarding at 3 pm. Within thirty minutes, we left Wheeler Station and were bound for South Carolina.

I was now very accustomed to these all-night train rides, and the prolonged, gentle rocking of the car put me to sleep relatively quickly.

In the early morning hours, our Atlantic Seaboard Railroad train made a stop somewhere in North Carolina, and we were served breakfast trackside.

By 11 am, we crossed the Virginia State Line and made a stop in Richmond just a few minutes past Noon. A contingent from the Red Cross was there to meet us, and the women passed out an assortment of cakes and coffee to the men.

Just four hours later, our train rolled into the terminal in Washington, DC. The Sarge informed us that we would transfer to a B&O train, but we would be fed sandwiches and coffee on the platform before leaving for Philadelphia.

Even though it was nearly 10:30 pm, a large crowd was on hand to welcome us as we pulled into Philly's station at 24th and Chestnut Sts. Several hundred people let out a thunderous cheer when they saw our troop train come to a halt at track Number 9. The boys had their windows wide open and were hanging their arms and heads out of the cars.

Most were cheering, as well, although some searched the crowd hoping for a glance at a familiar face. Alas, there were none to be had.

At Midnight, May 12, 1918, we boarded a New York Central Railroad train bound for Camp Mills, NY.

The Sargeant told us that the journey was slightly more than 150 miles and would take about three to three and a half hours to get there.

Located on Long Island, about 10 miles east of New York City, the camp would be our new home for the next few days. Then, we could expect to board a ship bound for Europe.

Our time there would be spent catching up on laundry, writing last-minute letters home, and doing a lot of praying.

I sent off one final letter to Stella during this time, for I did not know what lay ahead. Neither did I know where I would find myself.

After bringing her up to speed on the latest news, I closed with the following: *"Distance is just a test to see how far love can travel. Be assured that when this is over, I WILL be coming home to you. Love, Tommy!"*

Bill Hart, former A's pitcher
Image Source: Unknown

Connie Mack, Philadelphia A's
Image Source: Unknown

25

"INTO THE MOUTH OF THE DRAGON"

The USS Justica No. F 8261 sailed out of New York Harbor.
Image Source: Unknown

CHAPTER 25

"Into the Mouth of the Dragon"

After the routine inspections, we prepared to leave Camp Mills, NY, on the night of May 18, 1918.

At 0300 hours, under mysterious secrecy, our men were entrained for a short journey where we embarked on a ferry boat. The ferry took us to Pier 59 in New York Harbor.

By then, it was daybreak, and the 108th and 109th Field Artillery joined several thousand other troops in boarding the transport ship "Justicia," No. F 8261.

* *33 NOTE: The ship "Justica" was built by Harland and Wolff in Belfast, Ireland, the same as the "RMS Titanic." It was initially launched on July 9, 1914, as "The Statendam" for the Holland-America Line. The vessel was re-fitted for war duty later that year. For protection against U-boat attacks, its gray hull was repainted in confusing dazzle camouflage. It was handed over to the British on April 7, 1917, as a troop transport ship capable of carrying 4,000 troops. The steel schooner, with two masts, had 11 bulkheads and 18 water ballast tanks.*

With the morning sun shining brightly in a nearly cloudless sky, we left the pier. Two tug boats backed us out into the middle of the Hudson River, and we sailed under our own power past the Statue of Liberty. As I got my first glimpse of the famous green-clad Lady Liberty holding her equally famous flaming torch, I couldn't help but wonder if it would be my last.

Except for the rumbling of our engines, it was relatively quiet on the water. An occasional tug boat would sound its horns, and the crew would let out a cheer when they passed by us.

Later, a battleship honored us by having most of its finely dressed sailors standing at the ship's rail in full salute. As they went by, we could hear the ship's band on deck playing, "Over There."

When we left the harbor, per his orders, Colonel Asher Miner, commander of the regiment, assumed the ship's military command.

To the men, this seemed fitting and proper. We learned to sing a tune written about him when we served on the Texas border.

With the New York skyline at our backs, the men began to sing the song:

"The boss of all, there ain't no finer,
Our little 'old man' is sure a bird.
We'll ride through hell for Colonel Miner,
And ride right back if he says the word."

The song bore witness to the loyalty and affection that he earned over the years.

Col. Miner combined the strictness of a disciplinarian with an unusual kindness of nature. He not only revealed tireless energy and a genuine tactical instinct, but he had an absolute absence of fear. For these reasons, the men loved him.

Eventually, New York faded behind us, and on the horizon was nothing but water. A few errant gulls followed us for a while.

After one day at sea, "The Justicia" joined 12 other vessels, and the 13-ship convoy started for the other side of the Atlantic.

We were anxious to hear news regarding other ships during the crossing. One report stated that the troopship, "City of Calcutta," which left New York on May 2, had an engine failure midway across the ocean, and the vessel drifted aimlessly for 12 hours while repairs were being made. Talk about a sitting duck for U-boats.

As was the case with the long train runs to Texas and Georgia, card games took up much of the men's time while we were at sea.

If the game wasn't cards, it was indeed craps or some other form of gambling.

In one corner of the deck, a group of about a dozen men huddled around the players of one such card game. For a table, the men used a two-foot by three-foot wooden crate.

I preferred shooting darts to playing cards and never spent a great deal of time learning the finer details of poker. I was familiar with the basics, but the many poker variations, such as wild card, low ball, and split pot, weren't of much interest to me.

From a distance, I observed this high-stakes contest. O'Flaherty, an Irishman from the 109th Machine Gun Battalion, laid down his hand, which consisted of two pairs, aces, and sixes.

Sitting across the table was a hot-headed Italian, Guiseppe Constantino. He was grinning from ear to ear as he revealed his hand. He had three sevens. The grin turned into a devilish smirk as he waited for O' Flaherty's reaction.

The silence was unnerving as we all watched the Irishman's face turned beet-red.

It was no secret that the Micks and the garlic-eaters hated each other. Mistrust fueled this mutual dislike for each other, and these poker games usually resulted in throwing more gas on the fire.

"You Goddam cheat!" O', Flaherty yelled. "No! No way!" Constantino denied.

"I saw you hand-mucking with my own eyes," the Irishman accused his opponent.

   **   34 NOTE: A cheat may hand-muck a card or more than one card. When a cheat is "mucking," they are cleverly hiding cards to switch into their hand later.*

Several other men in the group claim they observed the mucking and joined in the fight.

Before long, things got carried away. There was a great deal of pushing and shoving amongst the men. The cards spilled onto the deck of the ship when the heavy crate overturned during the melee.

Constantino, who was outnumbered 11 to 1, was grabbed by several guys and physically carried to the ship's railing.

Although he was kicking and screaming, the alleged cheater was hung by his feet over the side of the ship.

With O'Flaherty leading the way, the mob insisted that he admit to his wrongdoing, or the rioters would drop him into the sea.

Finally, the Italian submitted to their protests and surrendered. In addition to being thoroughly embarrassed by the incident, Constantino attempted to compose himself once his feet were firmly back on the deck, but a large wet stain was clearly visible on the soldier's crotch area.

Not only was the man forbidden from joining in any other card games for the remainder of the voyage, but the guys hung the nickname "Pisshead" on the poor chap.

As for O' Flaherty, he found himself $27 richer over the disputed pot. During the scuffle, one of the other guys scooped the cards off the deck and handed the Irishman his winnings.

Most of the journey at sea was uneventful. Naturally, this boredom is what led to so many of those card and dice games.

It was almost a jolly interlude between the intensive training in America and the brutal fighting that was going on in France.

We managed to survive the darkened decks at night and the boat drills during the day. Still, it was primarily monotonous day after day.

A large detachment of nurses on board provided the necessary social element, and nightly dances took place in the saloon. However, the constant need to wear life preservers kept these hoards of young men at a safe social distance from their female counterparts. It was an ironic triumph of virtue over testosterone.

We took most of our meals in the mess hall, which was down in the steerage area, but occasionally we ate in the saloon. For a dollar a day, you could get three meals at 8, 12, and 6.

The only time there was any excitement was when there was a German U-boat sighting.

It seemed as though these U-boats prowed at every leg of our voyage. It was a common topic, especially as Mess. One of the guys revealed that he had seen two enemy submarines this week, and another reported that one of the ship's crew members admitted that somebody spotted three last night.

The most obvious detection was when a U-boat's periscope popped above the surface of the water. However, on rare occasions, the wake of the torpedo whizzing passed was definitely more frightful. Because we traveled in a large convoy for most of the Atlantic journey, that latter was infrequent.

A report from the "RMS Olympic," which had made its crossing about a week before us, had an encounter with a German U-boat.

We received word that just before 0400 on Sunday, May 12, submarine U-103 rose to the surface, expecting to find a large transport ship about a thousand yards away.

The enemy ship was about 995 yards off target, and the Olympic saw him first. The fifty thousand- ton vessel struck the U-boat on the starboard side just as it attempted to dive below the surface.

According to the rumors, the collision turned the sub over, and it went down under the ship. The German warship resurfaced just off the aft port gun, and the gunner put five five-inch shells into its side.

Two destroyers circled back to the Olympic and captured 31 enemy prisoners. The incident occurred north of Brest at the mouth of the English Channel.

   *   *35 NOTE: RMS Olympic was a British ocean liner. The Olympic had a long career spanning 24 years from 1911 to 1935. This included service as a troopship during the First World War, which gained her the nickname "Old Reliable." After the war, she returned to civilian use and served as an ocean liner throughout the 1920s and into the first half of the 1930s. The ship was the largest ocean liner in the world except by the brief tenure of the slightly larger "Titanic" (which had the exact dimensions but higher gross tonnage owing to revised interior configurations).*

Another soldier aboard our ship, The Justicia, indicated that he had sighted an enemy sub through his bathroom porthole while bathed in the tub.

We all laughed when he admitted that he started for the deck while wearing nothing but a lifejacket.

Once he realized his dilemma, he sheepishly returned to his cabin.

"Do you think," one of the guys questioned, "those submarines have wireless? Is it possible that they could send messages to other U-boats to track us?"

"No doubt," replied one of the others, "but I think we're pretty safe in this convoy," he added.

"I would give a month's pay to see a sub," one of the guys commented, "and a year's pay if he didn't see us!" He admitted.

A massive boom shook the vessel as we sat in the mess hall. Initially, it was unclear whether we had taken a hit or if we were firing upon an enemy vessel.

The unexpected blast not only startled all of us below deck but jolted us mentally. It reminded us that the war was real, and we could become an active part of it at any time - voluntarily or not!

To this point, the explosion was the worst sound I ever heard. It was a vicious attack on my psyche. I felt a little queasy. Not from seasickness. Not out of fear to fight. Not because of cowardness, but merely because it finally had sunk in that there was no turning back. There was no chance to change my mind. The fear of the unknown was playing with my emotions. The event quickly put an end to the boredom we had been feeling.

Within moments, the suspicion of a threat had thrown the entire ship into complete chaos. Men were scrambling in every direction. With panic clearly written on their faces, there was much shouting, yelling, and confusion. However, almost immediately, the pandamonium was replaced by the orderly, logical thinking that had been drilled into us for months.

The turmoil lasted only a few minutes when the loud shrill of a whistle made us aware that one of the ship's naval officers entered the room. Everyone rapidly stopped dead in their tracks, and the room grew deadly silent.

"Attention! Attention! Before you man the lifeboats and scramble for your life jackets, the noise you have just heard is not part of an enemy attack. It is the result of a scheduled drill to test the ships' guns that are assigned to our convoy. REPEAT! We are not under attack. As you were!" He stated.

Everything returned to normal, but it was evident that nothing would ever be normal again.

Additional U-boat scares would follow. Every time a black object was sighted not more than fifty yards away, we were on alert until the target was identified.

Rumors persisted that these sightings were mines, U-boats, patches of seaweed, or schools of fish.

Some even joked about seeing Moby Dick or some other sea monster, such as a giant squid.

During the week, drills were standard practice, and we often ran along with lifeboats swung out. There was much talk about the convoy changing course due to reported U-boat activity, but none actually transpired to our knowledge.

Throughout the voyage, some soldiers lived in fear. Several slept on deck, while others went to meals while wearing their lifebelts.

Whenever a plate accidentally dropped on the floor or a door slammed shut unexpectantly, it would trigger yet another panic attack.

Shortly after breakfast on Wednesday, May 29, a heavy fog rolled across the ship's bow. Before long, the mist was as thick as soup, and we temporarily lost track of the other ships in the convoy.

Before we regained contact with our escorts, we even passed a couple of ships bound for New York.

The fog finally lifted around 1600 hours.

That evening, we experienced some rough seas, and several times the waves crashed upon the deck.

At 0645, the morning of Thursday, May 30, we sighted land after 12 days on the open water. The west coast of Scotland came into view.

By 0800, the east coast of Ireland was visible. Many men came on deck to witness this superb spectacle where nature was invaded by modern warfare. With the green hills of Ireland on our right and Scotland flanking us on the left, we navigated the North Channel as we approached Liverpool.

Our impressive convoy of transports steamed over waters as placid as a lake. Overhead, in a cloudless sky, two dirigible balloons kept a watchful eye for danger, while a squadron of aeroplanes was also patrolling the area. They soared above our ships like giant seagulls.

Together they expertly escorted us through the Irish Sea's dangerous waters, and by nightfall, "The Justicia" docked in the port of Liverpool on the Mersey River.

We remained on the ship until the following afternoon when the regiment was permitted to disembark and march into Liverpool. Crowds of locals lined the streets to welcome the first American troops to enter the city. The regimental band played spectacularly, and our men carried the colors proudly.

With cheers and tears, the Brittains embraced us for coming to their aid after four years of suffering from the strains of war. The people looked to be badly poverty-stricken.

During the parade through the city, we made several stops along the route. Men, women, and children turned out to witness the pageantry, and during one of those pauses, I heard a small girl ask her mother, "Mama, will they see daddy in France?"

The woman smiled and nodded affirmatively as she tightly squeezed her hand.

The regiment marched six miles through the town and spent the night at a place called Knotty Ash Rest Camp on the city's outskirts.

On Saturday, June 1, after two days of rest, we hiked five miles and entrained at Stanley Railway Station, north of Prescot Road, Liverpool.

It was 0800 hours when we loaded into boxcars. The train stopped in Birmingham and Oxford. Along the way, we didn't see any wooden buildings but saw many fields of grain and lots of sheep.

Arriving at Winchester Railway Station at 1600 hours, we hiked to Camp Winnall Downs.

The regiment rested for three days at the camp recuperating from the arduous voyage and eating half-cooked mutton. Most of the boys are sick, but I feel very well. Some of the men caught colds during the trip, and the reprieve at Winnall Downs has allowed them to mend.

Those who are able have been hiking about 10 to 12 miles each day. Many of the houses in the area are built of stone and covered with straw.

As usual, word has it we are moving again. On Tuesday, June 4, we left Camp Winnall Downs. at 0700. It was a five-mile hike to the railway station.

We entrained once again on boxcars for South Hampton and arrived there at about 1000 hours. Our outfit spent the remainder of the day in a giant warehouse. At 1800 hours, we embarked on the channel boat Mona's Queen, No. C 0168, bound for Le Havre, France.

> *   *36 NOTE: The SS RMS Mona's Queen (II) was an iron-built paddle steamer, which served with the Isle of Man Steam Packet Company, She was the second vessel in the company's history to be so named, Mona's Queen. She served from 1885 until 1921. In 1917, during the First World War, the ship survived a collision with a German submarine while carrying troops from South Hampton to Le Havre.*

During the night of June 4-5, 1918, these men, who were part of the 28th Division, crossed the English Channel bound for France and were destined to join the fight.

"All things are ready, if our mind be so." — *William Shakespeare.*

"THE 108TH ARRIVES IN FRANCE"

June 5, 1918, the 108th disembarks in Le Havre, France
Image Source: Unknown

CHAPTER 26

"The 108th Arrives in France"

On Wednesday, June 5, 1918, The Monos Queen docked in the harbor of Le Havre, France. The port sits on the English Channel, Northwest of Paris.

Two days later, on the 7th, we got our first taste of 40 and 8's. This term refers to the wooden boxcars that are used by the military. These rail cars are capable of transporting 40 men or eight horses, hence the name.

The crude box cars were a pale comparison to the passenger cars we were familiar with back in the states. It was no wonder they smelled like manure, as the train had just returned from taking a load of horses to the front. Mostly, we got through it, although some of the fellows became sick to the stomach as a result.

Our regiment spent the next two days on those cars making the 389 km journey to Camp de Meucon, just outside the old french city of Vannes. The trip took us in a Southwest direction, to an area near the coast of the Bay of Biscayne. We arrived at the camp on Sunday, June 9.

Camp de Meucon was a mushroom city of barracks and stables sufficient to accommodate ten thousand artillerymen, two entire brigades, and the necessary complement of horses.

It had more of a permanent aspect than the American camps, owing to the scarcity of lumber. It was built primarily out of cement and stucco.

SFC Vogan told us that the installation was used as a Field Artillery Training Camp, Artillery Aerial Observation School, and an ordinance repair shop for mobile artillery.

The camp was hidden in an area of low sand hills, making it picturesquely and pleasantly situated.

Locultas, a tiny French village, lay on its western edge, while ancient stone farmhouses adjoined it here and there.

Primitive rural lanes, bordered with Beech trees, and pink flowering Foxgloves, led out into the surrounding green fields.

This remote region appeared to be quite charming and peaceful.

Many of our American officers were part of an advance detail. They arrived here in France several weeks ago to receive preliminary training from the French.

Initially, we were assigned barracks at Camp de Meucon with the rest of the artillery regiment.

In the back of the camp lay a long sandy ridge that served as a shooting range. Strategically placed observation towers and pyramids of stone gave the batteries an ideal setting target practice.

Captain Rene Descroix, one of the French officers assigned to the 108th, arranged for the artillery companies to train us on the French 155 mm howitzers, horses, and various other equipment pieces.

Descroix proved to be an exceptional instructor. He was able to bring important points to our American officers in a most impressive manner.

Since my stay at the camp only lasted a few days, I could scarcely get familiar with the base. I spent my time touring the French Field Hospital at the center and learning their procedures.

On Wednesday, June 12, the Sanitary Detachment received orders that our next assignment would be at Base Hospital 136, located in Vannes, Morbihan. The hospital was just a few kilometers from the camp.

The facility was part of a two-unit medical installation. A pair of four-story red brick buildings made up the hospital's main section.

The barracks assigned to us were part of the Caserne Quartier Senarmont. The French Thirty-fifth Field Artillery formerly occupied this section.

These quarters consisted of three large four-story buildings that also housed kitchens, a guardhouse, and stables. The complex included several other buildings surrounded by a twelve-foot stone wall. This enclosure was 760 by 860 feet.

The hospital, we were told, cared for approximately 3,000 surgical and medical cases. This caseload ranged from severe wounds and medical procedures to gas exposure, mild injuries, and illnesses, including psychiatric and mental disorders.

While the infirmary's bed capacity was 2,300, the average number of patients at the hospital at one time was typically between 1,000 and 1,500.

On Thursday, Sgt. Vogan called us into formation. Then, he gave us a briefing about the assignment. "Men, I have been ordered to set you up in pairs, and each team will meet with the commanding officer here at the hospital for your specific duties. His name is Commandant Claude Laurent. His office is on the hospital's first floor, just to the right of the main entrance.

"Your team assignments are as follows: Conner-Erdley, Connolly-Dohner, Hart-H. Haeberle, W. Haeberle-Hutchinson, Haliday-Gray, Kline-Kerr, McClain-Meissner, Quigley-Rafferty, Peters-Roth, Schalata-Schweppenheiser, and Warr-Zimmerling.

"Teams will meet with the Commandant every ten minutes beginning at 0900 tomorrow morning," he concluded.

"Dismissed!" The sergeant ordered.

Schweppenheiser and I met outside the Commandant's office at 10:20. We waited for Peters and Roth to finish their session.

Finally, at 10:30, a young, clean-cut Maréchal de Logis (Master Sergeant) ushered us inside.

The two of us were expecting the room's decor to be on par with what you would find for an officer of his stature, but the accommodations were quite the contrary in reality.

The stark, white plaster walls gave the nine-foot by twelve-foot room a gloomy, barren appearance. A single three-foot by six-foot window at the far end offered a minimal amount of daylight through its eight panes of glass.

On the right side of the window sat a small, rudimentary desk with a typewriter, accompanied by a similar wooden folding chair. This corner, we surmised, was reserved for the Master Sergeant.

In the opposite corner sat the Commandant on an equally primitive wooden chair behind a table. Two iron hooks were fastened to the plaster next to the window to serve as coat racks. At the officer's back, necessary documents and maps were pinned to a board hanging on the wall.

The only other item in the room was a small coal-burning parlor stove with its stovepipe disappearing into the ceiling.

The 54-year-old Laurent was bald on top, with a closely cropped horseshoe-shaped hairline. He also sported a medium-size mustache.

We exchanged salutes with the officer, and then he extended his hand for us to shake, followed by a warm smile.

The Commandant and his sergeant explained the hospital's layout, with the main floor being primarily offices, treatment rooms, operating rooms, and the basis for all medical procedures.

The remaining floors of the building, two through four, contained the wards for convalescing patients. The second floor was reserved for the most severe cases, while the third floor was maintained for those who were less critical. The top floor primarily cared for soldiers who suffered from amnesia, shell shock, and other mental impairments.

Commandant Laurent revealed that our assignments on the various floors would be on a rotating schedule enabling us to become familiar with a full range of cases and their appropriate treatment procedures.

In conclusion, the French officer explained that Master Sergeant Brodeur would post our duty assignments weekly on the board outside his office. Irvin and I were dismissed at that point. We saluted and politely left, thereby permitting the next team in for their meeting.

Later that day, we checked the duty roster, and the post revealed that Schweppenheiser and I would work the following week on the third floor. This news was a bit of a relief because it meant we would get our feet wet in a relatively straightforward section of the hospital.

First, we needed to report to the main nurses' station on that floor. Greeting us from behind her desk was an American Red Cross nurse, Irene Hamelin.

The thirty-something brunette was all business, and she instructed us to go down to the Central Supply Room on the first floor. She provided us with a list of needed items, including several packages of gauze bandages, tape, and bottles of alcohol.

While walking nearly the entire floor's length to reach the stairs, we came upon a senior French officer in full dress uniform.

The man appeared to be about sixty years old. With a gray goatee and piercing blue eyes, he stopped us in mid-stride.

"Pardon... excusez-moi, S'il vous plaît..." he muttered.

Irvin and I stopped immediately and saluted the gentleman, and he returned the gesture. "Oui! Oui! Monsieur," I replied, using just about all of my French vocabulary.

Seeing we were Americans, he attempted to explain his situation in English the best he could.

"I am an officer in the Army of the Third French Republic, Major Jules Humbert. I sent my aide to the kitchen 23 minutes ago to secure a pot of tea for myself and another doctor that I am scheduled to meet in short order.

"Could you gentlemen ensure that it is served in the conference parlor by precisely 9:28?" He insisted.

"Sir... Sir... we already have orders to pick up medical supplies for the nurses, sir," I begged. "Go and do it, private," he ordered.

"I have the complete run of this facility, and my orders supersede all others," he said, refusing to back down.

"Yes, sir," Irvin responded.

En route to Central Supply, we reported the incident to one of the French orderlies, and he assured us that he would take care of it.

When we returned to the nurses' station with the much-needed supplies, Nurse Hamelin instructed us to go down the hall to Ward 37A and spend some time getting familiar with the patients.

Our first encounter was a conversation we had with a British soldier who was recently wounded near Guillion. Aside from a few minor cuts and bruises on his forehead, it appeared that something had hit his right arm and shoulder the hardest.

"How are you doing today, lad?" I asked the man lying in bed number two.

"I suppose right now I'm in the pink, but just a few days ago, most would have told you that I'd be copping a packet," the man replied.

    *   *37 NOTE: Copping a packet was a slang phrase referring to the act of being killed. As a coping mechanism due to the war's horrendous nature, the men used creative descriptions to refer to death. Other such terms were: becoming a landowner, going home, being buzzed, drawing your full issue, being topped off, or clicking it.*

"Well, glad to hear it. Very pleased to learn you're doing so well," I responded.

"Well, I'm Corporal Schalata. You can call me Tom or Tommy," I explained. "and this is Private Schweppenheiser. We're here to give you a hand," I went on.

"What got you here in the first place?" Irvin inquired. "Sam... Sam Gladstone, here," he countered.

"I was with a British Supply company. We were hauling a wagonload of iron rations, me and Billy Slathers, we were... when a whiz-bang hit us on the right. I believe it may have been a Jack Johnson, but Billy, the poor lad, had no chance. A hunk of hot metal hit him square in the chest. He was done for."

    *   *38 NOTE: Iron rations were emergency rations that consisted of a tin of bully beef, some very hard biscuits, and a tin of tea and sugar. The term was also used to refer to enemy shell-fire. Whiz-bang was another term used by men in the trenches to identify shells by size, effects, or sound. Whiz-bangs were generally fired from high-velocity guns and gave you no time to duck. A Jack Johnson was the description given to a large German shell that delivered a thick dark smoke. Jack Johnson was a black American heavyweight boxing champion.*

After a few more minutes of chatting with the British soldier, we were on to the next patient, a private in the French Army. Soldat2.eme (Private) Martin Boulay.

"Hello, Monsieur, Corporal Schalata and Private Schweppenheiser, here. How are you?" I inquired. The young man winced with pain and politely nodded affirmatively.

Both of the soldier's arms were heavily bandaged. We determined that a shell exploded near his position. He instinctively drew his arms up to protect his face, and the shrapnel struck his limbs.

Irvin and I did our best to make him comfortable, and his only request was for some water. Schweppenheiser retrieved a pitcher from the nurse, and I did my best to help him drink.

After spending some time with a few more patients, we returned to the nurses' station for our next assignment. On the way, we ran into our friend, the French Major. This time he was dressed in a surgical gown and cap and explained that he was waiting on a nurse to assist him with a medical procedure.

When we explained our encounter with Major Humbert, the nurse responded by saying, "We have no record of an officer by that name, physician or not!"

Once again, we were assured that she would look into it, and she sent us to the Mess Hall for lunch. To my astonishment, there in the Mess Hall was Clay Jefferson serving up the chow.

"Clay," I exclaimed, "what in the world are you doing here?"

"Wells, Sir Tommy Sir," he said with a big smile on his face, "theys done run out o' French cooks here at this hospital, and so here I is."

"What a surprise! Great to see you again, Clay," I responded.

"Doc, this is Clay, Clay Jefferson. He's the fellow that took me to visit his grandparents. Remember that?" I explained.

"Oh, yeah," Schweppenheiser replied, "I remember that well. You guys almost didn't come back from that one!"

"Clay, this is my pal, Irvin Schweppenheiser. We often call him Doc," I said in introducing the two.

"Pleased to meet ya'. Any friend of Sir Tommy's is a friend o' mine," Clay stated while shaking hands with Irvin.

"We'll see you around, Clay," I replied as we gave a wave and proceeded down the chow line. In the afternoon, Nurse Hamelin assigned us to Ward 33B to visit some of the other patients.

Wouldn't you know it, again we came across our mystery French Major Humbert? Still dressed in his white gown, he stopped us in the corridor.

This time he was genuinely flustered and asked us to summon a nurse. "What seems to be the problem, Major?" Irvin inquired.

"I have a patient in the ward right here that needs his medicine," the Major began, "and I can't find the nurse!"

"I see, Sir," Schweppenheiser commented.

"And what is the medicine in question, Sir?" he asked. "Gâteau aux Pommes," the Major answered.

"Gâteau aux Pommes? Are you certain, Sir?"

"Yes! That's what I said, *gâteau aux pommes*, private. Didn't you understand me the first time?" the officer snapped.

"Of course, sir," he replied. "It's just that I never heard of that." "We'll go find a nurse and check on that, Sir!" I assured him.

Irvin and I turned around and reported back to Nurse Hamelin. "Are you sure that's what he said?" the nurse questioned.

"He claims that his name is Major Humbert, and he's looking for *gâteau aux pommes* to give to one of our patients?" She repeated in disbelief.

"Yes, ma'am. That's exactly what he said," Irvin confirmed.

"Do you know what *gâteau aux pommes* is, corporal?" the nurse inquired.

"No. Not really," Doc returned, "but it doesn't sound like a medicine to me," he noted.

"Apple cake," Nurse Hamelin revealed. "The man, officer or not, is asking for apple cake. I'll have to investigate this matter thoroughly. You men go back to your ward, immediately, and don't let this man interfere with your work at all," she commanded.

"Yes, ma'am," we both responded.

Before we left her desk, she informed us that we needed to wear a mask while visiting Ward 33B. "Several patients there have what they're calling the Spanish Influenza. It would be best if you were protected," she explained.

Armed with this new information, we hesitantly walked into the ward. The room contained just six patients, and the first soldier we visited was Corporal Melvin T. Crawford of the 38th Engineering Corps.

Crawford was born in Galena, IL, in 1897 and completed his military training at Fort Riley, KS. In the Spring of 1918, his outfit arrived in France, but he developed chills, fever, and fatigue within one month.

By the time he landed in the hospital, just four days ago, his skin had begun to turn blue, and he was having trouble breathing.

As we approached the man's bed, it was apparent that he was very sick. His face was expressionless, and his skin was now ashen.

We asked the man if he was experiencing any pain, and he reported that he wasn't. As a matter of fact, Cpl. Crawford almost looked euphoric, but we ascertained that this was due to the pain medication given to him.

During our training at the field hospital, one of the French physicians explained that Bayer aspirin was recommended but in limited dosage. Too much of the drug could lead to aspirin poisoning.

The nurse revealed that his temperature had risen this morning to 104 degrees.

Irvin and I chatted with the man for about 30 minutes. He told us about his family back home, and we did likewise. We hoped that the time we spent together would take his mind off his troubles and ease his burden. Finally, he grew tired and drifted off to sleep.

As we left the hospital to return to our barracks, we bumped into Clay once again. He told Irvin and me that a handful of men were meeting at a local tavern in the village, L'Oie Verte (The Green Goose).

"What do you think, Sir Tommy, Sir, can you join us?" Clay asked.

"Oh... I don't know. What are you guys going to do there?" I wondered.

"We's goin' to have a few beers, of course, an' play a game theys call here Bagatelle," he explained. "Bagatelle? What the hell's that?" I shot back.

"It's like pool.. ya 'know... something like balls and pockets... ya' know?" Clay described. "Sure, Clay. What do you think, Doc?"

Schweppenheiser just shrugged. Then, he nodded affirmatively.

"What time are you going, Clay, and where do we meet you?" I asked while trying to pin things down.

"I's gonna meet you in front o' yo' barracks at 1900 hours, okay, Sir Tommy, Sir?" Clay suggested.

As promised, my colored friend, Clay, was waiting on the street outside our barracks at the appointed hour. The three of us walked several blocks before turning onto Rue Joubert. At the far end of the street at No. 33, there was indeed L'Oie Verte.

Medium-sized gray stone about the size of cobblestones comprised the pub's exterior. Two large arch-shaped windows flanked each side of the front door. The woodwork was dark green, and a large wooded sign depicting a goose hung from an iron bracket.

The same gray stonework made up the interior walls. A long, ornately carved wooden bar anchored the right side of the room. The bar was curved at both ends and appeared to be about 18-feet long.

Several rows of liquor bottles lined the backpiece.

There were no stools at the bar, although the rest of the room had scattered about numerous wrought iron tables of various sizes. Providing seating were black, wooden chairs with arched legs. There were only a handful of patrons in the establishment at the time. Four of those were standing at the bar, while two others sat at a table near the window. All seemed to be heavily involved in conversation.

In the very back of the room sat three other American soldiers. They were from Clay's Mess outfit. He introduced his pals: Jesse Barlow, Harvey Miller, and Gerald Perlstein.

Next to them sat the odd-looking bagatelle table. While the piece of furniture may have been a distant cousin of the billiards or pool table, the green-felt tabletop and ivory balls were about the only similarities to that which we were accustomed to back home.

The table was about a foot and a half wide and six feet in length. In the center was a series of wooden pegs or posts. I took a quick glance and estimated that there were about two dozen of them, and they stood approximately three inches tall.

At one end of the tabletop, eight recessed holes were arranged in a circle and one in the center.

Sitting in these holes were nine balls; four red, four white, and one black.

Clay explained the rules and noted that there are many game variations with just as many configurations. The whole idea was to shoot the balls with a cuestick from one end and navigate the balls through the pegs and into the holes at the other end.

Our first mission was to belly up to the bar and get a beer. The barkeep, who introduced himself as Gaston, looked to be about 45 to 50 years old and sported a long mustache that was obviously waxed to a point. The man wore a green apron and had a white cotton towel slung over his shoulder. He informed us that the only beer available at this time was Bière de Garde. This style is a strong pilsner brewed over the winter to last well into the Summer months.

When Gaston placed the three pints in front of us, I winced just a little when I saw the brew's odd copper color.

Clay immediately reacted, saying, "Don't yous worry, Sir Tommy Sir, dis' tastes mighty fine. Might fine. You'll see!"

"Okay," I nodded. I'll have to trust you," I conceded.

Since this was our first night on the town since we left Camp Hancock, I suggested that we all join in having a shot to celebrate.

I was thinking some sort of whiskey or scotch, but one of the locals standing nearby turned to me and said, "Pardon, Monsieur, excusez-moi, S'il vous plaît, but if you're going to drink in France, you must drink as we do!"

The stocky man with a short grizzly beard pointed to a large colorful banner hanging on the wall behind the bar. It depicted a young woman in a long flowing purple dress. Draped around her neck were several bunches of grapes. At the bottom of the flag were the words: "Cognac Gautier Frères France - 1755."

"Cognac! Oui! Cognac! That's what you must drink!" The man insisted.

When I questioned the stranger about the exact nature of Cognac, he explained, "Monsieur, it is a double-distilled brandy made with fermented white grapes and stored in oak barrels. Hors d'Age or X.O. (Extra Old) cognac is aged for many, many years," he added.

"But... is it any good?" I begged of the man.

"Ma grand-mère boit du cognac et n'a toujours pas besoin de verres. Elle boit tout de suite de la bouteille," he replied.

With a furrowed brow, I looked at the bartender and asked, "What did he say?"

The man behind the bar left out a hardy laugh and said, "He says, 'My Grandmama drinks Cognac and still doesn't need glasses. She drinks right out of the bottle!'"

We all joined in the laughter, and the Frenchman gave me a vigorous pat on the back. I motioned to the barkeep to set us up with three glasses of the highly recommended Cognac.

The six of us sat at the table in the back of the room and took turns playing this strange version of pool.

I took a liking to my new friend, a bottle of Cognac, as I consumed a large quantity of this fine brandy.

Gaston approached our table with two long baguettes under one of his armpits and a plate of brie (a soft creamy French cheese).

From the pocket of his apron, he pulled out a knife, placed all of the items on the table, and said, "Bon Appetit!"

The man smiled, bowed slightly, and walked away.

By closing time, the Cognac really hit me. Clay and Doc had to help me back to the barracks and into my bunk.

The following morning Schweppenheiser roused me from a sound sleep and urged me to get up and get going. We needed to report to the hospital in less than 30 minutes. Just enough time to get dressed, have a French pastry, and a cup of coffee.

On our way to the third floor, I asked Irvin to fill me in on what happened the night before. "What the hell happened, Doc?" I asked. "I don't remember much of anything," I admitted.

"Well," he began, "Your buddy, Clay, took us to the Green Goose to play some pool game called Bagatelle. Next, you were introduced to Cognac, and by the end of the night, you agreed to be in a show to entertain the patients!"

"I what? Volunteered for what?" I exclaimed in disbelief.

"Yep! You, Clay, Warr, and Perlstein are going to be in some sort of skit or something to cheer up the fellas in the wards," Schweppenheiser explained.

"I don't believe it," I said while shaking my head. "How did I ever get myself in this mess?" I murmured.

"It was that special bloody X.O. brandy and that copper-colored beer," Irvin reminded me. "That's how!" he declared.

"Geez!" I replied. "What else could possibly be worse," I wondered.

When we reached Nurse Hamelin's desk, she was already prepared to give us the day's report.

"First, of all," she began, "Cpl. Melvin Crawford passed away last evening. I'm afraid influenza did him in. For the time being, stay out of that ward for your own safety," she ordered.

"Secondly," the nurse went on, "I got to the bottom of your infamous Major Humbert." "Oh, really!" Schweppenheiser responded in astonishment.

"Yes! Oh, the man is a French Major, that much is certain, but a doctor he is not!" The woman revealed.

"Really!" I chimed in.

"As I stated in the beginning, we have no staff members by that name. We do have, however, a patient on the mental floor that fits his description," she reported.

"Apparently, he escaped from his ward, and he has evaded detection for some time now," the nurse shared.

She concluded, saying, "He is now back where he belongs and has been safely confined to his room!"

Nurse Hamelin assigned us to another ward, and I walked away muttering to Doc, "Duped by a fruitcake! Well, that's just fine!

"I thought he belonged in Bughouse Number 8!" I added.

*   *39 NOTE: The expression Bughouse was a colloquial term for someone who was mentally impaired. It was a synonym for such phrases as crazy, nutty, looney, screwy, or batty. Bughouse Number 8 referred to a person who should be placed in a mental institution or asylum. The term came into use in the late 19th century. EG: "A person would go bughouse after spending a week with Aunt Margaret!"*

Apparently, the woman overheard my grumbling and questioned, "What was that remark, corporal?"

I felt like I was back at Our Lady Help of Christians battling with Sister Benedictus Carmella. I turned slightly towards her desk and replied, "Oh, nothing, Nurse Hamelin. Nothing at all!"

"OUR SHOW-BIZ DEBUT"

Clay Jefferson, Tommy Schalata and Joe Ward
Image Source: Author's Photo

Chapter 27

"Our Show-Biz Debut"

I still hadn't determined which was worse, drinking tequila in El Paso, Texas, or Cognac in Vannes, France, but now I was committed to performing for the patients here at Hospital No. 136.

Initially, I had no idea what was in store for me, but Captain Washington Mercher informed me that the show was indeed a big deal.

He explained that the entertainment would be a vital boost to everyone's morale, especially the patients. The officer hinted that a promotion could be forthcoming if I came through on this project. He emphasized that it would be a big lift for our outfit.

With that in mind, I assured him that I would give it my best effort.

By the end of June, I was assigned to join a handful of others who would be involved in putting on the show.

Under the French Sergeant Major Louis de Reims' direction, our troupe consisted of Clay Jefferson, Gerald Perlstein, Joe Warr, and myself.

The Sergeant Major informed us that rehearsals would take place two evenings per week, Tuesdays and Thursdays.

Commandant Laurent arranged for the production to take place on Sunday, July 14. This date just happened to be Bastille Day, known as 'la Fête Nationale Française.' The day is commemorated, much like our own holiday of Independence Day.

On Monday, July 1, Nurse Hamelin assigned us to Ward 32A, and our first patient was Private William Cassidy of the 16th Irish Division.

In March, the German Spring Offensive nearly wiped out Cassidy's forces near Ronssay. The outfit retreated following a disastrous effort in Operation Michael.

During the action, a sniper's bullet struck Cassidy in the neck. More precisely, his injury was in the area of the Sterno head or the Sternocleidomastoid muscle.

Although his wound required several months of recovery, the 18-year-old soldier's situation could have been much worse. Had the shot strayed just a little in any direction, the injury may have been fatal or caused paralysis.

As it was, the young man had temporarily lost mobility in his neck and has been unable to speak for the last 14 weeks due to the inflammation in his neck. The doctors, however, expected that he would recover eventually.

Cassidy communicated with Irvin and me through the use of a small chalkboard. The two of us spent nearly an hour with him, asking questions and trying our best to keep his spirits up.

"What are some of your favorite recollections of home?" Irvin asked him.

It took the chap a few minutes, but he finally scribbled on the board, "St. Malachy's." "Where is that?" I asked next.

"Belfast," he scribbled.

"What brings that to mind?" I pushed on. "Singing - in the choir!" Cassidy wrote.

Then, he took the chalk and angrily underlined his response several times before pounding his fist on the chalkboard in a fit of rage.

Irvin jumped into the conversation and tried calming the man down, saying, "Listen, William, the doctors are confident that you'll get your voice back in time. I know it feels like forever, but you just need to be patient. You'll see," he said assuredly.

"I can't! I can't! I can't!" Cassidy scratched out on the board, still visibly upset.

When I reached over to grab him by the arm, he took the chalkboard and threw it across the room.

Doc stood up and retrieved it and placed it on the table beside the bed.

At that point, Irvin and I agreed that we didn't want to agitate the fellow any further. Therefore, we assured him that his improvement was forthcoming and promised to check back on him later.

He nodded affirmatively and appeared to calm down. We urged him to get some rest, and the two of us left to complete our rounds.

Our next patient was Private Thwaite McNeill of the Ninth (Glasgow Highlanders) Battalion. The Highlanders were a Light Infantry outfit, and the 41-year-old Scotsman was suffering from trench foot.

We learned that soldiers who stood in the trenches in puddles of water and their own waste for extended periods were susceptible to the disease.

While the malady was not contagious, the men's feet could swell up to multiple times their average size and be completely numb. I suppose this was especially true for the Scotch soldiers who insisted on wearing their kilts in these wet and cold conditions.

Schweppenheiser and I approached the man's bed, "Good morning!" I greeted him. Private McNeill?" I inquired.

"Guid mornin! Thwaite McNeill, ay!" He responded. "How are you today, sir?" Irvin asked.

"Guid, so-so. An ye?" the man acknowledged. "Fine. We're both fine. Thank you," I noted.

"Can ye gie's a haund?" (Can you help me?), the Scotsman asked. "What do you need help with, lad?" I asked.

"A hae tae gang to privy," the man replied, meaning that he had to go to the toilet. Schweppenheiser countered, "I'll run for the nurse, pal. You just hang on a minute." "Coorie up!" (Hurry up!) The Scotsman urged.

"Irvin will be right back with the nurse," I assured the man. "Ye ar verra kin!" (You are very kind), he said appreciatively.

Schweppenheiser returned with the nurse in short order, and she asked us to leave the room. We did so while bidding Pvt. McNeill goodbye.

"Guid cheerio the nour!" (Goodbye), he acknowledged.

Irvin and I left the ward, and it was soon time for us to call it a day. We agreed that Cassidy and McNeill would require follow-up visits in the morning if that was okay with Nurse Hamelin.

The weeks seemed to fly by, and before we realized it, the time had come for us to entertain the men and women at the hospital.

The program "Home on the Range" referred to our local artillery range over at Camp Du Meucon, with a bit of good old-fashioned American western humor. The three of us would perform several comical skits, while Perlstein would accompany us on the piano.

Clay's personality had a naturally humorous side to it. Warr could be quite a character in his own right, and, I guess I fit the bill as a straight man.

The French Sergeant Major secured a couple of costumes that he found in an old wooden box in one of the storage closets. Clay dressed in a cowboy costume from the old west, I was handed a U.S. naval uniform, while Warr donned an outfit that resembled something from the Napoleonic era.

At two o'clock that Sunday afternoon, the curtain went up on the stage in Building No. 2 with Jerry Perlstein sitting at an old Erard piano.

He calmly sat on his stool playing the famous American tune, "Home on the Range." Following the title song, the private played "Oh, How I hate to get up in the morning," "Oh Frenchy," and "Don't Send My Darling Away."

Joe and I stood on the stage during his musical medley, and I just looked out at the audience.

The large hall was jam-packed with wooden folding chairs. In the front, closest to the stage, were soldiers in wheelchairs. Many had bandages on their heads, torsos, and limbs. Some were missing their arms, legs, or portions of them. Disfigured faces, eye patches, and other ghastly injuries were a grim reminder that these men have been through hell.

Although most of the patients wore broad smiles on their faces in anticipation that the entertainment would temporarily relieve them of their suffering. Others sat expressionlessly. Their blank stares suggested that life as they once knew it was left out on the field of battle. The sights, the sounds, and the smells that they endured evidently robbed them of everything they once had.

As I surveyed the room, row by row, the picture was much of the same. Along the walls sat other patients, primarily dependent on crutches and canes for mobility. Dozens of doctors and nurses, who could be spared from their posts, stood by their side to assist them.

During this time, it had occurred to me that this was just the beginning of my journey. My current assignment was merely an introduction to the real horrors of the war. I tried not to think about what lay ahead. However, I couldn't help but feel that this situation was inching me towards a dangerous cliff, and when I reached the precipice, I was destined to fall into some great abyss. Perhaps, I would never return.

Quickly, my mind focused on the present as I heard Perlstein's final piece conclude.

After the audience gave a rousing applause, Jerry gave a little ching-a-ling on the keys, and we began our monologue:

ME: "Well, Joe, isn't it great to be here entertaining all these great fellows?"

JOE: "Yeah, Tommy! I haven't seen so many smilin' faces since they stopped servin' that unidentifiable
hash down at the Mess Hall!"

ME: "You know, it's Bastille Day here in France. I think they call it 'la Fête Nationale Française,'
actually."

JOE: "What is that, Tommy? Is it something like our Fourth of July back home?"

ME: "Yes! Sort of. I heard the peasants revolted, and that's what started the French Revolution."

JOE: "Hey, did you hear about the French man who..."

ME: Hold it, pal. Don't say another word. We don't want to upset our French hosts. We have enough
trouble with the Germans. We don't need another battle on our hands."

JOE: Okay. Okay! I'll be careful!"

ME: "Say, Joe, what are you doing in that costume?"

JOE: "I am Napoleon!"

ME: "What do you mean by that? Why do you think you're Napoleon?"

JOE: "God told me!"

Just then, a voice from across the stage shouted, "I did not!"

It turns out the voice was none other than Perlstein, who was sitting there at the piano. That
joke earned a pretty good laugh.

ME: "Keep that up, fellas, and you guys will be roommates on the fourth floor!" That comment
drew a mixed reaction.

ME: Tell me, your highness, what's the worst advice you ever took from one of your generals?"

JOE: "Take Russia. What could go wrong?"

ME: "Say, Napoleon... do you think I could borrow some money from you?"

JOE: "Sorry, pal. I'm a little short!"

ME: "Okay... okay... let's get serious, now. You know, I heard one of the other fellows comment that
after the war is over, he would love to go to the south of France."

JOE: "Yessir, that would be NICE!"

After my partner delivered that pun, Perlstein gave another ching-a-ling on the piano.

ME: "Say, this is our first stop here in France. Do you have any idea what's in the middle of Paris?

JOE: "Sure, that's easy, Tommy... the letter R."

ME: "I was down at the tavern the other day. Do you know what one French man said to the other
French guy?

JOE: "I dunno, Tommy, what did he say?"

ME: "I don't know, either. I don't speak French."

Perlstein began playing the piano once again. Joe and I took our hats off, waved to the crowd,
and took a bow. I wouldn't say we were a huge success, but at least we managed to get a few laughs
from the guys.

Next, a three-piece band from the town paraded around the room and made their way to the stage. Leading the way was a short bald man playing the clarinet. He wore khaki-colored trousers with a matching button-down vest, white shirt, burgundy jacket, and a brown, derby-style hat.

Following him was the concertina player. While the bearded man wore a similar outfit, he sported a green bowtie. The man was a much heavier fellow, as well.

Bringing up the rear was a somewhat taller musician with a French horn. However, this chap wore a light blue jacket, navy blue necktie, and a well-worn, crumpled black fedora.

The trio stopped at center stage and entertained the boys with three French songs that were quite popular: "Ah! C'est la guerre," "La Madelon" and "La Chanson de Craonne."

As they finished, they took a bow and walked off the stage. The audience showered the men with whistles, cheers, and thunderous applause.

Perlstein played a couple of songs on the piano. Then, it was time for me to go back on stage with Clay Jefferson.

ME: "Isn't it great to be here with all these fine folks, Clay?"

CLAY: Sure is, Tommy, but... but..."

ME: "What is it, pal? What's the problem?"

CLAY: "Wait til' deez guys find outs I's the one servin' up dat hash youz was talkin' 'bout earlier."

ME: "Oh, I wouldn't worry about that. These fellows will complain about anything. Do you get many complaints down at the Mess Hall, Clay?"

CLAY: "Sure enuff! The other day one guy complained his food was too crunchy!"

ME: "Well, what was it?"

CLAY: "Chicken noodle soup!"

ME: "I see you're all dressed up like a cowboy, Clay. What's with the outfit?"

CLAY: "I jus' got transferred here to the western front!"

ME: "Oh, I see. What's it mean when your steer sits on your cowboy hat?"

CLAY: "Time to get a new hat!"

ME: "Do you know why they say a cowboy always dies with his boots on?"

CLAY: I's heard he doesn't want to stub his toe when he kicks the bucket! Dats all I knows."

ME: You know, Clay, every time I go to the picture shows, the cowboys are always riding a horse. Do you know why that is?"

CLAY: Dats easy, Tommy. I's sure knows the answer to that one!"

ME: "Well... what is it?"

CLAY: "Dats because da horse is way too heavy to carry!"

ME: "You got me there, pal!"

CLAY: "I gots a question for you, Tommy."

ME: "Shoot!"

CLAY: "Watch what you say around here..." (Clay left out a laugh while pointing a toy gun directly at me).

CLAY: "Here you go. Are you ready?"

ME: "Yeah, I'm ready."

CLAY: "If a cowboy rides into town on Friday and three days later leaves on Friday, how does HE do it?"

As I ponder his riddle, Clay looks out over the audience while making silly faces at me and laughing once again.

ME: "I think you got me, Clay. I have no idea."
CLAY: I's have to tell ya,' Tommy. The horse's name is FRIDAY!" The crowd roared when Jefferson let loose with that one.
CLAY: "I tells you what, Tommy, an' old injun taught me a neat trick when we wuz out in dat desert in El Paso..."
ME: "Is that right? What was the trick?"

Clay got down on the floor and put his ear on the stage. Then, he said, "A carriage. Six horses. Three black, two brown, and one white."
Perlstein ran his hands over the keys of the piano, imitating the sound of galloping horses.

ME: "Wow! You can hear all of that?!"
CLAY: "No, dey jus' ran me over."

Before Clay and I could stand up to take a bow, Perlstein started playing a song on the piano, and the entire room recognized it immediately and all joined in...
If you want to find the Colonel, I know where he is,
I know where he is, aww, I know where he is.

If you want to find the Colonel, I know where he is.
Home again on seven days leave I saw him I saw him Home
again on seven days' leave, I saw him Home again on seven days leave.

If you want to find the Captain, I know where he is,
I know where he is; I know where he is.
If you want to find the Captain, I know where he is
Pinning some more medals on his chest.

I saw him; I saw him Pinning some more medals on his chest,
I saw him Pinning some more medals on his chest.
If you want to find the Sergeant Major, I know where he is,
I know where he is; I know where he is.
If you want to find the Sergeant Major, I know where he is,
He's drunk upon the cookhouse floor. I saw him I saw him
drunk upon the cookhouse floor, I saw him drunk upon the
cookhouse floor.

If you want to find the Quartermaster, I know where he is,
I know where he is; I know where he is.
If you want to find the Quartermaster, I know where he is
He's drinking up the Company Rum I saw him, I saw him
He's drinking up the Company Rum; I saw him
drinking up the Company Rum.

If you want to find the Battalion, I know where they are,
I know where they are; I know where they are.
If you want to find the Battalion, I know where they are
They're hanging on the old barbed wire.
I saw them, I saw them! Hanging on the old barbed wire,
I saw them! Hanging on the old barbed wire.

Once again, the men cheered with approval, but then, the hall grew deafly silent.

The spotlight focused on a single soldier, who stood up near the back of the hall. He was an Irish lad, I could tell by the uniform, and even though it was quite a distance away, he looked quite familiar to me.

To my amazement, the chap began to sing "Danny Boy." The fellow had the most perfect tenor voice that I had ever heard.

Although you could sense the rest of the men of the 16th "Irish" Division wanted to join in, Pvt. William Cassidy sang the complete song solo.

Despite having no accompaniment, his crystal clear voice captivated the crowd. Some men smiled, while others wept, obviously reminded of better days back home. Even those who were not Irish couldn't help but find his rendition so pure, simple, and beautiful, yet chilling.

Without hesitation, Cassidy followed with another Irish tune, "Amhrán na bhFiann" or "The Soldier's Song" in English. Three hundred voices all singing in unison filled the air. In addition to the chorus, there were several verses, but the one that shall always remain with me is as follows:

"We'll sing a song, a soldier's song.
With cheering, rousing chorus
As round our blazing fires, we throng,
The starry heavens o'er us
Impatient for the coming fight
And as we wait the morning's light.
Here in the silence of the night
We'll chant a soldier's song."

"THE WAR GOES TO THE DOGS"

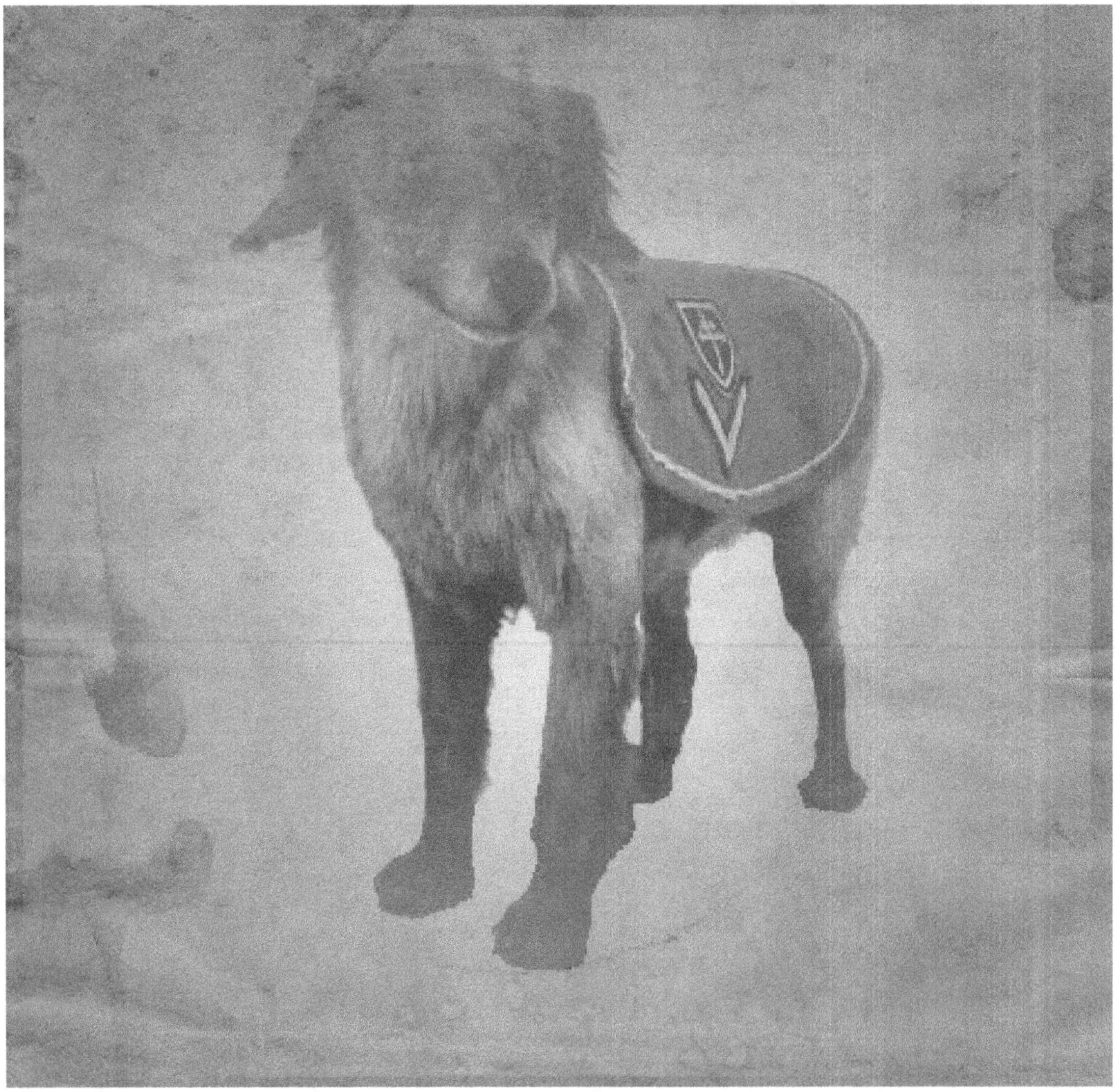

"Philly," served with Co. A of the 315th Inf., 79th Division
Image Source: Unknown

Chapter 28

"The War Goes to the Dogs"

After two months of intensive training and hard work, our outfit, full of pride, started for the front on Friday, August 9, 1918.

Under cover of darkness, our Regiment boarded those familiar boxcars known as 40 and 8's at a depot just outside Vannes, France, at 1900 hours.

Our CO informed us that our destination was Mézy-sur-Seine. This was in the center of the country near Versaille and Paris.

According to sources, the rail trip was about 472 km. Usually, the journey would be about eight hours in duration, but our ETA (Estimated Time of Arrival) at Mézy was two days later August 11.

About 25 of us jammed into one of the French blue and white boxcars, although its full capacity was nearly double that number.

The familiar smell of horse dung still permeated the interior. It was a pungent odor that reminded one of a mixture of wet dog and manure.

I was fortunate to have several of my usuals pals on board. Namely, Schweppenheiser, Wilson, Halladay and the two Haeberle brothers. We spent the time reflecting on the first leg of our journey thus far in France.

We looked back on that fancy French billiards game we learned to play at the Green Goose and the bughouse French Colonel we kept bumping into at the hospital.

Our gang sat on the floor together in one corner of the car. Directly in front of me was an eight-inch hole in one of the floorboards. The opening went straight through, and I could see the gray ballast between the rails pass beneath us. Only one of the upper panels, which served as a ventilation window, could open. The others appeared to be damaged or jammed.

After about two hours into the trip, one of the guys, Pvt. James Peters began to feel sick. We called the young soldier "Peachy" because he constantly commented, "that's peachy!"

Initially, Peachy got sick to the stomach, but then, he began to sweat profusely. The men tried to lift him to the opening on the side of the car, but he was too weak, and it looked as though he were about to pass out.

As a last resort, we laid Peters on the floor by the hole where at least a burst of air could pass through. He was pale and clammy, but the fresh air finally brought him around.

Fortunately, soon after the men revived him, our train made a stop near Saint-Guyomard for water, and we called the medics to check him out. They moved Peachy to one of the officers' cars for observation, and we didn't see him again until we arrived at our destination.

At approximately midway through our trip, just outside of LeMans, we stopped for a three-hour layover.

Col. Greble and his officers called the troops to formation trackside at the depot in La Chapelle-Saint-Album. Standing upon a large wooden crate on the railroad platform, he addressed the men.

"Men, the infantry outfits of the 28th Division already received their baptism of fire near Châteaux- Thierry. We are heading to be by their side," he began.

"Our 28th teamed up with the American 3rd Division and the French 125th Infantry Division on the River Marne. The Germans planned an offensive hoping to drive our Allies, namely the British Army, north into the sea, but thanks to intelligence from multiple sources, we knew they were coming.

"Although this German attack was to occur in the early morning hours of July 15, American and French artillery pounded the enemy before they could even charge from their trenches. Bravo to them!"

A roaring cheer by the men interrupted Greble's address. He acknowledged their approval with a slight nod of his head.

The Colonel continued, "At nearly zero hour, the enemy hit us with sneezing gas and poison gas along the riverbank. Our boys, however, were well-trained and were fully prepared with their gas masks. I know if faced with that situation, you will do the same!"

"The Germans surged across the river on boats and pontoons," he explained, "and still, the Allied Forces opened the fighting with a tremendous amount of firepower, and the German infantry took on severe casualties.

"I received a report directly from Lt. William Ryan of the 30th Regiment. He said, and I quote, 'Directly in front of us and down by the railroad, I could see German Infantrymen wearing overcoats, coming straight towards us in approach formation.'"

The Colonel briefly looked at his notes and continued, "The Lieutenant also observed, 'The German infantry and machine gunners came on at a slow walk...'"

"Regarding the 3rd Division, the brunt of the enemy attack fell upon Col. Edmund Butts' 30th Infantry and Col. Ulysses Grant McAlexander's 38th Infantry," he reported.

"I am proud to note that the 30th inflicted heavy casualties on the Germans, and our men went as far as to engage the Germans in the trenches and stopped them.

Again, the men burst into cheer.

"Five miles beyond the Marne River, Col. McAlexander's 38th faced a more difficult situation when the French hastily retreated leaving his right flank exposed."

Col. Greble added, "McAlexander bravely recovered, despite being fired upon on three sides, and held the Germans at bay. The 30th and the 38th defeated six German regiments. As an American fighting machine, we can all hang our hats on the fact that we proved our salt with the Allies," he commented.

"Our intelligence intercepted an enemy message from Lt. Kurt Hesse of the German 5th Grenadiers, who stated, 'I have never seen so many dead. I have never seen such a frightful spectacle of war.'"

"The enemy bulletin also reported 'On the other bank, the Americans, in close combat, had destroyed two of our companies. Lying down in the wheat, they had allowed our troops to approach and then annihilated them at a range of 30 to 50 yards.'

"You should take great pride in knowing the German officer stated, 'The Americans kill everyone, was the cry of fear on July 15—a cry that will cause our men to tremble for a long time.'

Col. Greble concluded, saying, "In the heat of battle, some of the American platoons were cut off and fought to the last man, while others bravely mounted a counterattack and broke the back of the German assault at the village of Mézy. I am certain you will also represent the 28th Division with the same honor and bravery!"

The adjutant dismissed the men, and we were left to mull around trackside until we reloaded for departure.

What the Colonel failed to divulge in his address was the disdain our troops developed for the French. This contempt was in light of their participation in the battle or lack thereof.

According to the scuttlebutt we heard, the French 125th Division withdrew without informing the Americans, putting the 28th Division's 109th, and 110th Regiments, in the middle of an awful ordeal.

Actually, four Pennsylvania companies of the 28th were attached to the French Division when they retreated without informing them. The riflemen became surrounded. Most of them were killed or captured. Only a few managed to fight their way south, where they rejoined their Division.

Rumors have been circulating that our boys were so incensed by the actions of the 125th that a French officer was allegedly shot in the back by an unidentified American doughboy.

As told to me, several eyewitnesses saw the officer carrying a French poodle at the front when the bullet struck him from behind. The dog survived. American authorities declared the occurrence an accident and declined to investigate.

Regarding Col. Greble's mention of Col. McAlexander, his contempt for the French was born much earlier in the war when he was trained in tactics by the French Army. The former Military Science Professor, McAlexander, was asked to comment on his experience with the French. He stated profusely that there was nothing that the French could ever teach him anything about war.

The man, who would later become the Rock of the Marne hero that day in July, was relieved of his command for the comment and was reassigned to the Inspector General's staff.

We also heard that the Second Battle of Marne followed on Tuesday, July 30. Working with the 28th Division was the 32nd. The men of the 127th Infantry, who were part of the 32nd, captured the tiny village of Cierges at about 1400 hours. The hamlet, situated in a hollow, was about six miles north of the River Marne.

The outfit continued on and attempted to capture Les Jomblets Wood and Bellevue Farm to the north, but a heavy hostile fire forced them to fall back from those woods.

In the early morning of July 31, the Division attacked and succeeded in capturing Les Jomblets and established itself about half a mile farther.

They told us that our troops repulsed a counterattack by the Germans made shortly after daybreak.

About 0900, however, they were driven back by a fierce German artillery barrage.

By afternoon the 32nd Division finally took and held Les Jombles due to the two regimental assaults.

Although there's no breakout of the casualties attributable to the fighting around Cierges, they were a significant part of the 4,500 killed and wounded the Division suffered during those nine days from July 30 to August 7.

The French nicknamed the 32nd Division Les Terribles and requested that the outfit remain in the sector.

Finally, our company detrained on Sunday, August 11, near Mézy.

It was still early in the morning when our train suddenly jerked to a halt and awoke many of the still slumbering soldiers.

As I exited the boxcar, I saw the battlefield outside the village. It was a scene of wreck and ruin. A road sign pointing to "Châteaux-Thierry- 24 km" was battered but still legible.

Looking eastward along the railroad track, I could see Hill 231 in the distance. At the foot of the hill on the right, I could barely make out the roofs of the village of Moulins, while to the left, a line of trees marked the mouth of the river, Surmelin.

At Mézy, what had been a picturesque little village by the Marne River with fertile fields and hills sheltering it, was now a shattered and bleak wasteland devastated by the conflict that passed through like a violent storm.

A shattered church tower overlooks a city park that is pockmarked and defaced by the bursts of a myriad of shells.

The ground, irreverently covered by the litter of war, is interrupted only by a smattering of white crosses marking the graves of the hastily buried dead.

From there, our Regiment marched towards our first camp near Cierges. As we made our way along the river, evidence of the intense fighting that took place here was a reminder of the devastation of war.

Along the riverbank, the legs of a half-buried German soldier protruded from the ground.

A smashed aeroplane laid in a heap across the road. Judging by its red, white, and blue tail markings, it was a French aircraft, probably a Hanriot HD-6.

Further down the road, we discovered piles of rifles, helmets, canteens, bayonets, gas masks, and other articles that men of the reclamation service were collecting.

These items, lost, discarded, or left behind in the heat of battle, are now useless to those brave men buried beneath those white, wooden crosses.

The stench of war hangs heavy in the summer air, and millions of flies carry out their own sorties as we walk this path of reality.

The road was busy with army trucks and ambulances, as well as dispatch riders on motorcycles.

Occasionally officers passed us by while riding in their olive drab Ford or Dodge sedans.

Piles of spent shells also lined the road, large and small caliber. Here and there, you see a hastily excavated dugout on the side of a bank, where some soldier sought shelter from the hail of bullets.

We heard through the ranks that the 109th Field Artillery had pushed through here about two days ago. They sought shelter in a patch of woods near the village of Fresnes. The area is about three- quarters of the way between Mézy and Cierges.

At nightfall, and the constant flashes of the guns to the north combined with the deep rumble of their distant roar seemed like the approach of a summer storm. Oh, if it were only so!

By morning we arrived at the camp at Cierges, only to learn that it was just a temporary layover. Soon we would be on the move again.

In the camp, I ran into Corp. James Conroy, who was walking a dog. I was taken back by the sight and went over to speak with the fellow.

"That's quite a dog you have there," I noted. "Yes, he is," Conroy responded.

"He's worth his weight in gold," the man continued.

"When this war's over, the Army owes this guy the biggest steak they can find," he added. The young man began to tell me the whole story about this unusual dog.

"The poor little chap has been in over a dozen battles and was wounded twice," he boasted.

According to Conroy, who was with the 102nd Infantry Regiment, 26th Division. The dog's name was "Stubby," and he actually out-ranked the soldier. Sgt. Stubby, an American bull terrier, possibly mixed with Boston terrier, was found by his master on the grounds of Yale University in April 1917. The pup was scrounging for scraps of food.

He began training the mutt and smuggled him into France with the rest of his outfit.

The dog's first action in the war came on February 5, when the 102nd was positioned at Chemin des Dames, just north of Soissons, France.

The unit was under massive attack from the enemy with heavy artillery fire and grenade assaults.

For several days the American Infantry Regiment suffered through these relentless strikes. Many of the U.S. soldiers fell asleep due to fatigue in their rat-infest trenches.

Just before dawn, the Germans unleashed a Mustard Gas attack, and Stubby, always on the alert, ran up and down the trenches barking and thereby alerting the men of the impending danger.

Some of his duties are to pull guard duty, warn the men of enemy movement in the opposing trenches, and clear the trenches of rats and other vermin that scurry back and forth. Stubby has been under constant fire day and night.

Not only is he a valuable watchdog in the trenches, but he once captured a German spy in the Argonne.

"While we were still in Chemin des Dames, Stubby heard a noise in the stillness of the night," Conroy recalled, "Stubby stole out of the trenches and recognized a soldier as a German. The enemy tried to deceive the dog, but he was too smart for him. Seizing the prisoner by the breeches, Stubby held onto him until help arrived."

"Alerted by the commotion," Conway went on, "our guys captured and imprisoned the spy."

"For his efforts that night, Stubby was given the Iron Cross medal that belonged to the kraut," he concluded.

In April 1918, during the Battle of Seicheprey, the dog was hit in the foreleg by a German hand grenade. The Army sent Stubby to the rear for convalescence, but the brave canine soon returned to duty.

Later, he was exposed to mustard gas, and they equipped him with his own gas mask. Stubby was so keen at detecting the whine of an incoming shell that he became quite adept at warning the troops when to duck for cover.

"On more than one occasion, he left the trenches and wandered into this sort of no man's land, between the U.S. and the German trenches. He stood by wounded soldiers until the medics could come and get them," Conroy added.

"Although the French tried to adopt him several times, he always returned to the American side," he concluded.

Conway revealed that following the Battle of Chateau-Thierry, the town's women made the pup a chamois coat. His heroism has earned him several medals, and he has his own set of dog tags.

    *   *40 NOTE: Stubby was just one of many dogs who were war heroes in World War 1. "Mutt" was a French bulldog who served with the U.S. 111th Engineer Battalion. He brought cigarettes to the men in the trenches, boosted morale, and calmed nerves during the intensive fighting. "Tom" was a French ambulance dog who saved the lives of many French soldiers who were wounded in the field. Then, there was "Rags," a French terrier, and a stray on Paris's streets. A U.S. soldier adopted him in the First Division. First Sgt. James Donovan taught this amazing dog to deliver messages on the battlefield and warned men of incoming bombardments.*

I patted the pooch on the head and went back to what I was doing.

While talking to some of the guys in my outfit, Bill Haeberle said he wasn't surprised by my story.

"You know we have our own dog here, as well," Haeberle stated matter-of-factly. "How's that, Bill?" I queried.

"Well, the guys over in the 315th Infantry, 79th Division, have a dog they call "Philly," he replied. "Really? What's the story there?" I questioned.

"She was a stray they picked up at Camp Meade in Middletown, PA.

Haeberle went on, "She roams the trenches warning the men about German raids. The pup has a fantastic set of ears on her. The krauts even have a bounty on her head. I think it's like 50 Deutsche marks or something like that. They say the mutt's been hit by shrapnel, gas, and everything else. Nothing stops her, though," he concluded.

"You say they call her "Philly?" I asked. "Yep. That's her name alright," he affirmed.

The night of August 13, we underwent the first tremendous air raid of our Regiment to date.

It was a cloudless night, with a bright moon. These conditions made every feature of the landscape clearly visible for the raiders in the sky.

The planes themselves were invisible against the midnight blue heavens.

Shortly after the orange glow of sunset had faded, we could hear the intermittent hum of the German planes in the distance.

As they drew nearer, the loud explosion of bombs punctuated the night. Suddenly, there was a rush of air, a flash of light, and a deafening roar thrust upon us. Chaos ensued as we all ran for cover.

When the danger had passed, there were no casualties in our area. However, one of the bombs exploded in the middle of a motor transport company in the woods across the road. Plenty of men were killed and wounded while most of the trucks were demolished and ignited the gasoline.

The spectacle kept the enemy planes circling the area all through the night, dropping bombs, not only on any military operations but on our troops, as well.

On Thursday, August 15, our Regiment moved into position near Courville, and it is while we were there, we fired our first shots in the war.

Courville, Sgt. Vogan informed us, was a picturesque village with about 400 inhabitants before the first German advance in May drove its residents from the town.

In addition to sitting amidst the beautiful, fertile countryside in Champaign, the French village had its own medieval castle.

The French converted the castle into a hospital and constructed an airfield nearby about a year ago. Like many of the others, we had passed through, we found the sleepy village primarily destroyed.

Near the town square, we saw the remnants of a Spad XIII American aeroplane. According to the men from one of the other outfits still assigned to the area, the plane belonged to one of our pilots, Lt. William Russel.

They say that Russel was flying with the 95th Aero Squadron. This unit was attached to the First Pursuit Group.

Just four days ago, on the morning of August 11, the lieutenant was a rear guard of a 13-plane patrol. Because he was flying into the sun, the American pilot didn't see a patrol of German aircraft flying towards him.

The enemy planes cut him off from his squadron. They attempted to rush to his defense, but the Germans separated him from the others once again. The group never saw the American flyer again.

According to one of the infantry units on the ground, Russel amazingly completed a difficult double reverse maneuver before being hit by enemy fire. The witness noted that his plane went out of control and crashed on the ground.

Our men reported that a handful of the local villagers, who had remained behind, pulled his body from the wreckage and buried him in the Courville Cemetery.

SFC. Vogan stated, "They hastily made a wooden cross and painted on it, William Russel, Aviateur American."

He affirmed, "This 24-year-old American flyboy is just another one of our many war heroes. It matters not if you're on the ground or up there," the sergeant said as he pointed towards the sky, "your dedication and bravery will help to win this thing!"

*   *41 NOTE: After the war, Russel's father, Henry Russel, left $10,000 in his will to the people of Courville. His donation went towards constructing a monument to remember his son, the American flyer, and a fountain to supply water for the townspeople.*

It was also on August 15 that the sarge informed me of my promotion to sergeant. My service with the P.A. National Guards, my exemplary work at Camp Stewart, Camp Hancock, and the French Hospital near Vannes earned me the promotion he told me.

Also making the rank of sergeant were Richard Connolly and William F. Haeberle. My good friend, Irvin Schweppenheiser, received a promotion from private to private first class. I was genuinely disappointed that Doc failed to make Seargent despite his valuable contributions in El Paso.

For me, the extra stripes meant that my pay would double from $3.75 to $7.50 per day. A sergeant first class earned a pay grade of $11.25 per day, while cooks and musicians also made $7.50.

Our battalion then moved to the right in the vicinity of Longville farm. This position was right near an area they call "Death Valley."

While the Third Battalion was moving again, Lt. Wesson of H.Q. Co. was severely wounded, and Clifton E. Collins, a Wagoner of Supply Co., was killed. They were our battalion's first casualties of the war.

It was a common practice to send new troops to the front lines in a quiet sector so they could get their baptism under fire, but as was our fate, this area turned out to be quite active at the time.

Within a few days, however, the Regiment was functioning as a veteran organization. Not only was the German Artillery fire severe, but their bombing planes were especially troublesome.

One of our batteries had 20 casualties in one day. The First Sergeant reported that the enemy had dropped more than six hundred shells in our area in that period. They consisted of high explosives and gas of 77, 88, 105, and 210 mm caliber. Every day the Regiment added more wounded and killed to the list.

The enemy sent many spies dressed in French uniforms or as French civilians among the batteries. Another trick the Germans played on us involved the hands on the Courville church clock.

Three men on routine patrol noticed the hands on the clock had changed positions several times. Apparently, this was some sort of signal for the enemy. From that point on, we had one guy in charge of watching this clock.

One afternoon, the man on duty saw the hands move, and a detail was dispatched at once to investigate. They found a civilian at the church, and the man immediately took flight. He was eventually captured and taken to Battalion H.Q. for questioning.

Later, we discovered a German dressed in a French uniform in a cave at a demolished farmhouse. The enemy soldier had a complete operating wireless outfit, and it appeared that he was sending his messages in code to the Germans.

Our men attempted to send a message to the German's, and they received a reply but could not translate it because it was in double code.

During our time in the area, the German Air Service was most active. Their planes were constantly over us, and for a time, the famous Count Richthofen Squadron operated in our vicinity.

*   *42 NOTE: Richthofen, "The Red Baron," was not among this squadron as he was shot down and killed earlier in April 1918.*

In one air battle involving eleven German planes and five Allied planes, four aircraft perished in the fight. One German and two American came down in flames or out of control, while the pilot of the other American was wounded but managed to land behind our lines near Areis-le-Ponsart.

Bombardments from the air often came at night, as well. Explosive shells and gas attacks were standard both day and night.

By August 28, the Fifty-Third Brigade had prepared all of the artillery in our sector to administer a massive attack.

Our unit, the 108th Field Artillery, fired 1,340 rounds of gas and 440 rounds of high explosives, while the 109th discharged 2,500 rounds of gas and 620 rounds of the other.

This barrage took the Germans totally by surprise and based on information we received from prisoners, we had inflicted more casualties with this three-to-one gas attack than we had at any previous point.

29

"THE GAS ATTACK"

The Pungent Smell of Gas was in the Air
Image Source: Unknown

CHAPTER 29

"The Gas Attack"

On the morning of September 3, we received information that the enemy was withdrawing from our front. Col. Greble ordered the batteries to fire on all the sensitive points according to gathered intelligence. Upon acting on these orders, we experienced very little shooting in return.

In the afternoon, forward observers reported that they detected several fires in enemy territory after this action.

Thus far in September, we have experienced unprecedented dryness in the area. These conditions have been highly favorable for the movement of our troops, guns, tanks, and supplies.

Rumor had it that Col. George S. Patton Jr., whom we last saw during our stay in El Paso, TX, was in the area with one of our armored tank divisions.

Many believed that the tank would be the one military vehicle that could win us this war. That opinion was easily understandable when you saw the boilerplates in action. They were indeed a scary sight. They rumbled along loudly, and their very appearance reminded one of something out of a Jules Verne novel.

Battalion HQ ordered us to set up our Field Hospital in a clearing near St. Gilles on Rue du Mont Saint-Martin. To the East, the area was densely wooded but in the West lay nothing but open pastures.

Hampering our efforts was an unexpected heavy downpour that began about 1400 hours and lasted until chow time at 1600.

Bill Haeberle was the first to be treated at the facility. During the storm, severe winds played havoc when eight of us set up the 20-foot by 40-foot tent. One of the ropes needed to stake down the canvas shelter wrapped around Haeberle's body and lashed him in the face. The line sliced his right cheek like a hog's belly. The poor guy needed six stitches.

I watched intently as French Major Seymour Dupois tended to the injury most efficiently. One of the nurses applied a three-and-a-half by three-and-a-half-inch gauze bandage to the wound.

Before long, others who were sick or wounded began to filter into our area.

During our training, soldiers were given instructions on treating themselves with basic first aid methods in the field.

In their packs, the army supplied each man with two gauze bandages (four inches by eighty-four inches), two compresses (three-and-a-half by three-and-a-half inches), two safety pins, and instructions.

The purpose of this dressing was to prevent the wound from further trauma and prevent loss of blood. This measure would also limit infection.

If a wounded soldier could not care for himself, a comrade or a stretcher-bearer could step in.

Most of our personnel received training on applying field dressings, controlling bleeding, splint fractures, and protecting the wounded from gas attacks.

The nurses assigned to our unit filled out a field card for each patient that received treatment. This form noted whether the soldier was very slightly wounded but able to return to action; slightly wounded and requires evacuation; seriously wounded; has fractures; severely wounded with attendant shock; gassed; psychoneurotic or just plain old sick.

Some of the treatments received by one of our physicians were: painting around the wound with iodine; injection of 500 units of anti-tetanus serum; one-fourth grain of morphine for the pain to those seriously wounded; control of hemorrhage through ligature, hemostats, or tourniquet; immobilization of fractures with wooden splints, and shock treatments such as blankets and hot drinks.

Our main goal was to stabilize patients and prepare them for transport.

Although it was not part of our assignment, a timely evacuation was always a challenge due to weather, terrain, and enemy fire.

Shortly, three injuries needed immediate attention. The first casualty involved an artilleryman from Battery A. During the storm, one of the horses reared up and slipped in the mud. Cpl. Leonard Pennypacker found himself under the fallen equine. His batterymates quickly went to his aid and pulled him out from under the 1,500-pound animal.

Without equipment to properly assess his injuries, an ambulance transported him behind the lines for further evaluation. However, one of the attending physicians believed the injured man had both his legs broken and a couple of ribs.

Our second case involved another artilleryman who received a concussion from getting whacked in the head. Two gun mates from Battery F brought Pvt. Calvin Craft in for treatment.

Once again, the foul weather caused one of the artillery pieces to slide down a ravine knocking the unsuspecting soldier off his feet. That guy was fortunate. Upon evaluation, one of the physicians determined that he had encountered no other injuries, and the gunner would be back with his outfit within a few days.

Amongst those injured was a familiar face, Milton Shomper, only now, it was Pvt. Milton Shomper of the Ordnance Detachment of the 109th Field Artillery.

The 26-year old Kensington resident worked with me at Baldwin Locomotive Works.

He was hauling a wagonload of ammo for Battery B when a shell exploded nearby. The wagon flipped on its side and Shomper was thrown to the ground.

Luckily, he, too, only sustained some minor cuts and bruises. However, his rude, sarcastic personality remained intact.

The two of us made eye contact and Shomper quickly began his verbal assault.

"Well... well, here I am in the bowels of France, and who do I have the pleasure of seeing, but Tommy Schalata.

"Where's Uncle Leo? Out getting you a cup of coffee?" He went on.

"I get to haul a wagonload of high explosives across no man's land, and here you are with your nurse's hat, a wet towel, and a bandage. Just like back home. Us poor guys get to the grunt work and yous guys drink coffee and play nursemaid," he ranted.

"Good yo see you, too, Milt," I replied.

"Someone will be over to check you out shortly," I assured him. I quickly left the area to avoid a confrontation.

Finally, Pvt. Emerick Hedrick, of Battery D, had his hand struck by a breechloader on his gun. When the battery was eventually able to commence firing, Hedrick's hand got caught during the recoil. Still slick from the recent drenching downpour, the piece gave the young lad a lesson in the importance of concentration.

Badly bruised and already entirely black and blue, Hedrick's lefthand wrapped in several gauze rolls reminded one of a leather baseball mitt.

By midnight, a few stragglers wandered into our tent with a variety of minor scrapes and bruises. For now, it was all quiet.

At 0130 hours on September 4, Col. Greble issued Field Order No. 5, directing the Regiment's advance. The Third Battalion relocated both batteries to an area near the Vesle River just north of St. Gilles.

The next day, the Second Battalion advanced to La Bonne Maison Farm, while the First Battalion took their position in the sand quarries on top of the slope north of La Bonne Maison. This spot was near the location of some destroyed airplane hangars.

The airfield at La Bonne Maison was built and used by the French in 1917. In late spring 1918, the Germans used the field during their drive towards the Marne. The enemy abandoned it sometime in July.

As for our own Second and Third Battalions, the units experienced little or no resistance when taking these positions.

That situation would change in due time, however. Enemy shelling was on the increase. With this constant harassment by opposing artillery, our men were instructed to dig holes in the ground to protect themselves from shell fragments. Officers sought cover in dugouts excavated in a wooded bank about one-half mile away.

The enemy bombardments offered a variation of high-explosive shells and gas canisters. This barrage saturated the atmosphere with poisonous fumes.

These attacks forced us to constantly put on our gas masks until the gas dispersed. Not a day went by that one or more men were wounded or killed.

From bumps and bruises, cuts and concussions, we advanced to massive trauma, amputations, and outright disfigurements.

From the time I spent training at the hospital near Vannes to this point near St. Gilles, I have seen with my own eyes the effects of this horrible mustard gas.

These deadly fumes can kill a soldier by blistering the throat and lungs if inhaled in large quantities.

Even men who were able to don their gas masks in time found that the mustard gas would produce terrible blisters all over their bodies as it soaked into their woolen uniforms.

Contaminated uniforms needed to be stripped off as fast as possible and washed. Not an easy chore for those in the heat of battle.

One of my first-hand experiences with this involved a patient in the hospital in Vannes.

Doc and I visited Lance Cpl. Ellsworth Crowley of the 14th (Light) Division of the British Fifth Army.

Crowley told us he was from the village of Bampton in Oxfordshire, England.

The poor lad had his face peppered with red blisters that ranged from pea-sized to that of a buffalo nickel. His misshapen eyelids, swollen and disfigured, not only affected his vision but proved to be extremely painful.

The same could be said for his arms and torso. The soldier's legs, however, were largely spared.

As the young Brit explained to us, he was standing knee-deep in mud in a water-filled, rat-infested trench. The thick muck, combined with the fact that he was wearing high boots, saved his feet and legs from the scourge.

A gas shell exploded near his position, just south of St. Quentin. Crowley and the others in his outfit had no advance warning of the strike.

His injuries occurred weeks before our visit, and still, his recovery was moderate at best.

*   *43 NOTE: The first gas attack in World War 1 took place on January 31, 1915, when Germany's Ninth Army fired 18,000 gas shells on the Russian lines. This attack occurred just west of Warsaw, Poland. The shells were filled with an early form of tear gas and proved to be largely unsuccessful.*

Two stretcher-bearers lifted a young man, barely 18 years of age, onto the operating table. The nurse cut the dressing off on his right arm, and he winced with pain.

Below his waist are two heavily bandaged stumps. On the left, what used to be his leg, is now cut off at the knee. His right leg now ends just above the point where his ankle once was.

Another French surgeon examines the entrance and exit wounds on his arm. The wounded man barks, "Listen, you bastard, you're hurting me!"

The physician raises his eyebrows and turns away, seemingly unfazed by his patient's outburst.

After all, this is war, and war has no pity.

The doctor returned to the operating table, poured some sort of liquid on the wound, and nodded to the nurse to dress the injury. Thankfully, another assignment called me away before observing what treatment was in store for the man's lower limbs.

The 107th Field Artillery was assigned the duty of destroying a German ration and supply train. This long string of enemy wagons traversed one of the nearby roads each night. These much-needed supplies enabled the enemy to withstand our constant pressure and incremental advancements.

Although it was too dark for observation, our infantry could clearly hear the rudimentary wagons rumbling when they crossed a small wooden bridge. Teams of horses pulled these heavy loads, and the distinct clippety clop of their hooves on the planks of the bridge gave them away, as well.

Captain Clinton Bundy, who was on a mission to disrupt these convoys, had a pre-arranged signal with the infantry when the enemy supply train reached the bridge. Battery B opened fire and continued for nearly an hour. In the morning, a scout patrol found the destroyed wagons strewn about the road and bridge. Neither a soldier nor a horse survived our bombardment.

This system was devised by Capt. Bundy and stopped several of these caravans before the Germans retaliated with new defensive gun positions. As a result, the 107th was the target of many high explosive and gas shells.

On clear nights, enemy aeroplanes raided our positions with their horrific bombs. Our return artillery fire netted limited results, and only the observation officer, who watched through field glasses, could estimate how effective our fire was.

Every night our own train of wagons, carrying rations and ammunition, traveled down the dangerously exposed road that ran from Arcis-le-Ponsart to Courville.

With several attacks and counter-attacks taking place, the Second Battalion sent a reconnaissance party to the vicinity of Villette on the morning of September 5. This action aimed to determine the feasibility of moving the 107th Field Artillery to a new point north of this road.

The patrol reported that this area was untenable because it was too close to enemy lines. Another circumstance in the decision was the fact that one of the three available bridges of this section was located near this point. Therefore, the 107th would remain just west of St. Gilles.

That evening, the Second Battalion took a new position in the vicinity of Baslieux. The Battalion's lead artillery unit followed the infantry across the river. The First Battalion was ordered to follow later that day. However, Major William B. Reilly later rescinded that order. The First remained active on the south side of the river.

Some observers reported that the Germans were quickly withdrawing. Our men saw them burning ammunition and supply dumps in the vicinity of Blanzy-les-Fismes. Better to destroy these items than to have them fall into our hands.

The First Battalion initiated a four-minute preparatory fire, followed by a rolling barrage on the morning of September 6. This artillery volley was in support of an Infantry attack by American and French troops northwest of Villette.

On the evening of September 6, the enemy became active once again. The Germans scored a direct hit on B Battery putting one gun out of action and wounding four or five men.

Earlier that same day, C Battery attempted to cross the Vesle River, but the bridges were not strong enough. During the operation, shots from the enemy wounded several of our men.

The guns of Battery D continued to fire both day and night. Positioned just in front of our Field Hospital, I felt like I was right in the middle of all the action.

The weather was calm this night. It was pretty dark, however, because it was a new moon. Only the stars provided a modest illumination.

This entire sector was not only overrun with incessant shooting and exploding shells; it was the epicenter of calamity and confusion among the men.

The roar of the incoming and outgoing shells was interrupted only by the yelling of these soldiers thrown into the heat of battle.

Although in my mind, I was prepared for anything, I tried to distract myself by thinking of Stella and my family back home. I was hoping to return safely into her arms, but the outlook at the time looked bleak.

I took out my pocket-sized prayer book and began reciting random prayers that I thought would see me through this nightmare.

In the midst of it all, one of our men wandered into the area with a bottle of vodka in one hand and brandy in the other. He offered a swig to whoever was in need. Several were willing partakers.

As I heard the shrill whistle of another incoming shell over our heads, I motioned to Schweppenheiser and Haeberle to get down.

"Keep your heads down," I whispered. "No shit!" Haeberle shot back.

Luckily, the enemy projectile overshot its target and landed about 30 yards beyond our position.

Despite the unrelenting blasts, I could hear the battery mates of Battery D chatter as they loaded the huge shells into the guns.

First came the order to reload, followed by the loud clang of the breech as the gunner slammed it closed and latched it. Then, a brilliant flash followed with a deafening roar.

Incoming shells yielded the same results. At one point, however, following a ghastly explosion nearby, I heard someone yell. Soon after, I could make out the sound of a frightful moan in the darkness.

I heard it again. Then, I detected the ghastly sound of someone uttering, "Uuugggggg!"

Immediately, I scrambled from my post under the tent to the site of the closest artillery piece. With my heart beating so wildly, I felt as if it would burst right in my chest. I stumbled through the blackness and tripped over a fallen body. Whomever it was, it was too late for the lad. In the pale light, I could see blood was dripping from his forehead. It began to pool around his right eye.

A few yards further, near another gun, I found a different man. Slumped over in a sitting position, I recognized the soldier as one of our gunners. Pvt. Kenneth Slocum.

At first, I was certain I heard a very soft moan and then a loud sigh, but I checked for a pulse, and he, too, was gone.

I sat there in the field. All was still for a while. It was quiet. "I'm safe," I murmured to myself out loud.

I could hear no sounds. No explosions. No yelling. No moaning. No murmuring. Nothing but quiet.

Then came another loud blast as a shell hit the ground nearby. Instantly, I recognized the pungent smell of gas. I reached around for my gas mask, but I realized it was too late as I fumbled in my search. I hunched over to protect my face as I buried my head in my lap. That's all I can remember.

"THE ROAD TO RECOVERY"

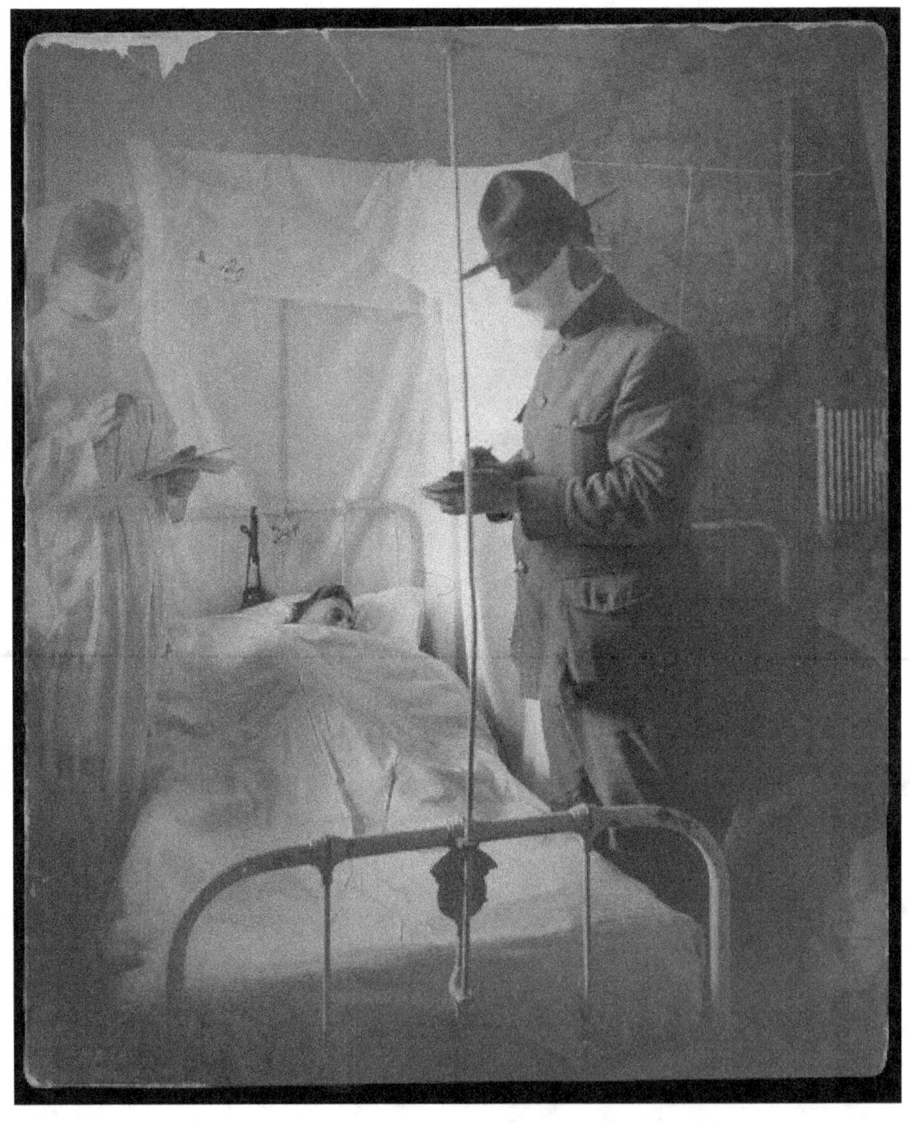

French Evacuation Hospital near St. Gilles
Image Source: Unknown

CHAPTER 30

"The Road to Recovery"

It was Saturday, November 20, 1896, and I found myself at the corner of Broadway and Woltz Ave. in Buffalo, NY.

My fourth birthday was approaching, and pop was taking me to Meunschmeyer's Variety Store for a birthday gift. Mom dressed me in my brown, woolen winter coat and a pair of high-button leather boots, also brown.

As we stood on the corner, waiting to cross Broadway, one of the city's brand new two-tone green electric streetcars came bearing down on us. The Buffalo Street R.R. Company recently introduced several of these modern machines to its line.

When the vehicle drew closer to the intersection, I was thrown into a panic upon hearing the wheels screeching on the steel rails and the loud clanging of the warning bell.

I froze momentarily as the trolley roared by. After it passed, I could see my father on the other side, desperately searching for my whereabouts. As he glanced back in my direction, he saw me with my arms wrapped around the black, wrought iron lampost. I was petrified and crying.

Immediately, he rushed to my side as I stood there, sobbing. He took his red handkerchief from his back pocket and wiped away my tears.

"Now, Tommy," he whispered softly. "It's okay. I'm here. I'll always be here," he said to console me. "I'll always be here," he repeated.

Next, I overheard, "Tommy! Tommy! Are you there? Can you hear me?"

The voice was distinctly different. Much louder and with a clearly urgent tone to it.

Slowly, I opened my eyes, and standing over me was a man in uniform that I was unable to identify.

The voice was familiar, but my vision was blurry. Almost foggy.

As the mystery voice continued to call me by name, my focus was becoming more acute. Finally, I realized that it was my friend, Irvin Schweppenheiser.

"Yeah... yes... er... what is it? Where am I? What happened?" I asked.

My panic was reminiscent of the recent dream I was having before he awakened me.

"You were gassed, Tommy," I heard Doc say, but before I could get additional information, I apparently lost consciousness again.

Next, I vividly remember flying in a Curtiss R2 aeroplane. The aircraft had a yellow fuselage and wings. I was operating the controls in the front of the cockpit. As I glanced over my shoulder, Stella was in the seat behind me.

We were flying over the city of Philadelphia. I traveled up Market Street until I reached city hall. I circled the plane around the Billy Penn statue, not once but twice before heading down Broad Street towards the Naval Shipyard in South Philly.

Stella was laughing and cheering during the entire flight.

"Tommy! Tommy! This is fantastic! I've never experienced anything like this!" She yelled from behind.

I could barely hear her over the drone of the engine.

"Hold on, Babe," I warned her as I dove to the left and circled to the Delaware River. I followed the river North until we were above her neighborhood near Cambria Street. I pointed at various landmarks along the way.

Suddenly, we flew into a thick fog. It was a wet, blinding mix as thick as pea soup. When it cleared, I looked over my shoulder, and Stella's seat was empty. She was gone! I guided the craft closer to ground level, but there was no sign of her anywhere.

I called out, "Stella! Stella! Where did you go?"

Shortly after that, I heard a woman's voice calling my name over and over and over! "Monsieur Thomas! Monsieur Thomas! Thomas..." the woman called.

"Veuillez vous réveiller," she said as I felt her tap my arm with her open hand.

In English, but with a distinctly French accent, she persisted, "Sergeant! Sergeant! Please wake up!" When I finally opened my eyes, I saw a young woman dressed in a pale blue nurse's uniform and white cap. Over the dress, she was clad in a white jumper with a red cross on her chest. She appeared to be barely eighteen years of age.

"Where am I?" I questioned. "What's going on?" I begged. "Make no mind of that," she replied.

"le physicien will explain to you when you are well enough. Do you wish something to eat or drink?" She inquired.

"You may have water, tea, broth? Nothing more," the nurse explained. "Where am I?" I pushed on.

"In due time," she assured me.

"Don't worry. There's time for that. It would be best if you got well first," this young woman pressed on in a soft, comforting voice.

"Broth, I guess," I relented.

I left out a heavy sigh, then followed with a noticeable wince of pain that caught her immediate attention.

"You hurt, Monsieur?" she asked while leaning in closer. I nodded affirmatively.

"My name is Margot," the nurse explained.

"I am going to get your broth and will give you a shot of morphine when you are finished. You still require more rest."

She flashed me a warm smile, then left the area. Within a few minutes, she returned with the broth. "Do you have any bread?" I begged.

"No. No monsieur. No bread. So sorry. You must wait," and the nurse was gone, again. I had just shut my eyes when Margot returned.

"Monsieur, time for your shot. I will help you roll onto your side," she instructed. I felt a sharp jab in my duff, and that's about all I recall.

It was dark. I smelled flowers. I heard music playing. Violins? Cellos? Suddenly there was a light in the distance—a dim light, but a light just the same. I walked towards that light and came upon the farmhouse painting that hung in the art museum back in Philadelphia.

There was the white house with the red tin roof—the front porch with the black dog laying on it. It was all there—the flowers, the oak tree, and the woman feeding the chickens.

I stood there, staring at the piece of art. It may have been a few moments, but it may have been longer. I had no concept of time. It was all visual. The more I gazed at the painting, the more real it appeared to be.

Suddenly, the woman turned towards me. She tossed a handful of feed at the chickens, and they responded by running to the spot on the ground where it had landed. There were three gray and black Barred Rocks, three Rhode Island Reds, four white Wyandottes, and a tall, handsome, brown rooster with iridescent green plumage on his tail.

The woman feeding the chickens seemed to look directly at me and smile, but at that very moment, a man approached her. He seemed to be coming from behind the house.

His approach startled the chickens at first, and then, the woman turned towards him.

I heard her exclaim, "Tommy, where have you been? Where were you? I was looking high and low for you? Whatever became of you?"

I kept hearing her voice again and again. Then, a bright light was shined in my face. So brilliant was the beam that I was forced to open my eyes. This time, standing at my bedside were the nurse, Margot, and two men I sensed were physicians.

The taller of the two moved the light away and began, "Young man, I am Major Perlmann. This is Captain Durand. He is a surgeon with the French Army."

The American officer appeared to be about six-foot-two inches tall. His long face sported a straight Grecian nose, a well-trimmed mustache, and a strong chin. The Frenchman was about five inches shorter from my vantage point and had a round face with a slight, pencil-thin mustache.

"What happened? Where am I?" I inquired.

The major explained, "You were gassed near St. Gilles. Mustard gas. You are in a French Evacuation Hospital. Captain Durand had to perform surgery on you here in the field."

"It is our opinion that you were not only exposed to the gas, but you must have ingested it somehow. In addition to affecting your lungs, it damaged a portion of your stomach, and Captain Durand, here, had to remove a section of it," Major Perlman revealed.

"It's very rare to see a case like this," he reported.

"Normally, Mustard gas causes skin rashes and blisters—inflammation of the lungs, etc. But rarely does it affect the stomach in this manner. That's why we think you may have ingested it somehow. It could have come in contact with some food that you ate," the officer surmised.

"Will I be okay?" I asked the two men.

The French captain bowed slightly towards me and smiled. Then, he spoke with a heavy French accent, "Monsieur, you should recover very well from my experience. We will send you to a hospital to recuperate for... well... say... oh, about three weeks... maybe a little less or a little longer."

"I see," I responded. "When can I eat?"

The captain offered the following advice: "That jeune homme, excuse me, my French, young man, it all depends on you. I would recommend liquids for a few days, and then we can try moving up with a goal towards solid foods, custard, eggs, and so forth."

"Any other questions, sergeant?" The major asked. "What day is it?"

"It's Sunday, September 8," Margot responded. "How long have I been here?"

"You were brought in here early yesterday morning," the major acknowledged while looking in the direction of the nurse. She nodded affirmatively.

"How long until I'm moved to the hospital?" I wanted to know.

He responded, "That depends on the resistance here in Death Valley and how soon we can mobilize, but I would venture to guess about two, maybe three days. Okay, son? You get yourself well," he concluded.

"Nurse Laurent will see to your needs," the major added.

With the consultation over, we exchanged salutes, and the three left the area.

I tried to close my eyes and get some rest, but this development was a lot to digest, both literally and physically.

On Thursday, I was given my first real food. My breakfast consisted of some relatively moist scrambled eggs, a slice of toast bread, and a cup of very weak tea.

While I sat in a chair beside my bed, three fellows walked into my area. As they approached, I was surprised to see that it was none other than Irvin Schweppenheiser, Harry Haeberle, and Roy Wilson.

"Hey, Fellas!"

"Hi, Tommy, how's it going?" Schweppenheiser yelled.

The other two gave out a yell, as well, but the nurse came running over immediately.

"Shhhhhhh! Hommes. We have some very sick soldiers here who need quiet and rest," she warned us.

"How ya' feelin', pal? Are they givin' ya' any grub, yet?" Harry inquired. "Oh, okay, I guess. I finally had some eggs this morning."

"Well, you look a hell of a lot better than when I saw you last," Irvin remarked. "You were out of it a few days ago," he observed.

"Yeah, I don't remember a whole lot. I guess it's good that I don't." "How long are you gonna be laid up?" Roy chimed in.

"Probably a month, the doctor says."

"What exactly happened?" I asked the guys.

"Our Field Hospital is set up near the hillside at Saint-Gillis.

It's about four kilometers from here," Haeberle began.

"If you remember, starting on Saturday, August 31, the enemy shell fire was severe. It kept up for nearly 24 hours straight," he went on.

"Actually, it continued for almost the entire week," Haeberle explained.

"Battery commanders reported on Friday, September 6, that about as much mustard gas was hitting us as the high explosives. One of the shells was a direct hit on a gun in Battery D. There was a private. Kenny, I think, was his name. He got the worst of it," Haeberle noted.

"You ran out to check on him," Harry explained. "He was dead. Although one of the mustard gas shells was a dud, it exploded before you could get back. Doc here carried you back to the hospital!

"Schweppy, here, got hit with the gas, as well, but not like you. YOU, pal, took the brunt of it," he added.

"Really?"

"Yes. Really," Roy confirmed. "Wow!" I exclaimed.

"Yeah, you're lucky, man," Harry declared. "How are you doing, Doc?" I asked. "Good! Real good!" He reported.

He continued, "I was feelin' pretty lousy for a day or so, but not like you."

"Say, Tommy," Wilson exclaimed, "do you remember that guy we shot pool with down at Camp Hancock? Harry Dommet, I believe, was his name."

"Dommet... Dommet..." I uttered. "Sounds familiar..."

"You know," Roy went on, "the guy from Lancaster. What did he say? He worked in a factory that made mouse traps, paintbrushes, and things like that?"

"Yeah, I remember him now. Wasn't he part of the Medical Detachment of the 108th Machine Gun Battalion?" I questioned.

"He ain't going back to Lancaster, as they say," Haeberle revealed. "Dead?" I asked, somewhat astonished.

"You got it. Dead," he responded. "No shit!" I blurted out.

"Got nailed by shrapnel the day before you... the fifth," Haeberle revealed. "Just a little over 19 years old," Schweppenheiser added.

"Wow! That's too bad," I lamented.

"That's no shit," Haeberle acknowledged, "one day you're shootin' pool with a guy, and later, he's being shipped home in a box to his mother, Ida."

"Oh! By the way, Tommy here's some mail that came for ya'. I thought you might want it ASAP," Irvin stated as he offered me the parcel.

"Thanks. I appreciate that."

Margot came over to urge the guys to wrap up their visit so I could get some rest.

The boys wished me a speedy recovery but warned me not to hurry back, insisting that I was better off where I was instead of being close to the action out at the field hospital. Naturally, I agreed.

The nurse ordered me to get back into bed where I could get some proper rest. I took her advice, but I was very excited to open my mail first.

After removing the twine and the brown paper wrapping, I eagerly opened the parcel. On top was a wax paper bag, and inside that was about a dozen of my mother's sugar cookies. The long journey reduced a few of them to crumbles, but just the faint aroma of something from home was a treat in itself.

I was tempted to take a bite of one of the cookies, but just as I raised it to my mouth, Nurse Margot passed by and shook her finger at me, saying, "Not cookies just yet, Monsieur Thomas. Not Yet. Perhaps, tomorrow," she scolded.

Just holding those cookies and smelling them gave me the feeling as though I were sitting at that kitchen table on Thompson Street with a hot cup of coffee.

At the bottom of the box was a letter stuffed in an envelope, and I could tell as soon as I opened it that it was from my sister, Helen.

July 23, 1918

Dear Tommy,

Pop says, according to the newspapers, you should be close to the action very soon. He has been following the war closely ever since you left.

The Spanish Influenza is starting to hit the country, as well. So far, we haven't had much to worry about here in Philadelphia, but it is already a problem in Boston.

I just celebrated my sixteenth birthday. Stella and Henrietta's birthdays will be following in September, but you already know that.

I hope and pray every night that you are safe. Father Movakowski taught us a new prayer to Jesus, asking him to protect all our boys fighting over there.

Every day I touch my necklace when I think of you and look at my special Christmas tree each night when I go to bed.

The family is all well. Veronica talks to Stella Zwolinski regularly. Her brother, Joe, is serving on the troop transport ship The USS De Kalb. She says that you are all Stella ever talks about, "Tommy this and Tommy that!"

I must go now, Tommy. Mother needs help doing the wash. Please take care of yourself and write when you can.

Your loving sister, Helen

Joe Zivie (Left) with Shipmate
Image Source: Author's Photo

Joe Zivie (Right) with deKalb commander, Warren R. Gherardi (Left)
Image Source: Author's Photo Image Source: Author's Photo

USS deKalb
Image Source: Author's Photo

"ROOMING WITH THE ENEMY"

Hospital ward with dozens of wounded
Image Source: Australian Broadcasting Corp.

Chapter 31

"Rooming with the Enemy"

Lucky for me, my move to the hospital would begin today, Tuesday, September 10, 1918. I soon discovered that my transit to a dispensary in the rear would be no easy task.

It is the practice to move wounded soldiers, like myself, from a Field Hospital or a First Aid Station to a safe point behind the front lines. These temporary facilities often have to be set up in shell holes, old gun placements, caves, cellars, and behind hills. They are very mobile, being almost constantly on the move to be close to the troops they serve.

The Hospital Corps carries supplies in pouches or sacks they call feed bags. There's always a shortage of dressings, splints, bandages, and litters. For several days, I was told, the corps personnel brought needed equipment to us near the front.

The men in the field generally receive two days' reserve rations in the field in the event they become stranded.

Several ambulance companies are operating in our sector, namely Nos. 109, 110, 111, and 112.

Initially, when I was wounded, they transported me from our own Field Hospital near Villette and then to the French Evacuation Hospital No. 5. This was about three and a half km to the south.

The path from Hospital No. 5 to the railroad junction near Courville was another four km. This would take place on a Sanitary Train. This is not a train, per se. It is a caravan of ambulances that transports the wounded from various collection points to other medical facilities. Most of these companies possess 12 horse-drawn and 36 motor ambulances.

Now, it was my understanding, that Ambulance Co. No. 116, which is primarily a horse-drawn unit, was going to take me to Courville. From there I would make the 133 km journey on an Ambulance Train to the American Red Cross Hospital No. 104 at Beauvais. I was told the infirmary recently expanded from 300 to 600 beds.

Another dangerous leg of the journey would take us through a small Fench village of Elise. This tiny hamlet was encircled by hills. Numerous caves and stone quarries gave the modest town great protection, but it was susceptible to gas pockets that permeated the valley from enemy shelling.

The route was also defined by a very narrow paved highway with mud shoulders. Road conditions made it impractical for automobiles. Many of the military trucks and other vehicles that used the road reportedly skidded off the roadway and wound up in ditches. Therefore, I had the good fortune to make the jolting journey in one of those awkward horse-drawn ambulances. The trip took us about three hours.

Meeting the Ambulance Train in Courville was delayed for 24 hours because it failed to arrive at the depot. Apparently, HQ Co. lost contact with it due to some oversight. They placed those of us who were being transported in a French barn until communications with the operation could be re-established. All told the process required 96 men from the Sanitary Train to transport the wounded on this mission alone.

The American Red Cross provided us with food and hot coffee en route to our destination, and that was appreciated by all, including those who were caring for us.

Since I was still on a special diet, I was offered some potato soup and coffee.

Finally, two British Wolverton Carriage Works 0-6-0 engines with 16 re-fitted passenger cars rolled into the station. They were a very odd-looking pair of locomotives (Nos. 6 and 7). They were like nothing we had ever built back at Baldwin, but we were anxious to get on board. I had heard that some of the earlier trains were primitive French locomotives pulling boxcars filled with hay. This unit was more like a hospital on wheels.

I was informed that some of the cars were converted to accommodate wards for injured soldiers. The train consisted of the following: one car for infectious diseases (24 beds), one staff car (eight beds), one kitchen and sick officers' (sitting car) with three beds for cooks plus 20 seats, nine ward cars (36 beds each), one pharmacy car (12 beds), one personnel car (33 beds), one train crew and storage car (three beds), one caboose with kitchen, men's mess, and two beds for NCO's.

Some of the larger units had the capability of carrying complete surgical cars and about 500 injured servicemen and 50 crew members.

To those patients like myself aboard this unit, the experience was both a blessing and a nightmare. I was relieved to be moving away from the front and the fighting, however, my bunk was small and uncomfortable. There were three tiers of beds and I was the lucky guy in the middle.

As my back sagged because of the flimsy mattress on my bunk, I kept getting cramps in my legs. Painful cramps, I might add. Because the bunk above me was so close, I could not move my legs or bend my knees to relieve myself of the pain. I was forced to turn on my side and work my cramping muscles with my hands as best I could. I spent more than an hour rubbing them to get some relief. Finally, I asked an orderly if there was some apple cider vinegar on board. This was an old remedy for cramping that I learned from my grandmother.

The young man brought me a small glass of water mixed with the vinegar. Soon after I drank the liquid, I felt some immediate relief.

Because most of us have been out in the field for weeks, the cars quickly became smelly and downright filthy.

Orderlies come through the car about once per hour. They bring us water, change our dressings, feed us and clean up as best they can. They tell me there are only two or three nurses involved in our care. Skilled physicians and surgeons are busy handling the most critical cases.

Friday, September 13, the ambulance train rolled into the station in Beauvais. Dozens of ambulances were on hand to transport us to the hospital. Although there was a large supply of motor vehicles, many horse-drawn wagons were pressed into service.

The trip was a bumpy ride of about three and a half kilometers. Bumpy due to the craters and ruts created by the intense shelling. The bulk of our journey took us along Rue du Wage and Avenue Corot.

One by one the ambulances pulled up to the main entrance and military and Red Cross personnel transported us into the four-story stone structure.

While the hospital at Beauvais was small compared to some of the others in service, it included 20 wards totaling 600 beds plus treatment facilities and storage buildings. Supplementary vacant land located between the hospital and the cemetery provided space for tents if additional patients needed to be treated.

The facility was without elevators, therefore we had to be carried up the stairs from floor to floor.

Many of the wards were designated for special treatments such as fractures/orthopedic, gas exposure, surgical recovery, plastic surgery, traumatic brain injury, contagious diseases, convalescence, and shell-shock/psychiatric.

Two orderlies transported me to Ward 33 on the third level.

As I suspected, I shared the ward with 29 other men.

If I had to describe my new temporary home with one word, that word would be "white."

Each of us had a plain white iron bed and a small white metal nightstand beside it. I was fortunate to have a bank of windows on the wall behind my headboard. The constant sunlight was a small beacon of pleasantness.

White plastered walls, white sheets and pillowcases, white blankets, and nurses in white uniforms completed the scene.

Every six feet, hanging from the ceiling was a green metal cone-shaped fixture containing a single light bulb. Simplistic to say the least.

It was a long journey from Courville, and it was strongly suggested that I get some rest. I closed my eyes and quickly drifted off to sleep.

The following morning I was awakened when an orderly came to my bed offering me some breakfast. My tray contained a bowl of hot porridge, a slice of melon, a small glass of milk, and a cup of coffee.

In the bed to the left of me was Kenneth King, another Pennsylvania boy from the Duncansville area. The rural town is just outside Altoona.

The 19-year-old private was also gassed near Saint-Corentin, just south of Villette. He had a shrapnel wound in the right arm and needed some help with feeding himself. I was glad to oblige.

On the right, I was surprised to find a wounded German prisoner. I was amazed to learn that the 30-year-old kraut from Wiesbaden, spoke somewhat fluent English albeit with a heavy accent.

Friederich Gustav Hartmann, who was an artilleryman with the German Seventh Army, was wounded and captured when we turned back their offensive. His outfit was among five enemy units that were overrun by our counter-attack. The Germans, we learned, had 24 field artillery batteries (144 guns) in the Seventh Army.

Hartmann appeared to be of average height and build with light blond hair and slightly protruding ears. He had a chiseled face with piercing blue eyes and a distinguished nose but without a mustache.

When I asked him about his injuries, the man noted that he had received bullet wounds in each of his legs and was bayonetted on the right side of his chest and in the left shoulder.

"During das early morgan hours, our batteries verr set upt aboutst three hundred meters from das river," he recalled.

"Hans vas loaden undt *Günter* vas trying to set das target," he tried to explain.

"A thick, milky fog rolled in from das river undt das blinden us. Vee could hear die enemy coming undt they verr firing during zee advance," he went on, 'but, quickly it vas alt quiet. Vee knew that they must be coming, but vee could not see a thing through zee soupy mist."

"Swiftly, shadowy figures emerged from zee haze and vee instantly recognized their uniforms verr green undt not zee usual gray of our men.

" Sey charged with gleaming fixed bayonets undt determined blood-shot eyes. As zee bullets whizzed past mein kopf (my head), mein life flashed in front of mein eyes until I was hit. First, a swift, burning pain in both mein legs. Then, a sharp, stabbing of steel buried deep in mein chest."

The German continued, "Vee verr all scared. I vas trying to save mein own Dupa (butt)... Mut verloren, alles verloren."

"What's that mean?" I inquired.

Friederich repeated the German phrase, but much louder this time.

"I am not deaf. I just don't know German. What are you trying to say?" I asked a second time. "If courage is lost, all is lost!" He replied.

"What happened to your mates?" I asked.

"Ich erinnere mich nicht mehr," he reponded in German. "...and that means, what?" I again ask for an explanation.

The man gave out a heavy sigh and said, "I remember no more."

The pioneer mumbled one more thing before he drifted off to sleep, "In Kriegszeiten Macht der Teufel Mehr Platz in der Hölle."

This time explaining to me, "In a time of war, the devil makes more room in hell."

Laying across the room from me was another Pennsylvania boy, Pvt. Benjamen Koehle. The 22-year old lad was from Tyrone, not too distant from my other roommate, Kenny from Duncansville. Koehle revealed that both of them were assigned to the 103rd Trench Mortar Battery, 28th Division.

Through our conversation, I learned that he had a broken arm, a dislocated shoulder, plus he fractured both his tibia and fibula.

" Initially, when we arrived in France, our battery was assigned to Camp de Meucon," Benny explained.

"After some intense training, we were loaded on 40 and 8s, and shipped to the front.

"Our unit passed through Chateau-Thierry and detrained at Mezy on the Marne," he went on. "How did you get so banged up?" I asked.

"Well..." he began, "we never did see any action, believe it or not.

"I was standing guard just outside a ruined church... get this name, I'll never forget it... *Église de la Nativité-de-la-Sainte-Vierge de Mézy-Moulins*," the soldier revealed, "and it was right around midnight. Suddenly, I heard a rumbling noise, and then, the entire wall behind me crumbled on top of me."

Benny continued, "It took six guys to dig me out. I thought for sure I was a goner!" "Geez," I exclaimed, "lucky for you that's all you got was a few broken bones!"

"Yeah!" He replied. "It's all on my right side, too! I just hope when I get back home I can still make sauerkraut, again!" The private bellowed.

"Sauerkraut?" I asked, quite perplexed. "That's right!" Benny stated proudly.

"Maybe you should ask Friederich, over here, he's a kraut!" I suggested.

"We make it every year back home, and it's my job to hand-crank the cabbage shredder. My pop will be pissed if he has to do it," he explained.

" Awww... I don't think you have to worry about that," I shot back. "I'm sure your old man will understand."

"You don't know him like I do!" he quipped.

Before we knew it the orderlies were bringing our lunch around, and I had had to scoot back to my bed.

Most of the food we received was typical French cuisine. My tray today consisted of a mixed salad, quail served with potatoes, a selection of local cheeses, and a fruit tart. I normally had a cup of coffee, as well.

Thursday, September 18 was a dreary, rainy day. There was a small white, wooden table in our room. We often used it to play cards, such as gin rummy, cribbage, or an occasional game of checkers.

Another chap in my ward, Elmer Shepellock, and I were engaged in a game of cribbage. "Shep," as we called him, was also from the Keystone State. He was a Phoenixville boy and was a member of the 111th Infantry of the 28th Division.

Somehow Shep and I got on the subject of movie theaters and he started bragging about the picture house he had back home.

"Yeah, Tommy," he began, "we've got a real nice one back home, The Colonial Theater."

" It was built in 1903, and I saw Mary Pickford there in a show back in 1915. She was great!" He bragged.

"I missed seeing Harry Houdini. He performed there last year, my family tells me. I hear they also had a brand new Wurlitzer organ installed a year ago, as well," he noted.

"Sounds great for a small town like that," I commented.

I'd be the first to admit that I'm not the greatest cribbage player.

When it comes to cards I prefer a game of pinocle, casino, or 500 Rummy. Shep was beating me easily, as was the case most days, and I just played along until the game reached its inevitable conclusion.

The following day, Friday, however, was bright and sunny. When the nurse made her rounds she informed us that the orderlies would be taking those of us who could be moved outside for some fresh air.

Shep and I were able to walk, while Kenny would be pushed around the gardens in a wheelchair. Joining us was another member of Phoenixville's 111th, Chaplain Wayne D. Jones.

He was tending to a badly wounded soldier in the field when a shell exploded nearby. Jones suffered several shrapnel wounds, but lucky for him, they were chiefly superficial.

Naturally, most of the landscape was destroyed by the effects of war, but still, the fresh air was good for the lungs.

A variety of birds were providing us with their sweet tunes, and it was comical to see several squirrels and their antics as they prepared for autumn.

The orderlies escorted us to one of the few oak trees remaining on the grounds. Shep and I sat on an iron bench and Kenny was parked beside us in his chair.

"So, what do you do for kicks back home, Kenny?" I inquired. "Oh... I do a lot of hunting and fishing," he responded.

"Is that so?" I probed

"Yes, I love the outdoors," Kenny acknowledged. "Anything interesting ever happen?" Shep asked.

"Well, I got lost in the woods overnight once," he admitted. "That's unusual," I countered. "Why don't you tell us about it."

Kenny began, "I was huntin' up at Miller's Point, one day. It was about 27 degrees and there was about an inch or two of snow on the ground.

"After not seeing nuthin' all day, I finally saw some deer tracks in the snow and followed them right into a swamp.

"It was getting dark, and I was startin' to get a little mixed up. I found myself walkin' in circles.

"By nightfall, I lost all hope of findin' my way outta there, so, I built myself a fire under a big ole pine tree.

"The next morning, I jus' kept walkin' towards the sun and found my way out to the road." He noted. "Geez," I exclaimed. How far back in the woods were you?"

"Oh... about three, four miles, I guess," he replied. "What happened then, " Shep wondered out loud. "I ran into a feller' from the highway patrol, and he yelled, 'Thank God, we found you!'

"I sez to him, 'found me? Found me? I knows where's I am now! Whatta' mean you found me, I sez." "What'd he say," I queried.

"He sez, 'I bet your hungry bein' out in the woods all those hours." " And you said?" Shep asked. "Nah! I had two snowballs for breakfast, but any chance you got a smoke, pal?" Kenny quipped. We all had a hearty laugh over that one, and it seemed like telling that hunting Kenny's story lifted pirits, as well.

"Say, Wayne," I chipped in, "Elmer told me a little about the famous Colonial Theater you guys have there in Phoenixville. What can you tell us about your town?" I asked.

"Well, he's right about the Colonial," the red-headed Jones began, "but we like to call our town "the gateway to Valley Forge," he remarked.

"Oh, that's where Washington stayed that one winter, right?" Kenny commented.

"Yes, that's true. By the way, you can just call me 'Reds.' That's what everybody else calls me.

"But more recently, we've had Buffalo Bill Cody, Buck Taylor, and even President Teddy Roosevelt ridin' through the park," he explained.

"Buck Taylor," Jones began, "he's known as 'The King of the Cowboys. He started his cowboy career with Buffalo Bill Cody, and he traveled the country with both Cody and Pawnee Bill, another famous cowboy showman.

Later, Taylor moved from California to Pennsylvania in 1897 to be superintendent of the Betzwood Stock Farm at Valley Forge.

"It was reported that he was killed when he was thrown from a horse that year, but those claims were false. He's still kickin' I might add.

* *44 NOTE: Buck Taylor, whose real name was William Levi Taylor was born in 1857. He died and was buried in the cemetery of the Valley Forge Memorial Chapel in 1924. Many other entertainers have used the name Buck Taylor, but he is the original.*

"Buck even served with Teddy's Rough Riders troop in Cuba and was a big supporter of Roosevelt," Jones revealed.

" As for Buffalo Bill, he's been to Pennsylvania more than 100 times... Altoona, Harrisburg, Coatesville, Phoenixville, you name the town, and he's been there.

"As a matter of fact, he opened his touring season in Coatesville in 1898. He rounded up his stock of six bison and a couple of hundred horses he had stored at local farms in the West Chester area.

"Occasionally, Cody wintered some of his animals at a farm just outside Phoenixville near the General Pike Hotel.

* *45 NOTE: Gen. Zebulon Pike, for whom the aforementioned hotel was named in 1810, discovered the famous Pike's Peak, in Colorado in 1806. Pike's expedition was part of the exploration of the Louisiana Purchase.*

"The following year, 1899, Buffalo Bill loaded his show on railcars in nearby Chester. All told, the troupe carried 329 show horses, 118 draft horses, six mules, six bison, 200 bushels of feed, and 12 tons of hay and straw from a local feed company. This feed only lasted one day, I'm told.

"Local eateries also had to cater meals to 780 crew members three times per day.

"Particularly during the winter," Jones went on, "seeing these famous cowboys and their performers, including Indians, was normal in our area."

"So, what about Teddy Roosevelt?" I questioned.

"Well, with Cody and Roosevelt both being outdoorsmen, and set on preserving the wild west, the two met several times," Reds explained.

"On more than one occasion they could be seen riding their horses through Valley Forge. The two were often joined by Buck Taylor since he had a connection to both men."

Jones revealed, however, "By the end of Roosevelt's term as president (in 1908-09), the two were no longer on speaking terms."

     *   *46 NOTE: Among the 191 shows Buffalo Bill performed in Pennsylvania, the last few years in the Philadelphia area included: Lancaster (April 22, 1911), April 24-30), Reading (April 22, 1912), and Allentown (April 23, 1912). Although the show went bankrupt in 1913, Cody signed a film contract to produce five reels and staged one week of shows in Philadelphia (May 22-27, 1916)*

"Wow!" I exclaimed, "I never realized these cowboy characters were such a big deal. I guess I never paid attention," I concluded.

After about an hour or so, the orderlies came and took us back to the ward.

Later that afternoon, Dr. O'Neil came to my bedside and informed me that I was being sent back to my outfit on Monday.

He revealed that his preference was to keep me there in the hospital for at least another week, but they were extremely short-handed at the front. Long story short, I was needed.

Of the more than two dozen men in my ward, it was the German who drew most of my attention. They all had interesting stories, but his anecdotes seemed the most compelling. He was a foreigner. He was the enemy. He was fascinating, entertaining, and all alone. For all of those reasons, I felt compassionate towards him.

Just before I shipped out, the subject of our families came up in conversation and Friederich explained to me his unique situation.

"Mein familie? Mein familie!" He began.

"For generations, zee Hartmann's in Wiesbaden verr in zee business of making, as you say... ah... paint. Vee calls it lackiermeister, meaning a laquer-maker."

"Mein Großvater (grandfather), Adolph...mein Vater (father), And Johann, mein onkel (uncle), Julius Karl... undt so on undt so on..."

Intently, he continued, "Vee all lived in a small house undt Schwalbacher Strass (Street), in Wiesbaden."

"Der Kaiser (Kaiser Wilhelm II, emperor of Germany)," the kraut revealed, "hast taken over our lacquer plant for der war unit made it into... as you say... hospital. Das future ist uncertain," he commented with a somber look on his face.

"Mein grossvater's bruder (brother), also namendt (named) Julius, went to Amerika with mein onkel, Johann George, many years ago!" The German recalled.

"Is that right?" I asked.

Ja! (Yes) Ja!!" The man nodded. "He was just a little boy," he added.

     *   *47 NOTE: The author's great-grandfather, John George Hartmann, did indeed come to America from Germany with his uncle about 1883. John's granddaughter, Elizabeth Hartman, (the author's mother), would one day marry Sgt. Thomas H. Schalata's son. Thomas E. (the author's father).*

One of the most beloved stories told to me by Friederich, the kraut, involved his drinking experiences at the local tavern in his hometown of Wiesbaden.

"In der vaterland... vee drink!" He began most animately.

"Vee drinks bier... vee drinks wine... vee drinks vater, but..." he said nodding his head and giving a wink of his eye, "vee drinks... mostly bier... but ja, vee drinks!"

"Das men," he continued, "vee drinks mostly at Der Eimer (The Bucket). Mein grossvater, mein vater, mein onkel Heinrich, mein onkel Walter, mein bruders Johann, Karl and Jurgen... vee allst drinks, undt drinks zum more!

Friederich continued, "Onst during der Oktoberfest, mein bruder, Jurgen, drank from der bar's famous wooden bucket.

He further explained that his brother passed out on the floor of the bar and nobody could move him. He was out cold.

"Mein mutter, Hilda, came undt said to mein vater, 'Why must he drink so much?' " "Poppa said, 'Being half drunk is wasted money!' "

Friederich threw his head back with a hearty laugh and said to me, "Zie liken mein story, Tommy? Zie liken mein story?"

"Of course, pal!" I shot back with a laugh of my own. "Of course, Fred," I confirmed.

As I look back at my unusual friendship with my German counterpart I came to the simple realization that when you stop fighting, you're just two people. Under these circumstances, you just have to look past the wartime atmosphere.

When you got to know someone like Friederich, I soon found out that he was just the same as I was. He was there to do a job he really didn't want to do, either and he had been ordered to do it.

The only sensible thing to come out of war is for old enemies to become old friends. Maybe someday...

German Hamburger Pioneer, possibly Friederich Gustav Hartmann
Image Source: Author's Photo

"MY HORRIBLE DREAM COMES TRUE"

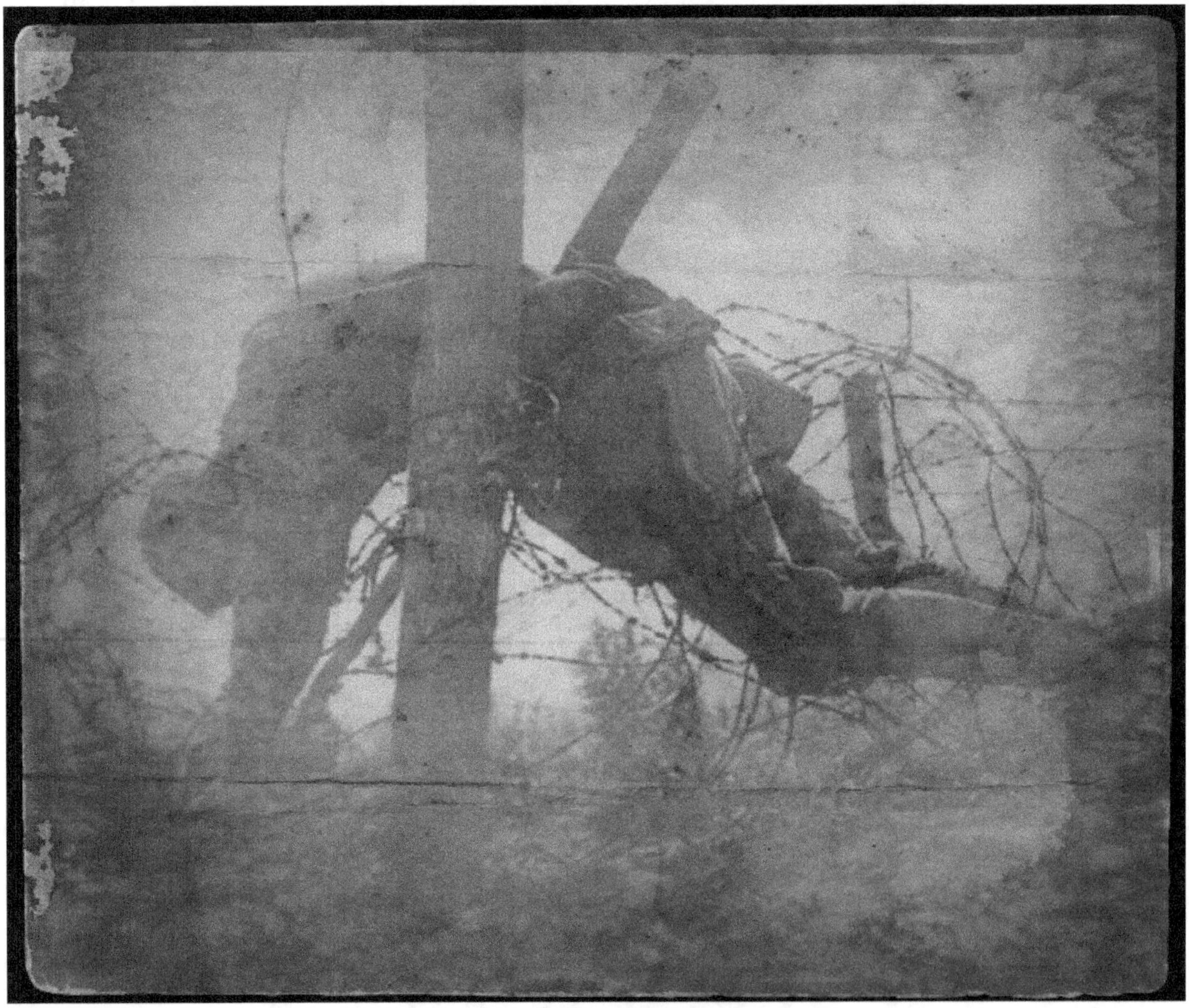

A casualty of war tangled in barbed wire
Image Source: Unknown

CHAPTER 32

"My Horrible Dream Comes True"

On my way back to Camp Hancock following my Christmas leave, I experienced a horrible dream. I had fallen asleep on the train that New Year's Eve and dreamt that I was part of a detachment that collected dead bodies and body parts on the battlefield. Now, when I returned to action with my unit, it appeared as though that dream was about to come true.

This region of the Argonne had been the quiet sector. Artillery only fired one or two shots per day, and the infantry practically nothing but guard duty. Then, on September 24, things began to change. Plans were made for a big offensive set for September 26. The offensive involved simultaneous assaults by four army groups - American, Belgian, British, and French.

To support the infantry attack, the Allies assembled: 2,700 guns, 189 small tanks (142 operated by Americans), and 821 aeroplanes (604 crewed by Americans).

With darkness, the roads so deserted by day suddenly became filled with panting horses, rumbling guns, caissons, motor trucks, and long columns of Infantry. Every available means of transportation was called upon, including small hand railway cars. A mule-driven narrow gauge train constantly furrowed ammunition and rations between the supply dump and the forward positions.

About 100 burros augmented the flow of materials northward. The donkeys were marshaled by men from the Wagon Company of the 304th Ammunition Train.

Motorized batteries emerged from their concealment of the woods towards the front.

The Infantry began moving stealthily in the uncanny quiet, measuring their distance in the process.

Those positioned near the front line for reconnaissance were issued French overcoats and helmets to maintain the fiction that there were only French troops in this locality.

For two days, the regiment was involved in the strenuous work of hauling tons of ammunition about five miles to our new positions.

Hundreds of trees had to be cut down to make room for the new battery sites. This had to be done quickly so that enemy aeroplanes would not discover our locations.

While the ammunition was being moved into place, the Germans did a considerable amount of shelling to hamper our efforts. During this time, we suffered substantial casualties, both killed and wounded.

Our regiment was finally able to respond at 2:30 am on September 26. The silence of the night gave way to the deep-throated roars of the great 155's. It seemed like the world was coming to an end as we fired three hundred and fifty-eight tons of shells in 24 hours. This included high explosives, gas, and smoke shells.

These high-caliber guns blasted relentlessly, splintering the darkness with a weird red glare accompanied by the pungent smell of battle smoke as it filtered down under the trees. The air was alive with whining, whistling, and streaming missiles.

The nature of the countryside with its extensive forests, rolling hills, and deep ravines made it easy for the Germans to defend.

The enemy used everything that modern warfare had developed to this point. They employed trenches and dugouts, miles of barbed-wire entanglements, countless machine gun nests, and strategically placed heavy artillery.

When the Infantry's First Battalion moved out, feeling their way in the darkness at 5:30 am, the artillery turned to a rolling barrage. The barrage advanced approximately two hundred yards every four minutes. Nine French batteries were held in position to protect the advance.

The roads were not only in terrible condition due to the bombardment, but they were severely congested with artillery pieces, ammunition trucks, and ambulances. All were trying to reach Varennes, a distance of about five miles. The horse-drawn section of the ammunition train succeeded in getting through to the batteries on the morning of September 27.

Adding to the traffic woes, the Military Police blocked all traffic during the advance due to General Pershing's anticipated arrival to observe the progression.

A Sanitary Train had a Triage at Clair Chenes, and one field hospital packed on trucks ready to move forward. There were also medical detachments with each infantry regiment, ambulance dressing stations near the front, and horse-drawn ambulances.

Over at the 107th Field Artillery, Major William T. Rees, Commander of the First Battalion, became sick. Captain Samuel A. Whitaker, of Spring City, PA, was placed in command of the battalion.

Machine guns were positioned in the very front of the French line, but almost on top of them were the 75's (75 mm), and close behind them were the 155's (155 mm).

When the smoke and mist cleared, you could see miles and miles of barbed wire and tanks moving ahead in the tall grass. One could only imagine that Colonel Patton was among them as he promised that fateful day in El Paso.

During most of the day, the 112th Infantry was assigned the slow, hard, dangerous job of cleaning up the Argonne Forest's eastern edge. It was there that the enemy had many inaccessible machine gun positions.

Over at the 109th Field Artillery, an enemy shell exploded in the dugout occupied by Captain Atherton. Two of his officers and two enlisted men were killed.

Colonel Miner, the 58-year-old Commander of the 109th Field Artillery from Wilkes-Barre, Pa, reported that his battery fell into position with the Infantry and the 108th Machine Gun Battalion. They were dug in northwest of Apremont and lay there all day.

While Colonel Miner was directing a platoon of guns, he was severely wounded in the face and lost his left leg.

Many of the roads and bridges in the area were destroyed by enemy mines. Therefore, detours around these huge craters became necessary. One of them was one hundred feet in diameter and forty feet deep.

While traveling on one of these temporary roads, the First Gun of Battery B of the 108th Field Artillery became stuck in the mud.

Colonel Edwin St. John Greble, who was 59 years old and a West Point graduate, jumped from his car in an attempt to get the gun out of the mire. In the process, the artillery piece struck a small mine. One of the gun's wheels was blown off, and the horses and men involved in the effort were all killed.

Miraculously, Colonel Greble escaped with only a small wound on his right foot. During the colonel's six days in the hospital, Lt. Col. John Hall was temporarily in command of the regiment.

During the advance, there were numerous German machine gun nests and snipers in the woods. The enemy constantly harassed our positions, but Colonel Greble ordered two hundred men to search the woods and mop up these German stragglers.

Privates James Braghetta and Eddie Bassi, of the 108th Field Artillery, Battery F, exposed themselves to enemy fire on September 29. The two soldiers made a heroic attempt to bring rations to their battery mates while under attack.

On September 30, the regiment gained Le Chene Tondu Ridge (Hill 245). This ridge had been heavily fortified by German machine guns. On that day, shellfire from a railroad gun behind enemy lines killed 14 and wounded seven machine gun company members. Also, the First Battalion took with them only reserve rations and slickers when making their advance. The balance of their rations was being brought up on a truck. Before it reached our men, it was hit by a shell and was utterly destroyed.

The fighting in that region continued for six days. One of the battalions found a German wagon train that had been caught in the fire. Our troops reported that the discovery was indeed a dreadful sight. Dead men and horses were found amongst their demolished wagons.

Two prisoners reported that their outfits had been literally wiped out by our heavy bombardment. This was the worst shelling they had seen during the duration of the war. So, high were the casualties that each company was left with less than twenty men.

Lieutenants Lester M. Smith and Willis P. Storer and five men from the 107th, Battery C, were killed on October 3, when a shell made a direct hit on their dugout. The seven American soldiers never had a chance.

On the 3rd, PFC George Breckenridge, of the 109th Field Artillery, placed himself in harm's way while dressing a wounded officer and another soldier under heavy shellfire. All three returned to safety without further injury.

On the night of October 4, the Third Battalion moved up to the left, in the heart of the Argonne, and on the following night, the Second Battalion advanced to join the Third.

German artillery began firing upon us from the hills beyond, but sufficient ammunition had not reached us to return fire.

But by the following afternoon, the First Battalion delivered four thousand rounds on the village of La Forge.

One of our batteries dropped over 15 tons of explosives on Chene Tondu in three hours. With nearly everything destroyed, the area appeared to be nothing more than a graveyard for dead Germans.

One captured enemy officer stated that his "infantry fought as though they were drunk," and his "artillery fired as though they were mad."

On October 8, these forces had advanced to Fleville.

From the observation post in a gravel pit, the Germans could be seen emerging from their dugouts. The enemy was obviously alarmed and bewildered. The Germans never thought that American artillery would dare advance so far. Nor did they realize, at first, where the firing was coming from. Those who survived could be seen scurrying back in retreat.

An enemy flag was raised at a hospital on the hill's very edge, and firing commenced. The battery did not fire at the hospital but over it. Had the situation been reversed, it is questionable whether an American Red Cross flag would have been so respected.

The battalion continued to move ahead on the 9th. Although, once the regiment took its position, it was relieved and was ordered to the old camp at La Croix de Pierre.

The Argonne's casualties were: killed - four officers, 128 men, wounded - 11 officers, 503 men.

My first mission on my return from recuperating in the hospital involved the dreadful task of recovering bodies. One of the sectors where recent action took place was assigned to Roy Wilson and me.

The two of us pulled a cart that contained wooden stakes, pieces of white cotton cloth, and a bucket filled with tools such as a shovel, wire cutters, a sledgehammer, and the like.

Dead soldiers remained precisely where they had fallen three or four days earlier. Many had been cut down in a recent German counter-attack.

Several had been pumped full of machine-gun bullets – mutilated beyond recognition. Sorting through this gruesome scene was not a pleasant chore.

An American private, identified by the red, keystone patch on his shoulder and a single stripe on his sleeve, was found in a ditch with a German bayonet buried deep in his gut.

    *　*48 NOTE: Although some men were issued the official red keystone patch, the insignia was not officially adopted until October 27, 1918.*

We were instructed to remove the identification tags from the dead. Many of these tags were already corroded from the weather and bodily fluids. Others had become embedded in the putrid flesh.

I pulled his dog tags, and Wilson recorded his name: Pvt. William Robinson. He was with the 110th Infantry.

The captain also required that we search each body for personal effects. Robinson had a leather wallet with family photos. Also, I discovered a small pouch that contained a rosary, a St. Christopher medal, and some change... fifty-seven cents to be exact.

I drove the three-foot-long wooden stake into the ground while Wilson handed me a piece of the white cloth to tie on top. This marked its location to the burial crew and informed them that the deceased had indeed been recorded.

Just a few steps away, a young German boy, not more than 15 or 16, was bent over a roll of barbed wire, his eyes were wide open, and his helmet lay on the ground at his feet.

We were assigned to record the recovered bodies from both sides. Therefore, it was our duty to document the identities of the enemy, too.

Wilson reached around the neck of the teenage infantryman and ripped his I.D. tag off. He read the information to me: Gefr. (Private First Class) Freiderich Faust.

In his breast pocket was a small, gold picture frame. Behind the shattered piece of glass was the photograph of a forty-ish woman with her hair pulled up into a bun. On the back, written in pencil, was "Mutter" (mother).

Besides the frame, the kraut had a gold pocketwatch on a chain. At the other end was attached a small penknife. The soldier also had two French francs and a few German coins ranging from pfennigs to half marks.

Wilson and I did our best to pry his body off the barbed wire and lay him on the ground. He was stiff as a board and literally frozen in that bent-over position.

Then, we marked the spot with an orange flag, designating it belonged to the enemy.

Some of the corpses were riddled with enormous amounts of shrapnel. Their remains were so badly torn that ribbons of flesh and muscle were exposed.

Such was the case of our next casualty, Pvt. William Peterson, also a member of the 110th. If it wasn't for his dog tags, we never would have been able to figure out his identity. Both arms and the right side of his chest were shredded. His steel helmet had a four-inch hole on top, leaving a portion of his skull exposed. It was enough to make you sick... I mean, seriously sick to the stomach.

Sadly, in his coat pocket was a small prayer book. Nearly a dozen family photographs were stuffed between the pages of the well-worn book... images, I'm sure, of his wife, kids, parents, and siblings.

Wilson commented that he actually knew the guy from the chow line in the mess tent. "Poor bugger," he said.

"Seemed like a decent guy based on the couple times I ran into him," Wilson described.

"I think he had a brother, or maybe it was a cousin or some kin to him over in the 109th," he added. "Yeah, tough break," I remarked.

"You know, Tommy, this is probably the hardest part of this damn war. It's difficult enough to stomach this sickening detail. Still, when you run across someone you that you actually know, that's what really gets to ya'" he admitted.

"I'm with you there, Roy," I agreed.

Our next stop is one that I shall never forget. Next to a pile of debris that appeared to be the remnants of a wooden wagon was the body of another American soldier. Two U.S. Army mules also lay nearby.

We turned the man over and I immediately recognized him as none other than Pvt. Milton A. Shomper. His face was instantly recognizable, especially the thick mustache.

Obviously, due to his sarcastic nature, I despised the man, but now that he was gone I felt sorry for the guy.

As we went about our task, I couldn't help but wonder what made him such an angry and resentful man. Was he mistreated as a child? Did his father run off, like so many other men of the time? Was it his family life or did other kids bully him at school? It could be any number of reasons that kept him from being a likable guy. I guess I'd never know for sure!

After I pulled his dog tags, I reached onto his right pocket and found two "Phillies" cigars, as they were his favorite.

In his left pocket was a photograph of a boy and a girl standing in front of a brick rowhouse that I presumed was their family home at 1804 E. Tusculum St., in Philly.

The two were standing in front of a set of six steps that led to a landing at the front door. The lad was wearing a pair of obviously dirty coveralls, a tattered long-sleeve shirt, and a cap. He appeared to be about 11 years old.

The boy had his arm around the little girl. She wore a plain, light-colored dress, high button shoes, and had her hair parted in the middle. She looked to be about three or four years younger than him.

Standing in the doorway was a thirty-ish woman. She was wearing a floral dress with a long white apron over top of it. A pure white cat sat on the stoop.

When I turned the badly crinkled photograph over, written in pencil was, "Milton and Myra Ann - 1903."

A seemingly innocent photograph taken 15 years ago offered no clue about the persona of one Milton A. Shomper.

The process went on until we ran out of stakes, and we ran out of daylight. We both agreed that we weren't going to run out of bodies.

Later, when we brought these I.D.'s back to the company, that horrid smell remained. So offensive was the odor that many of the soldiers required to handle them became ill themselves. Fighters on both sides gave their lives in hopes of ending this thing— as I mentioned earlier, the German dead lay among our guys.

Another detachment was given the charge of disposing of the dead horses, as well. They were an obstacle. Horses are enormous when they become bloated. Their bodies tend to swell to twice their average size. Their legs become immovable. They are as stiff and strong as steel posts. This situation requires the burial team to dig a ten-foot square hole that is six-foot deep. If the animal's legs were blown off, the ditch needn't be half that size. Otherwise, they were often removed with the help of axes and hand saws.

In a wooded area on the left, the remains of other soldiers were also left unattended. These men helped stop the Germans' seemingly last-ditch effort. Now, they lay littered on the ground and obviously disregarded. Tomorrow we would find out if that mission would also be assigned to us or if some other squad would pull the short straw.

The next day, October 10, Wilson and I were assigned to the woods' burial detail. The terrain was challenging due to the shell craters, mine holes, and other debris in our path.

I was in charge of pulling the cart while Roy was up ahead, scouting the way. Some of the tools and supplies spilled out when the wagon was upset. By the time I got everything under control, Wilson was about thirty yards ahead of me. Apparently, a dud artillery shell exploded near him, and I saw my buddy go down.

For a brief moment, I was dumbfounded. I panicked, and I left the cart where it sat and ran to his aid. Wilson was dazed, but I was relieved that I could see no visible wounds or blood.

"Roy, what happened? Are you okay?" I yelled. "Tommy. Tommy. Yes, I think I'm okay," he responded.

He made an attempt to get to his feet but immediately fell back to the ground. "Are you hurt anywhere?" I questioned.

I stood up, and while looking towards the camp, I waved my arms, signaling for help.

"No. No, I don't think so," he began. "My ears are ringing, and my head hurts like hell, but I don't feel any pain anywhere else," he reported.

Before long, Lt. Quinn ran to our position. He gave Wilson the once over, and the two of us helped him to his feet. We managed to get him back to my wagon and laid him in it.

I pulled the wagon with Wilson inside. Although he never complained of any pain, he noted that it was a terribly bumpy ride. Lt. Quinn carried the bucket of tools and occasionally assisted me through the rough spots.

When we got him back to the safe area, Roy was transported to the Field Hospital to be evaluated. The end result was that he had no injuries or wounds but would require about 24 to 48 hours to recuperate from the shock of the blast. It was a close call. Much too close for my comfort.

Wilson spent a couple days in the Field Hospital with other members of our outfit who also lay wounded. They were: Pfc. James Callan, Cpl. Paul Clopper, Pvt. Marty Conlin, Pvt. Eddie Lorillard, Pvt. Thomas Watchorn, Pvt. Dominick Bellevau (Battery D), Pvt. Eldred Miller (Battery D), Pvt. Daniel Nagle (Battery D), and Pvt. Irvin Thompson, (Battery E). The only artilleryman from the 108th that was reported killed was Pvt. Benneville Bertolit (Battery C) on September 27.

Fortunately, Wilson and I were reassigned to a more protected duty at the Field Hospital.

To this point, I was among the many in our company who were hit by gas. Others received wounds from incoming shrapnel, etc., but this was by far my worst experience of the war.

Before I saw my first action, I freely admit that I was consumed with fear. Fearful that I would not make it home to see my loved ones ever again, and terrified that someone would find me in much the same way as those I was tending to.

I wasn't cowardly in my approach to the action but sincerely afraid that I would be letting down two people who were genuinely depending on my safe return, my little sister, Helen, and my fiance, Stella.

I can never erase the images of the dead, their eyes open, their stone-like faces pale and chalk-like, their jaws dropped with mouths open and teeth showing. Their final expressions were captured for all eternity.

French Artillery Battery
Image Source: Author's Photo

Hidden German Artillery
Image Source: Author's Photo

Horsedrawn German Artillery
Image Source: Author's Photo

Life in the Trenches
Image Source: Author's Photo

"ADVANCE INTO BELGIUM"

There was little to be seen but wrecked houses and towns
Image Source: Author's Photo

Chapter 33

"Advance into Belgium"

On Wednesday, October 9, most of our regiment was relieved, and the men were sent to Camp La Croix de Pierre for several days of rest and policing up. I caught up with the rest of my outfit a few days later.

When I arrived in camp, I ran into one of our guys from the 111th Infantry. He reported that his outfit had just marched two kilometers from 6 am until 3 pm, and the only rations they had was one loaf of bread for every two men.

"The 112th," he said, "had been assigned to carry out vigorous patrols of the area in order to keep tabs on the enemy, and the outfit captured three German officers and 260 men." Sgt. James Uber of Company E, and PFC Oscar Dull, of Company C were killed in action at that time.

    *   *49 NOTE: Sgt. Clarence M. Jones, of B Company, was ordered to clear Hill 244 of the enemy. Jones led a patrol of seven men up a steep slope under intense enemy grenade fire. Four members of his patrol were killed during this action. The sergeant pushed on and silenced three machine-gun nests and 12 snipers. He sent one member of his patrol back with a message and held the position with his two other buddies for two hours before they were relieved.*

Doc was anxious to tell me about the good news that came our way while I was gone.

He informed me that before I arrived at La Croix de Pierre, our artillery detachment had to prepare for its first inspection. Initially, the officers of HQ Company inspected the Brigade's men and equipment over the course of three days. A march in review past Major General McNair followed. "We were not only told that the inspection was favorable." Schweppenheiser said proudly, "the general declared that our Brigade merited the enviable reputation as one of the fittest field artillery units of the American Forces!"

"Wow!" I exclaimed.

"Sorry I missed all the hubbub, but I'm kind of glad that I was able to avoid all the pain in the ass preparation that goes with it," I responded with a sigh. Schweppenheiser continued his update, "Secondly, when we marched out of the Argonne Forest, we were tired and dirty, but the word was quickly passed around that the regimental bathtub had finally arrived.

      *   *50 NOTE: This excellent delousing machine was given to the regiment by the City of Philadelphia at the cost of $10,000. During the first day alone, 1,400 men were given a hot bath under huge showers while their clothing was baked by live steam in another part of the machine. The American government had several of these machines in operation, but the 108th Field Artillery was the only one to have its very own bath furnished by its hometown.*

"Warm water, soap suds, and clean, dry towels were a welcome sensation that I had not felt since I can't remember when. Doc tried to recall, "Was it back in the hospital in Vannes?"

"Probably," I responded.

"You know, Tommy, I don't know about Haeberle and the other guys, but shaving is another chore that I sure missed. If my mom could have seen the whiskers I had on my face just half the time of the last few months, she would have given me a good scolding," he commented.

Speaking of Haeberle, Harry came strolling in at the tail end of Irvin's story with a couple of dusty bottles of beer cradled in his arms.

"Hey, boys! How 'bout a brewski?" He yelled. Harry passed one out to each of us sitting there, and Doc informed our new bartender that he was filling me in on the luxurious bath they had received.

"Hats off to Billy Penn and the City of Philly for giving us the bath that was so badly needed, and no thanks to Uncle Sam for putting us in this hell hole, to begin with…" Haeberle said in offering his toast.

"Here! Here!" Most of the guys followed.

"Na drzowia!" I added in Polish.

And so, we drank another round to Billy Penn and Uncle Sam.

As we were all sitting around shooting the bull, the third piece of information filtered down to us. The latest news was that Germany had asked President Wilson for terms for an armistice.

As this incredible story spread swiftly around the camp, we urged Haeberle to scrounge up some more beer to keep the celebration going. I don't know where his source was, but he managed to dish up a few extra bottles of the Belgian beer.

Before we grasped the enormity of the report, the regimental band was collected, and for the first time in many months, we heard the group play music. The orchestra members were proud of their impromptu performance, and the men in the outfit were rather enthusiastic over the whole affair.

Refreshed with dry, clean uniforms, the men sat in groups of 20 to 30 and listened while the band played such heartfelt number as: Stars and Stripes Forever, "The National Emblem," Anchors Aweigh," "The Marine's Hymn," "The Battle Hymn of the Republic," and "The Army Goes Rolling Along."

We all joined in during the last tune, and without a doubt, the gesture went a long way towards improving morale!

On Thursday, October 17, the regiment marched 22 km to St. Menehould. Our outfit bivouacked for the night on the outskirts of town. It was a cool, crisp autumn evening, and we slept well that night.

The next day we would be boarding a train bound for Belgium and the front. We had gotten very familiar with these train rides over the last few months.

The officers gave our outfit high marks when we left St. Menehould. Word was passed around to the men that Maj. Griffith T. Longstreth stated, "The entrainment was executed in well-nigh veteran fashion, and each train left its respective station with guns secured and lashed, horses in cars, and men properly clothed. The entire operation was accomplished absolutely on time!"

Once again, the 40 and 8's railroad cars had traces of hay lying about because they had previously transported horses.

A large pile of hay was piled up in one corner, and one could see movement on occasion. At first, we suspected a rat or some other varmint. Schweppenheiser went over and began poking around and discovered a small blonde-haired boy hiding in the heap.

The lad, dressed in tattered brown knickers and a soiled white cotton shirt, attempted to burrow deeper, but we soon dug him out.

After some intense questioning, we quickly learned that he was a young French boy of about seven years of age.

His name was Pierre, and he spoke a fair amount of English.

"What are you doing here, son?" I questioned the boy.

"Monsieur..." he began, "I am hiding from the Germans. They destroyed my village of Chaudefontaine. They killed my family. They ruined everything. I had nowhere to go... nothing to eat. Please help me, Monsieur!"

The poor boy began to cry softly. Doc and I scrounged a few crackers and some chocolates we had stashed away in our knapsacks.

Some of the other fellows managed to offer a few treats they too had squirreled away.

The unfortunate child was happy to have anything we could offer him. Haeberle gave him a drink of water from his canteen.

"What?... No beer, Harry?" I inquired.

"No, Tommy. That stuff ran out a while ago!" He chuckled.

"Besides," he quipped, "this kid is probably used to wine or something. This area is the champagne region, you know!"

After the boy quieted down, he was able to tell us more.

"My grandpapa operates a small vineyard in the area," Pierre began.

"First, the Germans destroyed almost everything with their big guns.

"Boom! Boom! Boom! They fired night and day," he explained.

"Then, their troops came through our farm. They had guns... bayonets... and they were, you know... mean!

"After they ruined our grapevines and other crops, they took our food and looted our houses. The swine burned down those houses that were left standing after the bombing.

"I hid with the chickens while momma, papa, and grandpapa met their death by those German beasts. I heard their pleas for mercy and their screams. Next, there were gunshots... three of them... Bang! Bang! Bang! I found their bodies in the meadow. It made me so sad.

"Next, the soldiers chased down the rest of the villagers and shot them, too! I heard the firing of their guns once again as I hid behind a giant tree.

"My sister, Suzette, ran to the woods. I lost her. I don't know what happened to her," he went on, almost crying once again.

"I told her to run! Run as fast as you can! I heard even more shots ring out but couldn't see what was happening," he whimpered again.

We took turns keeping the young French boy calm, and he continued to reveal more information regarding his plight.

His family indeed produced champagne from the grapes in their vineyard, and it sounded like they eeked out pretty decent lives for themselves before the war.

En route to the front, we passed through the cities of Chalons-sur-Marne, Epernay, Chateau-Thierry, and Noisy-le-Sec.

As our train rounded the outskirts of Paris, we made a stop. It was then that we turned Pierre over to the local authorities. They assured us the boy would be well cared for by the Red Cross, but I often wonder what became of the young man.

From Paris, our journey took us through Boulogne, Calais, and Dunkerque.

We could see a heavy fog engulfed the countryside for several kilometers during this portion of our route from the small opening in our rail car. In time, this fog transformed into a pounding rain. It was a nasty chilling rain, and the cold air could be felt coming through the boards of the railcar.

The rain was beating on the wooden roof of our car, and water began to drip on our heads. Initially, the rainwater was just a trickle, but over time this situation became more troublesome.

From the time we left the French capital, our trip would require three more days on this putrid train.

On Monday, October 21, at about 0200 hours, we made a stop at Wamnnebekem near Elverdinghe, Belgium.

Here, the First Battalion detrained while a light rain continued to fall. The dim lampposts that scarcely lit the area revealed that the rails and station platform had a glassy, wet sheen to them.

The First Battalion's orders merely stated that they were to camp somewhere in the vicinity of Ypres. Sgt. Vogan informed us that our stop would be next.

Our train traveled a mere five km south, and we arrived at the station in the Belgium town of Vlamertinghe. Most of the town was flattened from the intense enemy bombing. Unloading along the trackside was nearly impossible. By 0300, the rain once again turned into a complete downpour. The mud in places was over a foot deep, yet a large sign nearby read, "Drive slowly to avoid raising dust!"

In the Fismes sector, we had seen destroyed houses and towns, but nothing like the devastation that was before our eyes. This territory was ruined and blackened beyond description. Four years of war turned it into a world of complete desolation.

A large pile of rubble, mostly stone and wood, sat along the left side of the road. The only thing recognizable amongst the ruins was an iron cross and a wooden sign in French: "*Église Sainte-Brigitte.*" (Church of St. Bridget).

I thought I had seen the worst of this war back in the Argonne with twisted ropes of barbed wire and equally twisted torsos and contorted faces, but here the enemy left behind remnants of their machinery and artillery pieces. An assortment of military equipment and other gear could be seen strewn about the battlefield like children's playthings.

Rats, the size of groundhogs and gofers, scattered momentarily but returned in swarms while knawing on the unburied dead. We had previously seen various rodents during the times we spent in the trenches, but these scavengers were downright vicious and quite fearless.

From Vlamertinghe, we marched another fifteen km. in the driving rain towards the city of Ypres. The marching was bleak over these shell-torn roads. The roadbed was peppered with holes that were filled with water. One of the fellows came up with a name for the road, "The Three M's: the Muck, the Mire, and the Morbid."

Even though the men and horses were well-rested from the long train ride, the march was slow. Both man and beast were simply fatigued from the previous action.

When one team of horses could not drag a wagon or an artillery piece up a hill, the men replaced that team with one from the rear. Officers sent the most unserviceable horses to a mobile veterinary hospital.

Due to these conditions, our 15 km journey required about 18 hours to traverse.

As we approached Ypres, there was little to be seen but wrecked houses and towns. It was a mass of crumbling stone. The red-tiled roofs of some of the dwellings remained in tack, or a solitary chimney defied destruction, but the war spared little else.

When we reached the other side of the city, we departed by way of the Menin Gate. This passageway was made famous by British and Commonwealth forces throughout the war. The entrance is situated on the eastern side of the city at Menenstraat (Menen Street) and the Ypres Canal/River.

> *   *51 NOTE: Thousands of British and Commonwealth forces marched through the Menen gate during World War 1 between 1914 and 1918. More than 80,000 of their unmarked graves are located in the area. The Ieperlee (or Ypres-Ijzer Canal) is a canalized river and flows via the city of Ypres (Ieper).*

The river is 17 kilometers (11 mi) long. Its name is derived from iep, the Dutch word for elm. It gave its name to the city of Ypres. In the 11th century, the river's canals were built to link the town to the sea. The town had a thriving cloth industry.

Upon leaving the city, we started on a long hike across "No Man's Land," and for nearly 30 km, we saw no habitation of any kind.

According to our maps, we were passing through towns and villages that no longer existed. Signboards marked their locations, but the rest of the area was a vast wasteland. Places like Frezenberg, Zonnebeke, Broodseinde, Tyne Cot and Paendale, all the way to Roselare.

The unmistakable roaring sound of an aeroplane engine could be heard in the distance as we trekked across this desolate landscape.

At first, we were hoping to catch a glimpse of America's flying ace, Eddie Rickenbacker, but he was reportedly more than 300 km south of us in France.

We also knew that while Belgium's own aerial hero, Willey Coppens, often operated in this area, he was shot down about a week before our arrival. The Belgian flyer survived the dogfight but was hit in the leg, and his limb had to be amputated. That certainly would have put him out of commission.

What we were seeing amounted to Allied airdrops of rations and ammunition.

For guys like us, seeing these magnificent flying machines was still a novelty. As they soared high above us, their majestic, colorful winged crafts were something to behold. Each country had its distinctive color combination, and they indeed appeared to be works of art to those of us on the ground.

We learned the plane markings rather quickly. Most of the Allied aircraft had some sort of circle designation. The British planes had a blue ring with a white ring inside and a red dot in the center. The French, however, bore the exact opposite: red, then white, with a blue dot.

American aeroplanes could be identified with a red outer ring, followed by a blue inner circle and a white dot in the center.

An aircraft with a red outer circle, a yellow inner circle, and a black dot in the center was Belgian.

However, the fuselage could be painted in any number of colors, including green, brown, blue, and gray. Many times the tail was decorated in red, white, and blue.

Coming directly toward us on the horizon was a French Spad SX111. When the aeroplane flew directly above us, the pilot dipped his wings to the right to recognize our forces. Many of our men all gave a hearty cheer to the airman. Some waved their helmets in the air.

After the French plane circled the area and flew out of sight, we observed two British aircraft approaching from the rear.

The pair of Sopwith Dragons roared right over our heads, performing the daring maneuver of doing a barrel roll while changing positions from left to right and so forth.

The guys fully appreciated their bold exercise and went wild. Many of the troops broke rank and cheered with approval. Our officers told us that British, French, Belgium, and American aeroplanes dropped more than 15,000 rations for the boys and 65,000 rounds of ammo throughout the month.

    *   *52 NOTE: Allied sorties included supply drops, aerial observation, bombing runs, and strategic attacks against enemy troops and aircraft. However, by the end of October 1918, the British Royal Air Force would lose 47 aircraft and claim 61 German planes.*

On Thursday, October 22, Major William Taddonio, a clean-shaven officer from the medical detachment, personally made the rounds visiting with the boys. The major accompanied Sgt. Vogan in handing out the enormous bundles of mail that had finally come through.

Sure enough, there was a letter from Stella. It was some correspondence from home that I had longed for and now fully appreciated its arrival.

October 9, 1918
Dear Tommy,

I hope all is well and you are safe wherever you are. We haven't heard from you in such a long time. Since you were in the hospital, I guess. We can't help but wonder what is happening to you overseas.

While the weather has been tolerable over the last several weeks, I'm afraid the Spanish Influenza has paralyzed the city. I don't know if any of you over there are coming down with the ailment, but it has become a genuine concern here at home.

Several hundred sailors at the Philadelphia Naval Base became ill around September 18.

Ten days later, the city put on a vast Liberty Bonds Parade to raise money for the war effort. According to the local newspapers, officials were expecting about 10,000 to attend the event, but more than 200,000 lined the streets to watch the spectacle.

The papers reported that a 30-year-old policeman was the first death in the city from the sickness.

The city's health director has warned that thousands of cases may develop if the people are careless, and the epidemic may get beyond control.

My brother, Joe, read in The Evening Bulletin that more and more cases are being reported every day. Hotels, barbershops, restaurants, and lunch counters are still open, but employees must cease work upon the first sign of the flu.

They are trying to shut down the theaters, too, but people are protesting over such a fuss.

Many people I know are out of work due to this epidemic. Fortunately, I am still working at the arsenal, and Joe has his job at the chemical plant. I guess we're both needed because of the war effort.

It makes me wonder, nonetheless, who is safer these days. Those of us left at home or you who must battle the evil forces of the war.

As far as my family goes, we have all been spared of this disease thus far. I am sorry, because my sisters are out of work at the hosiery mill.

I have not heard from Veronica or anyone in your family about their health, but I assume they are in the same boat as we are.

They are still playing baseball games, but the people in attendance must wear masks over their faces.

This whole thing scares me so! I hope and pray that we all make it through this scourge.

Please know, my love, that I think of you always and long for the day you return to me. May God and His angels watch over you.

Since I spend most of my leisure time reading and writing, I have written a special poem just for you. I hope you like it.

"A Dream"

Stay! Oh stay, thou happy vision,
Stay still, over my senses reign.
Can it be that I've been dreaming,
If so, let me dream again.
Let his hand be once more leaning,
Gently on my faithful breasts.
Let his eyes, so full of meaning,
Turn to mine, and tell me that I am best.

I will ask Joe to pen a letter to Veronica to inquire about your family. Perhaps, Veronica, or your favorite sister, Helen, can write you with the latest news from home.
Waiting and praying for your safe return,

Love,
Stella

* *52 NOTE: The Spanish Lady, as the sickness was named, killed 139 Philadelphians in one day in the week following the Liberty Bonds Parade. During the next month, the Influenza would take the lives of another 12,000 in the city. A third of the Earth's population, or about 500 million people, were infected by the sickness, and the mortality rate was believed to be between 50 and 100 million people. During this period, one must remember that no anti-flu drugs or vaccines, antibiotics, or mechanical ventilators existed. The City of Brotherly Love not only led the nation in deaths but clearly wrote the book on how to mishandle a pandemic.*

War-ravaged Belgian Street
Image Source: Author's Photo

Belgian townspeople amongst the rubble
Image Source: Author's Photo

Destroyed Belgian railway station
Image Source: Author's Photo

Passing through France into Belgium
Image Source: Author's Photo

The devastation of war
Image Source: Author's Photo

34

"THE DAY OF THE SAINTS"

Chaplain tends to his flock in the field
Image Source: The British Library

CHAPTER 34

"The Day of the Saints"

On October 28, the Regiment passed through Roulers, Belgium, on our way to the front, spending the first night at a ravaged chateau at Iseghem.

The river Mandel and the canal Roeselare Leie run through the city of Iseghem. Along one side of the canal, a large shoe and brush-making factory once existed, but bombing had also reduced it to rubble.

The Germans used the chateau as a prison camp to hold wealthy Belgians during their occupation.

When we arrived, we quickly discovered that they left the landmark in deplorable shape. It was in ruins, quite frankly.

It was devastating to see what remained of the once-stately structure. What seemed to be a grand circular drawing-room was divided up into smaller offices. Nearly every wall had a hole bored through it, and sections of stovepipe ran in every direction.

The German's obviously hauled away most of the finely-crafted furniture. The chateau had broken glass and other debris everywhere.

Surprisingly, reams of paper littered the floor. It appeared unusual because the enemy burned all the rest of the available wood, paper, and such to keep the woodstoves going. They must have left in a hurry!

A large park surrounded this once beautiful estate, and nearly all of its mature, stately trees were destroyed by shellfire. Replacing the former lavish gardens were huge craters, muddy ruts, and more rubble.

By afternoon, we received word to clear an area inside for ourselves to spend the night. We were tired from the long march but grateful to have a dry place to sleep.

Several patrols combed the town, and in the basement of what had been a butcher shop on Roeselaarsestraat, they found three young German soldiers. The trio had barricaded themselves in a storeroom on the property.

Making the initial discovery was Cpl. Leonard Jenkins. He reported hearing a muffled thump, then a squeaking noise coming from inside the storeroom. When he entered the room and knocked over some crates, the three came out quickly with their hands in the air.

The young chaps wore typical German infantry field uniforms with corduroy, knicker-style trousers, and knee-high leather boots.

Across each of their chests were ammo belts, albeit empty.

In addition to the packs on their backs, each man carried a Mauser Model '98 rifle slung over his shoulder.

The shortest of the three had oversized, protruding ears. The obviously very young man was also the only one who had a long sword hanging on the front of his uniform. It appeared to be an Imperial German Artillery Officer's weapon. The fellow must have claimed it from a fallen comrade.

One of the officers at Division Headquarters interrogated the men, and they actually turned out to be boys. There was Freidrich (age 15), Klaus (age 16), and Wernher (age 18). They were part of an infantry outfit in the German's 26th Reserve Division. Freidrich and Klaus, we learned, were brothers.

While all three remained expressionless for the most part, the middle soldier was continually observing what was going on and keeping an eye on us. He remained calm throughout the questioning.

Major Harold Hellyer ascertained that the unit had relieved the 16th Bavarian Division Southwest of Roulers on October 4-5. However, the 26th passed through here sometime in the last two weeks. Allied intelligence told us that the division was currently in Deynze, about 28 kilometer's away. Therefore, the three, it was determined, either voluntarily or accidentally, were left behind.

Hellyer was an up-and-coming young officer. He was clean-shaven, and his face had very bold and strong-looking features.

Personality-wise he was generally all business but was well-liked and respected among the men. The Headquarters Company planned to send the prisoners behind the lines for further interrogation.

Harry Haeberle found a dozen bottles of wine left behind by the Germans, and another wooden crate of Belgian beers, mostly Abbey-styles, whatever they are. Naturally, we were excited to try some.

The tempting aroma of coffee began to permeate the building. However, we never got an opportunity to taste it. A handful of enemy planes passed over, dropping several bombs, and the men used the coffee to douse the fires. Although the bombs hit relatively close, no severe damage resulted.

About 30 minutes after the bombing stopped, Harry returned, toting a big fat goose by the neck in his right hand, and a loaf of bread in the other. We didn't even realize he was missing.

The crafty Haeberle traded a bottle of wine to one of the local Belgians for the bird. He said the old man that he swapped with was happy to make the deal.

"Whattya gonna do wit' dat?" one of the guys asked.

"Cook it up, of course. What do you think I'm going to do with it?" He shot back.

Once a perimeter around the city was established, the division commander issued an order for strong patrols along the outskirts as part of our defense.

While there was still a little daylight, I showed Haeberle, Schweppenheiser, and Harry Dohner a room that I found in the chateau's cellar. It may have been the servant's quarters because mattresses, blankets, and other items were on the floor. It was dark and quiet down there. Hopefully, it would be a good refuge if the enemy bombing resumed. We prepared to turn in for the night.

I collapsed on a mattress in one corner of the room. Schweppenheiser, who always seems to draw the short straw, had to sleep on the bare floor with just a blanket.

We could hear some of the others stirring upstairs from time to time, but we only detected a dull thud when an occasional shell burst nearby.

I fell into a deep sleep but awoke about four hours later. My initial response was to go up to the street level, get some air, relieve myself while I was up, and return to my spot. The rest of the guys slept through the night.

In the morning, the aroma of coffee filtered down to our lair, and it was time to get up and move around a bit.

The food supply hadn't caught up with us yet, so it was slim pickings for breakfast. The sarge passed out rations of some kind of canned meat.

One of the officers also found a local bakery still operating in the village, so he made a deal to get several dozen loaves of bread for the guys.

We were also lucky to be visited by Mr. B.O.H. Oliver, a representative of the Y.M.C.A. Oliver was a civilian but remained a constant companion of the men in all their activities. During the fighting, he was always going from battery to battery with any supplies he could obtain. This time he brought with him some much-needed grooming supplies and edible items such as nuts and candy. The guys always appreciated his special treats.

The word came down that we were moving out at 1100 hours. I decided to grab a quick shave while I had the opportunity and a fresh pack of razor blades.

Haeberle and Dohner chose to explore the town a little before we headed out. Irvin stated that he was going to examine the rest of the chateau and its grounds.

Although the Belgians were relieved to see our arrival, not everything about us Americans was appreciated.

One of the guys in our outfit, Jimmy Peters, was later scolded by one of the locals, "You men marched through our village in columns of three, with your rifles presenting arms with like broomsticks."

The man went on, "Your cursing and foul language are obnoxious and embarrassing to us," he said. The villager criticized, "Many of you were boasting about what you're going to do to the Germans but you have no discipline, it seems.

"What is just as odd is the fact that we watch as the officers and rankers slap each other on the back like they're pals or something."

The two Harry's returned, Harry Haeberle and Harold Dohner, and gave their story.

"I found a cellar under a paint-makers shop, and it was loaded with potato-mashers (German hand grenades) and barrels of ammunition the Jerry's left behind," Haeberle noted.

"If the bombers woulda hit that place when we wuz in there, I'd be chattin' to St. Peter right about now," he laughed.

"Anything else interesting?" I queried.

"Nah, not really. The krauts took everything that wuz worth anything," he replied. In mid-conversation, Irvin walked into the room, ready to tell us what he found. "Well, Doc. What did ya find on your mission?" Haeberle inquired.

"A few trinkets up in the attic," he noted.

"I found a bag of coins in a box and a gold ring. I haven't looked them over yet, but they seem kind of interesting.

"There's a pile of dirty dishes in the kitchen sink and spoiled food on the table. It looks to me like somebody left in a hurry, right in the middle of a meal," Doc went on.

The four of us went outside for a smoke. The day was damp and overcast, but there was no sign of imminent foul weather.

As we stood on the driveway in front of the chateau, Fr. Mackenzie passed us on his way inside. "Good morning, fellas!" he greeted us.

"Morning, padre," Hoeberle replied.

We all saluted and remarked to ourselves that we hadn't seen the chaplain for quite some time.

The priest must have heard us as he walked by and stopped dead in his tracks. He turned, looked directly at us, and said, "But... I'm sure I'll be seeing all of you at Mass on All Saints Day, right fellas?"

"Yes, Father. You can bet we'll be there," Haeberle answered as he continued to be our spokesman.

Unfortunately, religious services were hit or miss in the field. The war dictated whether there was room for God in these hellish conditions.

Open-air services took place when the danger was held at bay. One of the priests assigned to our outfit often said Catholic Mass in a small tent in a remote area, and the officers authorized those who could be spared to participate.

By now, the perception was that the war was going in our favor, and we all hoped and prayed that the end was in sight.

With All Saints Day approaching Friday, November 1, Fr. Mackenzie met with Col. E. St. John Greble, the 108th Field Artillery Commander, and requested permission to celebrate a special Mass on that day.

The colonel told the reverend he could arrange the service as long as conditions permit. Any enemy resistance would negate the whole thing. Fr. Mackenzie said he could live with that.

As we moved out of Iseghem, the 107th Field Artillery moved in and took our place. The Germans proceeded to bomb the city once again. They made every attempt possible to demoralize us, but we weren't giving into their plan. Besides, there were essential railyards at Ingelmunster and Iseghem and a crucial ammunition dump on the outskirts of Lendelede.

The colonel and the Battalion Commanders went forward to reconnoiter.

On October 29, we marched about 15 kilometers passing through that small town of Lendelede. Only the two walls of the church and tall spire of Sint Blasius (Saint Blaise) remained standing. It was a sight that we had seen many times.

The march went through Ingelmunster, Oostroosebeke, Oyghem, and we took our position in the vicinity of Desselghem.

The 107th Field Artillery was in a position in the vicinity of Oostroosebeke. The divisional front extended along the railroad line from Waereghem in the North to Wortgem in the South.

Since Desselghem was only one kilometer behind the front lines, we set up at Garverken on the road to Audenard. The divisional front spanned a distance of about five kilometers.

Once again, German bombers were active during the night, especially in Lys, between Oyghem and Desselghem.

The brigade set up headquarters in an abandoned village schoolhouse. The two-story stone building had a red-tiled roof, and the locals claim it dated back to 1873.

The commanding general and his French associates held several conferences to determine the best plan to attack the Germans.

Amazingly, stoves, heating apparatus, and culinary equipment were collected and proved to be both useful and resourceful.

We observed officers from both sides coming and going at all hours of the day and night.

In particular, one old French colonel with a nicotine-stained mustache resembled a caricature of the famous German General Von Hindenburg. He wore a long black overcoat reminiscent of a priest's cassock. Many remarked that he was the most faithful henchman of all the French camp's followers.

He arrived at H.Q. on the first day of our stay at Desselghem and had breakfast, lunch, and dinner with the staff.

When General Price inquired through an interpreter whether he would spend the night, the Frenchman declined, saying, "Ten thousand thanks, but he would go home for the night."

Upon receiving the colonel's reply, the American General sarcastically inquired whether he could expect the colonel by 2:30 a.m. the following morning.

Once again, the French officer replied, "Ten thousand pardons, he feared that would be impossible," but with a dazzling smile, he promised to be on hand by 6 a.m. for breakfast, and he made good on his promise.

We received word that the plan of attack had for its objective a reclaiming that portion of the front from Waereghem to Audenard on the Scheldt River, a distance of twelve kilometers.

Choosing artillery positions in Belgium proved to be much different than that of France. The mostly flat terrain put us at a disadvantage.

Gun placements, in many cases, were behind barns or under the cover of tree rows.

Observation posts were also a point of contention. Windmills and churches provided the most viable spots, but the Jerry's rarely made a wrong guess when firing upon our observers.

On the night of October 30, over at the 109th, their batteries moved into position South of Garvirken on the road to Oudenarde, supporting the Ninty-first Division.

The attack, scheduled for the early morning hours of October 31, would hit Spittaals-Boschen. There is a strip of woodlands in the center of the sector that bristled with enemy machine-gun nests. The German's rearguard held this target, and these men were clearly battle-tested.

The second objective would be the Cruyshautem-Wortghem Railroad Yard, while the last leg of the attack would focus on the ancient and historic town of Audenard and the Scheldt River's crossing. This operation would be known as the Lye-Scheldt Offensive.

At precisely 5:30 a.m., the Fifty-third Field Artillery Brigade and attached French Artillery fired a four-minute rolling barrage. An attack by our infantry followed. When the guns began shooting, it marked the first American artillery to fire in Belgium during the four years of war.

During the engagement, Captain Thomas N. Troxell, of the 109th, was severely wounded while making a personal reconnaissance of enemy machine-gun positions. The operation was successful, and the batteries advanced four kilometers to a position South of Waereghem.

Troxell was one of the few casualties who arrived in our field hospital, set up in a girls' dormitory within the city limits. We managed to patch up the Captain and send him off to a French Hospital.

Other injured men suffered mainly shrapnel and bullet wounds, all minor. One infantryman was pinned beneath by a fallen tree from the shellfire, while another was buried by debris when an enemy shell exploded inside a brick building.

The following day, our forces advanced another fourteen kilometers near Oyeke, where Battery D fired two hundred rounds at a crossroad used by the Germans. This engagement turned out to be the last hostile fire by our Regiment during the war.

The charge continued on November 1, with infantry patrols reaching Audenard. General Price ordered the batteries to advance, and H.Q. was established in Chateau Nokere, South of Cruyshautem, a venerable edifice with paneled walls and superb furniture.

However, the recent occupation by the Boche, left the place filthy. They left the drawing-room and the music rooms littered with vermin-infested straw.

*   *53 NOTE: Boche - Pronounced [boʃ], is a derisive term used by the Allies during World War I, often collectively ("the Boche" meaning "the Germans"). It is a shortened form of the French slang portmanteau alboche, itself derived from Allemand ("German") and caboche ("head" or "cabbage").*

At Noon on November 1, Fr. Mackenzie received the go-ahead to celebrate Mass behind the chateau in a small sheltered clearing.

General Price gave about two dozen of us permission to attend the unique service. We could hear artillery pieces firing in the distance, but there was no sign of any enemy aircraft in the area.

Fr. Mackenzie read the Gospel:

"When Jesus saw the crowds, He went up the mountain, and after He had sat down, His disciples came to Him. He began to teach them, saying, "Blessed are the poor in spirit, for theirs is the Kingdom of Heaven. Blessed are they who mourn, for they will be comforted. Blessed are the meek, for they will inherit the land. Blessed are they who hunger and thirst for righteousness, for they will be satisfied. Blessed are the merciful, for they will be shown mercy. Blessed are the clean of heart, for they will see God. Blessed are the peacemakers, for they will be called children of God. Blessed are they who are persecuted for the sake of righteousness, for theirs is the Kingdom of Heaven. Blessed are you when they insult you and persecute you and utter every kind of evil against you falsely because of Me. Rejoice and be glad for your reward will be great in Heaven."

He followed the reading with a vital message fitting for the day.

"Today, men, is All Saints Day. We commemorate the holy people we call saints—beginning with Jesus' apostles and those who followed over the centuries.

"While it is a good thing for us to emulate these selfless followers of Jesus Christ, many other saints walk among us. Men and women just like you.

"Many of these saints are in your ranks. You may be one of them, yourself. Some of those courageous soldiers are no longer with us.

They have already given their lives in this great war, and unfortunately, some of you may join them before it's over.

Some of these saints fought the gallant battle. Some of these saints heroically saved the lives of others. Some of these saints confronted unrelenting danger for the greater good, and we all know there is no greater sacrifice.

As Jesus said in the Gospel, we just heard, "Blessed are the peacemakers, for they will be called children of God."

"I am going to keep my homily brief. Therefore, in conclusion, we don't know when God will call upon us to sainthood, but we all have it in us to answer that call.

"Neither do we know the hour of Jesus' return, but we need to be prepared.

"Fellas, join with me in singing the hymn you probably learned many years ago as a child, "For All the Saints."

"For all the saints, who from their labors rest,
Who Thee by faith before the world confessed,
Thy Name, O Jesus, be forever blessed.
Alleluia, Alleluia!

Thou wast their Rock, their Fortress and their Might;
Thou, Lord, their Captain in the well-fought fight;
Thou, in the darkness drear, their one true Light.
Alleluia, Alleluia!

For the Apostles' glorious company,
Who bearing forth the Cross o'er land and sea,
Shook all the mighty world, we sing to Thee:
Alleluia, Alleluia!

O may Thy soldiers, faithful, true and bold,
Fight as the saints who nobly fought of old,
And win with them the victor's crown of gold.
Alleluia, Alleluia!

And when the strife is fierce, the warfare long,
Steals on the ear the distant triumph song,
And hearts are brave, again, and arms are strong.
Alleluia, Alleluia!

The golden evening brightens in the west;
Soon, soon to faithful warriors comes their rest;
Sweet is the calm of paradise, the blessed.
Alleluia, Alleluia!

But lo! there breaks a yet more glorious day;
The saints' triumphant rise in bright array;
The King of glory passes on His way.
Alleluia, Alleluia!

From earth's wide bounds, from ocean's farthest coast,
Through gates of pearl streams in the countless host,
And singing to Father, Son, and Holy Ghost:
Alleluia, Alleluia!"

"Finally, we all pray that the end of this terrible war is close at hand, but let us prepare ourselves for whatever the Lord has in His plan. May the Father, The Son, and the Holy Spirit protect you and keep you safe, my brothers. Amen!"

Three German Soldier Boys
Image Source: Unknown

35

"FINALLY... THE END"

American troops celebrate the Armistice
Image Source: Flickr

Chapter 35

"The End of The War to End All Wars"

Many of the other outfits in our division, such as the 107th Field Artillery, had to be quartered in barns and sheds near their gun positions.

Our men were surprised to find many Belgians occupying the few farmhouses that were still standing. The half-starved locals continued to work in their fields despite intense machine gunfire.

To illustrate just how scarce food was in the area, I am reminded that when one of our horses became so wounded or injured that he had to be shot, the animal was led into a field to be disposed of.

This was a signal to the local villagers, and once the animal was put down, the local population butchered the beast and distributed the meat. The carcass was usually picked clean.

Some good news came our way when a captured German prisoner informed us that Lt. J.H. Smith, commander of the 107th Field Artillery's Battery C, had not been killed but was a prisoner in the hands of the Germans.

Although the officer had been wounded in the chest while trying to establish a forward observation post, his wound was not critical.

For our outfit, the 108th Field Artillery, choosing artillery positions in Belgium was much different from those in France.

Not a place could be found that answered the requirements as prescribed in the books. The flat terrain forced us to set up placements behind rows of trees or behind barns. We could only hope there was a minimal flash that would give away our positions.

After participating in several attacks, on November 2, the regiment moved forward to Wortegen and took the position on a general line northeast of the town as far as Oycke.

We began firing in the direction of Audenarde, and the batteries no longer required prepared maps. Instead, they relied on their early experience in the field to aid in their firing. Besides, what French maps were available were difficult to decipher.

Once again, we set up a temporary Field Hospital to the rear, but we were ordered to unpack from the wagons only those absolutely needed items.

I drew a shift working at the Field Hospital and was involved in two cases during that stint.

Our first case involved one of the horseshoers from Battery A, Pvt. Harry Ash. He was kicked in the area of his left arm and shoulder. We needed to put his arm in a sling and give him a shot for pain.

More severe than Ash's injury was an incident involving one of the gunners, also from Battery A, Cpl. Edward Callahan.

Callahan suffered a laceration and burns on his right hand as a result of the gun's recoil.

The physician on duty gave him five stitches and instructed me to bandage up the soldier's hand. I was given the task because we were shorthanded on nurses at the front.

After applying the gauze dressing, I began to wrap his hand, and I distinctly heard a woman's voice from behind me.

She asked, "Tommy, are you sure you know what you're doing?"

I was heavily involved in the procedure, and my determination to get the job done forbade me from turning around.

I promptly answered, "Yes, I know what I'm doing. I've done this a hundred times over the last six months. What's it to you?" I fired back.

The mysterious voice softly responded, "I am just here to watch over you. I have always been here to protect you."

Upon hearing those words, I couldn't help but turn around. Standing there in front of me was my grandmother, Josephine. She was wearing a black dress with a black shawl over it.

I blinked my eyes for just a second, and she was gone. Turning back around, I said to my patient, "Did you see that?"

He responded, "I didn't see nothin'. Who the hell are you talking to?" "Nobody," I answered. "Nobody. I guess I'm just hearing things."

The rest of my shift at the Field Hospital went without incident. Thank God! Our division was relieved by the French on November 3.

The outfit was ordered to move back to Desselghem on the nights of November 3 and 4. News also filtered down to us that Austria had signed an armistice. Could the end of the war be far behind, we wondered?

Rumors circulated that the Germans blew up the bridges over the Scheldt River (L'Escourt Fleuve) and the canal. These would have to be rebuilt quickly if we were to advance.

The engineers of the Ninety-First Division were feverishly engaged in their reconstruction in order to permit passage of our artillery in this sector.

Many units were sheltered at various positions northeast of Harlebeke. It was there we found lodging and enjoyed a few days of much-needed rest.

Once again, we took advantage of the opportunity to clean up in the concrete bathhouses the Germans constructed during their occupation here.

Also, on November 7, the word was received through Division Intelligence that German envoys would pass through our lines that night.

A renewed optimism pervaded the whole brigade at that time.

That would change, however, on November 8. We were on the move again in the midst of heavy rain and congested roads. The commanding general was ordered to plan for a forward movement. We were to prepare for an attack on Sunday, November 10.

German bombers were very active in the area, especially at night.

On clear moonlit evenings, we could easily see the giant Zeppelin-Staaken R.VI bombers flying overhead. These enemy aeroplanes boasted four engines and required a ten-man crew that included four gunners.

Their likely target was a large ammunition dump of gas shells located several miles behind our line. For that reason, we were required to carry our gas masks with us at all times. Should the dump be blown up, we would be protected.

During our stay in this area, King Albert of Belgium paid a visit to our regimental headquarters. The king was accompanied by Queen Elizabeth and the Crown Prince. The Belgian monarch was most cordial to our officers, and his visit lasted several hours.

Our outfit moved temporarily into position on the ninth, but the following day (November 10), we closely followed the infantry advance and crossed the Scheldt River in the vicinity of Oudenarde.

Two of our batteries, A and E, crossed the river on pontoons. Some of the men and horses had to actually swim across the body of water.

Brigade headquarters was established in some rooms in a chateau, which adjoined a convent near the Scheldt River.

When Lt. Mayer approached the gentle sisters with the request to set up headquarters within the chateau, their faces showed an obvious deep concern.

The feeling bordered on terror, as the order had spent the last several days confined to the cellars of the structure, listening to the destruction of their convent above their heads. The beautiful cathedral was just a stone's throw away.

After some gentle persuasion, the lieutenant convinced the women that the American soldiers meant no harm and would not interfere with their work of mercy.

In the morning hours of November 10, in Cruyshautem, the church bells called the villagers to their devotions while the French Infantrymen fraternized with the Belgians with full mess kits.

The French were advancing towards the River Scheldt, as well.

During the night of November 10, the officers planned the attack, which would occur the next day.

That night was a very restless one for me. On the one hand, we heard rumors that the war could be over at any time. On the other, the brass was preparing for another attack. Nobody wanted to become another casualty of the war so close to the end.

I decided to pen a letter to Stella and turn it over to the chaplain, Fr. Mackenzie.

November 10, 1918
Dear Stella,

> *We are hearing rumors that the war is all but over, but we plan to unleash another attack in the morning. You know that I am not a coward, but I do not wish to be just another victim of the war after all I have been through.*
>
> *With each passing day, I long to return home to your loving arms.*
>
> *Tonight, more than ever, I look back over the experiences that have brought me this far.*

From the long train ride to Texas to the baseball games, the boxing matches, and the fantastic flight of Dargue and Gorrell that saved many lives, these are memories embedded in my mind.

I look back at the months I spent at Camp Hancock, including my visit to the farm of Clay's grandparents. All of these experiences and the training I received there were put to good use.

It seems like only yesterday that we spent our last Christmas together, and that is a memory I cannot erase from my mind.

Add to those encounters our trip across the ocean and our journey across France to this place in Belgium, and I find myself filled with nightmares that I cannot talk about yet, yearn to forget.

Just the other night, I had a visit from my grandmother, Josephine. Do you remember we visited her grave when I was home for the holidays?

She appeared when I was bandaging a patient and revealed that she was there to watch over me, but there's a part of me that wonders if the angels sent her to collect my soul.

After six months of living hell, Stella, I must admit, I fear tomorrow most of all. It seems as though my life hangs in the balance, and not knowing what tomorrow brings is the most frightening of all.

Hopefully, by the time you receive this letter, my worries will have proven to be for naught, and it will be only a matter of time before we are reunited once again.

I send you all of my love, and I pray to God that I may safely come home to you.

Tommy

On the morning of November 11, I was awakened at four, and within an hour, our batteries went into firing position for the last time near the village of Maeder. All of our guns were prepared for a barrage that was to take place at 9:45.

New orders were received, however, at 9 AM:

"Headquarters 91st Division,

(Secret) November 11, 1918, 8:30 o'clock "Field Orders No. 33

"In compliance with orders from Marshal Foch, hostilities along the entire front will cease at 11:00 o'clock, French time, November 11, 1918.

The line held at that hour will be reported and will be held by a strong line of outposts. The remaining troops will be billeted as near their present locations as possible. Communication with the enemy is absolutely forbidden. All officers and non-commissioned officers will take the necessary steps to see that every man is informed of this fact.

"William H. Johnson,

Major-General U.S.A. Commanding"

In a drizzling rain, we heard, the German delegates joined representative of the Allies on a railway car in the Compiegne Forest and made the end of the war official.

World War 1, labeled as the war to end all wars, would come to a fitting conclusion, at the eleventh hour, of the eleventh day of the eleventh month of 1918 (November 11, 1918).

As the news came of the war's conclusion, one of the soldiers in our outfit reported, "Our wireless picked up the message that the hostilities were over."

Then, all at once, everything stopped. It was precisely 11 AM when all firing on both sides ceased.

The sensation to everyone was a novel one, and it took some little time to become accustomed to walking around in broad daylight in view of the enemy without some qualms of fear.

One of our guys, PFC James Rafferty, walked out in the open and did not know what to do.

When everything went silent, he dropped to the ground and remained there until he saw Lt. George Quinn walk out in front of the men.

The lieutenant yelled, "It's all over, the war is over, it's all over, and you can go home now!" We started getting up pretty fast after it got quiet, and some of the boys were hugging each other.

Surprisingly, there was no jubilant celebration. No hollering. No shouting. Nobody throwing their helmets in the air.

With me at that time were Irvin Shweppenheiser, Harry Haeberle, Bernie Halliday, and Barney Roth. The five of us took turns shaking hands and embracing one another.

"We made it, Tommy," Schweppenheiser beamed. "Yes, we did, Doc," I replied.

"I never thought we would ever live to see this day," Halliday noted.

"Me neither," Roth admitted.

"Awwww, You guys are all babies," Haeberle squawked.

"This was an adventure! Something to tell our kids and grandkids," he added.

"Maybe for you, Haeberle," I quipped.

"Most of this I want to forget," I confided.

The others agreed, and we all walked away, looking to meet up with some of the other guys in our outfit.

Though everyone felt that the conclusion of the armistice meant, in effect, the close of the war, across the entire field, we could see that there was no shouting or cheering, no demonstration of any kind.

Men and officers went quietly about their work or souvenir hunting. In fact, now that the fighting was over, everyone felt the privilege of getting all the war trophies that could be had.

Before noon men were over the lines and fraternizing with our foe, swapping bread or cigarettes for pistols, helmets, iron crosses, buttons, or anything else that belonged to the other side. We were surprised to learn that the Germans were quite friendly on the whole.

Quite fittingly, one of the men over at the 111th Infantry stated, "as the hour approached, desultory rifle and artillery fire continued until the very last minute, and then, peace came at the stroke of 11 o'clock."

"Our men knew not what to make of it. It was possible to walk in the open and not be shot at," he concluded.

It seemed to all as if a terribly heavy weight had been lifted off our shoulders.

Shortly afterward, all that could caught a few hours of sleep, the kind they had not enjoyed for months. For others, their restful sleep was eternal.

"EPILOGUE"

Tommy and Stella finally got their farmhouse in 1946

EPILOGUE

With the strain of fighting over, the period following the Armistice was trying. Everyone talked about the possibility of sailing home by Thanksgiving, but nobody fully realized what an enormous undertaking it would be to transport two million men across the ocean.

Initially, the men spent a great deal of time hiking after the Germans just in case the Armistice failed to keep the peace.

On November 18, the regiment left Oycke and marched towards Brussels. They reached Maeter that night and remained there until the next day.

For the next several days, the outfit continued to move forward north by northwest, passing through the Belgian towns of of Strypen, near Sottengem, Hundelgem, Beirlegem, and Bayegem. The regiment journeyed west through Dickelvenne, Cavere, and Petegem, finally reaching Thielt on November 26, my grandfather's birthday.

His outfit remained in the quaint Belgian city for two weeks and celebrated an improvised Thanksgiving Dinner while there.

On December 7, the hike continued through Menlebeke, Ingelmunster, Iseghem, and Roulers, stopping for the night at Oostnienwkerke. This town was just on the edge of "No Man's Land."

While crossing "No Man's Land," the regiment saw remnants of towns that no longer existed. They were marked by signs, and that was about all that remained.

Finally, the men reached Proven, an old English campsite, and they settled there for about one month.

While the men carried on their usual duties and inspections at the camp, my grandfather recalled that they "had truly learned what wet weather meant."

"We seldom saw a clear day at Proven," he noted.

"There was mud and rain everywhere all the time," he recollected.

Also, during their stay, the unit celebrated its 79th Anniversary of existence on December 11 and Christmas a few weeks later.

Many Russians, who were prisoners of the Germans, were let go to roam the country. Several of these soldiers made their way into camp and were eager to do chores in the kitchen in exchange for food.

From January 4 through 6, 1918, the regiment entrained just beyond Proven to return to France.

Two days later, these forces arrived in Lavaland marched onward to Entrammes. The men were billeted at various points in the area.

On January 30, the 108th Field Artillery, along with regiments of the 53rd Field Artillery Brigade, was inspected and reviewed by General John "Blackjack" Pershing.

All units were officially returned to the 28th Division during their stay in the area, and the 108th Field Artillery became a fully motorized Artillery Battalion. Tractors, trucks, automobiles, motorcycles, and traveling machine shops had finally arrived.

As my grandfather awaited his return home, several letters were both sent and received during the passing months.

By February, the news from home revealed that the Spanish Influenza had passed. Fortunately, both the Schalata and Zwolinski families had escaped the scourge of the deadly disease. Others, however, were not as lucky. Several neighbors in Bridesburg perished, as a result, including an eight-year-old Irish boy, Timothy Carrigan.

The lad was not only seen pulling his wagon around the neighborhood while delivering grocery orders, but he also collected rags and newspapers for the war effort.

The big blow for my grandfather was hearing the news that his good friend and boss at Baldwin Locomotive Works, Uncle Leo, was also one of the influenza's victims. The loss of his fiery but fair Italian mentor was difficult for him to accept.

From March 10 through 17, he was granted leave to visit Hautes Pyrennes in southern France. The trip included a tour of the religious shrine of Lourdes.

By March 19, the regiment turned in all ordnance equipment, and the horses were released by the end of the month. With everyone ready to go, the regiment moved forward to a camp at Le Mans, joining the infantrymen of the division.

On April 19, the French Cross de Guerre (war cross) and the Distinguished Service Cross were handed out to many men and others from the division.

On that same day, the regiment left for St. Nazaire, France, arriving there on Easter Sunday, April 20.

After the routine inspections, minus Battery C, the regiment boarded the USS Peerless and set sail home on May 1.

Battery C, however, left Port three days later, on May 4, aboard the USS Calamares.

The voyage home was a happy, uneventful one despite the crowded conditions, although one of the men remarked, "the first four or five days were rough. However, after the first two weeks, it wasn't so bad."

Initially, the ships landed at Hoboken, NJ, on May 14. Then, they sailed on to Philadelphia, arriving there on May 16.

For miles down the Delaware River from the Port of Philadelphia, dozens of boats all gaily decorated with flags met the Peerless and cheered the men home.

The 108th Field Artillery accounted for 33 killed and 276 wounded. That the outfit did not suffer more casualties was almost miraculous by all accounts.

My grandfather went through final inspections and examinations before receiving his final discharge papers. He rejoined his family amid several days of jubilant celebration. You can be sure my great-grandfather had a lot to say about that.

My grandfather returned to Baldwin Locomotive Works in 1919, initially in the main plant as a detailer. Still, on the recommendation of Mr. Robinson, he was transferred to the Hog Island facility.

He spent one month as an inspector of hulls and five months as an inspector of machine installation.

For 14 years, beginning in 1921, he was employed at American Engineering Co., where he served as a temporary all-around inspector primarily in the machine shop and the fabrication of steel and iron.

His employment was off and on due to ill health from his service in the war.

As far as Stellla Zwolinski goes, she finally married my grandfather on January 21, 1920, at St. Laurentius Catholic Church.

Apparently, the winter of 1919-20 was a brutally cold and icy one

Tommy told Stella, "We need to get married. It's too cold for me to be traveling back and forth between my house and yours."

Family legend also states that their wedding day was so icy that wooden boards had to be placed on the steps so that attendees could safely enter the church.

My father was born in Philadelphia on March 29, 1927. He served in the US Army, the Reserves, and PA National Guards for 39 years.

His time in the service included the occupation of Germany following World War II and working for the Stars & Stripes Military Newspaper.

He finished his career with several years of service in the 28th Division.

Tom and Stella remained in Philadelphia until June 20, 1946, when they finally purchased the farm that was always a part of their dream.

As they often referred to it, the old homestead was located in Warwick Township, Chester County, PA.

It was said to be an old Indian Trading Post and referenced as land deeded at one time to William Penn's family. My grandfather restored the property to its original grandeur and lived there with my grandmother until his death, January 22, 1963.

* *54 NOTE: Many of the photographs in this book and especially those in the Epilogue are part of my grandfather's personal collection. He evidently obtained images of German soldiers and officers during his postwar service overseas. Of particular note, pictures E1, E2, E3 and E4 have been developed from silver-gelatin dry plated glass negatives. This photographic process was in use from 1873 through the 1920s.*

Duty Status Leave Card

———

Leave is Granted, on a Duty Status, to:

Name ..THOMAS. SCHALATA,.........................

Rank.. SGT,......Co. or Unit. SANITARY. DETACHMENT,...........

Regt. or Organization. 108th. FIELD. ARTILLERY,..............

To visit ....HAUTE. PYRENEES..................Leave Area

Reservation No................... Through the Leave Areas Bureau

To arrive on ...., 1919

Signature of Commanding
Officer Granting Leave..............................

Rank and Organization Colonel. 108th. U.S.F.A.

Captain Adjutant

Duty Status Leave Card Page
Image Source: Author's Photo

Entrammes road to monastery
Image Source: Author's Photo

Monastery in Laval
Image Source: Author's Photo

Stella and Tommy's Wedding Photograph
Image Source: Author's Photo

(E1) Prussian Officer Pioneer
Image Source: Author's Photo

Sottengem Railway Station, Brussels Belgium
Image Source: Author's Photo

Unidentified enemy officer
Image Source: Author's Photo

(E2) German Guarde Pioneer
Image Source: Author's Photo

(E3) German Enlisted Soldier
Image Source: Author's Photo

(E4) High-ranking German officers. Believed to be in the photo (left to right) are:
Field Marshall Paul von Hindenburg, Gen. Erich von Falkenhayn, Gen. Ludendorf,
Friederich Adam von Bernnhard, and Obers Lieutenant Friederich Ritter von Haack.
Image Source: Author's Photo

ABOUT THE AUTHOR

Tom Schalata, a native of Pottstown, PA, enjoyed a 40-year career in both advertising and editorial while working for the following Pennsylvania newspapers: The Guardian, Pottstown; The Daily Republican/The Phoenix, Phoenixville; The Daily Local News, West Chester, and The Tri-County Record, Morgantown.

A graduate of Peirce College, Philadelphia, he was the editor-in-chief and sports editor, of the college newspaper, The Peircetonian.

In addition to The Bloody Bucket, Schalata has published the following works of non-fiction: A 40- year History of Performance Inc., a Pottstown-based car club, From Poznan to Pottstown: A Family History, and The Gospels According to St. Stephen's, a 90-year history of St. Stephen the Martyr P.N.C.C. (Polish National Catholic Church).

Also, he has authored two previous books in the genre of historical fiction: The Trunk and Kolęda: A Polish Christmas Carol. Both novels focus on Polish history and heritage.

Schalata currently resides in Stevens, Lancaster County, with his wife, Donna, and yellow lab, Stanley.